Burials

Books by Mary Anna Evans

The Faye Longchamp Mysteries
Artifacts
Relics
Effigies
Findings
Floodgates
Strangers
Plunder
Rituals
Isolation
Burials

Other Books
Mathematical Literacy in the Middle and High School Grades:
A Modern Approach to Sparking Student Interest
Wounded Earth
Jewel Box: Short Works by Mary Anna Evans
Your Novel, Day by Day: A Fiction Writer's Companion

Burials

A Faye Longchamp Mystery

Mary Anna Evans

Poisoned Pen Press

First Edition 2017

10 9 8 7 6 5 4 3 2 1

Library of Congress Catalog Card Number: 2016952024

ISBN: 9781464207501   Hardcover
      9781464207525   Trade Paperback

Poisoned Pen Press
6962 E. First Ave., Ste. 103
Scottsdale, AZ 85251
www.poisonedpenpress.com
info@poisonedpenpress.com

Printed in the United States of America

For Tony, who is soon to be a Sooner

Acknowledgments

I'd like to thank all the people who helped make *Burials* happen. Tony Ain, Michael Garmon, Rachel Broughten, Amanda Evans, Robert Connolly, Kelley Morrow, Vinci Cully Barron, and Leroy Cully read it in manuscript, and their comments were incredibly helpful. Deputy Chief Daniel Wind III, of the Muscogee (Creek) Nation's Lighthorse Tribal Police generously spoke with me about the complex issues related to law enforcement on tribal lands. They get credit and my gratitude when I get things right, and they are absolutely not to blame when I get things wrong.

As always, I am grateful for the people who help me get my work ready to go out into the world, the people who send it out into the world, and the people who help readers find it. Many thanks go to my agent, Anne Hawkins, and to the wonderful people at Poisoned Pen Press who do such a good job for us, their writers. Because I can trust that my editor, Barbara Peters, and the rest of the hardworking Poisoned Pen Press staff will ensure that my work is at its best when it reaches the public, I am free to focus on creating new adventures for Faye. I'm also grateful to the University of Oklahoma for providing the opportunity for me to teach a new generation of authors while continuing to write books of my own.

And, of course, I am grateful for you, my readers.

Chapter One

Powerful forces are constantly at work on a human body that is buried under five feet of red clay. Every cubic foot of that clay weighs a hundred pounds. For simplicity's sake, presume that the body is six feet long. No, make that five feet long, because this body once belonged to a woman, and a small one, at that.

Perhaps her buried form was two feet across at its widest point. It was probably less, but let's use two feet for convenience. Thus, she'd offered ten square feet of surface area to the five-foot depth of the clay soil that had crushed her. Simple math says that this fifty cubic feet of soil had weighed—and still weighs to this day—five thousand pounds.

It weighed two and a half tons.

Two and a half tons of downward force will break bones. It will press the flesh from those bones. It will force the air out of decomposing lungs.

Over the years, the overbearing clay moved ceaselessly, swelling when wet and shrinking when dry. Every rainstorm shifted the clay. Some of the motion was vertical. Some of it was lateral. This slow shimmy had disarticulated her bones, leaving them in a configuration that was almost the natural shape of a woman who lay on her bed asleep, but not quite.

The clay had dyed her bones red.

Still she waited for someone to find her. Had she been able to wonder, she would have asked whether anyone had ever even noticed she was gone.

Twenty-nine years is a long time to go without a proper burial.

Chapter Two

Faye Longchamp-Mantooth sat with her knees pressed against the airplane seat in front of her. Her husband Joe's lanky legs were encroaching seriously on the tiny personal space a major airline considered ample for a full-grown adult, but where else could he put them? Faye and Joe had jammed themselves into these seats because some requests can be sidestepped and some cannot.

When a friend asks for help moving, there are ways around saying yes. If you say you have to work, he's not going to press you to give up your overtime pay. If you remind him that your kid plays baseball on Saturdays, he'll understand.

Other requests can be refused outright. When a stranger asks you to donate to a political cause that is not your own, it isn't rude or even unexpected for you respectfully to decline.

But when a man's father calls and says to him, "I'm ready to scatter your mother's ashes," there is no honorable way to say, "Dad, let me check my calendar. I'm not sure I can get on a plane to you any time soon."

Faye's husband was an honorable man who had adored his mother, and who was still surprised to realize how much he loved his old man. Faye loved both of them. When their bank balance didn't cover the plane tickets, the two of them had scrounged up a tiny consulting job that she could do while they were in Oklahoma. Sure, it would cut into her family time, but this trip wasn't about her. It was about Joe and his dad.

Joe would hate it if she said so, but he looked so much like his dad. They had the same bone structure, dark hair, strong jaws, broad shoulders, sturdy legs. Their eye colors were different—Sly's were black, while Joe had his mother's green eyes—but their sharp gazes were the same.

Faye hoped her husband was happy to be making the trip from Florida to Oklahoma to see Sly, but he hadn't said a word since the "Fasten Your Seatbelts" sign came on.

• ● ● ● •

Joe Wolf Mantooth hadn't been home since he was eighteen. He'd left on foot when his mother's body was hardly cold. His abortive attempt to say good-bye to his father had gone so poorly that Joe was never sure whether the man actually understood that his son was going away.

He'd found Faye in Florida. With her help, he'd gotten an education, had kids, built a business. Together, they'd made the first home he had known since his mother died.

Joe had been past thirty before he boarded his first airplane. Now he sat beside his educated and accomplished wife, munching stale pretzels like a man who belonged in the sky. He knew intellectually that he was successful in all the ways that mattered, but he didn't feel it. All he felt was regret that his mother would never know how far he had come.

Faye knew his body language well enough to know that this was a good moment to rub his shoulder and mumble something that sounded like, "You should try to get some rest." He was grateful for the caring gesture, but he was still more grateful that she didn't press him to talk. Faye always knew when to leave him be.

Joe wished Faye could have known his mother.

Patricia Mantooth, whose education had ended with a GED, would have been intimidated at first by his wife and her big words and her doctorate, but they would have bonded over recipes for blackberry cobbler. They would have squabbled over the best bait for catfish, but they would've gotten over it. Joe took a moment to imagine his tall ivory-skinned mother and his tiny brown wife dangling hooks in the water while his children gathered berries for the cobbler.

His mother's and his wife's looks had contrasted in every way, although their sharp wits and loving personalities were very much the same. Patricia's hair had been long and red, and it had hung in ringlets. Faye's hair was a short, sleek black cap. Patricia's eyes had been green. His wife's were a dark brown, almost black. The image of the two women side by side was a beautiful one, but it hurt, because they were never going to meet in this life.

Joe looked down at the countryside, dun-green agricultural squares crossed with the random dark squiggles of a tree-lined creek. When they got to Oklahoma, the dirt would be red where the creeks cut into it, so red that he'd be able to see it from all the way up here in the sky. In all her days, his mother never set foot on an airplane. She would have been transfixed by the sight of the natural world from this unnatural angle.

Patricia McCullough Mantooth had loved the outdoors as much as Joe had loved her. When he remembered his mother, that's where she was, outdoors, sitting on a creekbank with a cane pole in her hand. Afternoon sunlight was shining on auburn hair and skin that always freckled and never tanned. She lived her whole life in crummy little houses where no amount of scrubbing would ever lift the stains from the floor. In Patricia Mantooth's world, outside was always better than in.

Joe's memories of his mother smelled like biscuits and gravy. She had possessed the poor woman's knack for miracles, so she'd been able to turn flour and grease into a meal that tasted like love. But once the meal was over, she had never lingered inside where the air was old and musty. She'd gone outside and she'd taken her only child with her.

Sometimes, Joe's father had been there as they sat with their feet in the creek, watching minnows flit around their ankles through clear water stained tea-brown by fallen oak leaves and pine needles. More often than not, he'd been on the road, doing what truckers do. When Joe missed his mother, he went outside and found a place to put his feet in cool water, and it usually made him feel better. He could not believe that his father had kept that woman's ashes indoors all this time, cooped up in a cheap urn.

Fifteen years is a long time to go without a proper burial.

Chapter Three

Archaeology and gunfire would not seem to go together, at least not always. So why was Faye spending the first minutes of her Oklahoma consulting gig crouched in the shadow of a dusty pickup truck with the sharp crack of a gunshot still ringing in her ears?

She heard silence now. No, not total silence. She heard the rapid breathing of the man crouched beside her and she heard the pounding of her own heart. She smelled the funk of both their sweat. She tasted the dust kicked up by their terrified feet and knees as they scrambled out of the truck and hit the ground. They were huddled on the driver's side because the sound of the first gunshot had clearly come from the passenger side where she sat.

So had the second shot that followed it as soon as they opened the truck door, as if saying, *You're wondering if these shots are for you? Look what happens when you make a move to protect yourselves.*

A moment later, when her client heaved his bulky frame forward and peeked around the front bumper of his truck, the third shot sounded.

The timing of this third shot obliterated any sense of denial that Faye might have harbored. The first shot had come the moment they stopped the truck. The second had come when they opened its door. The third had come when her client, who was reputedly a very smart man, made his foolhardy move. Yes, someone was definitely shooting at them.

Why was she here? She was on vacation, for heaven's sake.

"Hunters?" she asked hopefully.

Her client, Dr. Carson Callahan, shook his big shaggy head and said, "Doubt it. Too close to the road. Nothing's in season, except maybe squirrels."

"I should call 911."

Carson was quicker with his phone. "No, I've got it. You're not from around here, and I know how to tell them where we are. I don't trust their navigation system to find us way out here."

He punched in the numbers and the beeping sounds assaulted her ears. She needed quiet to listen, in case the shooter came closer. She wished Joe and his hunter's ears were with her.

No more gunshots came and Carson's calm voice was soothing. He was saying things that were unintelligible to an outsider, things like, "We're out past the old Simpkins place, upstream from that swimming hole south of the highway. Yeah, that's the place. Go through the second gate and over the cattle gap." It was good to know that help was coming.

She tried to listen past his voice to hear footsteps or heavy breathing or any sound that might be bringing danger. She heard nothing. Any shooter who might be coming their way was doing it on very quiet feet.

And then she did hear something. A voice, not far away, was saying, "Carson? Is that you? Help me."

There was a moment of silence while the person calling to them gathered enough breath to shout again.

"Help! Can someone help me?"

● ● ● ● ●

When the police arrived, Faye already felt like she knew the person trapped at the edge of a wooded area that began about twenty feet from where she crouched.

If she got on all fours and peered under the truck, she could see him lying in the thick underbrush. All she really saw was a dark shadow, but the shadow was a person and that person was scared. His name was Kenny Meadows. He was one of Carson's employees, and he was living a nightmare for no other reason than that he'd gotten to work a little early.

"Kenny? Are you hurt?" Carson had called out.

"No. Well, I'm not shot. I scraped myself up when I hit the ground, but I'm not hurt bad."

"What happened?"

"I was standing over here, looking for a mockingbird I heard singing in that tree, and *boom*. The sound was so loud that I thought a gun went off right next to my ear. I took cover in these bushes and now I'm afraid to come out."

Carson had admitted that they were afraid, too, then the three of them had waited together for help.

Every so often, Kenny had called out, "Are you there?" and they'd assured him that they were. Faye was about to jump out of her skin, but she had Carson right beside her. Kenny was lying on the ground, alone, waiting to see if someone with a gun was coming for him. She knew how scary that was.

After one of Kenny's bids for reassurance, Carson asked him if he still heard the mockingbirds and he said yes. The sound of the birds calmed Faye a little bit and it seemed to calm Kenny, because his lonely questions came further and further apart.

Carson and Faye were still crouched by the truck when a shiny-clean white SUV pulled up next to them. Faye felt safer, less exposed, crouched with this vehicle on one side of her and Carson's pickup on the other. The driver rolled down his window to speak to them.

"You two all right? And Kenny?"

"They sent you, Roy? What did we do to rate the police chief?" Carson asked.

"I've only got so many people. One of them is working with the fire marshal on a suspicious warehouse fire close to Muscogee. Two more are busy trying to track down the idiots who keep vandalizing cars at the casinos, and you know the tribe wants that one solved. And I've got some working with a federal agent on a meth lab they just busted south of Okfuskee, plus doing regular ordinary police work that's got to be done. I'm all that's left, so you people get me. Lucky you. Get in the back and keep your heads down. We're gonna go get Kenny."

Faye hauled herself up into the back seat of a vehicle that sat a little too high off the ground for her to get in easily. Carson jumped in right behind her. The seat was broad, but they huddled close together. If asked, she would have said that they were leaving room for Kenny, when the truth was that they were both too scared to give up the comfort of human contact.

The chief steered his car into position between Kenny and the wooded area where the shooter had been. "Get in," he said, but Kenny was already squeezing into the back seat with Faye and Carson.

"We're going to go up that gravel road I just came in on," the chief said, "and we're going to sit next to the highway while we wait for the K-9 unit. If there's still somebody out there, Bleck will run them down. That's one fine dog."

"You don't think there might be somebody with a gun out by the highway?" Kenny asked. He sat hunched over in his seat, using the car doors for cover.

The chief turned to look at the people behind him. His black hair was cut short and his brown skin was showing its first creases. There was no hint of a smile on his face, yet he still managed to look kind. "There could be somebody with a gun any place," he said, "but your odds of getting shot in a car sitting by a busy public road with the police chief in it are pretty low. Besides, your shooter is probably already a mile away. More, in a car. Everybody around here knows Bleck. Nobody wants to be around when he's on the job."

He reached out to shake Faye's hand. He shook it, just once, and she was not surprised to find that his palm was calloused.

"Roy Cloud. Pleased to make your acquaintance."

● ● ● ● ●

Bleck had made quick work of searching the wooded area where the shooter had hidden. It was a sizeable patch of trees covering a low hill surrounded by pastures and row crops. The patch of trees was big enough to get lost in, so it was certainly big enough to hide a scary person with a gun. Faye worried for the officers searching it.

Bleck's famous nose had found no trail, and neither he nor his partner had found bullets or casings to prove that anyone had ever shot a gun there. Faye, Kenny, and Carson sat with the chief in his SUV and tossed around ideas about what exactly had just happened.

"There's three of you that heard the shots. I know for a fact that Kenny and Carson have good sense. Doctor Faye, you look sensible, too. If you three tell me somebody was out there, I believe you. From the sound of it, I'd say that someone was shooting at you people. What exactly are you doing out here that might upset somebody that bad?"

Faye watched Carson push his hair back from his face so he could look the lawman in the eye. His hair was too short for a ponytail and too long for a man whose job required him to lean forward for hours on end. The sun had put premature wrinkles around his mouth and burned the ends of his brown hair to the color of ash. Carson was a massive man, heavy with muscle but not fat, yet he didn't have the look of a bodybuilder. He looked like a man who moved dirt and rock, day in and day out, using a body that was built for his work in a way that Faye's was not.

He also looked to Faye like a man who didn't often sit still. She could tell that the time they had spent hiding behind his truck, motionless, had been hard on him.

"We're starting an archaeological excavation today," Carson said, gesturing at Faye, himself, and two technicians who had arrived after the shooting stopped. "That backhoe is costing me a lot of money," he said, nodding his head at a machine so big that it hardly needed pointing out. Carson's workers were standing in its shadow. "Those people are costing me a lot of money, too. How soon can we get started?"

"You sure you don't want to call it a day?" Cloud asked. "Send your people home and let their nerves settle down?"

Faye looked across the grassy area being used as the parking lot for this rural archaeological site. Two of Carson's field technicians were standing with the backhoe operator, a slender dark-skinned man who was leaning against his truck and looking impatient.

Faye knew that Carson's work plan for the afternoon was critical to keeping the project on schedule. He was not going to want to send everybody home just because they were nervous.

"No, I don't want to call it a day," Carson said, proving that Faye already knew her client pretty well. "The last time work was suspended at this site, it stayed suspended for twenty-nine years. You just told me that nobody's lurking in the woods, so okay, there's nothing to worry about. It's time to get to work."

"You sure about that?" Cloud asked.

"I've got some security guards coming to help me make sure nobody shows up and starts shooting again. What else do you expect me to do? If I hold off work today, will we somehow be safer out here in the woods tomorrow?"

"Can you really get security guards here that fast? It's not like we're sitting in downtown Tulsa."

"I know some people who work security at the casinos. They'll be very happy to spend their time off earning an extra paycheck."

Roy grabbed hold of the passenger headrest, using it for leverage so that he could turn and get a better look at the people in his back seat. "You got the budget to pay security guards all summer? I don't even have the budget or the personnel to assign anybody to stay here with you today. I'll make sure somebody drives by and checks on you several times, but that's all I got."

"I can pay the security guards for a while. We're going to have to take this thing a day at a time. But know that I am not going to be intimidated into shutting down my project. I've worked too long and too hard to make it happen."

All eyes were on the backhoe, a massive yellow thing that looked angular and hard against the soft green of the trees. When it started digging, the project would officially begin.

Carson was still talking himself into doing what he wanted to do. "I'm not even sure there's anything to be afraid of. It was pretty scary at the time, listening to those gunshots, but maybe it was just hunters. Really, really stupid hunters. And maybe we were so scared that it seemed like the shots came whenever we moved. Your officers checked out the woods. I hired the guards. We'll be fine."

"Can any of you think of a reason somebody wouldn't want this project to happen?" Cloud asked.

"Carson's the tribal archaeologist for the Muscogee (Creek) Nation—" Faye began, but her explanation was cut off by a hurry-it-up nod from the police chief who knew the business of most everybody in his little hometown. "So you know that," she said, and her train of thought came to an abrupt halt.

She started again, hoping she might be able to tell Roy Cloud something he didn't already know. "The tribe will be building a park here, once Carson finishes this project that's designed to make sure that the construction won't be disturbing cultural remains. The park will offer fishing, swimming, boating, camping, playgrounds, an archaeological museum," Faye said. "You'd think the community would be in favor of that."

"You'd think," Carson said, "but people can get touchy about archaeology when it's their own history that's being disturbed."

Roy Cloud looked like he was thinking something that he wasn't saying.

They were interrupted by a racket that started loud and got louder. All the people present—Faye, Carson, Carson's employees, the backhoe operator, two security guards just getting out of their vehicle, and Chief Roy Cloud—whipped their heads toward a black van that was approaching fast enough to raise a dust cloud off the dirt road leading into the woods from the highway. People were hanging out all its windows, hollering something unintelligible.

Carson mumbled, "Oh, for the love of all that's holy," as he jumped out of the SUV and jogged toward the spot where the van had parked. "This is just like 1987 all over again."

"You thought she was going to take it lying down this time?" Cloud said as he and Kenny jogged after him. Carson just shook his head and kept running.

Faye hustled to catch up with them, wondering what had happened in 1987 that involved a van full of people making a lot of noise. She also wondered who "she" was.

As they passed the workers, Faye saw one of them turn his eyes to the approaching van and say to Kenny, "Would you look at that? You'd think thirty years hadn't gone by."

Kenny didn't respond.

A half-dozen young people boiled out of the van. In less than a minute, they were lined up beside the van, holding neatly hand-lettered signs. The slogans ranged from a Crazy Horse quote— "One does not sell the land people walk on"—to Chief Joseph's "My heart is sick and sad." Faye had to admit they'd chosen some of her favorites. The apparent leader's sign was larger and he had used his own words to make his point: "Let our ancestors rest in peace. Archaeology is an assault on our culture."

The driver pulled a handmade drum out of the back of the van and handed it to one of the protesters who immediately began a pulsing rhythm. Some of the protesters used rattles to add to the beat. With an initial shout from the leader, they began singing a call-and-response melody with a visceral power that made Faye want to stop and listen.

Carson looked at Roy Cloud. "Can we do anything about this?"

"This is tribal land. The people have a right to assemble."

Carson closed his eyes and let out an explosive breath. "All right. Let them protest. There is nothing they can do to stop this excavation. I did a mountain of paperwork to get it approved. It's legal. The tribe didn't just approve the work. They're paying for it. Everything we do here will be conducted with respect for the past and for their ancestors. And she knows that."

"In cases like this, she doesn't really respect government approval. Nor tribal approval. Nor any paperwork. That can't be a surprise to you."

Carson stood with his fists on his hips. He answered Cloud with a simple shake of his head.

"The press will be here any minute," Cloud said. "You know she called them in plenty of time to disrupt the beginning of this dig."

"Of course she did."

"And you know that the news about the gunshots you heard this morning will get out. Kenny will tell Mickey, because he tells Mickey everything, and Mickey is constitutionally incapable of keeping his mouth shut."

Carson was too upset to answer Cloud with anything but another headshake.

"I'll meet with the press," the police chief said. "It'll keep the rumors down."

"Good. Because I don't intend to give any interviews. I lost the whole morning and I have work to do this afternoon."

"Fine," Cloud said, "but I have to ask you this. Is it possible that she had something to do with the shots you heard this morning? Could she maybe have been trying to shut the project down?"

Carson's free-floating anger found a focus in Roy Cloud. "No. No! She wouldn't have risked hurting—" He stopped for another explosive sigh. "She wouldn't have risked hurting anybody. She would never hurt anybody at all."

Chapter Four

Faye wished that the earnest young man wearing two long braids and a long-suffering expression would quit banging on that everloving drum. She rather enjoyed the voices of the singers, but the drumming had wormed its way into her nervous system and stayed there. He'd been beating that drum for nearly an hour straight. He'd drummed through Cloud's efforts to speak calmly to the newspaper reporter who showed up to cover the protest. He'd even drummed while the group's leader was giving the reporter an interview.

This seemed counterproductive, since the point of a protest was to let the public know about a cause. How was the reporter supposed to write about the protest if he couldn't hear what the demonstrators had to say?

When Cloud had mentioned the "media," Faye had pictured someone, and maybe several someones, speaking seriously into a video camera. Plus a few newspaper reporters angling for an interview. She'd forgotten that she was in Sylacauga, Oklahoma.

Maybe if somebody had actually been shot, a TV crew from Tulsa or Oklahoma City would have driven out for the afternoon. As it was, the press coverage was limited to a single reporter for Sylacauga's weekly newspaper. Roy Cloud gave her an interview, then left after telling Carson to call him if he needed anything. The reporter followed him down the dirt road that wound through trees that obscured the main road and made Faye feel like she was further out in the wilderness than she actually was.

Shortly after noon, the backhoe operator was finally poised to take a literal bite out of this project. Soon enough, Faye and Carson would be doing the work they loved. It would be accompanied by singing and chanting protesters and clattering rattles and the constant dull banging of a small handheld drum, but things could be worse.

"When I got the e-mail from Joe saying that he was coming home for a visit and bringing his archaeologist wife," Carson said, raising his voice so she could hear him, "I had no idea he'd married Faye Longchamp. Your paper on archaeology/community interaction during your work with the Sujosa people in Alabama was amazing. My dissertation advisor said that every archaeologist planning to work on tribal lands here in Oklahoma should read it, and she was so right. Since I'm doing this project for the Muscogee Nation, your analysis of the Sujosas' interactions with your project team is totally on-point."

Carson turned to look at his field technicians, who were waiting patiently for him to give them something to do. Shouting over the protesters, Carson said, "I've just got three workers here in the field now. We're not doing an extensive excavation. Ordinarily, three field techs would be plenty of people with shovels but, frankly, these three worry me a little."

Faye had been hired to review Carson's work plan and assess whether his team needed extra training, so this was the most important thing he would say to her all day. "Why exactly do they worry you?"

"They're all older. Not elderly, just older, but a shovel bum's work is hard on a body. Any body."

Faye squinted in their direction. She saw gray hair, but all three workers stood tall and moved with confidence. "I wouldn't write them off because of their age, not at all. Maturity counts. Much experience?"

"Some. Two of them are in their early sixties but they stay in shape. They've done a respectable amount of this kind of work. The other one did a bit of fieldwork, but it was long ago. She actually got close to earning a master's in anthropology before she quit to get married. She was out of the workforce for a long time until her husband died late last year. After that, I hired her to be my assistant. She's been real helpful in the office, but we haven't done any fieldwork. That means she hasn't held a trowel in her hand since I was in elementary school."

Faye gestured at the only other woman who wasn't part of the irritatingly noisy protest group. She was tall, with dark brown hair cut short. "That's her?"

Carson nodded. "Her name's Emily Olsen. She's a good bit younger than the other two, maybe mid-fifties."

"You say she has some field experience? I wouldn't have guessed it by looking at her."

Even from this distance, Faye could see the woman's milk-white skin and soft abdomen.

"Yeah, she has experience. Well, some. She worked on one excavation, a very long time ago, but she's spent the years since then raising a son who's grown now and lives in Tulsa. It seems her husband left her enough money that she doesn't have to work, but she's not the type to sit around and watch TV and wait for her kid to remember she's alive. I like her. She's enthusiastic and smart. I guess I'll find out right quick how useful she's going to be in the field."

"What was her early experience like? If she was working at a volunteer site in the Yucatan, that's not much help to you."

"Actually, the location of Emily's earlier work is the most interesting thing on her short résumé. Her one and only archaeology job was here."

"In Oklahoma?"

"No, I mean right here at Sylacauga. She was part of Dr. Townsend's crew back in 1987."

Now this was intriguing. Even after twenty-nine years, stories about the notorious Dr. Townsend still surfaced whenever American archaeologists gathered to drink and gossip. No one ever suggested that she wasn't brilliant, and no one ever suggested that her early research wasn't still cited for its meticulous approach. She had done good, solid work until the day she walked away from an unfinished project and never came back.

This was that unfinished job, and Carson's job was to salvage what he could of Dr. Townsend's work. More specifically, he was the tribal archaeologist for the Muscogee Nation and he intended to finish what she had done for them here at the Sylacauga site.

Actually, if Faye wanted to be official about it, Carson worked for the Muscogee (Creek) Nation. The tribe's legal name acknowledged both their traditional name for themselves and the not-too-creative name that Europeans had given them because they tended to live near creeks.

The tension between those two names acknowledged the complex history of a civilization that had been forcibly packed up by the United States government and moved nearly a thousand miles west on the Trail of Tears. They had left a trail of graves holding people who didn't survive the trip, scattering remnant groups like breadcrumbs all along the way. There were federally recognized Muscogee or Creek tribes in Alabama and Oklahoma. There were state-recognized tribes in Alabama and Georgia. Faye knew of tribes without governmental recognition in Florida, Alabama, Georgia, and Texas, and there were probably more.

As best as she could tell, local practice was to use the European word "Creek" most of the time, and she usually followed suit. Joe called himself Creek, and her own family had always used "Creek" when referring to their distant ancestors. In legal issues, it made sense to use the official tribal name, but "the Muscogee (Creek) Nation" was bunglesome on the tongue. Faye had trouble deciding which to use, so she muddled along, inconsistently choosing one name or another.

Whatever she called Carson Callahan's employers, they had hired Dr. Townsend's one-woman cultural resources firm way back in 1987, hoping that the Sylacauga site could be developed as an archaeological park. Instead, the woman had left them with an open excavation, uncatalogued finds, unpaid employees, unpaid bills, and no money left in the budget to finish the work.

The tribe's contracting department, inexperienced in dealing with archaeological work, had paid Dr. Townsend's bills on the assumption that a bill for eighty percent of the work meant that eighty percent of the work had been done, but it hadn't. Not even close.

The tribe had hired another contractor to pick up where Dr. Townsend had left off, but their estimate of the cost for completing the work was far more than the Creeks had wanted to spend. To the tribal leadership, going forward with the project looked a lot like throwing good money after bad. What was more, it looked like a good way to get embarrassed again. They had already been embarrassed quite enough.

Rather than trying to track down their runaway contractor, they had paid the bills and made sure that the employees got paid. They had paid another firm to fill in the excavation and make sure the artifacts found by Dr. Townsend's crew were properly curated, then they had walked away from their losses.

Carson, a Sylacauga native, had been fascinated by the failed excavation for his entire life. It had been a foregone conclusion that he was going to badger his new employers into reopening it. The only question had been how much time would pass before the day that he found a way to pick up where the 1987 team had left off.

This was that day. The Muscogee (Creek) Nation had wasted a great deal of money the first time they tried to develop this site. It was up to Carson to make sure it didn't happen again.

If Dr. Townsend had wanted to continue her career as an archaeologist, running away from an active contract and leaving her client holding the bag would have made it impossible. Careers don't bounce back from such things. But she clearly hadn't wanted to keep being an archaeologist.

Rumor had it that she'd moved to a mountain cabin that she'd owned for years, cutting herself off from friends, coworkers, lovers, everybody. Or maybe she hadn't had any friends to leave behind. Her reputation for pure meanness bore out the idea that she'd found other people burdensome.

Dr. Townsend's parents had both died in the year prior to her abrupt departure. The gossips thought maybe she'd inherited enough money to walk away from her job. It made some sense that a woman like that would have withdrawn from the world the instant she'd accumulated enough money to make it possible.

"What has Emily told you about the earlier work?" she asked.

"Not much that I didn't already know. I've been the Creek's tribal archaeologist for five years, but I've been busy monitoring run-of-the-mill construction projects and roadwork for all of that time. This is my first opportunity to do work here that I consider important, even groundbreaking. This is a fascinating habitation site, quite old, but it's a big question mark in a lot of ways. Everything I know about this site comes from studying the artifacts Dr. Townsend uncovered and left behind. And her field notes. She left behind more notes than artifacts."

"The tribe wasn't interested in going forward with the work she'd started?"

"Nobody but me has ever thought there was more to this site than the handful of stone tools they found in 1987. The tribe just wasn't interested in spending the money to continue her work, so I've done my best with what I had. I did my master's work by studying Dr. Townsend's finds and field notes—'excavating the collection,' some might say. I carried that work forward into my dissertation as much as I could. The notebooks, in particular, are…interesting."

Faye had known colleagues who were this obsessed with one particular site. Sometimes they were right. "What do you mean when you say the notebooks are interesting?"

"She was a true scientist, meticulous about recording everything—the time of day, the weather, the precise coordinates of every find. I can't describe to you how detailed her notes and sketches were. Just imagine an old-time archaeologist recording every last little thing because he's working without a camera."

He wasn't telling her everything.

"I don't think that was what you meant when you said 'interesting' in that tone of voice."

"Well, her very professional sketches were a big contrast to her unprofessional sniping about her crew, her client, the job. Everything. I mean, who puts that in their field notes? I was actually pretty excited when I first read those notes. I thought I was seeing evidence that she'd planned to walk away from the job all along. Why else would you call your client a fat bastard in notes that he might eventually see?"

"Are you saying you *don't* consider calling her client a fat bastard to be evidence that she was planning to abandon the work?"

"I did, until I talked to people who knew her. You know how people are at conferences after they've had a few drinks. Their lips get loose."

This was why Faye did her drinking at home with Joe.

"According to people who worked with Dr. Townsend, her notes were always that way. They think that calling people names in writing kept her from screaming at them in public. Maybe it worked sometimes, but everybody says she did a lot of screaming anyway."

"But she kept getting work? Why?"

"Because she was that good."

Carson had done a thesis and a dissertation on the woman's work, and he'd published some impressive papers on it, too, so Faye was going to have to take his word for that.

"Did her notes give you everything you needed to do this job? What about after she left? If the firm that closed the excavation did a crappy job, you're in deep trouble."

"That's why it's so helpful to have some of Dr. Townsend's workers onboard. Emily, in particular, remembers a lot of details from the time after her boss ran away. The firm the Creeks hired to close the excavation went bankrupt years ago, but I have Emily to tell me about their work. Her description makes it sound like they did everything by the book. I don't think we'll find any surprises when we open it back up."

"We've talked a lot about Emily, but what about the other two workers? What do you know about their skill level?"

Faye pointed at two men wearing red baseball caps. No one else but the backhoe operator, Emily, and the security guards was there, so they had to be Carson's paid employees by process of elimination. She recognized one of them as Kenny, the man who had bonded with them while they waited for Cloud to arrive.

Kenny was dark-skinned, broad-shouldered and maybe a little taller than average. She could see a scrape on his chin and another one on his arm, which reminded her of their traumatic morning. Kenny had been so scared by the gunshots that he'd thrown himself at the ground, face-first. She would have done the same.

His eyes were hidden behind dark sunglasses, but he looked like he was keeping everyone and everything under surveillance. He stood, arms crossed, next to Carson's other paid worker, who also wore dark glasses. His body language said that they were friends, but Kenny was doing none of the talking.

Kenny's talkative friend was remarkably similar in build—not tall and not short, well-muscled and sturdy—but his face was paler and it was framed by a blond-and-gray beard.

"They don't worry me nearly so much," Carson said. "They're both teachers at the middle school in Sylacauga. In case you haven't noticed, the site's called Sylacauga and so's the town."

"Doesn't that get confusing?"

Carson smiled. "Sometimes. But if you don't call things what the locals call them, it gets even more confusing."

Faye watched Kenny interact with the man at his side. They didn't look at each other as they talked. Instead, they stood looking into the distance as if they'd both noticed something fascinating. The man who wasn't Kenny talked constantly. He punctuated his chatter by occasionally stopping to spit. Sometimes Kenny spit, too.

"So you found two middle school teachers willing to spend their summer vacation sweating for just about nothing. You can't possibly afford to pay them much."

"No worries. The state of Oklahoma makes me look like I'm made of money. Oklahoma doesn't even pay its teachers enough to eat on the regular, so most all of them get summer jobs every year."

"It's not just Oklahoma that shorts teacher pay."

"I hear you. It just so happens that my personal middle school teachers love what they do. They also love Sylacauga, both the town and the site. They were born here and they'll die here, so they're willing to teach for the little bit that Oklahoma pays them. And they love archaeology almost as much as they love living in Sylacauga. They worked here in 1987 for Dr. Townsend, and it wasn't their first summer project. If there's been a summer dig within driving distance of here during the past thirty years, those two guys worked it. They're worth a lot more than I'm paying them."

Faye hoped Carson was right. "So tell me about your teachers who would rather be archaeologists."

"They worked for Dr. Townsend, just like Emily, but they've got even less to say about her. About the only word my father's said about her in twenty-nine years is 'bitch.'"

It took Faye a second to realize what Carson was saying.

"Wait. You're telling me that your dad's gonna be working for you?"

He nodded toward the blond-bearded worker. Carson looked absolutely nothing like Joe, but for the second that his head inclined toward his father, the archaeologist reminded Faye of her husband. Carson looked exactly as excited as Joe would be by the prospect of working side-by-side with his dad for months on end.

"It's not like I'm in a huge metropolitan area, crammed with experienced archaeologists who want to work for cheap," he explained. "Dad's experience at this site goes back to when I was maybe eleven. I lived for the times he brought me out here with him. Dr. Townsend seemed like a goddess to me, just as beautiful and just as scary. I never said a word to her, but she's the reason I'm an archaeologist today. Anyway, yeah. That's my dad. The one with the beard. His name's Mickey. I'll introduce you in a minute."

Faye wanted to pat Carson on the hand and say "There, there," but she could add eleven and twenty-nine. It made no sense to treat a forty-year-old man like a child, even if he did present himself more like a teenage surfer than like a professional who was almost as old as she was.

Nodding at Kenny, she said, "I don't know much about him, other than that we spent half the morning being scared witless together."

"Kenny? He's Dad's best friend and he always has been. They're next-door neighbors. They hunt together. They watch football together every weekend. Everybody should have a friend like that. Kenny teaches earth science. Dad teaches biology, because there was never going to be much for him to do in Sylacauga with his other degree, the one in anthropology. And Dad will never, ever leave Sylacauga. They've been teaching at the same school all my life. Kenny caught me shoplifting bubble gum at the convenience store when I was nine."

Faye wasn't sure how she'd feel if she had to be the boss of two men who remembered what she looked like with her baby teeth. "What did he do? Make you take the gum back and confess? And I suppose he told your dad."

"Nope and nope. He paid for the gum. Then he put me in his car and drove. I was dead-sure that he was taking me to jail. Two hours in that car, driving around backwoods Oklahoma, and Kenny never opened his mouth. After he gave me enough time to think about what I'd done—more than enough time—he took me home. Still never said a word."

"So you've basically got two dads working for you."

Carson gave a single slow nod. "They're good at the work. They're damn smart. They're reliable as the sunrise. I'll survive."

Her phone vibrated in her pocket. Faye let it wait.

"How's the Muscogee tribe to work for?"

"Great. Our relationship has always been totally businesslike. That makes plenty of sense, because they're businesspeople in a big way. They run eleven casinos and thirty smokeshops and God knows what else. They don't make mistakes in hiring and training their project managers any more, so the Dr. Townsend problem will never happen again. This project is small potatoes to them, but they're paying close attention. This is their heritage and I'm digging it up."

"It's not just the Muscogee tribe who'll be watching to make sure you do this job right. Uncover human remains or burial goods, and everything will get more complicated and it will cost more."

Carson nodded impatiently, as if to say *Everybody knows that.*

"The Creeks want to build a museum here as the centerpiece of an archaeological park," he said. "They want to showcase history right where it happened, and that history might go back a very long way. As in a thousand years back."

Faye raised an eyebrow, but did not say what she was thinking, which was, *Everybody thinks their site is the biggest and the oldest.*

Carson was on a roll, so much so that he didn't even notice Faye's skeptical eyebrow. "Dr. Townsend believed the Mississippians were here, and so do I. Nobody else has ever thought they were so far west. This park could be like no other, and I want to see it happen. So do the Creeks, but they also want to make money."

Faye looked around at the land with its low trees and rolling hills and big sky. It had its own beauty, but it was nothing like the lush southeastern lands where the Muscogee had lived before being forced to walk the Trail of Tears. "Do you blame them for wanting to make a little money?"

"Oh, hell no. If people want to lose their money at the tribe's gaming tables, I'm happy for the Creeks to have it. The park will be an excellent place for gamblers to send their families while they feed slot machines. If the families are having a good time here, the gamblers will be able to stay long enough to leave a few more dollars at the blackjack table. I know how this works and I completely understand what my employer wants from me."

The backhoe operator beckoned and Carson excused himself.

As Carson walked away, Faye's phone vibrated again, twice in quick succession. She didn't like to text on company time. It was probably Joe and it was probably nothing, but three texts so close together could mean something was wrong with one of the children.

She slid her phone out of her pocket, took a quick peek, then pocketed it again. Joe's urgent messages had been:

Dad aint stopped talking since u left

he's on his 8th cup of coffee & that can't b good

may have to kill him or run away frm home again

Faye liked her father-in-law quite a lot. Okay, she loved Sly and so did Joe. But there was no denying that they'd both been irritated when he'd played the mother card to manipulate Joe into coming for a visit. They would have come eventually, but Sly's insistence that they scatter Patricia's ashes on her birthday had yanked a knot into their schedule.

College-bound Amande was scheduled to take her SATs on the very day of Patricia's long-delayed funeral. Little Michael was already booked for a week of prepaid and expensive riding lessons. Faye had thought this was excessive for such a small child, but she'd kept her mouth shut because she knew her husband very well. The child might as well be comfortable in the saddle when Santa left a pinto pony under the tree. And yes, she did expect Joe to bring the pony indoors for its Christmas morning unveiling.

The family had decided that Faye and Joe would fly out for the funeral, with Amande and Michael coming after the SATs and the pony riding. She hoped this made Sly happy, and she hoped he wasn't making her husband too miserable.

Joe was a grown man. He would survive spending a day alone with his dad.

Chapter Five

The backhoe rolled to the lip of the excavation. The first part of this dig was going to go fast. Faye hoped that Emily had been right that the excavation was closed properly after Dr. Townsend's dereliction of duty.

Any archaeological project can be interrupted by time or foul weather or, unfortunately, lack of funds. A decades-long hiatus like this one was unusual, but it sometimes happened, and there was no way to know how long any closed excavation would stay closed. That's why it was so important to close it right.

The armchair archaeologist might think, *What's the big deal? Fill in the hole. When the project starts back up, open the hole again.* But the professional knows that there is a right way to close down an unfinished excavation that may someday be reopened, and that's what Carson was doing today. He was reopening an old, unfinished excavation.

The 1987 dig had been far more extensive than the one Carson had planned. Based on Dr. Townsend's field notes and his own preliminary remote-sensing data, he intended to reopen a five-meter-by-five-meter segment of a trench that had been thirty meters long, five meters wide, and a meter deep.

This was the area where Carson thought his team was most likely to find cultural remains. If they found nothing, then the Creeks could feel reasonably confident about building their visitor's center on this spot. If they did find something significant,

Carson would be a very happy man and the visitor's center would just have to be built somewhere else.

Presuming proper field technique had been followed in 1987, a layer of plastic had been placed carefully at the bottom of the excavation. Then a backhoe had refilled the hole with the same soil that had come out of it. It had been screened first, of course, for artifacts and other important clues to the past, but its stratigraphy had been completely scrambled. It was impossible to put it back the way it had been before, so there was no point in trying.

This was why Carson could tell the backhoe operator to dig quickly. There was nothing left to learn from the soil above that all-important plastic.

The operator looked down at Carson. "Want to tell me one more time what you need done? Once this machine has done something, you can't undo it."

Carson gestured toward a rectangular area marked at the corners by stout stakes. "That's the spot. When you get down about a meter, slow down. We'll be looking for a layer of plastic."

The man nodded, then walked back to the backhoe and settled himself in the operator's seat. Carson watched him go, so intent on his work that he jumped when his father walked up behind him and tapped him on the shoulder.

"Son, you sure you want to do this today?" Mickey asked. "I keep thinking about those shots you heard this morning. Do you really think those guards are keeping anybody safe here? It's not like they can stop bullets."

"Dad—"

"You know what your mother would say."

"If I'd listened to her, I'd be doing a nice, safe desk job right now. Maybe I'd be managing a nonprofit or working for a government agency. The only element of risk would be whether I could make it to retirement before I put myself out of my misery. How long has it been since I let Mom tell me what to do?"

"Not as long as you think. Was it really your idea to buy that house down the street from her office so she can poke her head in the door any time of the day or night?"

Carson grunted.

"Your mother's very good at getting a man to do exactly what she wants, and all the while he's thinking he's a free agent. Ask me how I know."

"Yeah? Well, she can't get me to delay my project for a single minute more, and neither can you."

"It's your funeral," Mickey said.

Hearing those uncomfortable words, Faye thought about the morning's unexplained gunshots. To his credit, Mickey winced at what he'd said and withdrew, taking his spot beside Kenny. Emily joined them, and Carson's crew of three stood beside one of the corner stakes as their project got started.

Carson and Faye joined them as the backhoe began digging. The security guards slowed their patrols as they looked over their shoulders at the big machine. Faye felt as excited as everyone looked. There's something about watching heavy machinery operate, up close, that has the power to turn anyone into a three-year-old.

The backhoe's sharp blade hit the dirt and scooped a load of dry, loamy topsoil into its bucket. Fine, dry particles hung in the air.

A small motion of the operator's hands swiveled the metal beast a quarter-turn, and the great clod of dirt fell to the ground. The bucket took another bite of ground, digging into the red-clay subsoils, and dumping them into the growing pile of backdirt. Instead of slumping into a pile the way Faye's native sand would have, the hard clay broke into two big pieces surrounded by scattered crumbles and dull green grass.

Repeating the motion again and again, the operator opened the ground ahead of him and raised a pile of soil to his right. The air filled with the smell of disturbed soil and hot diesel fumes, and Faye liked it.

The backhoe never tired. As its blade traveled down, Faye stood at Carson's side and tried to calculate how much he was spending on labor and equipment rental, not to mention those security guards who weren't in his budget. She wasn't sure of the exact number, but it was a big one.

"How'd you get your employer to revisit this job now?"

"Tourism in this area is up. People love those casinos."

Faye knew this was true. Her father-in-law was a regular at the nearest one, when his bank account allowed it.

"Antiquities protection laws make it tricky to do this kind of work anywhere, these days," she said.

"I told the tribe that I thought putting a park here would get the tourists to stay an extra day. The tribal leadership must have thought I was right, because they went ahead. They had to get a lot of people to sign off, but this project has friends in high places. Favors were exchanged, backs were scratched, and surprise! The dig was approved. Obviously, I was thrilled."

While they talked, Carson never took his eyes off the moving backhoe. In his right hand, he clutched a meter stick that he would use to gauge whether the operator was getting close to the target depth. The backhoe operator never even gave him a chance.

Just as Carson was walking to the lip of the excavation to measure its depth, the operator slowly extended the backhoe's arm to its maximum length. He used it to scrape the bottom of the hole, as gently as if he'd reached out his own finger to dab a bit of food off a baby's chin. Translucent plastic glinted through a thin layer of residual dirt.

Faye suppressed a grin and the desire to mutter, *Show-off.*

Carson hurried over to speak to the man operating the big yellow machine, talking fast and pointing, as if the operator hadn't just demonstrated that he could do this job with no help from anybody.

Working slowly, the operator exposed more of the plastic, while keeping the sides of the excavation straight and the corners square. Eventually, though, he reached the limits of what heavy equipment can do. It was time for the shovel bums to take over.

Carson's workers jumped down into the open excavation like people who were happy to use the shovels in their hands. They quickly cleared the bulk of the dirt that remained atop the plastic, then they lined up at the far edge of the plastic, ready to start rolling it back at Carson's signal. He gave it.

The slippery film was awkward to handle, but they had most of it out of the hole before Faye's contracted eight hours were up, and she was glad. She wasn't ready to walk away. Not just yet. Archaeology was usually slow work, so this dramatic peeling-back of the earth made her heart race. She at least wanted to see undisturbed soil emerge before she left.

Carson was darting back and forth between Kenny and Mickey as they rolled up the big plastic sheets. Faye hung back, partly to stay out of the way but mostly to let Carson handle his own project.

When she thought she couldn't stand being on the sidelines a second longer, Carson glanced over his shoulder and held up a hand, beckoning her to join him as he went back down into the excavation. He had hardly lowered the hand before she was down in the unit with him.

The sides of the pit were gray-brown at the surface, shading quickly to red as the depth grew greater. Its bottom was like kiln-fired pottery, flat and hard and the color of brick. This was the natural state of Oklahoma dirt. There was no question that this was as far as the previous crew had gotten.

Kenny and Mickey had hauled the plastic up top, and Carson was helping as they worked hard to handle the unmanageable film as it billowed in the wind. Emily had lingered in the open excavation. Faye hoped she wasn't a slacker, but Emily didn't seem lazy. The tall woman was stooped over, taking small steps as if something under her feet felt wrong.

Faye was already moving in Emily's direction when the woman looked up from the area of disturbed soil, as long and narrow as a small human body. The soil had sunk as much as three inches in some places. The depression's corners were square and its sides were so straight that they had to be human-made.

Emily raised her head and met Faye's eyes for just an instant. There was only one word for the expression on her face, and it was horror.

Faye was at Emily's side in three strides, and this time it was her turn to beckon Carson as Emily dropped to her knees and started digging.

Faye didn't think Emily's technique showed enough care. "Hang on a minute, Emily. Let's get Carson to come take a look." Emily didn't seem to hear a word she said.

"Carson," Faye called out, "can you get down here?"

Carson handed his corner of the billowing plastic to Mickey and headed for the rim of the excavation. The scraping of Emily's trowel on exposed clay filled the open pit.

Part of Faye's brain knew that something bad was about to happen. Something really bad. It was telling her to protect herself, and it was making her adrenaline flow. Time slowed and her senses sharpened. The metallic smell of iron-rich soil was strong. She could feel the sun's heat baking the back of her bare neck, and she could feel the slight coolness of her own shadow on her hands and arms.

She looked over Emily's shoulder as she dug, saying, "Really, I think you should wait for Carson."

The older woman's hands were white as bone and scattered with brown blotches left by time. They were in constant motion and they never slowed down.

Faye recognized the sound of metal on bone before she saw the human femur emerge from the clay. Scraps of khaki-colored twill fabric surrounded it.

Faye grasped Emily's shoulder. "You have to stop," she said. "Carson will need to call the law. The tribe should know, too."

The woman never faltered in her digging.

"Emily!" Carson said as he jumped into the pit and rushed toward them. "What do you think you're doing?"

Emily proved she hadn't suddenly lost her hearing by shaking her head, as if that was an adequate answer to his question. She kept her trowel moving, never once pausing to study this grisly thing she'd found.

Now that Faye was getting a good look at Emily, she could see that the woman's dark hair was heavily streaked with white.

Creases marked the back of the hand that was wielding a trowel, wielding it as confidently as if it hadn't been decades since she last worked here.

Raking the sharp edge of her trowel across the hard-packed clay, Emily carved away a thick layer of soil that was a slap in the face of a professional archaeologist's conservative technique. She did it again. And again, faster, raking deeper into the soil with every pass. The cheekbone of a human skull emerged.

"Emily, stop," Carson said, reaching out to grasp Emily's wrist. "I mean it."

Emily shook his hand away and kept digging. Carson grabbed her wrist again and reached for the other one, but he was too hesitant about it. He moved like a man who had been so big for so long that the fear of hurting people was deeply engrained.

At five-foot-nothing and a hundred pounds, it would have taken a lot for Faye to hurt this woman who was nearly twice her weight, so she had no worries that she might accidentally hurt Emily. She reached out to grab Emily firmly by the waist.

Emily dodged them both and moved ever faster, knowing that they weren't going to let her flout the law forever. She was uncovering the skull too fast, shoveling the soil away too quickly to know whether there were artifacts mingled with it.

No, not artifacts. Clues. This was not just an archaeological dig that Emily was botching with shoddy technique. This was a crime scene. The shreds of fabric surrounding these bones were of recent manufacture, and Faye had seen a zipper among the cloth cradling the femur Emily had uncovered.

Faye's hand found her phone. Carson could handle Emily, if he could just make himself use his strength against someone who was smaller than he was. Somebody needed to call the police.

The high-pitched tones associated with the numbers nine, one, and one again, sounded at the Sylacauga site for the second time that day. They pierced the dry air and bounced off the sides of the open excavation. They were as manmade and artificial as the straight sides and right-angled corners of this woman's open grave.

For it was a woman. Faye was almost sure of it. The grave wasn't sized for a full-grown man. The portion of the femur that had peeked through the soil had looked too slender to belong to a man and too long to belong to a child. Faye would have called it gracile.

The lovely sound of the word "gracile" echoed pointlessly in her brain as Carson grabbed Emily by both shoulders and tried to haul her away from the buried skeleton. As Faye waited for the emergency operator to answer, she evaluated the portion of the skull that Emily had covered.

The chiseled shape of the cheekbone and chin also looked female. Above the exposed cheekbone, obvious fractures radiated from a distinct depression. If Faye had to guess, she'd say that someone had struck this woman a hard blow with a blunt instrument.

Only seconds had passed, but Faye hardly remembered why the phone on the other end of the connection was ringing. A voice broke the silence for Faye as she stood fascinated by Emily and her frenzied breaking of taboos.

"Nine-one-one. What's your emergency?"

Before Faye could begin her explanation—"My name is Faye Longchamp-Mantooth and I'm an archaeologist at a dig that has uncovered a human burial"—Emily completely let go of any semblance of proper technique. She turned the point of her trowel into a weapon against the unyielding clay, hacking at it, scraping, gouging.

Carson wrapped both arms around Emily, trying to get her to stop, but she was a large woman and a strong one. She was struggling so hard that Faye wasn't sure he could stop her from digging without hurting her, and it was plain to see that using physical force on another human being was something that Carson just did not want to do.

"You know better than this, Emily!" he said. "What's going on with you?"

Emily wriggled her right arm loose, aiming her trowel at the hollow between jaw and clavicle, as if clearing the soil's weight from the throat of a choking woman. She was wielding it with enough force to splinter any bones in its way.

The emergency operator was calmly asking Faye to state her emergency as Carson finally used his muscled body with force, shifting Emily's body hard enough to throw the frantic woman off-balance.

"You're fired, Emily. Fired." Carson sounded like he'd rather be saying anything else but this. "This is completely unethical, and you know it."

Emily was powerfully built, broad-shouldered and thick through the middle, and even Carson couldn't overpower her instantly. She gave the trowel one last raking jab and uncovered something that glinted, sparkled, glittered.

Lowering her torso almost to the ground, she shifted her weight so far forward and down that Carson was thrown off-balance. Without looking back at him, Emily shook herself free, frantically raking her thumbnail at the thread of silver to free it from the soil.

The end of the silver thread was fused by clay to the dead woman's sternum.

Faye wanted to say "Leave her alone. Let her rest in peace," but her voice wasn't working. The emergency operator had noticed this, because she was speaking slowly and plainly into the phone, as if trying to communicate with an injured person descending into shock.

"Ma'am. Ma'am, can you hear me? Are you okay?"

Emily was rubbing at the end of the strand of silver, trying to free it from a bone that had long been stained red by the Oklahoma clay. When an irregular object broke free of the bone, she cupped it in one hand and rubbed at the encrusted dirt with the other.

"I knew it!"

She flung the object at Carson, who reflexively let go of her shoulders and caught this thing that was flying at his face.

"I should have known she never left. She would have said good-bye. I should have known that something terrible had happened to her." Weeping, Emily stretched herself over the grave, facedown. Her tears made muddy spots on the exposed curve of a red-stained cranium.

Mickey and Kenny had jumped down into the pit and run to Carson, who was studying the silver chain on his open palm. He held it out for them all to see. It was attached to a large pendant in the zigzag shape of the Greek letter sigma.

His father took it from him, cradled it in his hands, and bowed his head over it. "She wore it all the time. Dr. Townsend, I mean. Her first name was Sophia."

The voice in Faye's ear was growing insistent. "Ma'am. I need you to tell me if you're safe. I'm sending you some help."

Faye found her voice. "Thank you, Operator. I'm fine. Perfectly okay. Just let me tell you what kind of help I need. I need the medical examiner and I need whatever law enforcement agency has jurisdiction in murder cases around here. The tribal police? The sheriff's office? The FBI? The Bureau of Indian Affairs? I have no idea. All I know is that we've found the body of a woman who hasn't been seen around here in nearly thirty years. The condition of the body suggests that she was murdered. Her name was Dr. Sophia Townsend."

Excerpt from the field notes of Dr. Sophia Townsend
June 3, 1987

If that simpering woman doesn't stop forgetting to label the sample bags, I may have to kill her. Even if she finally figures out how to do that simple-minded task, I may have to kill her anyway. She asks constantly whether her field technique is improving, following me around like a mongrel dog, so I think I shall call her Ladybitch.

As for her fieldwork, no. It is not improving. She handles her trowel like a butcher hacking the gristle out of a chuck roast, but she cries when I say so. I'm giving her a week to give up the weepy shit. If she can't manage it by then, I'm killing her.

Her blond and handsome colleague gets to keep his job, because he handles his trowel like a scalpel, but I shall call him Idiot. I haven't told him that I find him attractive, not yet, but he surely expects that I do.

His buddy has earned the nickname of Stupidface. He does not handle his trowel like a scalpel, or even like a butter knife, but I still hold out a little hope for him. He learns by watching and doing. (Unlike the fatuous Ladybitch.) Stupidface will develop some skill and he doesn't talk much, so I think I'll be able to stand having him around until his technique improves. The Hulk talks even less, which makes him a lot easier to stomach.

All four of them have gorgeous faces and toothsome asses that somewhat compensate for their deplorable lack of skill. This is, of course, why I hired them.

Chapter Six

"What now?"

Carson dropped into the front seat of his truck where Faye sat waiting for him. He looked like he wanted to go somewhere deep in the woods and just throw some rocks at a tree that never did anything to hurt him. He also looked like a man whose dream project was in jeopardy. Faye would have stayed with him for moral support as he waited for the complicated situation to play out, but Roy Cloud was back to investigate the second crime of their day, and he was beckoning her.

The Sylacauga site had morphed quickly from an archaeological dig to a crime scene. The 911 operator had wanted to send emergency medical personnel immediately. If she hadn't been standing on the lip of an open grave, Faye would have laughed at how many different ways she'd had to say, "She's dead. She's really dead. Seriously, there's nothing here but some old bones," to forestall an onslaught of paramedics.

Faye had done enough work with law enforcement to know how much they hated medical personnel tramping through their crime scene when the victim was beyond help. The medical examiner did still need to officially pronounce the bones dead and take possession of what was left of the body, though.

The Creek Nation's Lighthorse Tribal Police had sent a first responder to take control of the scene. She had barely paused to introduce herself as Kira Denton before diving into the task at hand, securing the perimeter.

The tribe had sent someone who seemed very important. Cloud had walked her around the site, showing her where the shooting had happened and showing her what was left of Sophia Townsend. She'd had intense conversations with Carson and Cloud, before leaving in an expensive but not flashy black sedan. Faye didn't have to be privy to those conversations to know what they were about. The tribal government wanted everyone to know that they were watching.

The medical examiner arrived soon afterward to confirm that the woman who had been reduced to a sad collection of bones was indeed dead. He checked in with Denton before crossing the crime scene tape she'd draped around the rim of the open excavation.

This seemed to Faye to be a logical enough place to put the boundary. For all these years, the body had lain two feet under a plastic sheet buried three feet underground. Faye could think of no way that any evidence could have survived elsewhere, but something might have survived under that sheet at the bottom of the old excavation. She didn't know what it might be—footprints? a single strand of hair with miraculously surviving DNA at the root?—but a case like this would require investigators to play long shots.

Cloud had talked to Carson first. It hadn't taken long. How much, really, could Carson know about a woman who was dead and buried when he was a child?

Now it was Faye's turn. She and Cloud sat face-to-face in two folding chairs that were just outside the crime scene tape and within eyeshot of the open grave. When he said, "Tell me everything you know," she did.

Faye told him every snippet of gossip she'd ever heard about Dr. Townsend's odd disappearance. Then she told him about the day's events that had led up to the discovery of bones that were probably Sophia Townsend's. After that, she cast about awkwardly for something else useful to say. She came up dry, but her time spent working on a Mississippi Choctaw reservation prompted her to ask an unrelated question.

"Jurisdiction on tribal lands confuses me, Chief Cloud. Is this your case to investigate? And is it going to stay that way?"

"You tell me and we'll both know."

When Faye laughed, he said, "I'm serious. Kind of serious. Jurisdiction on tribal lands confuses everybody. If this is a murder or manslaughter—and it sure looks like one of those things— then, you're right, the jurisdiction isn't mine. It's federal. That means they've already assigned someone to the case and we'll have some top-notch forensics people on the scene tomorrow as soon as they can get out here to us. But you've got to understand how stretched thin those people are. There's not going to be a lot of evidence to be found here, so they might decline to prosecute. It happens more than you'd think."

"I'm guessing you're not happy about that."

"This is tribal land. My land. If I can get justice for that woman by staying involved, I will. I'll be real nice about it, so the feds won't mind too much."

Faye thought that the Muscogee (Creek) Nation seemed to have been lucky in its choice of police chiefs.

Chief Cloud changed the subject from the death of Sophia Townsend to archaeology, asking Faye for some background on why Carson had hired her. His manner was low-key as he asked her a series of softball questions about her professional background as the topic of conversation somehow made its way back around to the events of the day. What was the significance of the layer of plastic? What did they hope to find beneath it? He seemed genuinely interested and not at all intimidating, although she thought the capability for steely interrogation was in him.

None of Faye's answers could have been any surprise to Cloud after his interview with Carson. He took notes as she spoke, despite the fact that he was recording the conversation. Somehow, those notes taken in longhand on a pad of lined paper made her feel like he took her words very seriously. They made her want to tell him something helpful. They made her dig deeper into her memory than she might have if his cheap disposable pen hadn't been traveling deliberately over the yellow paper and leaving a thin trail of black ink behind.

Roy Cloud himself made Faye wish she knew something helpful to tell him. She found his broad, calm face comforting. Trustworthy. She wanted to give Cloud the key he needed to crack this case open, but she didn't have it. All she had was a question that had been bothering her ever since Emily freed Sophia Townsend's necklace from the bones that had once encased her heart.

After Faye had told him every last thing she knew about the case, she asked her question.

"How is it possible that nobody realized that Dr. Townsend was missing? All these years, nobody ever asked whether she'd really turned into a mountain hermit? Can that be true?"

Detective Cloud's poker face was not perfect, because she saw what his eyes did when she asked this question. The lids dropped a millimeter, darkening eyes that were already black. Then he lifted them and held her gaze. There was an entire murder investigation being launched behind those eyes, but he only said, "That's something I'm trying to find out."

He moved to dismiss her, but she said, "Wait. Have you learned anything about the shooting this morning?"

"If I had a suspect, I could ask for an alibi. If I had any clues, I might be able to come up with a suspect. If I knew for sure somebody was shooting at you, the whole thing might turn into a federal case. As it is, well…I've got someone looking at videos from all the businesses along the highway between here and town, but they get a lot of traffic. The shooter would have had to have stopped at one of those businesses and done something that told us that this person, out of all the others on the videos, should make us suspicious."

"That's a long shot."

"Tell me something I don't know."

Cloud gave her an appraising look and apparently decided to tell her what little he did know. She was, after all, one of the people who'd be in the line of fire if the shooter came back. "I've got one long shot that isn't quite as long as the others. I've got somebody looking frame-by-frame at video from the security cameras at a church just a mile down the road from here. A person who's trying hard can cover that mile pretty fast, even on foot. Somebody fast might've been able to cover the whole distance before I got here. That's where I'd park if I wanted to come in on foot so that nobody could get a look at my car."

"And?"

"The cameras don't show a single car or truck in the parking lot this morning. They do, however, show the shadow of one vehicle as it passes just outside the range of the cameras at just the right time of day to be our shooter. The driver had to leave the pavement and drive across the grass to avoid those cameras. That just doesn't seem like an accident, do you think?"

Cloud raised an eyebrow as if he actually did care what she thought and was going to wait until she responded.

Faye said, "I'm going to say it's no accident, since it's the only clue we've got, isn't it?"

"If God loved me more, there would be tracks in that grass that I could match to a set of tires, but no. All God gave me was a shadow. That shadow comes into the parking lot about dawn and it leaves right after you people called for help."

He held his hand out, palm down, then whisked it to the side as if to emphasize that the person who cast the shadow was really gone.

"You can't do much with a shadow," Faye said.

"No, you can't. But you can ask yourself who would know how to stay out of camera range."

"A really smart and experienced criminal?"

"Maybe. Or maybe the head of the church's facilities committee. Or maybe just a member of the church who pays attention. Or maybe someone who works for the security company that installed the cameras. I know some people who go to that church and I know some people who do security. I'm on it."

Then he sent her away to sit beside Carson in the cab of his pickup, where she asked him the same question she'd asked Cloud.

"Do you really think that nobody realized Dr. Townsend was missing?"

Carson shrugged. "I'm not the one to ask. Ever since I was a kid, I've been hearing people say that she got sick of people and went off to live in her mountain cabin. I took the gossips at their word. All those people telling that story must've thought it made some sense."

"Except," Faye said, "for maybe one person who knew exactly what had happened to her. That would be the person who started spreading the story about her mountain cabin to cover up the fact that she was dead. Murdered."

Carson's two remaining workers, Kenny and Mickey, were standing a stone's throw from the truck. She wondered if they could hear her and Carson talking. She could hear their voices through the open window, but the constant wind made the words indistinguishable.

Their chatter had an uncertain rhythm. The words came in spurts. Sometimes they halted unexpectedly. Sometimes they sputtered out. Dead silence might have been appropriate out of respect for the dead, but it would have been damned uncomfortable. Instead, they'd settled on stiff, awkward conversation. They were surely pondering the fact that their summer jobs were now a lot less secure than they'd thought, and she was pretty sure that their personal budgets depended on that income.

There's no rulebook on how to behave after watching a long-dead body being unearthed. Carson had been in elementary school when Sophia Townsend died, and Faye had been in Florida, still in her teens. She felt confused, but not bereaved, and Carson seemed to feel about the same.

Both Kenny and Mickey must have known Sophia Townsend fairly well. Faye found them to be unreadable. The dead woman had been their boss for months. Yet their eyes were as shielded as if they were still wearing sunglasses in the deep shade of the trees that nearly surrounded the open excavation.

The other witness who'd known Dr. Townsend, Emily, was taking her turn in the folding chair across from Cloud. Emily was considerably further away than the others, but Faye could just make out the woman's troubled face.

Emily was the only person in sight who was obviously grieving for Sophia Townsend. She'd said that Sophia's parents had died just months before their daughter disappeared. No one could recall any mention of other family members. Was it really possible that no one but Emily had missed her?

Maybe. According to Carson, the people who remembered her were unanimous in saying that Sophia Townsend had been a very unpleasant person. Faye had already known this, just from years of hearing archaeologists gossip. She supposed it was possible that someone so difficult could be completely without close relationships.

But Sophia Townsend had certainly had professional relationships. An entire crew of archaeologists that might have included several more workers besides these three had been working for her when she died. How could they all have swallowed the notion that their boss had simply decided to stop coming to work?

Someone had started that story, and Faye wanted to know who it was.

Chapter Seven

It had been nearly an hour and Faye still sat beside Carson, making small talk while the police did their work. Not much had changed, other than that Faye had realized how late it was. She shot off a text to her husband to tell him she might be a while and why.

Emily was now settled onto the chair opposite Cloud. Before the investigator could begin speaking, the medical examiner approached them quickly, signaling that he needed a word with Cloud.

Cloud and the medical examiner huddled like two people who didn't want their conversation heard. Every now and then, they stopped talking and took a long look at the truck where Faye and Carson sat.

"I think we're about to have some company," Faye said.

A few minutes later, Cloud and the medical examiner proved her right by heading their way.

Instead of approaching Carson, Cloud stuck his head in Faye's window, which caught her off-guard. At the end of the day, she'd be back at her father-in-law's house, and her involvement in this job would be over. She was hardly more than a bystander. Why would he seek her out instead of Carson?

"Dr. Longchamp-Mantooth," Cloud said, "I've been thinking that you might be important to this investigation, and I guess I've been right. The medical examiner here thinks he's going to need some help."

The medical examiner leaned in her window, jostling Cloud out of the way. He shook her hand saying, "The name's Gerard. Nice to meet you, ma'am. I'd be grateful to have an archaeologist on-hand while we proceed. This ain't any ordinary case. Anybody can see that. Plus we just found this. We've got some time before the forensics people get here to decide how to proceed, but we need to all be on the same page and we need some real specific archaeology expertise here. Check this out."

He held out his phone. On its screen was a close-up photo of a small red-stained sphere protruding from a pile of dirt. Gerard had put a quarter next to it, giving the photo a sense of scale.

"May I?" she asked.

He handed over his phone. Faye pulled a magnifier out of her pocket to get a better look at the object's surface patina. She could see a hole that seemed to have been drilled straight through.

"It's some kind of bead, right? Really old?" Gerard asked. "Maybe pottery? My daddy used to plow up old beads out by the river. I'd go out in the fields after a big rain, and there they'd be. I've still got a big jar of 'em. Lots of times, somebody had scratched designs in the wet clay to make 'em pretty."

Faye could see why he'd think this was a pottery bead. It had taken on the color of the red dirt where it had been buried, so it looked like it had been molded from clay.

"Good guess," she said, "but no. This doesn't look like a pottery bead to me. The clay has stained it red, but nobody made this. I'm pretty sure it's a pearl, and a big one. But I do think you're right that it's very old. My gut tells me that it's been in the ground for a lot longer than Sophia Townsend."

"No joke?" Gerard said, leaning over for another look at the picture.

Cloud nodded. "The creeks and lakes around here are full of mussels. They're good eating, if you salt them good and don't mind chewing. Every now and then I find a pearl in my dinner."

Faye was still studying the photo. "I don't think this came from a mussel. I don't think it came from anywhere around here, actually. I'd say it was a saltwater pearl."

"If it's really old, like you say, how in the heck did they drill that little tiny hole?" Gerard wanted to know. "I figured you could mold clay around a twig to make a pottery bead, but… wow. They made that little hole without a power drill?"

Faye prepared to tell him exactly how it was done.

Cloud cut off her incipient monologue. "Could I see that?"

Faye handed him the phone.

"Are you a hundred percent sure it's old? Do you think she could have been wearing a string of pearls when she was killed?" Gerard asked.

"Maybe. It's hard to say from just this picture, but that hole doesn't look machine-drilled to me."

Cloud put on his reading glasses to get a better look at the photo. "I hear you saying she was maybe wearing a string of pearls when she died, but that don't make a bit of sense. Not if she was out here working. Pardon me if I'm wrong, Doctor Faye, but I don't think you archaeologists dress up much when you're on the job."

Being called "Doctor Faye" made her want to laugh, but Faye enjoyed the way Chief Cloud said it, so she let it slide. She gestured at her own work attire—a lightweight olive drab shirt, long-sleeved to protect her skin from the sun, over a matching pair of cargo pants. "As you can see, I'm not dressed for a cotillion. You think maybe she had a date, but she came out to work for a few minutes first?"

"There's no place nice enough to wear pearls in Sylacauga. Not unless you like to wear pearls while you chew on barbecued ribs," Cloud said. "Oklahoma City, yeah. Or Tulsa. Maybe she was on her way to one of those places. But with who?"

"Just as likely, she got killed someplace else and the creep brought her body back here to get rid of it," Carson said.

"I still think this pearl is old, so old that she wouldn't have been wearing it. Don't you agree, Carson? I also think it's significant that she was buried here," Faye said.

She looked at the excavation and imagined the earlier one that had been standing open when Sophia Townsend died. It would have been as wide as this one, five meters, but it would have been much longer. She pictured the thirty-meter trenches that she knew Sophia's crew had opened and thought that Carson had been singularly unlucky to pick the five-square-meter spot where Sophia Townsend's body waited.

"Finding her body here means that the murderer had to be someone who knew there was an excavation and knew where it was," Cloud said. "Say she was killed while being mugged on the streets of Oklahoma City or was maybe even the victim of a serial killer—the murderer wouldn't have known there was a handy pit in the woods a few miles outside of Sylacauga. How many people would have known that? Her employees. Her friends—"

Gerard, the medical examiner, interrupted him to say, "Friends? If she had any of those, or any close family, don't you think they would've missed her when she dropped out of sight? Everybody here's telling me that nobody ever reported her missing."

"Her client. That's who would have known where the excavation was." Carson quickly added, "I mean, the contract manager for the Muscogee (Creek) Nation, the one who hired her. Her client."

He emphasized the word "client," as if he couldn't think of any other way to explain the consulting archaeologist's relationship with the person who paid the bills. "His name's Phil Smithee. Phil learned his lesson after letting this project spiral out of control. He's moved way up the ladder since he was the contract manager who didn't keep a close enough eye on Sophia Townsend and her spending. These days, he heads up the tribe's purchasing department. He's over everything, casinos and all. He would have known where she was digging. Lots of people would have. It's not like it was some big secret she was working out here."

Faye felt sad for Carson. He was so clearly trying to make the list of suspects longer, so that his father wouldn't be one of only three people on it.

"I know Phil, and I'm not surprised to hear that he dropped the ball on this job," Cloud said. "He's marginally competent—which is better than the incompetent fool he was when he managed this job—but just being competent is more than most people can do and it's usually enough to get a job done. He can tell me if anybody else who knew Dr. Townsend is still around. And maybe he can dig up a file with a list of everybody that worked for her. Nothing says it was just these three, you know."

He looked at Carson as if a thought had just occurred to him. "You don't have a list, do you?"

Carson shook his head again. "She doesn't call them by their names in her field notebooks, and those are the only documents I have from the original dig. Kenny, Mickey, and Emily are from Sylacauga, so I know them personally. That's how I knew they worked here in 1987. I don't have any way to know anything about Dr. Townsend's other employees, though I'm pretty sure there were more. I guess we could do the obvious thing and ask the three of them."

He handed Gerard back his phone, then started to speak again, but the medical examiner interrupted him. "Wait. I've got another picture to show you two archaeologists. That woman, Emily, the one who you said was doing the digging when the body got uncovered? Well, she sure wasn't careful about it. She left that pearl laying in a pile of dirt by the body, and she uncovered part of something else while she was at it."

Faye thought she could see Carson's blood pressure go up when Emily's unprofessional behavior was mentioned. A puff of air escaped his pursed lips, then he said simply, "That's why she doesn't work for me any more."

Gerard thumbed the screen of his phone to scroll to the next photo, then held it out for Faye and Carson to see. After one glance, they said in unison, "We've got to get down there," jumped out of the truck, and started running. The police chief and medical examiner, both fifty-ish, had to work hard to keep up with the younger archaeologists. Faye didn't look back, but she knew they were behind her.

Carson's security guards, who were still patrolling in case the morning's random shooter came back, turned quickly when they heard the pounding steps of four people. When they saw that the four people were the tribal archaeologist, his consultant, the medical examiner, and the police chief and that they seemed to be on a mission, they went back to their silent patrolling.

Officer Kira Denton, who also heard them coming before she saw them, could see that they intended to jump her crime scene tape. She was having none of it. Proving that she took her job seriously enough to stay in top physical condition, she outran all four of them. She turned to face them with one palm signaling for them to stop.

"Halt!" Her voice was surprisingly strong for a woman of average size.

"They're with me, Kira," Cloud said. "You know I'm not going to let them mess up the crime scene."

"It's my job to make sure ingress and egress is orderly, and I plan to do it."

"You always do. But do you really need to make a big deal of this when you can see that you're dealing with me and not a homicidal maniac?"

"Maybe you are a homicidal maniac. I've never been real sure, Chief."

Keeping herself between the four of them and the crime scene tape, Denton reached for a pad of paper sitting on a chair beside the top of the ladder. "Nobody enters the crime scene without stating their business and signing themselves in. And being admitted by me."

Cloud started to speak, but she shut him down quickly. "Nobody gets in without my say-so. Not even you, Chief Cloud. Especially not you."

Maybe Denton was joking or maybe she really did insult her boss all the time. Faye couldn't tell. The four signed the paper quickly, but Denton took her time getting out of their way. As he stood at the edge of the pit, Cloud muttered, "The way people talk about Sophia Townsend reminds me of you, Kira. So sweet and charming."

Carson was the last to approach Denton's checkpoint. As he made a move to join the others, Cloud made a motion with his hand that said, "Not yet." Kira Denton walked to stand beside him as silent backup.

He took the phone out of Gerard's hand, pointed it at the two archaeologists, and said, "Tell me exactly what you see in this photo. Tell me why you broke out running just now like two startled deer when you saw it. And I mean for you to tell me right now."

"Do you see that figurine poking out of the ground? It could be really important." Faye pointed to the photo displayed on Gerard's phone. It showed the red-stained surface of a half-buried figurine.

It was encrusted with dirt, but the shape of a woman's eye, cheek, and jaw were clearly distinguishable, and her sloping shoulders protruded from the earth. A few inches away, her swelling hip also rose slightly out of the soil. Her waist, her legs, her belly, all the rest of her waited beneath the surface. Faye could hardly breathe for the thought of bringing her to light after all these years.

Gerard had spent some time studying the figurine before he brought the photo to her, and he wanted to share his theory. "She's carved out of stone, right? What a beauty."

"Yes, she's a beauty," Faye said, sorry to have to tell the man that he was wrong again, "but no, she's not stone. Someone made her out of clay a very long time ago."

"At least we can presume she's made out of clay until we check her out. She looks a lot like clay figurines that were found at Spiro Mounds," Carson said. "This could tie the two sites together. Even better, if we can prove that the Sylacauga people were also the Spiro people, we have a chance to remedy, just a little bit, one of the worst crimes against history ever committed in America."

"Well, now you've got my attention," Cloud said.

Faye nodded at Carson to explain things to Cloud. Spiro and the people who once lived there were his professional turf.

"Spiro is an important Mississippian site east of here. It was built about a thousand years ago," he began. "One of the mounds was still more than thirty feet tall into the early twentieth century. The mounds at Spiro stood more or less intact until the Great Depression, when some men leased the property so that they could 'mine' them for artifacts. It's hard to describe the destruction they left behind. Pits, shafts, even tunnels—they completely honeycombed the biggest mound. And at the heart of it? They found and destroyed a—well, let's call it a time capsule, because that's what it was."

The archaeology-loving medical examiner said, "Dear God."

"The Spiro people had built a chamber out of logs at the center of the biggest mound, filled it with treasures, then sealed it with clay. Nothing like it has ever been found in North America. Maybe anywhere," Carson explained. "The looters destroyed it. They sold what they could and trampled the rest into what was left of the mound. Because of this, there are artifacts from Spiro Mounds in museums all over the world, but not nearly so many here in Oklahoma as there should be."

Roy Cloud's face was very still. Faye had lived with Joe long enough to recognize the expression of a peaceful man working to quell a murderous anger.

"The sealed chamber had created unique conditions that preserved fabric, lace, feathers, wood," Carson said. "It was like an American King Tut's tomb. Eventually, the looters were forced to stop, and Oklahoma passed an antiquities law to keep looting like that from ever happening again. And what did the looters do in response? Boom." He flung his hands outward, miming an explosion.

"What are you saying?" Cloud asked.

"They used black powder to blow the rest of the mound to oblivion," Faye said. "Out of sheer spite."

Gerard was looking at his phone. "This little statue. Are you saying that finding it means that there might be stuff here like the stuff that got blown up at Spiro?"

"If we're really lucky," Carson said, "there could be a whole town beneath our feet that was built by the same culture. I'm here to try to find it."

"That would make up for losing the American King Tut's tomb just a little bit, wouldn't it?" Cloud said. He peered over the lip of the excavation and considered the grave at its bottom. "I don't want this thing messed up. We work together with the feds real well. Have to. Jurisdictional issues around here are always weird. I'm sure those forensics people coming tomorrow are really, really good at what they do, but they can't possibly have any more experience at a site like this than any of us do. That's because there's probably never *been* a site like this."

Faye couldn't disagree.

"No disrespect to them intended," Cloud said, "but I want the Creek Nation to have its own archaeologist working alongside them and I don't want to wait God knows how long for our purchasing people to hire somebody who's never even been here. It's tornado season. We can't afford to let a twister tear everything up. That's why we came to talk to you, Dr. Longchamp-Mantooth. The federal investigator—the name's Fred Bigbee—has cleared you and me to go down there tonight. I had to promise I wouldn't touch anything, but he's allowing me to photograph the scene and you to document the bones where they lay."

Faye still wasn't exactly sure why the police chief and the medical examiner were talking to her, instead of talking to the very qualified tribal archaeologist managing the job where the body was found. Nobody in the world knew as much about this site as Carson.

She began, "I'm sure that Dr. Callahan and his team can help—"

"I'm sorry but we need you." Cloud interrupted her with the crisp efficiency of a polite man who currently had no time for the niceties. "Dr. Callahan's team is made up of three people who could, in theory, be suspects in this case. Well, two people and Emily, who he just fired."

Faye began saying "But Dr. Callahan himself wasn't here—" but she stopped herself.

Carson *had* been here. He'd been an eleven-year-old kid, but he'd been on this very spot with the victim and her crew. He'd known all the suspects. He'd even known the victim. And his father was on the list of suspects. There was no way that Roy Cloud or the coming federal agents were going to let Carson Callahan muck about in this crime scene.

This was a murder case, maybe a capital murder case. Faye could see that she was their best option for solving it without compounding the tragedy of Spiro by mishandling the archaeology of this probably significant site. There was nothing for her to say but, "I'll help you in any way I can."

"Thank you," said Cloud. "My budget isn't anything to write home about, but I am very glad to have a consultant of your stature on the case."

"For this?" Faye said. "I'd do it for free."

Cloud laughed and said, "You're a helluva businesswoman, Doctor Faye." Then the laughter died. "But I'll pay you anyway. I want my own person watching over what the FBI's folks do with the forensic investigation. Just in case. Are you willing to do that?"

Faye answered simply, "Yes."

Carson was looking at him expectantly, but Faye knew what Cloud was going to say.

"I'm sorry, Carson. Until we clear your dad, I just can't have you in the crime scene. That goes for Kenny, too. I know what he means to you. Until those two are cleared, you can't be in the excavation, not even as an observer."

Carson made an odd sound, as if he wanted really badly to say something but he knew better.

"Denton here," Cloud gestured at the pugnacious officer at his side, "will admit Dr. Longchamp-Mantooth to the crime scene, but you need to stay on the other side of the tape, Carson."

Officer Denton glowered over Cloud's shoulder to show that she would take any measures necessary to keep Carson where he belonged.

"Mind you, Dr. Callahan, I'm not saying that I think your dad did it. I don't have a clue who did it. I know how bad you want to be down there digging up another King Tut and his treasure, but it can't be helped."

Officer Denton logged Cloud, the medical examiner, and Faye into her records, initialing their signatures. Then she let them pass. Locking eyes with Carson, Denton forcefully drew a line through his name.

As Faye stepped down into the excavation, she caught Carson staring at her. In his eyes, she saw anger at fate for separating him from the defining moment of his career. She saw anger at Cloud, too, for his part in that. Perhaps she saw a son's anger at his father just for being on the planet, a state of mind that had been around since Oedipus. And she thought maybe—probably—she saw anger at her for stepping into the role he so desperately wanted to play.

Chapter Eight

It was a strictly hands-off situation. Faye crouched in the dust with her magnifier, her camera, and her field notes, and she examined Sophia Townsend's grave as closely as she could without actually touching anything.

Cloud was taking pictures. He'd started by backing up against one wall of the excavation and taking a photo, then walking in a circle around the grave, just a few degrees at a time. If the crime scene had been a clock, Roy Cloud would have been taking pictures at twelve o'clock, one o'clock, two o'clock, and all the way back to twelve. When he finished doing that, he'd moved all the way in and circled Sophia Townsend's body again to take close-ups.

Still not finished with preparing a baseline set of photos of the entire crime scene, he stood next to the grave and turned around in a tight circle with his back to the grave, taking a set of pictures facing outward. If Sophia Townsend had still had eyes, these pictures captured what she would have seen from her vantage point.

Two younger officers were setting up a temporary shelter over the grave because Cloud was taking no chances. It was just a tarp hung on head-high posts, but it was better than nothing.

"The weather center says they can't say much about tomorrow's chance of rain, but today's looking good. We may get a few drops this afternoon, but no real rain to speak of. That's good because there's not enough daylight left for anybody to excavate those bones right tonight," Cloud said. "This tarp will keep those drops off Dr. Townsend until tomorrow. If the meteorologists are wrong and we get one of those evening storms that come around this time of year, there's not a thing we can do to keep that grave dry."

Faye looked up at the two people standing above them, watching. Denton hadn't budged from her assigned post. Carson seemed to have assigned himself permanently to the spot right across the crime scene tape from Denton. He'd fetched his binoculars from the truck and was studying Faye's every move.

This was hardly necessary. Roy Cloud had finished taking about a thousand pictures and he was standing two feet behind Faye, watching her at point-blank range to make sure that she touched nothing and damaged nothing. If Faye had done anything that Carson needed to see, Roy Cloud surely had a picture of it.

Faye was pushing her luck with the ever-watchful Cloud, by kneeling to bring her face within inches of the half-buried pearl and figurine. "If I could just figure out why they're here and why they're at this depth, I'd be happy. This makes no sense."

"If it didn't look like a murder," Roy said, "I'd say that some-body loved her and buried her with things she'd treasured when she was alive."

So Roy Cloud was a romantic. Faye wasn't surprised.

The fractures on Sophia Townsend's skull spoke against Cloud's romantic notion, so he and Faye just stared at the figurine, pearl, and bones. It was as if they thought the buried things might jump out of the ground and explain themselves.

Under magnification, the figurine's clay surface showed impressions of its maker's fingers, which was pretty cool when she thought about how many years it had been since its maker's hands had gone to dust. She itched to sift through the backdirt that Emily had piled up while uncovering a corpse. Who knew what else she could have dug up in her frenzy to find Sophia Townsend?

The bones looked just as they had when they first emerged from the ground, red-stained and lonely. Faye took several photographs of the network of fractures marring the skull.

She was startled when Cloud dropped to a crouch next to her. "Tell me what you see."

"Well, I mostly see that Emily made a mess of uncovering this burial. See that mark on the sternum? And that one on the mandible?" she said, gesturing with her pen. "They're fresh. Toward the end, Emily was hacking at the ground hard enough to gouge bone."

"No wonder she didn't notice the pearl or the figurine. And no wonder Carson fired her."

"No joke. She was looking for the silver necklace that would prove to her that Sophia Townsend was the person buried here. And she found it. I don't suppose you've got any doubt that this is Dr. Townsend?"

Cloud shook his head. "Not with that necklace around her throat. Gerard's gotta earn his pay, so he'll do his best to prove it beyond a shadow of a doubt. It's not likely that Sophia Townsend's dental records can be had after all this time, but you can bet that Gerard has already started looking for them. And he'll try to find her relatives, of course."

"I know of a case where a skeleton washed up on a beach after a hurricane," Faye said. "The upper left arm had obviously been broken. Someone came forward with a picture of a woman who had been missing for forty years. She had a cast on her left arm. We were able to prove it was her. I can't tell you how it felt to put that case to rest. And her. It was good to give Abigail Williford justice after forty years."

"Some cases turn personal. It sounds like this one turned personal to you."

"She washed up on my beach."

Cloud was silent. Faye, still crouching by the grave, looked back over her shoulder at him, wondering why he didn't speak. It seemed that Roy Cloud was not a man who talked just to fill the air with words. Joe was like that but, in Faye's experience, it was a rare quality.

After a time, he spoke. "That's pretty personal, Doctor Faye, finding a woman's bones on your own land. Maybe you felt about her the way I feel about anybody who dies on tribal land. It's my land. Partly mine, anyway. I feel responsible."

Faye nodded but said no more. Cloud had said exactly what she was feeling.

"As for Sophia Townsend," he went on, "maybe her medical records will tell us something that proves whether these are her bones, but it's been a long time since she died. Doctors and dentists retire and their files were on paper back then. Things get lost. In the meantime, the necklace is enough to prove it to me. That and the fact that even a cursory web search of her name should turn up something if she were still alive, but it just doesn't."

He pulled his phone out of his pocket. "I mean, I should be able to find out plenty of things about Dr. Townsend with nothing but *this*. I did a web search that pulled up a few articles she published in the seventies and eighties, but other than that? Nothing."

Faye's eyes traveled over the curve of Sophia Townsend's bare cranium, as if that would tell her something about who the woman really had been. "From what people say about her, she doesn't seem like the kind of person who would have hung out on Facebook."

"She's not just absent from social media. She's absent from the whole Internet. She hasn't even got a White Pages entry. I can't find a phone number or an address anywhere. Even a mountain cabin has an address, unless it was built illegally and totally off the grid."

"It's as if she died before there was a World Wide Web," Faye said.

Cloud poked around on his phone. "It says here that the World Wide Web was invented in 1989. She did die before that."

"There you go."

Cloud's eyes stayed on the bones in front of them. He said, "And it's as if she died before we required standardized addresses so that calling 911 would bring help when people called for it. Maybe mountain cabins really didn't have physical addresses back then."

"Was 911 even available everywhere back in 1987?" Faye asked.

Cloud shook his head and waved the phone at her. "Not according to this amazing machine I keep in my back pocket. I was a grown man in 1987 and I still have trouble wrapping my brain around how much the world has changed."

"Same here."

"As I recall, private detectives made a real good living back then, running down information that I can find on my phone now. Working this case is like climbing into a time machine. I might have to do the legwork the old-fashioned way, but I can do it. There aren't many advantages to not being twenty-five years old any more, but that's one. I know how to roll up my sleeves and look through a file drawer for paper evidence."

Faye was using her thumb to estimate how long the exposed femur was. "How do you plan to go about doing that old-fashioned legwork?"

Cloud laughed. "Well, I'll do my best to keep my own paws out of the file drawers, because I've got other fish to fry. This is where federal jurisdiction comes in handy. I can find out about tax delinquencies and mortgage defaults and such around here in the 1980s, but this isn't where Sophia Townsend owned her cabin. The FBI has much longer arms. It would sure help if I knew where that mountain cabin was, but there aren't that terrible many places around here that have what most people would call mountains. Lots of Oklahoma is flat as a pancake, but not all of it. My money is on one of the counties east of here. The land has got some elevation and it's close enough to drive back and forth every weekend."

"What do you expect to find?"

"I expect to find that Sophia Townsend stopped paying her bills in 1987, just like I expect her dental records, if they still exist, to match the teeth we're looking at right now."

"We're going to have to be smart about how we dig here. Here's an example," Faye clicked the button that turned her pen into a laser pointer. She used it to make a red dot on an area of bare dirt that still bore the scrape marks left behind by Emily's trowel. "It's going to be really tricky to get the left jawbone out of the ground without disturbing stuff like that."

"Like what? I don't see anything, and my eyes aren't as old as all that."

Faye pulled a flashlight out of her pocket and shone light over the spot, parallel to the ground. "See that?" The rays of light, raking across the surface at a different angle, revealed a domelike bump about the size and shape of a contact lens.

He turned his head to the side and leaned down so far that his cheek nearly touched the ground. "I do. Is that another pearl?"

"I can't answer that question, but it's about the right size. And so's that." She moved the laser pointer's red dot a few inches to the right. Then she moved it again. "And that."

"You're saying we may have three more pearls buried here?"

"Maybe more. We won't know until we look."

"You're worth every cent I'm paying you and every cent I should be but I'm not. Do you see anything else I should know about?"

"I do. Those pearls, if they're pearls, are in the area between the skull and collarbone, very near the vertebrae. And they are at a slightly lower level than the vertebrae. Now imagine that those neck bones still had flesh on them."

"If those bones were still inside a neck, the pearls would be beside it, but lower. Is that what you're saying?"

"Yes. And see where the figurine is, right up next to the clavicle but slightly below it?"

"You're saying that the figurine was underneath her body, too?" Faye nodded.

"Were they there already? Did the killer coincidentally pick a spot for the grave that was on top of some really important artifacts that have been waiting here for a thousand years?"

"No, I don't think so. I can't even say that the artifacts are the same age as each other, not without lab tests or undisturbed stratigraphy. If they aren't the same age, then it's even less likely that they waited patiently together for Sophia's body to join them. I've seen pictures of pearl necklaces and similar figurines from Spiro, but they've got wildly different dates. I mean, like…

hundreds of years of difference…so that argues against these things being buried at the same time."

"But here they are together."

"Yes. And if I'm right that they're of different ages, there are only a few situations where you'd expect to find them together. Usually, it would be because somebody brought them together on purpose. Now look at this."

She used the laser pointer to point out a rectangular patch of darker red soil on the bottom of the rectangular grave. It was so obvious that even Cloud's inexperienced eyes were able to see the difference in the soil colors, once she pointed it out. The smaller rectangle lay under the skull and the neck, extending about halfway down the length of the sternum.

"It looks to me like a second hole was dug below the grave and below the pearls and figurine. I think it was shaped like a box." she said. "I have no idea why it's there."

"Who dug it? And who buried the artifacts on top of it? Sophia Townsend? Her killer? Somebody who's been dead a thousand years?"

"I don't know," Faye said. "I just know that they're here."

Faye had done all she could do with the daylight available. She had scrutinized the condition of the bones, pearl, and figurine. They had been photographed and documented in her notes. She and Cloud had made sure they were covered in case of rain, to the extent possible. She'd visually inspected the floor of the entire excavation, in case something had been waiting there for the twenty-nine years since the protective layer of plastic was laid in 1987, and she had found nothing.

Standing beside the old bones, Faye watched Carson's security guards making their rounds. Kira Denton was debriefing Roy Cloud, and the other two officers were still fussing with the canopy they'd hung over the grave.

Sophia Townsend had been alone so long that all the activity around her seemed noisy and intrusive. Faye had never before understood so fully the meaning of the age-old wish for the dead to rest in peace.

It was time to leave Sophia Townsend be, even if just for the night.

She climbed out of the excavation for the last time that day and found Carson, unmoved and frustrated, in the exact place she'd left him.

"What now?" The man was so upset that he was almost twitching.

"What you need is some patience," she said.

"I've been patient. Very patient. What I need is a beer. I waited here all afternoon while they questioned all three of my workers. Then they all three hung around even after the police released them. Should I pay them for the whole day? The two who are still working for me, I mean. Not Emily. Oh, you know what I'm saying."

Faye grabbed the man by both elbows and steered him toward his truck. If he was going to melt down, he didn't need to do it in front of his employees. He certainly didn't need to melt down in front of the police.

"You can't pay them indefinitely if the investigators don't release the crime site soon. But today? Yes, I think you should pay them for today."

All Carson could say was "My budget." He got in the truck and laid his head down on the steering wheel.

"Your budget is what it is. Unexpected things happen. Smart managers pad their budgets a little, and you're smart."

Carson grunted, and Faye thought that the tone of the grunt said, *Yes, I did pad my budget, but I didn't expect to lose the padding on Day One.*

"I called Joe a while ago," Faye said. "He should be here any minute."

Carson's wordless grunt said, *I can't afford your husband and I can't afford you, either.*

"Joe's not on the clock. He just wants to say hello to an old friend. And I'm not on the clock, either. If you're able to dig again before I leave, I'll be back on the job as if nothing ever happened."

Carson raised himself to vertical and stuck out a hand. "It's a pleasure doing business with you."

"Any time."

He took a silent moment to look at his father and Kenny Summers standing idle under an oak tree like two smokers taking a break. Emily was sitting alone with her back against a pine trunk gazing with dull eyes at the pit where Sophia Townsend lay dead. Carson didn't bother giving Emily a glance, so Faye knew he was still angry with her.

Of course, he was angry with Emily. She had broken a generous handful of taboos and thoroughly earned being fired from the job.

Carson watched the three of them for a while, then he said, "I guess I need to rethink everything."

Stepping out of the truck, he gave Faye a follow-me jerk of the head, so she got out, too.

Kenny took a step in Carson's direction, interrupting him before he even started to talk.

"We can't do this, Carson. We can't disturb that woman with our digging. She needs to be left alone to rest. Anybody can see that this site was never meant to be dug up. We shouldn't have done it in 1987 and we shouldn't do it now."

Faye noticed that Kenny had been willing enough to bend those convictions to take this paying job. Twice.

"I differ with you on that, Kenny," Carson said. "I think that finishing Dr. Townsend's work is the best way to honor her memory. She's in a better place and she doesn't need the body lying at the bottom of that excavation now. She wouldn't want her bones to stand in the way of getting this important work done."

Kenny didn't answer him. He just stepped back, standing shoulder to shoulder with Mickey. Faye didn't doubt that Kenny would be coming back to work. He might not like the job as well, now that Sophia Townsend's body had been uncovered, but he still needed the money.

Carson started talking, and it was clear that he'd been thinking through these words ever since a lonely corpse had surfaced in the middle of his excavation.

"I've been blaming Sophia Townsend for thirty years of neglect of this site. Well, maybe I was wrong. Maybe she planned to get up the day after she was last seen and come to work, just like she did every day. We can't know what was in her head, but there has to be a reason everybody was so quick to believe she'd run off. The police are trying to find the answer to why she died. I just know I'm going to finish the work she started. That's as good a memorial as an archaeologist can have."

With one hand on the truck door, he turned to face his employees one last time.

"You might as well go on home. You can stay home, Emily, and you'll get your paycheck for the time you worked before I fired you. Dad and Kenny will be paid for all of today and after that—well, I don't know. I'll let you know when we're able to get back to work. I promise. As soon as I know, you'll know. Have a good evening."

Chapter Nine

Joe opened the door of the truck where Faye and Carson sat. She scooted to the middle of the bench seat as he dropped down beside her and said, "You two making plans for a big dig? One with lots of paying work for Faye and me?"

"Yeah, eight whole hours of your wife's time and none of yours," Carson said. "You were expecting more than that?"

Joe laughed and stuck out a hand. "So how're you doing? Last time I saw you, you were taller than me. And heading off to college, I think."

"I was! That was a long, long time ago, wasn't it?" Carson reached around Faye to grab Joe's hand with both of his and shake it hard. "I remember thinking I was so grown up and you were just a kid. How much older am I? Two years? Three?"

"Something like that. Who would've thought we'd ever wind up in the same line of work?"

"Not just in the same line of work. You've passed me up, little buddy. You've got an established business. You got married. And you married up! I mean, really up. Look at this woman. And she's smart, too."

Faye laughed until Joe let go of Carson's hand and put a possessive hand on hers. That's when she realized that these guys were serious. She decided to keep her silence until they finished the manly tallying of status points that would, she presumed, establish that Joe was no longer Carson's "little buddy."

"Got a couple of kids, too," Joe said, holding out his phone so Carson could assess the quality of his offspring.

Faye wondered how many college credits of anthropology had been earned by the three people sitting on this pickup truck's bench seat. She also wondered if either of the others had noticed that the way they were maneuvering to assert primacy was just classic. Right out of a textbook.

Carson looked at Joe's phone and made admiring noises. "I never would've thought I'd get this old and still be single. It's time to settle down and start a family. It really is. My parents have been praying for grandchildren for so long that they think maybe God's going deaf. Man, I put everything aside to get that doctorate."

Yep. Carson knew he was losing the battle over who had the better personal life, so he had no choice but to play the PhD card.

Joe and his bachelor's degree couldn't counter it, so he squeezed Faye's hand a little tighter and scrolled through his phone for more kid pictures that were even cuter, if such a thing could be possible. It was time for Faye to stop this.

"Joe hasn't been home to Oklahoma in years, and I've never been here at all. Let's get out of this truck and look at it before it's too dark to see."

• ● ● ● •

The three archaeologists walked away from the pickup and the excavation and the dead body of Sophia Townsend.

They followed a faint path, almost a rabbit's trail, that led through the thick woods surrounding Carson's worksite. A recent wildfire had burned through the underbrush, leaving a black swath that was rapidly going green with new growth. The burned area crossed the narrow path and extended through the woods away from the excavation.

A clear creek skirted the base of the hill where they stood. Faye saw no dramatic scenery, no craggy mountains or rushing river, only pastures and hay fields stretching out toward a line of low hills. The whole scene was overwhelmingly green, with the earthy soil of new-plowed fields and the near-black of the far hills offering a sharp contrast. A charcoal gray cloud billowed on the west horizon. Faye couldn't have said why the silver-blue sky looked enormous, but it did.

Joe was looking around, spinning in a slow circle to drink it all in. Until this moment, she'd had no idea that he was homesick.

They stood silent for five minutes or more until Carson raised a hand and pointed east.

"The mounds at Spiro are that way, as the crow flies. Spiro is said to be the westernmost Mississippian outpost of any significance—but the spot where we're working is indisputably west of Spiro. You know what that means?"

"If you find something significant, you win," Joe said. "That's what it means. You'll rewrite that part of the history books."

"Maybe we did it today. Maybe that figurine and that little pearl were what I came here to find."

Yep. They were back to establishing primacy, but this time they were competing with the entire field of archaeology, instead of with each other. Faye figured that was progress.

Carson was finished with talking about his personal life, since Joe was winning in that arena, but he could talk all day about archaeology.

"We know that the people at Sylacauga traded with Mississippian cultures as far away as Ohio. We've found the lithics to prove it." he said. "Well, Dr. Townsend did, back in eighty-seven. It beggars the imagination to think that they weren't in touch with the people at Spiro, just a day or two away by canoe. Frankly, I think they *were* the Spiro people."

"Spiro's always seemed small," Faye said, "compared to the other big Mississippian sites."

"Exactly." He spread his big hands and made a big gesture toward the verdant hills to the east to emphasize his point. Carson was born to work outside. Indoors, he would be forever breaking things.

"Do you have anything that can be carbon-dated?" asked Joe.

"Not yet, but I budgeted for thermoluminescence if we find any potsherds. You can bet that I'll start reading up tonight on carbon-dating pearls. I'm not sure it's right to take a sample of something as potentially significant as that figurine, but maybe sampling just one of those pearls would be okay. It's just so exciting to find something that's indisputably different from anything found here before. And to find it on the first day? Amazing. All these years, we've had nothing to work with but the few finds left from Dr. Townsend's work. I've squeezed all the information out of those artifacts that I can, and I'm mightily tired of writing the papers that should have been written by Dr. Townsend. God rest her soul."

He bowed his head.

"I'm feeling pretty awful right now. All these years, I've been thinking terrible things about her. Saying them, too. I thought she'd walked away from her responsibilities—to her client, to her workers, to history—and all the time she was lying dead in the ground. Murdered."

He looked at Faye and Joe for confirmation. "She had to have been murdered, don't you think? I can't think of any other reason for her to be buried like that, in secret and with a fractured skull. And it looked like she was still in her work clothes. God."

"It's the only explanation I see," said Faye.

Carson started walking back toward the excavation quickly, as if he felt responsibility tugging him. Faye and Joe followed.

"All through grad school, I kept hoping that I was missing something in those dusty old storage boxes she and her crew left behind, but the boxes never gave up anything but field notebooks and stone tools. No wood, no fibers. If she even found any seeds, they were lost in the confusion when she disappeared. You can't carbon-date something that was never alive."

"No, you can't," Faye said. "But reopening Dr. Townsend's excavation gives you a chance to put a date on this place. Pray for charcoal left behind on a very old hearth."

Carson walked even faster. "That's why I picked this spot for the excavation. Remote sensing showed an anomaly that was big enough to be significant. It could have been a hearth or something else datable. Who could have expected that it would be the bones of Sophia Townsend?"

When they got to Carson's pickup, he reached into a Styrofoam cooler sitting on its tailgate and offered them both a beer, but Faye pushed aside a layer of ice and found a soda. "We're both driving."

Carson, who didn't seem to be as finicky about driving under the influence, sucked down half the bottle before he spoke again. Rubbing a thumb over the water condensed on its label, he went on talking archaeology as if he'd never stopped.

"Here's my theory, and I know it's unorthodox. I think the Spiro site itself was ceremonial, not residential, because the bulk of the population didn't live there. I think they lived here around Sylacauga."

He held out his hands, palms down, making circles that encompassed the land outside the pickup cab. "And I don't mean that the Spiro people moved here when their civilization started to decline. I think they were always here, leaving the priests at Spiro alone to do their magic. The soil was better here and the creeks were more productive. Spiro couldn't have supported a population anywhere near the size of a city that could be built at Sylacauga."

"Not while Spiro was supporting its priest class," Joe said.

Carson nodded like a man who was surprised to hear that his little buddy had amassed some expertise. "Exactly."

"Do you think the populations mixed at all?"

"Sure. The Arkansas River isn't that far from here by water. They could have paddled downriver to Spiro for festivals and camped. They'd have been fed as part of the ceremonies, so they could travel light. People have done a lot harder things for religion."

"People who travel light don't leave much of a mark," said Joe, who never carried anything bigger than a backpack. "Except maybe they left canoes and rafts behind at Spiro, if they walked home instead of paddling against the current. Wouldn't that be something awesome to find?" Joe said.

Carson's face lit up. "It certainly would. One day, I'm going to build a traditional canoe and try to paddle this far. I'd have to portage around dams that weren't there in Mississippian times, but I think it could be done. Anyway, maybe the pearl and the figurine are exactly what we came here to find."

Faye had worked with people who were this obsessed with a site. If the murder investigation continued hampering his project, Carson wasn't going to take it well. He already wasn't taking it well.

"Like I told you on the phone, Faye, Dr. Townsend could have rewritten Oklahoma history, if she hadn't abandoned the job...."

Carson's face went red. "I've got to learn to stop saying those kinds of things. It's such a shock to know that she's dead. God rest her soul."

● ● ● ● ●

Sylvester "Sly" Mantooth cradled a chipped and stained coffee cup in a pair of hands that had handled much more potent drugs than caffeine.

Nicotine, for sure. He couldn't have denied the yellow stains on the fingers of his right hand if he'd wanted to, but he didn't want to. In recent years, Sly had learned to own his mistakes. If a man approached his time in a penitentiary properly, this was his first lesson.

These hands had handled alcohol, for damn sure, and a lot of it. The love of alcohol, first his father's and then his own, had marked the first fifty years of his life. He still missed his whiskey, but he didn't miss the man he was when whiskey got the better of him.

And drugs. Dear God, the volume of drugs these hands had handled during his short drug-smuggling career. He could never know what those drugs had done to the people who used them, and he was going to have to live with that for the rest of his life.

Sly had been a trucker since he got kicked out of boarding school, but if he could have rolled together every dollar he'd ever made on hauling legitimate loads, the total wouldn't touch the money he'd gotten to move those little bags of white powder. Until he got busted. The money had come too late to save Patricia from the cancer they couldn't afford to treat, and Sly believed in his heart that this was part of his punishment for running drugs.

These hands didn't deserve to hold anything better than a chipped and stained coffee cup, but they were soon going to be holding his little grandson again. Sly knew that he didn't deserve that joy, but he was going to grab it.

The night before, they'd pounded a hello on his son's back, because he wasn't real sure he knew how to hug a grown man. Both of Faye's little hands had fit easily in their grip as he told her hello and didn't tell her how grateful he was to her for making his son so happy.

He'd tell her. One day, he'd tell her.

Sly had a lot of practice at hiding his feelings, so it hadn't been all that hard to keep the surprise from his eyes when Joe had hung up the phone and told him that Sophia Townsend's body had surfaced.

She was back. After all these years, she was back.

Chapter Ten

Faye saw no chance that she and Joe would be getting away from the Sylacauga site any time soon. Roy Cloud had said he had no more need of her till morning, but she knew that Carson would not be leaving until Cloud and the medical examiner finished their work and left his precious excavation to the tender care of Kira Denton.

Faye couldn't bring herself to leave Carson sitting alone thinking about the corpse of a woman he had known hidden at the bottom of an excavation at an ancient site he'd spent his entire adult life studying. Even if she could have justified walking away from Carson by telling herself, *I just met him today. How much do I owe him, really?* there was Joe to consider. Long ago, Joe had been close enough to this man to earn the nickname, "Little Buddy." Joe had walked away from Carson once—and his father and his memories of his mother and the whole state of Oklahoma—but Faye knew that he wasn't going to do it now.

Faye was worried about Carson. He'd nearly drained his beer and she saw the telltale sidewise glances of a man who really wanted to go pull another one out of the cooler. He was a big man who could surely metabolize a lot more alcohol than she could, but pounding two beers and getting right behind the wheel was a bad idea in Faye's book. She'd already decided that she or Joe would be driving Carson home if he reached into that cooler again any time soon.

Carson was putting up a good front, but he had to be stewing over losing control of his site to the police. And to her.

Good-hearted Joe was a lot more suited than Faye to making folksy small talk, so she was letting him do that.

"This is beautiful country, ain't it?" he said. "Not many people, though. The Creeks think they'll be able get people to come to a park way out here?"

Carson knew the answer to this, and answering it made him perk up a bit. "People already do come out here. That creek we saw drains into a lake that the locals have always used for fishing and swimming, but the Creeks can't develop the property into a moneymaking recreational area, not without encroaching on the archaeological resources. Even back in eighty-seven, Dr. Townsend knew that building a tackle shop on top of a burial site wouldn't go over well around here."

"Nor is it legal now," Faye said.

"It was illegal here then, too. Oklahoma had a burial desecrations law and an antiquities law even before the federal government passed NAGPRA to address the same issues. We had to. Remember that you're in the old 'Indian Territory.' We've always needed to work with tribal leaders. Not that we've always done the best job. Nope. Not saying that. I'm just saying that every now and then, we do okay."

"NAGPRA must've come in right after this site went dormant," Joe said. "It changed everything."

Carson was trying to maintain the affable mask that almost covered his intelligence and ambition—and tonight, anger—but his hands drummed restlessly on the steering wheel. "This is embarrassing, but I was a little relieved when the bones turned out to be Dr. Townsend. If they would've been old, NAGPRA red tape would've stopped the project until the legal stuff could be figured out. Also, the Creeks would have been completely justified in pulling me off this site for good. It's their land. If they'd rather leave an ancient burial alone and cancel developing the park, then that's their right. As it is, once the crime scene is released, we're good to go."

"You may be good to go, but I think you're going to have a really, really jumpy crew. Unexplained gunfire and a corpse? All in one day? You're lucky they don't have many other options for summer jobs," Faye said.

"No kidding," Carson answered, but then he immediately turned the conversation back to his project. This single-mindedness was not a surprise to Faye. She'd been watching Carson all day long and this was the way he operated.

"Even back in 1987," he said, "Dr. Townsend was trying to do things right. Up until…until the end. She'd been meticulous up until that time."

"Maybe somebody should have suspected that she didn't leave on purpose," Faye said.

"That's bothering me a lot today," Carson said. "They say she treated everybody around her like dirt and ran off to the mountains every weekend. She didn't rent a place in Sylacauga, not even a room where she could move in some of her own stuff. You know what it's like to spend months in the field."

"You want to make yourself comfortable," Faye said.

"Exactly. Unless you're Sophia Townsend." Carson took the last swig of his beer and put the empty bottle in a cup holder. "She took a room at a cheap motel out by the interstate. Same room every week. Drove in early on Mondays and checked out every Friday morning. Anybody could see she lived out of her suitcase, because it was in her back seat all day every Friday. Even I noticed it, at my age. I remember hearing that the last time anybody saw her, she had that suitcase in the back seat, so it must've been a Friday."

"People can choose a way to live. It don't have to be the same way everybody else does it," Joe said.

"True," Carson said, "especially archaeologists. We're independent-minded people who tend to go our own way. People who knew Dr. Townsend personally weren't surprised when she decided not to finish this job, but I've been living with her work for years. I should have known that a scientist of her caliber wouldn't walk away from her project."

"It must have been strange today, uncovering the body of someone you knew," Faye said. "What do you remember about her?"

"One time, I saw Dr. Townsend get right up in Kenny's face and scream awful names at him. I told Mom and she told my dad to keep me away from her after that, and he mostly did. Sometimes, though, I begged enough that he sneaked me out here."

"Your dad was always fun to be around," Joe said.

"Yeah and he's smart. Smart enough to do my job, actually."

Carson kept talking like a man who had years of troubles and unanswered questions.

"Dad's always said that he didn't understand how Dr. Townsend could have screwed up the budget so bad. Everything was running smooth. Nobody was drawing any overtime, because she would've had a screaming fit before she would've paid it. You tell me how she could have spent her whole budget without finishing the work. Accounting is just adding and subtracting. I make sure I have money in my bank account before I spend it. It's not that different."

Faye knew a little bit about the kinds of bad luck that could bust a budget. Broken equipment. Unexpected site conditions. Even the weather. Carson knew those things, too. He was just too wrapped up in this project to be forgiving of Sophia Townsend's leaky bank accounts.

Carson pushed a hank of hair behind one ear. It immediately fell back into his face. "Dad usually won't talk about Dr. Townsend. And I've tried."

"Except that one time he called her a bitch?" Faye said.

"Well, yeah. Kenny doesn't talk much, but he'll say more than Dad will about their old boss. Usually, Dad will just say that she wasn't a people person but, like I said, there was that time he called her a bitch. Kenny calls her that all the time. When you've got two Sunday-School-teaching men who act like their tongues would fall out if they said a curse word, and you hear them both saying things like that about a woman? When you know they were both raised in a time when you didn't speak ill of a lady? I have to wonder what she was really like."

"Nobody else has anything to say about her?" Faye asked.

Carson wiped a bead of sweat off his wide forehead. "Nobody but Emily. She's never argued when Kenny cussed Dr. Townsend, but after today…well, it looked to me like she was very, very close to her late boss."

"Or she wanted to be," said Faye.

Carson wiped his hair off his forehead again. The man needed a hat to keep his hair out of his face. Faye would have shaved her head before she'd have gone out in the sun like that.

Carson shrugged and spread his hands. "Oh, I give up. I don't like to talk bad about the dead, but Dad did open up about Sophia Townsend just once, and there's no way to soft-pedal what he said. He told me she worked people till they puked. Dad says he had to talk Kenny down more than once when she told him he was lazy, like all his people. Kenny's full Creek."

"Charming woman."

"No joke. She had nicknames for them all. Dad's was 'Idiot.'"

It seemed that Carson did own a bandanna. He yanked it out of his back pants pocket and used it to wipe his face. Faye suppressed a maternal urge to tie it around his head.

"Going by what Dad told me, Dr. Townsend's crew hated her, and she didn't get along with her client any better. Bottom line? She just wasn't *happy*. Oh, I think she was sometimes. I remember her staring down into the excavation like she could see right into the past. I think she loved archaeology but she didn't like being an archaeologist."

"Did your dad say where he thought she went when she disappeared?"

"Same thing as everybody else. She had that little weekend place and he was as sure as he could be that she'd gone there. It's where I've been picturing her all this time. Nothing fancy, just a bedroom, a little kitchen, a bathroom. Enough space for a piano and a lot of books. And a garden out back. When you don't like people, what else do you need, really?"

As someone who chose to live on an island, far from everyone but her immediate family, Faye couldn't judge someone else who wanted to do the same thing.

"Maybe we're reading too much into all the talk about Dr. Townsend's bad temper," Joe said. "That pearl and that figurine— they're worth a lot of money. Thieves will kill a woman just for her jewelry. If they're robbing a house, they'll kill anybody that gets in the way."

There was a place in Faye's heart that had never healed after robbers murdered her friend Douglass. It ached.

"That almost makes sense," Carson said, "except they left the valuables behind."

"It makes sense if she resisted and the robbers killed her by accident," Faye said. "After that, maybe they decided it was better to bury the artifacts with her, rather than sell them and risk being convicted of murder. She—"

Carson broke in. "If she got killed during a robbery, then anybody could have done it. Not just the people who were working with her. Right?"

Carson was still worried about his father, and Faye didn't blame him. Kenny Meadows, his second father, was a suspect as well. Carson had a lot riding on the results of this murder investigation.

Joe hadn't picked up on Carson's fears, so he kept hammering on the possible guilt of both of his friend's fathers. "Other than people who worked right here, who else would have known that she'd found artifacts worth stealing?"

"Anybody could have known that," Carson said. "If my dad found something cool, he told my mother about it over dinner that very night. Same for Kenny and his wife. Their wives told their friends. It's a small town. You remember what it's like to live here, Joe."

"I'm sure Cloud will be talking to everybody about what happened that summer," Faye said. "Well, everybody who remembers 1987."

Faye was watching Carson's face, hoping he would respond to her reassurance that the detective wasn't necessarily out to get his father. His expression stayed taut. Why?

Faye walked her logic back. For someone to have killed Sophia Townsend for the artifacts buried beneath her, the killer would have had to have known that they existed and that she had them. Something about that logic made her feel as perplexed as Carson looked.

● ● ● ● ●

Roy Cloud had left the folding chairs where he'd been conducting his interviews. He walked toward them as Faye, Joe, and Carson watched with all the excitement of three people who didn't want to answer a single question more.

Pausing by the passenger window where Faye sat, Cloud said, "You can send your security guards home, Dr. Callahan. Denton will be here all night, earning a little overtime. I've got someone driving by to check on her now and then. You can sleep easy. I'll be back tomorrow about sunup. I expect you'll be here by then, Dr. Longchamp-Mantooth. Any problem with that?"

Faye said, "No," wishing he hadn't made it so clear that Carson was being left out of the ongoing investigation.

Cloud told them to have a good evening and left. Now that he was gone, Carson had no reason to stay, not unless he planned to guard the guard. Faye was certainly ready to go find some supper. Joe must have been, too, because as soon as Carson said, "I guess I might as well get on home," they were both were out of the truck, hurrying away from the awkward conversation and waving good-bye. As she slid into the driver seat of their rental car, Joe cranked his father's truck.

They flicked their headlights on to beat back the coming night, and the beams illuminated Kira Denton on the far side of the excavation. She moved with purpose, checking out the woods surrounding her post.

Faye was chilled by the air conditioner that she'd set at full blast when it was a lot hotter outside. As she fumbled with the car's unfamiliar controls, her thoughts chilled her as well. She'd finally figured out why Carson had looked so perturbed.

Faye had read everything Carson had ever published on the Sylacauga site, and Carson had read every one of Sophia Townsend's surviving field notebooks before he wrote those papers.

If those notebooks had mentioned artifacts as significant as the ones that had just been found, Carson would have written about them in his papers, so Faye would have read about them. No, he wouldn't have just written about them. He would have searched high and low for that figurine and that possible string of saltwater pearls, and he would know that they weren't where they should be, safely ensconced at a curation facility.

Faye racked her brain for a good reason that the figurine and pearls had been omitted from Dr. Townsend's field notes. Had she found them that last day? Was she killed before she had time to finish her notes? Had she hidden them, planning to sell them to fund an early retirement?

Maybe the pertinent notebook had gone missing. Or maybe Dr. Townsend's team didn't find the artifacts at all. Maybe someone else had pulled them from the ground.

But if Sophia Townsend wasn't the one who found those treasures, then who did? And why were they buried with her?

Excerpt from the field notes of Dr. Sophia Townsend
July 31, 1987

Ladybitch found a potsherd today. It was about the size of my palm, so it had no business being in the backdirt. It was way too big to miss, but somebody missed it, and I suspect Stupidface and his sloppy field technique. He's always in a hurry to move more dirt than Idiot, just like he'd like to earn more money than he does and drive a bigger truck and have a prettier wife. It's an asinine way to live, but being a man means that you spend your whole life in a pissing contest. I guess that's why they're born with the equipment for a pissing contest.

Now, let's think about this. The county sets Idiot's salary, same as it does Stupidface's. The school system hired them both on the same day, so they will make the exact same salary until the very day they retire. Or die. Neither of them can afford much of a truck on that salary. And I can't see a lot of difference in the prettiness of their wives. This means that I have to watch them jockey for primacy with their trowels all day, every day.

Their trowels, like everything else about them, are exactly the same size.

Stupidface's futile flailing with his trowel evidently gouged up a clump of dirt big enough to hide a rather large potsherd, which wound up in the backdirt pile. It might never have seen the light of day if I hadn't told the terminally inept Ladybitch to sift through all that dirt. I told her that her job was to uncover the tiniest things, because they are so often the most important.

This is true, in general. In Ladybitch's case, I just gave her that job to keep her from breaking something important.

And what did she do with the potsherd, a lovely bit of ceramic art, delicately etched by a long-ago some-one with the eye of an artist? She broke it in two places.

Either I'm going to have to kill these people, or they're going to be the death of me.

Chapter Eleven

It was long after midnight. Roy Cloud knew he would be up the rest of the night working this case, so it only made sense to plan his next steps now, before he was punch-drunk from sleep deprivation.

Roy's classes at the academy had not covered this coldest-of-cold-cases scenario. Since graduating, he'd spent twenty-four years fighting crime in the employ of the Muscogee (Creek) Nation and he'd taken more continuing education courses than he cared to remember. One would think he'd have gained some education or experience during all those years that would be relevant to this case, but one would be wrong.

A thirty-year-old corpse—skeleton, really—was not unheard of. He'd worked cold cases that old. He'd solved a few. Sometimes an investigator got a lucky break and nailed a perp who'd walked free for a really long time.

This cold case, though. Holy hell. The victim had been unearthed by people who had known her personally before she disappeared all those years ago. What were the odds of that?

Usually, when you found a dead body that had been dead for a while, you had a case file to help you get started. You had interviews with witnesses, with loved ones, and with persons of interest. You had alibis to check. You knew when the victim was last seen.

Cloud had none of these things. He absolutely wouldn't blame the FBI if they declined to prosecute this case. The odds of solving it were so low compared to the effort it was going to take to glean even the tiniest clues.

Fortunately, Cloud was not a man who gave up easily, and he was in the mood to sift everything he knew for tiny clues.

The victim had disappeared without a word and nobody thought it was worthwhile to call the police. This made no sense.

A huge number of missing persons cases kicked off with a call reporting that someone had failed to show up for work. People who have jobs tend to show up, because people who have jobs like to keep their paychecks. Yet he was supposed to believe that not once during all the time Sophia Townsend had been gone had any of her coworkers turned to one of the others and asked, "Whatever happened to our old boss? You don't think something happened to her, do you?"

What were the odds of *that*?

Cloud called bullshit. By all accounts, Sophia Townsend was so relentlessly unpleasant that she might have been murdered on the spot by a stranger she reamed out for pumping her gas too slow. But she also might have been murdered by one of these people he'd talked to today, and the evidence pointed in that direction. Would anyone else have driven her here and buried her at the bottom of her own excavation?

At the very least, they all must have suspected that Sophia Townsend had come to harm, but they'd kept their mouths shut to avoid trouble.

At the worst? One of these people had killed her and concocted a story that made the others believe she'd voluntarily walked away.

After her body went in the ground and a backhoe covered the grave with tons of soil, her killer couldn't have expected that her bones would ever surface again. But they had. So it was entirely possible that one of the calm and relaxed people watching that backhoe operator do a bang-up job of digging a great big hole had known that a dead body lay at the bottom of it.

Could anybody really be that gutsy?

After due consideration, Cloud decided that even if Emily, Kenny, or Mickey had killed Sophia Townsend, turning down this job wouldn't have been an option for the murderer. Passing up a good job in Sylacauga would have looked too suspicious. It would have been far smarter to take the job and stand bold and confident on the lip of the newly reopened excavation, pretending to be surprised by the abandoned grave at its floor.

Or, and this was a thought that Cloud was going to need to ponder, maybe the killer had made one last-ditch effort to stop that backhoe from uncovering Sophia Townsend. Maybe the killer had been prowling with a gun that very morning, terrorizing Kenny Summers, Carson Callahan, and Faye Longchamp-Mantooth and hoping that somebody got scared enough to call off the excavation.

It could have happened. An archaeologist who was less driven than Carson might have decided that the project wasn't worth getting killed over. The Creeks, too, could have gotten cold feet. If somebody got shot on their land, they could be defending against an expensive lawsuit. Almost as bad for an organization that depended on tourism, the publicity would have been just terrible.

So where did all these things leave Cloud and his investigation? Nowhere that made any sense.

One thing was for sure. He would be a fool to put his full trust in anything any of these people told him about what happened back in 1987.

A murder scene that was also an archaeological dig made the situation still more off-kilter and repetitive, like a skipping record playing the same tune again and again. The metaphor made Roy smile, since most of his witnesses and all of his suspects were old enough to remember when music meant vinyl and only vinyl.

Like a skipping vinyl LP, this story hiccuped, jumped backward, ran forward a bit, then hiccuped again. People whose job it was to find buried things from the past, including dead bodies, had found a buried thing from the past. And it was a dead body—the dead body of a person who had, in the past, been looking for buried things from the past.

Roy Cloud was getting vertigo just thinking about it.

The fact that the crime scene had also been an archaeological dig at the time of the murder, where the victim and suspects were digging up even older buried things, made things weirder yet again.

And now the archaeologists were telling him that the silver necklace found around Sophia Townsend's decomposed neck dated to 1987 or thereabouts, but the pearl found beneath her body might have been pulled from an oyster that had been dead for a millennium.

The clay figurine with it? Maybe even older.

Roy liked to read science fiction, but this real-life story felt like an overcomplicated time-travel novel. He'd started drawing a flow chart in his notebook, just to keep track.

Dr. Faye Longchamp-Mantooth had seemed quite comfortable with this case's recursive flow of time. Roy decided he wanted her to help him with his flow chart, because he didn't know some basic things like how many people would have worked on Dr. Townsend's team. Five? Ten? Fifty?

Probably not fifty. Roy Cloud had worked for the Muscogee (Creek) Nation for his entire career, and he was in fact an enrolled member of the tribe. He knew that his tribal leaders were skilled in business. There was no way that they'd pay for fifty people to dig up this site. Roy was sure of that much, but he needed Faye Longchamp-Mantooth to tell him how many they did pay, and he didn't want to wait until morning to find out.

It was long past a normal person's bedtime, but murder cases don't run on the clock. Roy found Dr. Faye Longchamp-Mantooth's number, newly saved to his phone, and he called her with a single tap of his thumb.

"Hey there, Doctor Faye. I want to get a few things straight," he said. "The clothes and the silver necklace belong with the body, right?" he asked. "But the pearl and the little statue that were underneath the body were really old?"

"I'm pretty sure. Well, except for the canvas bag. I showed you the shreds of canvas sticking out of the ground around the antiquities, remember? Under the skull? I think we're going to find that the figurine and probably the pearls were buried in a bag that was new in 1987."

This was just great. Even the ancient stuff that was making his life difficult was complicated, because somebody—probably the killer—had gone to Walmart and bought a brand-new bag to bury it in.

"There's a canvas bag in that grave, too?" he asked her. "Oh, yeah. You did show me that. What else? Jimmy Hoffa?"

Cloud was a little afraid that she was too young to get the Jimmy Hoffa reference and he was going to have to tell her a long story about a mysteriously missing 1970s union boss. She laughed, and he was relieved.

"Nope. No Jimmy Hoffa," she said. "I think we all agree that those bones belong to the woman who was heading up the dig here back in eighty-seven. Detective Cloud—"

"Call me Roy."

"Sure thing. Roy, did you see the size of that pearl? It was fit for a queen. I'm so glad Emily stopped digging when she did. If there really are more pearls buried there, she might have damaged them or even lost them."

"Yeah, I did think that pearl looked bigger than any I've ever seen in person. I can't imagine drilling a hole in it with a little sliver of sharp rock, which I guess is how they did it back then."

"And the canvas bag. Remember I showed you the plastic thread around its handle? Attached to what's left of a price tag? I'm guessing the bag was brand-new."

What do you know? Roy thought. *It was brand-new, I got something right about this weirdo case already. I bet we even find out the bag came from Walmart. But I wouldn't have seen that little plastic thread without the help of Dr. Faye Longchamp-Mantooth.*

The archaeologist kept telling him about all the things she'd noticed about the ragged wad of dirty old fabric. "The tag is pretty well gone, I'm afraid. It was plastic-coated, so it held up a lot better that Sophia Townsend, but it's probably illegible. Maybe you've got some technicians who can reconstruct enough of the printing to find out where it was bought. I don't know if that'll do you any good after all this time, but it's something."

Roy grunted in agreement. The woman knew her stuff. "Get some sleep, Doctor Faye, and I'll try not to keep disturbing you. It's hardly fair, considering the little bit that I'm paying you."

Roy broke the connection before he realized that he'd never asked Dr. Longchamp-Mantooth the question that had prompted him to call. He decided to save it for their next conversation, because he was sure there would be another one soon. In the meantime, he decided to go bother Vernon McAlester, the Creek Nation's project liaison. Vernon never had much to say, but people talked more when you showed up in the middle of the night.

Roy had known Vernon a long time, but then he'd known everybody around Sylacauga for a long time, especially if they were Creek. Vernon probably wasn't thirty, so he couldn't know anything that wasn't in the project files. Still, Vernon could surely dig around in those files and find out how many people were on the crew. Even better, maybe he could get their names. And maybe he knew some other helpful things.

As Roy drove through the night, his mind conjured up images of Sophia Townsend's bones amid a fine scattering of pearls. It conjured up the faces of three people who had never, not in nearly thirty long years, been willing to publicly ask what had happened to that poor woman. He wondered whether Mickey Callahan, Emily Olsen, and Kenny Meadows were sleeping tonight.

His mind also conjured up the face of Kira Denton, left behind to guard the artifacts that went with Sophia Townsend into the ground.

Denton was well-trained and well-armed. There was no pressing reason to expect trouble to find her. Roy wasn't overblessed with available personnel, so he had to stop somewhere when it came to asking people to work all night.

Still, despite all the rational reasoning that said his officer would be okay, he knew that he needed to raise Denton on the radio and listen to her tell him everything was fine. And he knew he'd be checking on her again, more than once. She would probably get sick of his voice. Given her disposition, she would probably tell him so, but that was her problem.

• • ● • •

Joe woke because Faye wasn't beside him.

He wasn't surprised that she was up. He had always slept better than she did. He'd tried to teach her to let go of her worries and sink into sleep, but she just couldn't do it. This was the price she paid for having a fine mind that never really stopped to rest.

But Faye was a considerate insomniac, so she always got out of bed instead of disturbing him. Tonight, after what she'd seen, Joe thought he should probably go look for her.

He followed the light at the end of the hall and found her by the fireplace, in front of the easy chair covered in brown-flowered cloth where his father had sat for Joe's entire life. On the fireplace's mantel sat the urn where his mother's ashes waited for closure, but Faye's eyes weren't on the urn. They were on the coin-sized object in her hands.

Joe watched her study one side of it, then run a fingertip over it before turning it over to repeat the process.

"Whatcha got?"

She held out something that Joe recognized. He'd seen it sitting around the house for years—on his father's chest-of-drawers, in a bowl of interesting junk that stayed on the coffee table, on a spot on the mantel right in front of where Faye stood—but he'd never given it much thought. He was pretty sure he'd seen it in the houses they'd rented before this one. It had always just been there.

He picked it up from her palm and, for the first time, he realized what he was holding. "Wow. We've gotta ask Dad where he found this. But maybe Mom found it. We've had it for a long long time."

He thought, *If my dead mother found it, we'll never know where it came from,* but he didn't say it out loud. He just said,

"It's Mississippian, ain't it?" running his finger over the surface just as she had.

It was a potsherd with a gentle curve, as if it came from the side of a large ceramic pot. Before it was fired, someone had taken a sharp implement and carved a design into its soft clay surface. He felt and saw a series of concentric curves, like a rainbow. Below was another design made of short curving lines that made him think of a feather.

"Mississippian?" he asked.

"Yeah, I'd say so. Maybe Carson's not wrong to think that they lived around here."

She reached her hand toward his, touching the old thing on his palm lightly with her fingertip. She traced its outline, pointed on one side and with a deep notch on the other, and said, "It's shaped like a heart, don't you think?"

"Yeah. I always did think so."

"Maybe that's why he keeps it next to your mother's ashes."

Joe gently set it back on the mantel, propped up against the urn.

"We need to go out there," Faye said.

Joe said, "Where?" but he knew exactly where she wanted to go.

"Think about it. Somebody killed Sophia Townsend. Tonight is the first time since 1987 that the killer has had any reason to worry about being caught."

Joe's attention hadn't left his mother's urn. In 1987, she'd still been alive. Healthy. Strong. Cancer had been the furthest thing from her mind.

"And that's not all," Faye continued. "Back in 1987, somebody buried a canvas bag holding priceless artifacts underneath the dead body of a murdered woman and let them be covered by five feet of dirt. That person obviously never intended to come back to get them. It was like burying a stack of thousand-dollar bills. It was like burying the Mona Lisa."

Joe put 1987 and his mother in the past and thought about what she was saying. "So we need to go out in the middle of the night to check on artifacts being guarded by an armed officer… because why?"

"It's not the middle of the night. By the time we get there, it'll be almost sunup. Anyway, we need to go out there because one person just isn't enough to protect the place. What if there are more priceless artifacts still buried in the ground and somebody out there knows about them? People talk. Gerard, the medical examiner, was so excited by those pearls and that figurine that he's probably blabbed about them to the whole world. By now, every crook for miles around knows what we found today, so we're not just up against the murderer who put them there."

"You think the murderer is still alive?"

"Could be. And I can see what Sylacauga's like. I don't think anybody's ever left here but you. Anybody that was here in 1987, even Sophia Townsend's murderer, is probably still here. You're the exception that proves the rule."

Joe was stupidly pleased to hear that she though he was a special case.

Faye was still talking, running through every detail that had been running through her mind when she should have been sleeping. "It would be too easy for anybody with a rifle and a night scope to pick off Officer Denton, walking away with things that would bring a fortune on the black market. It could happen. Don't forget that somebody was already out there with a gun this morning."

Joe couldn't argue with her logic. He almost never could. In some ways, Faye was a slave to logic. He started looking for his moccasins.

Faye wasn't through sifting through all the logical possibilities, despite the fact that she was succeeding in getting him to leave the house when he should be asleep. "And there may be more amazing things buried there," she said. "Only one person knows."

"You call the detective yet? Somebody could shoot us as well as they could shoot the officer he left guarding the place. There's a lot of hunters around here. A lot of 'em probably have night scopes."

Faye nodded. "I was planning to let Cloud know. I'll call him now."

"You say one person ain't enough. How 'bout three? Is four enough? If we go out there, will we be making Officer Denton any safer?"

"That's why I'm calling Roy Cloud so he can meet us out there. I hope he can bring more officers with him. Maybe Agent Bigbee's people will be here soon. The woods need to be alive with people. Anybody hoping to grab those artifacts needs to look around and say, 'I can't take on an army, so I'm going to get the hell out.' So, no, we're not enough, but we would improve the odds."

Joe always traveled with weapons, but when he flew, he packed them in his suitcase and checked it. Airport security people wouldn't understand why he was carrying two stone knives and a weighted leather bolo that could take down a man at fifty paces. He went to their room and opened his suitcase, pulling out a knife and the bolo and slid them both into the bag hanging at his waist.

Then he pulled the other knife out of his suitcase and handed it to Faye. He'd made it for her, but she refused to carry it on a regular basis. This time, she took it.

Roy Cloud had known the truth for a while. He'd known it when he finished his fruitless interview with Vernon, the Creeks' young-and-therefore-useless contract officer. Vernon had been two years old in 1987, so he knew nothing that wasn't in the project files left behind from Sophia Townsend's dig. He'd said that the project's 1987 records included the contract, Sophia's bills, and nothing else. No record of how many employees she'd hired. No list of their names. Nothing. Her bills weren't even itemized, so they could hardly be more useless.

Vernon had suggested he talk to Phil Smithee, who was the boss of his boss, and who was the man who had let Sophia Townsend mismanage her budget in 1987. Roy, not being stupid, had spoken to Phil hours before and learned nothing, because Phil was still an idiot. He'd risen to a position of responsibility and appeared to be discharging that responsibility well, but that didn't mean that he wasn't an idiot. It meant that he hired good people to help him feign competence.

Roy couldn't imagine how Phil had kept his job after paying Dr. Townsend all that money and having nothing to show for it. As a member of the tribe who funded that paycheck, Roy was royally pissed off at Phil. Vernon McAlester seemed to be following in Phil's barely competent footsteps, so Roy's trip to his house had been wasted.

As Cloud had left Vernon's house, he'd tried to raise Kira Denton on the radio. She'd answered him every other time he'd called, but this time she didn't. This couldn't be a good thing.

He'd been sure of the truth when she also failed to answer her cell phone. As he'd accelerated to the top speed that the country road beneath his tires would allow, he had called for backup. Imagining how dark it must be in the woods surrounding the open pit, he'd said, "Bring night scopes, heat sensors, lights, a dog. Bring it all." And then he'd let Agent Bigbee know what was going down.

As much as he hated to give up trying to reach Officer Denton, he did it, so that he could radio Brian Hannity, the officer he'd asked to check on Denton throughout the night. Hannity didn't answer, and he didn't answer his cell phone, either. Something wasn't right.

After driving away from Vernon McAlester's front porch light, after long minutes spent driving away from the city limits of Sylacauga, after a timeless time spent studying the Milky Way's foggy stripe emerge as the moon left the jet-black sky, Roy had finally admitted to himself that he needed still more help. So he called for it.

"Cloud here, calling for more backup. I'm going to need a helicopter."

For how else would he find a fugitive fleeing in utter darkness, unless he had someone in the sky?

He tried time and again to raise Denton and Hannity on the radio and on the phone. When his cell phone rang, he grabbed it, hoping they were calling him back to tell him their radio was on the fritz. Later, they could all laugh about it, except Denton didn't laugh when she was on duty.

His phone rang and he grabbed for it, hoping.

His hopes were for nothing. The ringing phone's screen didn't say, "Kira Denton." It said "Faye Longchamp-Mantooth," so he let it go to voice mail. He appreciated that the archaeologist wanted to help solve Sophia Townsend's death badly enough to lose sleep, but he couldn't talk to her now. The Townsend murder was a cold case that had waited twenty-nine years for his attention. It could wait another day. All he could think about now was the safety of Kira Denton and Brian Hannity.

He tried a few more times to get ahold of Denton and Hannity. Eventually, he gave up and just drove.

• • ● • •

Faye was glad for Joe to be at her side in the front seat of their parked rental car, knowing that their arrival had tripled the number of people in the dark woods surrounding the Sylacauga site's open excavation. And its open grave.

Or perhaps they didn't triple the site's population. There was no way to know how many people were in those woods. Perhaps Kira Denton wasn't out there any more. Perhaps someone dangerous had come back to fetch those valuable pearls and that priceless figurine. Perhaps that someone had come back to make sure no one uncovered evidence that would reveal a murderer.

In the grassy clearing between their parked car and the edge of the excavation, they could make out nothing more than shapes and shadows. Nothing more than a warm glow lit the eastern horizon. The moon had set, so they would have no light to help them until dawn came.

They had brought flashlights, but it would have been nuts to venture into the unfamiliar woods with nothing but their pale beams. For now, they had only the stars and the diffuse light of the sun's rays striking airborne dust far above their heads. Faye and Joe could probably have managed the few short feet over open ground to the excavation in the darkness. They might even have been able to do it without falling into the pit, but venturing out of the car seemed like a good way to get shot by a police officer who didn't know they were friendly.

"What now?" Joe asked.

"We should get down. Anybody could be out there with a gun," Faye said, and they slid down in their seats until the tops of their heads hardly reached the bottom of their car windows.

"Is Cloud on his way?"

"I left him a message. If he got it, he should be here any minute." Faye listened to the darkness and watched the sun's glow reach a tiny bit further into the eastern sky. Keeping her head down, she rolled down her window and listened to the night's silent air. Then she said, "Something's wrong."

"And you know that how?"

"Nobody could have missed us just now. Loud engine. Headlights on bright. We weren't even trying to sneak in. Denton should have already been checking us out. We should see her flashlight coming. We should hear her yelling 'Who's there?'"

"That was your plan? Come out here and see if we could flush her out just by showing up?"

"Yes, and don't laugh. I figured if we rode out here, Officer Denton would come out to greet us. I figured we'd be helping her just by being here. Safety in numbers. But somebody got to her before we did."

"So you're saying that there may be a bad guy out there, but there aren't any good guys."

"Not any more."

Chapter Twelve

Faye could hear the approaching vehicle before she could see it. Headlights off, it approached them at a speed that was more than safe. It roared toward her so fast that she reflexively flung her arms in front of her face to stave off the impact.

Swerving in from behind, the SUV stopped mere inches from the passenger side of the car where she sat. If she'd wanted to flee, she couldn't have opened her door wide enough to get out.

Joe's hand closed gently around her upper arm, and she could feel the smooth curve of his own stone knife between her skin and his palm. She reached into her purse and retrieved hers. The sound of the handbag's clasp opening, then snapping shut, was as loud as a snapping tree trunk in the silent car.

Then the other car's window rolled down. Chief Roy Cloud leaned out of it and through Faye's open window. He glared down at where she sat slumped in her seat, and his face was so close that she could feel the heat of his breath on her cheek.

He hissed, "Are you people out of your minds? This place isn't safe. It isn't safe at all."

Faye was still listening for the sound of the officer who should be approaching, weapons at the ready, demanding to know what they were doing there at this hour. She heard nothing.

"We know it's not safe," she said. "Your officer is in trouble, and we don't know what to do about it."

Joe had leaned out his own open window, listening. He was moving his head slowly from side to side, trying to assess the direction of a sound that only he could hear. Faye had long ago learned that his hearing was better than hers, so she wasn't surprised that she heard nothing but ordinary night sounds. A moment later, she heard the sound of engines and turned around in her seat to see two more cars approaching.

It had hardly been an hour since she had stated that, in this place and at this time, safety could only be had if the woods were alive with people. Maybe she was about to get her wish.

Joe's hand grew tighter around her upper arm. "Listen."

All Faye could hear were the sounds of approaching engines, until the two speeding cars pulled to a stop behind them. When they cut their engines, there was a single moment of silence and Faye could tell by the twitch of Joe's hand that he still heard something she couldn't.

Then the silence was broken by Roy barking into his radio. "Cloud here—"

Joe leaned far across Faye and reached a long arm into Roy's car. Grabbing the police chief by the shoulder, he said, "I hear something over that way." He pointed out his window toward the excavation or perhaps beyond. "Somebody's calling for help. If you and your people will be just quiet for a minute, maybe we can find her."

As she tried to listen, another noise, much louder than the cars' engines, assaulted Faye's ears. A bright light swooped in from the west, accompanied by the whapping sounds of helicopter blades. Under any other circumstances, she would have seen the coming chopper as an emblem of hope, like the cavalry cresting the hill in a black-and-white western movie. At the moment, she just wanted it to be quiet so that Joe could do what he did best.

Joe was doing all he could to be heard above the din. "Chief Cloud! Did you hear me?"

"I did, and I'm on it." Roy paused just long enough to look Joe in the face and say, "Thank you." Then he returned to barking orders into his radio, laying out a plan to send the helicopter away, so that Joe could hear. After that, she knew he would ask the helicopter pilot to cover his officers from the air while they searched for their missing friend.

Joe got out of the car and waited for Roy and his officers to gather themselves. Faye stopped slumping and sat up in the car, ready for action. Roy Cloud didn't know it yet, but Faye knew that her husband would be going into the woods with his officers, whether it violated police protocol or not. Joe was not an arrogant man, but he was completely aware that there weren't many trackers with his skill.

Roy Cloud also didn't know yet that Faye was going with them, too. In her years with Joe, his skill with woodcraft had rubbed off on her. She would never have Joe's eyes and ears, but she had her own intuitive ways. She also had a logical brain that never stopped sifting through clues, trying all the ways that they could fit together until she found the right one.

While she waited for Joe to locate the source of the cry for help, Faye had sat in the front seat of this unfamiliar car and studied the lay of the land. She remembered that Denton had stationed herself on the far side of the pit from where they sat.

Faye had tried to use her binoculars to get a look at the area where she thought Denton might be. It was still too dark. Fortunately, she had sat in that truck the evening before with Carson and Joe for two or three everloving hours, at least, facing in that direction. She could summon up the view at will.

The underbrush in that area was thick, too thick in most areas for an intruder to approach without warning and too thick for a faraway shooter to get a good shot. There was only one spot where it would be easy to pass quietly through the trees. Faye remembered the scorched area cleared by wildfire that she'd seen the previous afternoon. By removing the undergrowth, the fire had opened a spot where Officer Denton could get a clearer view of her surroundings. It had also made a narrow opening in the underbrush where trouble could approach. Faye suspected that this was where the unseen shooter who had terrorized her, Carson, and Kenny had stood less than twenty-four hours before.

When she told Cloud she intended to go with his officers to search for Denton, he said, "The hell you are."

"But I think I know where she is. It's where I'd be if I were her."

"Tell me."

So Faye had pointed at the spot. The darkness was so deep that she could barely see the pointing index finger at the end of her arm. "Over there. Does that help you any?"

Cloud had cursed, then he had assigned her to an armed officer with a night scope and a heat sensor who would be glued to her side. Then he had cursed some more, because Joe was approaching with a light in his eye that said he too expected to risk his life tonight.

Roy Cloud didn't know what Faye and Joe could do yet, but he would soon. In the few minutes left before daybreak, their skills might save a life or two.

· • ● • ·

The source of the cries for help was found quickly, but it was not Kira Denton. Brian Hannity, the officer assigned to swing by and check on her periodically, was lying crumpled in a corner of the excavation.

"I heard gunfire, two shots, so I left my vehicle and ran toward it. Being stupid, I forgot you said there was a big hole in the ground, Chief."

Cloud's voice was gentle. "It's not stupid to be so dead-set on helping your fellow officer that you run in the direction of an active shooter. It's not the way to live to a ripe old age, but it isn't stupid."

"Where's Kira, Chief?"

"I don't know."

· • ● • ·

Faye wouldn't have wanted to be a lurking fugitive, listening to the officers taking possession of the woods, tree trunk by tree trunk. They took cover behind each tree of any size, used their heat sensors and night scopes to assess their surroundings, then moved forward with their firearms drawn. With them came powerful lights and the voices of well-trained people focused on a single goal. They were here to find their fellow officer.

Bleck and his partner were on the way, but the chief hadn't wanted to wait. If all went well, Kira Denton would be safe and sound before Bleck's famous nose came on the scene. If not, Bleck would find her. Or he would find her body, but Faye didn't want to think about that.

Overhead, the helicopter hovered, shining its light wherever Roy Cloud told the pilot to shine it. The noise of its blades was constant. It rattled Faye's heart in her chest.

Their first goal was to find Officer Denton, but their second goal was to track down the person who had fired two shots in these woods for Brian Hannity to hear. Cloud had mustered everybody he could and he had deployed all the resources he had, but there is always a limit to what is humanly possible. The truth is that the world is big and there are only so many officers of the peace. It was entirely possible that a fugitive could get past the officers patrolling the perimeter, and it was entirely possible that the helicopter pilot would be looking in the other direction when it happened. All they could do was their best.

Faye moved into the woods with the second wave, behind the officers in the forefront who had cleared their way. She pointed out a path to the spot where she believed Kira Denton would have stood guard and the man at her side radioed it to everyone else. After the first wave of officers had cleared each area, Faye and her companion moved in behind them.

When they reached the clearing where Denton should have waited, Faye was heartsick to find it empty. She had been so sure.

She stood in the middle of the open patch and spun in a circle, imagining where she would go if she were a police officer under attack. After spinning once with her gaze focused outward, she spun again with her eyes and flashlight on the ground. The officer at her side handed her his night scope, so she spun again.

On this pass, she saw a dark streak that shook her faith in everything. She had so wanted to be wrong about Kira's safety. She had hoped they would find her hiding, even injured, but the streak of blood at her feet was too dark, too wide, too terrifying.

"Here!" she said. "She has to be nearby. She was bleeding too much to get very far."

The smear led across the clearing in the direction of the excavation, growing broader and darker with distance. Between the clearing where they stood and the open pit, the body of Kira Denton lay huddled behind a cedar tree. She'd been shot through the chest.

● ● **●** ● ●

Faye and Roy watched the paramedics maneuver the stretcher carrying Brian Hannity through trees and brambles.

"Well, our killer is a good shot. Came damn close to putting a bullet through Kira's heart," Roy had said, wiping his eyes. "But that don't mean a damn thing. The countryside is full of good shots around here. I know kids who could do that."

The approaching stretcher carried Brian Hannity, who had been lucky enough to only break a rib and a leg. He had also banged his head against the ground hard enough to knock him unconscious.

A meter is only slightly more than three feet, and that isn't very far to fall, but Brian Hannity had been running at top speed in the dark. He'd had no warning that he was about to hit the ground hard until his feet left solid ground and he launched into the air. He hadn't even had time to throw out his arms to cushion his fall.

If he had fallen with his head cocked at a slightly different angle, he might have broken his neck. At another angle, he might have suffered a head injury very like the one that killed Sophia Townsend. As it was, he had lost a dangerous amount blood from the places on his leg where broken bones protruded through the skin.

Brian Hannity had been lucky enough to be lying unconscious and quiet in a corner of the excavation in the critical
moments after Kira Denton's death. The shooter, who hadn't
had any reason to suspect that he was there, failed to notice
him in the dark, even while descending into the very same hole.
Despite his concussion, Brian Hannity had woken with enough
clarity to know that he did not want this person to see him, so
he had hidden there without a sound until he was sure that the
intruder was gone.

Hannity had passed in and out of consciousness after the
shooter left and before the police arrived, but the sounds of voices
and sirens and gathering cars and an approaching helicopter
signaled that these were people who were not trying to kill him.
This had seemed like a good enough time to stop playing dead.
He'd called for help until Joe had led a team of paramedics to
the spot where he waited.

As the stretcher passed, Roy ran to Hannity's side. He trot-
ted alongside the fast-moving stretcher, holding the wounded
man's hand and listening to him talk. The paramedics carrying
Hannity wanted him in a hospital, immediately.

Hannity had begun calling out information as soon as Roy
drew near, like someone who kept remembering things and
wanted to make sure he got them said. And maybe he was right
to worry. Faye could see that mud was ground deeply into the
terrible injuries on his leg. He could already be succumbing
to infections or exposure or shock or the stress of long-term
unrelieved pain.

Hannity never stopped giving evidence while he was being
carted to a waiting ambulance, trying to spit out the information while he still could.

"Didn't see who done it." Fear made his voice loud and his
words fast. Faye could hear every word.

"Kira was on the far side of the pit. Heard a shot. Couldn't get
her to answer me." He paused to drag some air into one damaged
lung and one good one. "So I headed her way. Wanted to help."

"That's what good partners do. And you're a good partner." Faye had seen Roy's eyes sweep Hannity's body from head to toe, assessing his condition in much the same way a physician would have. His glance lingered on the man's torn pants leg, stiff with blood and filth.

"Thought I could get to Kira if I used trees for cover. I went over the edge with my ears still ringing from the shot that took her. Guess I'm too clumsy for the bad guys to find me."

"Don't say that. You didn't do anything wrong," Roy said to Hannity as the stretcher passed where Faye stood. "Nothing."

"Laid there on the ground for a long time. Don't know how long I was out. When I woke up, somebody with a flashlight was right down in the pit with me. Digging."

Faye wanted very much to be at the bottom of that pit. She needed to see what the shooter had done to Sophia Townsend's grave and to the artifacts buried in it, but she had to wait until Agent Bigbee was ready to let her go down there. Until he and Roy Cloud were sure the killer was gone, she would be sitting here watching the police get control of the scene.

Later, when Cloud and Bigbee gave the all-clear and when the sun lit the place where Sophia Townsend had lain for all those years, Faye would be able to see what was left there. But not before.

Excerpt from the field notes of Dr. Sophia Townsend
June 30, 1987

My fellow archaeologists are full of shit.

I haven't gone to a professional conference in years, because I endured enough of their shit when I was in graduate school and during my abortive academic career.

I'm good at what I do. I am. But I don't suffer fools gladly, so I burned through five graduate advisors before I escaped with this PhD that qualifies me for a job that barely puts a roof over my head. I got this worthless degree by finding the least competent professor in the department and making myself indispensable.

No, that's not true. I acquired a graduate advisor by making myself so indispensable to Henry the Ass that he had to listen to me call him an ass whenever the situation demanded it. I made myself so indispensable that he was even afraid to hit on me. This made me something of a folk hero among my fellow female graduate students, whom he pawed regularly.

I got my degree by writing a seminal paper that would assure his bid for promotion to full professor when he slapped his name on it as first author...then refusing to hand it over to him until he signed my application for graduation.

I was justified. He would have kept me as his galley slave forever if I hadn't forced his hand.

The last time I went to a professional conference, Henry the Ass was presenting a paper and I attended the presentation. He started sweating the minute I walked in.

During the Q&A session, I asked him a question about "our" paper that could only have been answered by someone who had read and understood it. Then I walked out and left him to flounder in front of hundreds of colleagues. And I did it quickly, before I was tempted to put him out of his misery by answering the question for him.

Back in graduate school is when I got into the habit of using my field notes to...um...express myself. Henry the Ass certainly never looked at them. My clients don't.

If I should ever make an earth-shattering discovery, yeah, future scholars might comb through my notes to glean new insights on my work long after I'm dead. They might find my notes entertaining. Or, to put it more honestly, future archaeological scholars might comb through my notes in hopes that they might be able to cobble together a paper of their own out of tiny scraps of my original work, overburdened by great gobs of their own inanity.

Psychological scholars might use the quirks of my field notes to write a few papers of their own.

This is how academia works. If you can't come up with a new idea, steal somebody else's.

Cut it up. Repackage it. Pretend it's new.

Fortunately for me, my career has been a long chain of boring jobs. Boring potsherds that are no different from anybody else's. Boring flint tools that are no different from anybody else's. And this job, with the lovely Muscogee name of Sylacauga that somehow looks Greek, too...it will be no different.

It will be no different.

No one will read the final report. No one will read any paper I might choose to write about it, and let me be honest and say that I'll never get around to that.

I don't know if I'll do this kind of work forever, but I'm doing it now, so here I am. I might as well amuse myself by insulting Henry the Ass in this notebook he will never see, and by using my dwindling sex appeal to wreak some havoc.

Today, I tortured poor Ladybitch, who keeps dating men because she has no idea that she likes women better.

Tomorrow, I believe I will unbutton an extra button at the top of this faded work shirt. I'll pull on my tightest work pants, the ones that make my thighs look like they did when I was twenty-three. And I'll spend the day pitting Idiot and Stupidface against each other and against poor Ladybitch.

If the Hulk were still here, I might feel a few sexual fireworks myself, but he has decamped. I must make do with what I have.

Watching two thirty-something-year-old men and one twenty-something-year-old woman suffer with the hots for the same thirty-seven-year-old body is somewhat entertaining. It makes working in this flat, hot, Godforsaken corner of nowhere almost tolerable.

At the end of the day, as always, one of them will be invited to stay late to "help me finish putting away the tools," and the other two will go home alone with their own useless tools, knowing that they lost today's contest for my affections.

Yep. That should be fun.

Chapter Thirteen

After Kira Denton's body was found, Faye watched Cloud and his officers shift from searching for their friend to a full-out manhunt. The traditional word "manhunt" made Faye wonder whether the shooter was a man or a woman. At the moment, the shooter was a genderless shadow who might or might not be waiting in the darkness of the thickly wooded area that surrounded the Sylacauga site's open excavation. Could that same shadow have been responsible for the gunshots that had terrified her just a day before?

Possibly, probably, the shooter was gone. Possibly, probably, the shooter had fled after killing Denton, after failing to kill Hannity, after stepping down to the floor of the excavation to muck about with history and its relics.

Had there been time for a clean getaway?

Perhaps the shooter navigated in the dark through trees and the surrounding pastures, presumably to a waiting car. Or perhaps not.

The risk that someone was waiting behind a tree to take out more of his officers had been too great for Roy Cloud. As soon as the edge of the sun had cleared the horizon, the chief had deployed the helicopter to pin down any fugitive still on-site, then he had deployed the search team and Bleck to search, tree by tree, the woods beyond the spot where Kira's body had lain.

Faye's stomach growled and her groggy brain wished for its morning coffee. The thought of coffee reminded her of Sly, who seemed to be staving off his cravings for alcohol with a steady flow of caffeine.

"We should have told your dad we were leaving. Or at least left a note. He'll be worried."

"Didn't think we'd be here this long. He's still asleep, or we would've heard from him by now. I'll text him. He'll check his phone as soon as he gets up, so he'll know where we are before he has time to get worried."

"Good idea," Faye said, and then Sly was immediately gone from her thoughts. She leaned back in the passenger seat of their rental car, thinking of Kira Denton.

Faye had never heard Denton speak a pleasant word, but the woman had gotten the job done. She had died getting the job done, just like Sophia Townsend. Faye didn't have to like either of them to admire their dedication, their drive, their competence.

Faye had been raised to be nice, trained by her genteel Southern mother and grandmother to behave just like they did. Most of the time, those genteel ways didn't stand in the way when Faye needed to get something done. Usually, they provided a nice social lubricant that made her life run smoother.

But sometimes they slowed her down. Sometimes people took advantage of her gentle nature. There had been times when Faye had wished she could be more like Kira Denton and Sophia Townsend, willing to let people dislike her, if need be.

It was possible that some people thought that the deaths of nasty people mattered less than the deaths of lovable ones. Faye wasn't one of them. She grieved the deaths of two people so prickly that there might not be many others to grieve them. She figured she owed Kira and Sophia that much.

• ● ● ● •

The text from his son came before Sly had finished spooning dark-roasted coffee into a filter. He hadn't even known that Faye and Joe were gone. It wouldn't have felt right to disturb his married son's time alone with his wife. Sly had been counting on the warm, brown smell of brewing coffee to lure them out of their bedroom to visit with him.

He looked forward to his time with the two of them, just sitting around and talking about nothing. They were young, and just sitting around was something that never occurred to them. At home, they had children to tend and jobs to do. Here, away from the children, they never thought to use the time to relax. Instead, they'd found a way to bring their work with them, though as a man with a come-and-go job and bills to pay, Sly could hardly blame them for that.

But even when the work was done, they didn't know how to be still. Faye wanted to drive up past Tulsa to a national park where she could see a prairie full of bison. Joe wanted to take Sly's battered john boat to the river, so he could show Faye some of his favorite fishing spots. They'd even invited him to join them.

These weren't bad ways to spend their time, and they were exactly the way that people their age did spend their time. Trouble was, the phrase "spending your time" came to have a different meaning when a man got to be Sly's age and noticed that there was only so much time left.

While the coffee dripped, he put on his reading glasses and studied the screen of his phone. Joe's text said that there was trouble out at the Sylacauga site, where they'd found what was left of Sophia Townsend. It made him sad to think of what time had done to a strong, vital woman. And sexy. He might as well admit it. The woman had possessed a sex appeal that he was hard-pressed to explain.

Usually, a man could point to the things that made a woman appealing. Big eyes. Big boobs. Curvaceous hips. Long legs. Long flowing hair. Had Sophia had any of those things? Nope.

She had been a small woman with boyish hips and close-cropped black hair. Not big boobs and not small ones, either. If her eyes had been big, he'd never noticed. All he had noticed was the way she looked out of them at the world and found it wanting. Maybe that was the secret to her appeal. A man wanted her to look at him and let him know that he was enough. And not just men. That's what Emily Olsen had wanted, too.

Sophia had bedeviled him, flirting and then pushing him away. She'd made him lewd promises that had succeeded in their aim, which was to distract him from his wife. For the rest of his days, it would pain him to remember how Patricia had looked Sophia over with her own intelligent eyes, sizing up the competition.

He should have told Patricia how he felt about her. He should have told her every day.

But what was a man to do about temptation? What is there to do about temptation, other than to remove oneself from it? He hadn't done that. He'd gone to work for three weeks, twenty-one days, and he'd let Sophia play him. Then the day had come when he just couldn't do it any more, but he could have never explained why.

She'd played him against his friends, too, so now he didn't have those friends any more. He wondered if they even remembered why they had grown apart.

It had been so long. So many days in a man's life were alike, going to work and coming home just the same as always. When Sly looked back, there were thousands of days that stayed just out of reach, but only dozens of days that stayed clear in their joy or grief. This was the way of time, an ever-moving thing that was always just beyond his grasp.

He remembered some things about that summer. Mickey Callahan had been as obsessed with Sophia as he had, and so had Kenny Meadows and Emily Olsen. The woman had cost Mickey and Kenny their marriages. Sly still wasn't sure how he'd been lucky enough to keep his.

Sly wondered whether Carson Callahan knew why his parents divorced. He was old enough now to understand the power of a woman so sensual that the air around her vibrated with sex, even when she was wearing worn army surplus pants and not a drop of makeup. If Carson had been unlucky, he had gained personal experience with a woman who had both Sophia's powerful sexuality and her fondness for using it to turn the people around her into toys.

Sly knew men like that, too. At any given bar, they were working the room until they found a woman whose needs made her vulnerable. Or a man. It didn't really matter to people like Sophia who it was they sucked dry. He wondered if Emily ever told her husband of twenty-five years that she had once been crazy in love with a woman. Judging by his daughter-in law's description of Emily's behavior when Sophia's bones came to light, Sly would say that Emily had never stopped being in love with a woman.

After all this time, Sly remained amazed at how easily people had swallowed the story that Sophia Townsend had run away to the mountains. Everybody had shaken their heads and said, "Well, she never liked anybody much and she did like that cabin. Can't say that I'm surprised."

That was bullshit. Sophia Townsend needed people. She needed people to bedevil. Quite frankly, she needed people to torture.

The people who lived in the town of Sylacauga had not been sorry to see the back of Sophia Townsend. Now the law would be looking for the person who killed her, and they would quickly figure out which of the locals might know something about her death.

Sly Mantooth had known the dead woman. He had worked for her for a little while, although nobody seemed to have remembered that. Yet.

It was no big secret that he had loved her a little. He gripped the chipped, stained coffee cup and waited for a knock on his door.

●　●　●　●　●

Faye braced her trembling legs as she half-stepped and half-jumped into the excavation. She hadn't realized what the tense day and night and morning had done to her, and the crisis wasn't over.

Everything was in flux. Hannity was still in serious condition. A careful search of the woods had uncovered no shooter and no identifiable footprints on the hard-baked soil. Threatening clouds blew overhead, and Faye couldn't take her eyes off them. She had lived through countless coastal storms and a single Category 5 hurricane, so she had seen clouds roil and blow before, but she'd never seen ordinary everyday clouds move the way the clouds in Oklahoma did.

As a scientist, she understood that she was standing at the crossroads of the North American climate, where the jet stream brought icy air from the North Pole to mingle with the hot, wet air blowing off the Gulf of Mexico. As a human being standing underneath the turbulent clouds as they fled across the sky, she felt awe.

She also felt fear. A thunderstorm at this moment would be a disaster, washing away almost any hope of finding Sophia Townsend's killer. The weather forecast had changed overnight, predicting heavy rain, winds, thunder, lightning, maybe even hail. Bigbee and his forensics team were coming as fast as they could, but Sylacauga was a long way from nowhere. The team was racing a monster thunderstorm and losing.

Cloud had decided that it was too risky to leave Sophia's bones in an open hole that could be flooded any minute, and Bigbee had agreed. As soon as he gave the go-ahead to start without him, Cloud had beckoned Faye to clamber into the excavation with him. Scattered raindrops were hitting the hard dirt, so they might not have long to salvage any information Sophia Townsend's grave held.

Those bones and the things buried with them were the only clues they had in the Townsend investigation. Even that evidence could be gone or destroyed now by the person Hannity had seen digging the night before. Faye had no idea whether the pearls and figurine still waited in the twenty-nine-year-old grave she was about to visit. The ghoulish image of a shadowy figure packing up Sophia's bones and hauling them away shook Faye to her core.

As Faye drew near, she knew things were bad. It was easy to see that someone had been digging in Sophia Townsend's grave.

She walked to the gravesite and crouched beside it. Roy Cloud stood behind her, careful to keep his shadow away from the area where she needed to work.

"Gone," she said. "It's all gone. Not her bones, but everything else."

Sophia's bones had been disturbed but gently. The bones that had composed the top of her body—skull, vertebrae, ribs, clavicles, scapulae—had been neatly stacked beside her pelvis. The intruder had then dug a deep hole into the vacant space left behind.

Faye looked with wordless regret at the disturbed soil where the Mississippian artifacts had been. Every last pearl was gone, pried out of the hard clay. The figurine had been taken. Even the cheap canvas bag was gone, with not a stray fiber left to show that it was ever there.

She sat back on her heels and said, "At least we took pictures."

That was cold comfort for the loss of the most spectacular finds she'd ever seen while still in-situ.

Then the adrenaline-fueled trembling in her hands returned as she saw the size of the hole left by the intruder. It was far bigger than necessary for the retrieval of just the figurine and the pearls. She could only wonder what else had been waiting just below Sophia's bones, below the pearls and the figurine.

"Do you remember the rectangle in the bottom of her grave?" she asked. "The darker soil? That's what they dug up. All of it."

The intruder had left a box-shaped hole as deep as her arm was long. "Do you see that?"

She moved aside so that Cloud could look. He said, "It looks to me like somebody dug up something fairly large, maybe the size of a case of beer or even bigger. What do you think it was?"

"I have no idea, but it wasn't just the pearls and figurine."

Faye didn't know what to do with herself after she had stated that disturbing fact, so she did what she did best. She went back to documenting the current state of Sophia Townsend's grave, photographing the rearranged bones and sketching them to account for the differences between the human eye and the camera lens. Every gust of wind brought a few more raindrops.

As she sketched, she watched Gerard and one of Cloud's officers crouch beside Sophia Townsend's body, preparing to excavate it as tenderly as a mother lifts an infant from its bed. After the bones were safely removed and packed into paper bags, Faye examined the hole in the soil that had been beneath them. It was rectangular in cross-section, with loose dirt around its rim where someone had worked to get a strong enough grip on the box to yank it out of the ground.

A hard edge in the soft soil caught her attention and she said, "Look at that. I think it's a potsherd."

She freed it from the soil and brushed it clean, holding it up for Cloud to see.

"I'm pretty sure it's Mississippian." She was so startled by the pattern decorating the potsherd that she spoke too softly and he asked her to repeat herself. "Mississippian. You know, like Spiro Mounds. About a thousand years old. Carson's going to have a coronary when he sees this."

The potsherd had four sides and it was about the size of four or five postage stamps. It was incised with an intricate design, a rainbow-like pattern of concentric semi-circles bordered on one side with a stylized feather.

"And that's good?"

"If it's Mississippian? It will make Carson's year. If this is what I think it is, this will make his career."

"So it's valuable?"

Faye's eyes kept returning to its shape, which was vaguely like an envelope, a square with a triangle sitting on top. It bowed outward slightly, as if it came from the side of a large round pot.

"Valuable? No, not really. It's valuable to science, but a collector wouldn't bother with it. The pearls and the figurine? Yes. They have intrinsic value. You could sell them for big bucks, but not this."

"Can you tell anything by where you found it?"

"It's in disturbed soil, so no, not much. I'm not sure it's been here long. I searched the surface yesterday, and it wasn't here. It's right where you'd expect it to be if it fell out of that canvas bag when the thief dug it up, so that's what I think happened. I wonder what it was doing in there."

Cloud studied the hole. "Maybe the thief threw it on the ground because the two artifacts in the bag with it were worth a lot of money, but it wasn't worth carrying out of this hole. And who knows what was in that box underneath? Maybe something even better. Do you think it was just a lucky accident that they came to steal two things and got away with three? Or did somebody already know the box was here underneath her?"

Faye couldn't stop looking at the potsherd. "I don't know. They probably already knew. Why else would you keep digging after removing the canvas bag?"

"It stands to reason that the person who knew the box was here would be the person who buried it."

She nodded, still looking the engraved patterns on the sherd. "And it stands to reason that the person who buried those things under Sophia Townsend's body is the same person who put her in the ground."

Chapter Fourteen

Faye stood on the porch of a strange house, listening to rain pound hard on the roof above her. They had been lucky to get Sophia Townsend's bones safely out of the ground before the storm hit. Agent Bigbee and his people had arrived an hour later and they'd stood in raingear alongside Faye and Roy, looking at the way the falling drops pockmarked the water standing in the bottom of the excavation.

Then they'd all gone back to the police station, shed the raingear, and wiped their wet faces before sitting down to discuss the case. In the end, it made no sense for anybody but Bigbee to stay in Sylacauga, especially when they had access to Roy's excellent photodocumentation of the site before the rain. Sophia Townsend's bones were ready to go to the lab and the rain had washed away any hope of finding much more.

Bigbee had praised Cloud's work on the case, saying, "You've salvaged this case, Roy. The storm could have cost us everything. Let's you and me sit down and go over the interview notes you took yesterday."

"You and me" didn't seem to involve Faye, so she had excused herself. On her way to the car, she texted Roy to say that she needed to spend some time with Sophia Townsend's field notes. She figured he could share that information with Agent Bigbee, or not, as he saw fit.

Not many minutes later, after driving through heavy rain being blown sideways, Faye stood on Carson's front porch saying the same thing she had to Roy: "I need to spend some time with Sophia Townsend's field notes."

Faye said this politely and in a pleasant tone, but Carson couldn't have been happy to hear it, nor to see her standing on his front doorstep with an annoying request.

Carson answered Faye with, "I'm sure Roy Cloud would appreciate your unbiased opinion on what they have to say," and he too spoke politely, but his face said a lot more.

Carson looked violated. There was no other word for it. It was as if Faye had said, "I need to search your house. I'll be rifling through your underwear drawer and inspecting the sheets on your bed. If you keep a diary, I'll be reading that, too."

The look passed quickly and Carson was himself again, anxious to help with the investigation and willing to talk about his work with a fellow professional who had spent most of the day doing work that he'd spent his whole career waiting to do.

Carson's home was a small, gray, wood-framed house dating to the mid-twentieth century, old enough to be architecturally interesting but not old enough to be expensive. It suited him.

The floorboards of the porch creaked under her feet. They had been recently swept but not recently painted. Carson pushed open the screen door and let her into a living space much like the house's exterior, clean but far from new. The floor was covered with freshly waxed linoleum tiles that reminded Faye of her childhood schoolrooms. The furniture spoke of thrift shops and parental hand-me-downs.

He gestured for her to come in, so she followed him across the room. Carson was big, no question. Dirt is heavy, and he had broad shoulders made for lifting it.

Walking behind him, Faye could see the muscles of his back, overdeveloped from neck to waist. They showed through his thin cotton shirt. His thighs strained at the dirt-brown cargo shorts covering them. Below their hems and above his socks, calf muscles bulged. She wished she were half as well-constructed for her work. She also wondered how big Carson had been when he was eleven. Then she wondered at herself for even thinking that a child that age could have done something so horrible.

"I think you'll find the notebooks...um...fascinating," Carson said. "Do you need the originals or can you make do with photocopies?"

Faye considered the question. She'd prefer to see the notebooks just as Dr. Townsend had written in them, but they were a direct physical link to the place and time of the woman's death. That made them evidence and she shouldn't be handling them.

"I probably need both. I need to take the originals to Roy Cloud and Agent Bigbee, at least for now, but I'll also need a set of copies to review. I guess it's possible there could still be fingerprints on the originals—"

"Underneath years and years of my fingerprints. And my dissertation advisor's. Not to mention several other experts I've consulted over the years. And, I suppose, the prints of the archaeologists hired to close the excavation back in 1987 could be there, too. But I'm sure Roy Cloud is enough of a miracle worker to find something useful under all that old skin oil."

Faye almost took a step backward to retreat from his sarcasm and frustration, but she held firm. "I hear you. There are probably no useful prints left on those notebooks, but disentangling all those prints is a job for the police, don't you think? And, oh, I don't know—couldn't they find hairs or fibers or something? The odds of using them to find Sophia's killer seem pretty low, but this is an oddball case. We're going to have to turn over every rock that might have a clue under it."

"Then we shouldn't make Roy Cloud wait even a second," Carson said as he pulled open the door of a coat closet. "He's the boss of everything now."

He lifted a banker's box off the top shelf and shoved it in Faye's direction, as if challenging her to carry it as easily as he did. When she grabbed it, he said, "The originals. Here you go. Tell Cloud to make sure his people take good care of them."

The box was heavy, but not unmanageably so. If Carson was hoping to see her stagger under it, he was going to be disappointed.

She carried it to the dining room table and set it down next to stacks of paperwork, then lifted the lid. She knew better than to add her name to the long list of people who had left fingerprints on those field notebooks, but she did want to look at them.

The box held a dozen or so blue bound notebooks. She had expected there to be more, but now she remembered that Sophia Townsend hadn't even finished out the summer at the Sylacauga site. She hadn't had time to fill shelves and shelves of notebooks.

Some of the books were stained with smears of red dirt, and those smears made Faye sad. They made Sophia Townsend real. They made her an ordinary person who got dirty sometimes. They made her nothing more than a woman doing her job and living her life, expecting that she had fifty years left to do those things.

These notebooks held Sophia Townsend's thoughts. Their pages were covered with her handwriting. One of them might have been the last thing she held in her hands.

"Don't worry. I'll treat them as gently as irreplaceable artifacts," she said.

"That's what they are."

Carson's face softened as he looked at the notebooks, like a father looking at his children. How many hours had he spent with them over the years?

Faye said, "Yeah, they are," and carefully put the lid back on the box.

Carson didn't seem to have anything to say. He just stood there like a man wishing she would go away.

Faye couldn't give him that wish yet. "What about the photocopies? Do you have a set I can copy so that I don't have to handle these? If I have my own set, I can take notes right on the pages and you'll still have yours for your work."

Carson turned away. He walked silently to one of the bookshelves that lined his living room walls and gathered an armload of three-ring binders, each of them completely filled with paper.

Putting them in another dusty box, he said, "These are my copies. You'll see years of my notes in the margins, but I left her handwriting just as it was."

"If you tell me where to go to make another set, I'll do that now and bring yours right back."

There was an awkward pause. Faye could almost see the man's thoughts. He knew that her request for his copies was justified. Considering that she was working on a murder investigation, he obviously should give them to her, but he hated doing it. He didn't want to risk not getting them back.

If Faye let him down, who knew when Cloud would release the originals so he could make another set? Besides, it was a hard thing to swallow, sharing something so central to his work with someone who had barged in and taken it over.

He made a decision and it did not involve handing the copies over to Faye.

"We'll need to run these through a copier so you can have a set. The copy shop's downtown. We'll go together."

• • ● ● •

Downtown Sylacauga was a single line of storefronts along a six-block Main Street. A row of squatty brick buildings faced the north side of the street. Most of them had green awnings, with a few renegades sporting brown ones or even no awning at all. One of them had a bay window framed in wrought iron that had once been painted black. It protruded from the store's bricked front, its dulled metal shone dimly in the sunlight, and it sagged, all at the same time.

The Depression-era buildings housed locally owned diners and shops that had survived because McDonald's and Walmart were not interested in a town the size of Sylacauga. Who wants to drive an hour for a hamburger or a tube of toothpaste?

Across the street from Main Street's businesses, a railroad track ran past a white-painted feed-and-seed store and a cluttered salvage yard as it hurried out of town. At the city limits, the boarded-up depot had been waiting for years for one of those trains to stop.

Only storekeepers with a certain entrepreneurial spirit were to able survive in Sylacauga, and that spirit was on display all along Main Street. Someone was running at least two businesses within any given storefront, with the most prosperous-looking buildings housing three. Wayne's Signs, which Wayne ran out of the feed-and-seed, seemed to be making good money on signs big enough to accommodate the businesses' unwieldy names. Shelly's Dress Store and Coffee Shop sat next to Max's Shoes, Dry Cleaning, and Alterations. Beyond them was Dottie's Drugstore, Floral Designs, and Cell Phone Repair.

A long row of parking spaces ran in front of the row of shops, and more of them were occupied than Faye would have expected. Sylacauga's merchants were reaping the benefits of a captive audience.

Donna's Hair Salon had a sign in the window advertising a copy shop and the services of a notary public. Faye decided that this must be where Carson was taking her. How many copy shops could there be in Sylacauga?

The massive wooden door to Donna's Hair Salon glowed warm and brown beneath years of shellac. It opened into a large space floored with about a million tiny black and white tiles. The smell of acrylic nails and hair dye completely swamped any trace of copier toner, but a sign saying "Copies this way" told Faye that they were in the right place.

The sign led them to a small wood-paneled room holding a single copy machine, which was in use. A business-suited woman with shoulder-length ash-blond hair looked up from her work and said, "Hello, dear. I'll just be another minute."

Carson said, "No worries, Mom. Take your time. Is the law firm's copier on the fritz?"

"You know I don't use the company machine for personal things."

"Mom. You're a partner. It's your machine."

"I only own a third of it, and you know how Larry and Sue feel about this."

She held up a flyer with the heading, "Eight Reasons Why Archaeology is Cultural Appropriation."

Carson was too irritated by his mother to remember to introduce Faye. He gave the flyer a dismissive wave of the hand and asked, "Does anybody sitting in our current legislature know what cultural appropriation is? Or care?"

"That one is for universities. This one is for the legislators."

She held up another flyer that read, "Eight Reasons Why Archaeology is Bad for Business" and Carson laughed out loud. Faye had to admit that the woman had style.

"Mom," Carson said. The woman didn't look up from her photocopying. "Mom, it hurt my feelings that you sent a bunch of flunkies yesterday to protest my dig. My work isn't offensive enough for you to come yourself? Do I need to be more aggressive about appropriating culture if I hope to get your attention?"

"It's your own culture you're mucking about in, dear. You should care. I would have been there yesterday, trying to make you care, but I don't have time to be a hands-on protesting radical walking the picket lines. Not any more. I can have more influence as a hands-off lobbying radical. I was at the state capitol yesterday, trying to get the legislature to pass some laws that will annoy you to no end."

Carson finally remembered Faye, jerking his head in her direction. "This is a colleague of mine, Dr. Faye Longchamp-Mantooth."

The woman looked up from her photocopying and extended a hand. "I'm Alba Callahan, Faye. It's very nice to meet you."

Faye didn't know how she had expected Carson's mother to look, but it was nothing like the woman in front of her. Alba Callahan did not look like a genteel old lady who spent her time musing on how proud she was of her son and his PhD. She looked like an attorney at the peak of her career who had no plans to slow down.

Alba Callahan moved like a woman who had played basketball in high school and still made it a point to keep herself in shape. Her blond hair was streaked with white, but Alba made gray hair seem stylish and intentional. She looked as if she'd gone to a salon and gotten silver highlights. Her black suit was well-cut, with long straight pants, a petal-pink silk blouse, and a jacket that nipped in at her trim waist.

Faye had not expected a woman who was the mother of a forty-year-old man and who lived in Sylacauga, Oklahoma, to make her feel so frumpy.

Carson took the box so that Faye could shake his mother's outstretched hand. Faye could have sworn she saw the woman check the ring finger of her left hand.

A flicker of disappointment crossed Alba's face, and then she said, "Wait. Did you say Mantooth? Are you young Joe's wife? I heard you were coming to town. Everybody's heard, actually. Sly hasn't talked about anything else for weeks. He cornered me at the pharmacy last Tuesday."

Instead of letting Faye's hand go, she clasped it with her other hand, too. "I'm so happy to meet you. Patricia was—" Her voice cracked and she covered by squeezing Faye's hand hard. "She was a lovely person and my good friend. We used to volunteer at the school library together. My goodness, that was a long time ago."

Her hands unfolded, palms up, as they slowly released Faye from their grasp. Even Alba's hands moved like those of a dancer or an athlete.

"I still miss her," Alba said. "I'm so happy Joe found you. Patricia would have loved to meet you. I know all your good points already. Sly made sure of it."

Faye had changed her clothes and boots when she left the site, but Alba's effortless elegance made her want to look down and assess the cleanliness of her soles. No matter how hard she tried, Faye was almost always a little bit dirty.

Alba squared up her stacks of paper and slipped them into her briefcase. "The copier's all yours." As she passed Carson on the way out, she stopped for a hug.

Alba must have seen Faye cringe as her son's sweaty arms crumpled the expensive suit, because she said, "It'll wash." When she released Carson, there was a petal-pink smear of lipstick on his cheek.

She waved a languid hand as she left, saying, "So nice to meet you, Faye."

After the copy room door closed, Carson said, "Just so you know, Mom fought the Sylacauga project tooth and nail. Mom believes in protecting the ancient sites, and I do mean protecting them from people like me. She's against anything that poses any risk of disturbing cultural items or, God forbid, human remains. That means she would prefer that we never build a road in this county, not ever again."

"What did she do to try to stop your project?"

"She lobbied the legislature. She took out ads. She went door-to-door with a petition. She argued with the Creeks until the very minute they gave me a budget for the job. You name it, she did it. And remember, these are my employers that she's harassing."

"Having met her, I can't say that I'm surprised to hear that she sticks to her principles."

"She made me look bad in front of my boss and she nearly sank my project. My own mother. She tried to stop it the first time, too, all those years ago. She's lost this battle twice now, and she doesn't lose many."

Faye could believe this.

"She believes in protecting the ancient sites," Faye said. "So she represents the Creeks? She's their lawyer? No, that doesn't make any sense. They gave you a budget to do the project. They *want* this work done."

Carson shook his head. "No, she doesn't represent the Creeks. She *is* Creek. An enrolled member, in fact. She just doesn't agree with the tribal government when it comes to excavating on tribal land. Or any government excavating on any land, for that matter. Mom doesn't think there's any reason good enough to risk disturbing the dead."

Faye's head turned involuntarily toward the copy room door where she'd last seen the light-haired, light-skinned, light-eyed woman who was, despite appearances, a citizen of the Muscogee (Creek) Nation. She knew better than to make presumptions, but she'd done it.

"I can't picture your mother standing outside in the sun long enough to protest. She's so…well, elegant is the only word for it. Did you see the heels on those pink shoes?"

"Mom wasn't so polished when I was a kid. She had a serious punk phase in the eighties. Nothing but torn jeans and band t-shirts. I was seven before I saw her wear any color that wasn't black. But anyway, yeah. She's done her share of standing outside in the sun, protesting stuff. I've done my share of standing out there with her, wondering why my mom was so angry. Back in the day, she held sit-ins. She chained herself to fences. Stuff like that. I'm told that her one face-to-face conversation with Sophia Townsend went very, very poorly. Dr. Townsend had my mother arrested."

Faye tried to imagine how a face-off between the two women would have gone. She wasn't sure which one would have been scarier. "Civil disobedience didn't get her the results she wanted, so your mom decided to go to law school?"

"Exactly. When I started middle school, she started law school. She still works for social change. These days, though, she works like a lobbyist, shaking hands and calling in favors. She hasn't been back to jail since she lost her bid to stop Sophia Townsend from ripping up history."

"And yet you chose to be an archaeologist."

"I was a really well-behaved kid. When I decided to rebel, I did it in a big way."

That statement made Faye snicker. She pulled the top off the box of binders. Running into Carson's mother seemed to make Faye only the second most annoying woman Carson had seen that day, and that had made him friendlier. She took advantage of this chance to ask him some questions. "What about you? Are you a citizen of the Muscogee (Creek) Nation?"

"It's complicated. To be enrolled, you have to be a blood descendant of someone who was listed as Creek on the Dawes Rolls, which the government compiled more than a century back to make it clear who was a member of what tribe. As time passes, it gets more and more likely that an enrolled Creek might look like Mom. Or me, I guess," Carson said. "I could be enrolled because of Mom, but Dad's not Creek and they didn't raise me in the culture. It would feel dishonest. What people consider themselves to be has less to do with what they look like and more to do with their upbringing. And their level of interest, I guess. Joe knows way more about the traditional ways than I do, but he taught himself, which I respect enormously. Did he ever fill out the citizenship forms?"

"There are things Joe doesn't talk about and that's one of them. I always thought he wasn't a member because his mother was white."

"Guess again. Joe's mom could trace her family all the way back to the Dawes Rolls, and that's been the gold standard for proving membership for a really long time. Even when he was my little buddy, Joe didn't care for paperwork and government stuff. I think that's why he never applied."

Faye opened the top binder and pulled out a chunk of pages. Putting them in the photocopier's feed tray, she pressed the big green button.

The chunk-chunk of a copying machine at work filled the little room. Faye hoped that Carson's resentment of her was gone for good, but she doubted it. More likely, he was able to rise above that resentment because he enjoyed sharing his local knowledge. Some people would have called it gossip.

"Kenny's not enrolled, though he'd love to be. He's very proud of his heritage, very traditional. His whole family is, but they don't have the paperwork to prove it. Maybe my little buddy's right about how much those papers are worth."

"How do you know everybody's business?"

"Around here, people just know."

The shushing sound of paper exiting the copier was a white-noise backdrop to their conversation.

"Emily?"

Carson snorted at the idea. "Nope."

"Roy Cloud?"

"Enrolled, and related to half the government of the Musco-gee (Creek) Nation. Just so you know who you're dealing with."

Faye felt a little wistful that she didn't have the paperwork to connect her to her Creek ancestor, her great-great-great-great grandmother Susan Whitehall. Given that Susan was born in the Georgia wilderness before the American Revolution, the necessary papers had never existed. She knew even less about her African ancestors and, given the clean break with Africa brought about by slavers and slave ships, that would never change.

The chunking sound stopped and she fed the copier another stack of paper. "Do you have insider knowledge of anybody else's bloodlines?"

"Sophia Townsend. She was Creek and she spoke the language."

Faye was so surprised that the words "Get outta town!" fell out of her mouth. "All this time we've been talking about her, nobody ever said she was from here. I had the impression that she was an outsider."

"Just because she was Creek didn't mean she wasn't an outsider here in Oklahoma. She was from Alabama. I think that may be why Roy is so dead-set on shadowing the FBI on this case. Just because the federal government has decided it's in charge when it comes to violent crimes, it doesn't change how Roy feels about Sophia getting murdered here, among her people."

"Did she come from a traditional upbringing? Do you know?"

Carson shook his head. "I don't know a thing about her family or even whether she was enrolled in the Creek tribe there. I just know how she sounded when she talked. You can hear it in the way a person pronounces their vowels. Nasal sounds are different. So's the…I guess 'tonal range' is what you'd call it."

"I think I know what you're saying. Roy Cloud's voice has that sound, doesn't it?"

"Yep. It's a quiet, calm way to speak. When I went away to college, I missed that sound a lot. Does Joe speak the language?"

To Faye's ear, her husband and Roy Cloud sounded nothing alike. "Joe didn't grow up speaking Creek, but he taught himself a little after he left home."

"I didn't think I could hear it in Joe's voice, so that makes sense. But I certainly did when Sophia Townsend talked. After all these years and all the time I spent studying her work, she still fascinates me."

"Why? I mean, other than that we just dug up her grave."

Carson delayed answering by stacking the first batch of copies more neatly than they strictly needed to be stacked.

"It's a hard thing," he said, "navigating a traditional upbringing and a career in archaeology. Not many try. The ones that do? I think they either struggle every day to do the right thing and honor their ancestors. Or they just do their work and try to forget where they came from."

Faye remembered a Choctaw man in Mississippi who had found his own way to honor his culture and still pursue his love for archaeology. It hadn't been easy. "How do you think Sophia dealt with that conflict?"

"I was just a kid and I didn't really know her. From what I've heard, she was the kind who spent every waking minute trying to forget where she came from."

They fell silent, each of them taking a stack of pages and loading it into a binder. As the pages passed beneath her hands, Faye saw black smears marking the copies where faint remnants of red clay had lingered for so long on the originals. They gave her hope that a forensics lab could tease a fingerprint out of those smears of dirt, though what Cloud could do with it was anybody's guess.

The smears also reminded her of how hard it is to completely remove red dirt from absorbent surfaces. Slick surfaces like metal and glass were easily wiped clean, but paper? Unfinished wood? Bone? Human skin? These things hang onto red clay. They stain.

Sometimes scrubbing will take off the stains. Sometimes heavy-duty soaps or detergents can do the trick. But there are situations when nothing will remove the stain but time.

Kira Denton had been dead less than a day. The person who killed her had knelt by her grave to dig up a figurine, some pearls, and a mysterious box that was large enough to be awkward to carry. It was inconceivable that the killer had accomplished these things without getting dirty. Filthy.

If the killer was one of the archaeologists, then a little bit of dirt wouldn't be noteworthy. If the killer wasn't one of the archaeologists, though, ground-in dirt could be hard to explain.

Stained clothes can be shed, as evidenced by the monumentally dirty clothes waiting in a plastic bag in the trunk of Faye's rental car.

Stained skin? Not so much.

Photocopying is a slow and mindless task, and even Carson couldn't talk all the time, so Faye had a lot of time to think these things through. She came up with no answers, other than that she needed to call Roy Cloud as soon as she could conveniently slip away from Carson. It was hard to stand next to him, knowing how he would feel if he knew what she was about to do. He would view her next action as a stab in his back.

She stood at the machine, feeding it sheets of paper and thinking about paper and clay and skin and hands. Mostly, she thought about Alba Callahan's graceful hands.

They had been remarkably unwrinkled and free of age spots as they waved in the air and clutched Faye's own hands so warmly. Alba's nails had been shorter than Faye would have expected, and they had been painted with a polish dark enough to cover almost anything, but there had been nothing else remarkable on the backs of Alba's hands.

This was not true when she flipped them over. Staining the rough areas at the base of each of her palms, there had been a barely discernible reddish tinge that was the color of hard-baked bricks.

The stains on Alba Callahan's hands were the deep orange-red of Oklahoma clay.

Excerpt from the field notes of Dr. Sophia Townsend
July 28, 1987

I would sell my mother to find a potsherd.

Or a bit of charcoal from a very old hearth. Or a bone fragment. Or a shell. Or a pile of nutshells where someone sat down and hulled a pile of hickory nuts. But I've given up on finding something that was once alive and therefore suitable for carbon dating, so I'd settle for a potsherd that I could send to a lab for thermoluminescence testing.

I can't find one.

So I've been reduced to desperate measures, shipping stone knives and bird points to a professor in Canada who is probably unbalanced. He says he can get detectable amounts of blood and plant residue off their surfaces. He claims he can then get radiocarbon dates on the blood and plant material, but that's probably bullshit. I can't imagine that he can get enough organic material for his equipment to see, but he insists that he can. My regular lab certainly can't. He hasn't managed it so far, despite the number of American dollars that I have sent across the border.

I also mailed a couple of flint tools to him for thermoluminescence tests, but that only works if the rock was heat-treated to make it easier to shape or...hell, I don't know...if it fell into a fire by accident because its maker got drunk. No luck.

Of course, I had no luck. I've had no luck with any part of this godforsaken job.

For instance, I'm saddled with Stupidface, who thinks that a teaching certificate in earth science gives him a right to an opinion on how I run my project. He insists that relative dating works just fine and I shouldn't get all worked up over a lack of objective laboratory data. He's under the impression that we can guess the age of everything we uncover by its place in the stratigraphy.

That's what I consider his approach to be. Guessing.

"If this tool is found below that one, then it's older," he says. "Study the layers of soil. You don't need a lab to tell you how old these things are. To do lab tests of something, you have to destroy it just to get a sample. Is that why we're looking for old things? To tear them up? How does that respect the person who made them? The soil will tell you how time passed here. Listen to it speak."

Sorry, Stupidface.

In my world, dirt doesn't talk. I want to establish a date for this site that can't be torn apart by small-minded academics infatuated with their own unsubstantiated theories. I don't want to lead from weakness, justifying my position by saying, "Look! This spear point was found one centimeter above that one and three centimeters below the other one. They were all found in soil that is indicative..."

Oh, I can't even pretend to write in academic bullshit doublespeak. I certainly can't stand up in front of a crowd of small-minded hacks and listen to them tear my academic bullshit apart.

Relative dating just doesn't work for me. I want lab data.

I want objective dates to hang my hat on, and I will have them. I will find something that is inarguably datable, and I will find a certified lab to put its stamp of approval on that date. Then we will know the age and significance of this site.

Make no mistake. This place is significant.

And that is why I would sell my mother for a potsherd.

Chapter Fifteen

"So Alba Callahan doesn't strike you as a woman to get her hands dirty?"

Roy Cloud didn't sound like he had grave concerns that Alba might be guilty. Maybe a criminal investigator who knew all his suspects personally didn't have the most clear-headed judgment.

Faye wished they were face-to-face, but he was out doing detective things while she was trying to get back to Sly's house for a little of the family time that had brought her to Oklahoma. She had called Cloud because she figured it wasn't all that important to be face-to-face when she had nothing to say but "Alba Callahan's hands look suspicious, so question her before she washes them."

"You don't think she's capable of murder?" Faye asked. "Is that because you've known her a long time and you think she's a good person? Or is it because you don't think she could pull it off?"

"Oh, Alba's one of the most capable people I know. If I had to name the person in Sylacauga most capable of planning and executing a convoluted killing and cover-up like Sophia Townsend's, it would be Alba. Most killers aren't smart enough to get somebody else to bury all their evidence under five feet of dirt for thirty years. Alba's that smart. And she had a couple of motives."

He hadn't risen to Faye's baited question of whether he thought Alba was a good person.

"A couple of motives? I know Alba opposed Dr. Townsend's work at the Sylacauga site. What's her other motive?"

"I see that you aren't tapped into the Sylacauga gossip machine yet. Alba's motive is very clear-cut. She and Mickey broke up because he was sleeping with Sophia. The really interesting thing is that Kenny was, too."

"Well, that sheds a little light, doesn't it?"

"Hang on."

The entire process of Cloud ordering a cheeseburger and a root beer, from "Can I take your order?" to "Have a good day!" seeped out of her phone. Now Faye was hungry.

She heard Cloud take a big slurp of root beer. "Sorry. When I'm working a new case, I eat all my meals in a rolling car. I'm on my way home from utterly failing to find any record of where Dr. Townsend's cabin was. I dropped the ball when I didn't ask her employees if they knew its location, so I'm calling 'em all back in tomorrow."

"They're gonna hate you for that, if they don't already."

"Alba Callahan probably does hate me already. I interviewed her this afternoon, probably right before you saw her. Did she look nervous? Rumpled? Guilty? Please tell me she looked guilty so I can arrest her and go home."

"Sorry to break it to you, but no. There wasn't a rumpled hair on her sleek blond head. I did not get the sense that you had intimidated Alba Callahan into confessing to murder."

He sighed. "Not surprised."

"Why do you think she would've looked nervous?"

"I don't know. Maybe because I asked her if she murdered Sophia Townsend."

If being asked by a police chief whether she'd committed murder didn't rumple Alba Callahan, Faye figured nothing would.

"What did she say?"

"Alba said, and I quote: 'I didn't kill Sophia Townsend, though God knows she had it coming. If I'd done it, you would never have found her and you never would have been able to prove a thing.'"

He laughed, but his laugh was broken off by an audible bite of the cheeseburger.

Still chewing, he said, "You know, Doctor Faye, I kind of believe her."

Faye wasn't in the mood to listen to him eat, so she said, "Well, if you find somebody whose alibi you don't believe, just let me know. Otherwise, I'll busy myself with reading these field notebooks until I talk to you tomorrow. I want to see my family before they go to bed and I need to sleep at least a few hours."

"Wait! One more thing!"

Faye hoped he'd let her hang up before she had to listen to the cheeseburger wrapper crackle again. "Yes?"

"Before you worry too much more about the dirt stains on Alba's hands, why don't you drive past her house?"

"Is it urgent? Can I do it tomorrow? And why?"

"She's got the prettiest yard in town. Prize-winning antique roses. Crape myrtles. Blueberry bushes. All that jazz."

"And…?"

"She does all the yard work herself. Alba knows how to look top drawer—hair, clothes, shoes, bag, everything. But her hands are always a wreck. I think she's got red mud underneath her skin in some places. It's like she has dirt tattoos."

Blueberries, flowers, and prize roses. Faye wouldn't have thought those beautiful things could make her feel so stupid.

"Really. Go look at her flowers. They're great. She and my late wife used to pass plants back and forth all the time. They both had the greenest thumbs. Charlotte always said that if Alba stuck a wood pencil in the ground, it would take root and grow into a tree."

"Now I feel like an idiot."

"Don't. Just because Alba grows pretty flowers, it doesn't mean she's not a killer. Remember that, Faye. Alba's got enough anger in her to fuel more than one murder. And she's not the only one."

Faye hung up the phone and drove. Roy Cloud sure knew a lot about everybody in Sylacauga. She might find him affable and down-home, but if Sophia Townsend's killer had also spent the last twenty-nine years in Sylacauga, Cloud and his insider knowledge would be terrifying. So who was he talking about when he said that Alba Callahan wasn't the only angry person in town?

Emily Olsen was angry and sad and grief-stricken over a woman she had loved. But was she angry before Sophia Townsend's bones appeared?

Faye thought of Emily's life. Her husband was dead, probably years before his time. Early widows had good reason to be angry. She had at least one child, but Faye had gotten the impression from the way Carson mentioned her son that he didn't come around much. Emily could be angry about that.

A fifty-ish widow with no kids to keep her distracted from her grief would have enough free time to work up a powerful anger at fate. Emily could be looking at forty more years that promised to be no more fulfilling than this one.

And maybe Emily's last forty years hadn't been as fulfilling as people might think. Maybe she would have been happier spending her life with a woman. She might be angry that she'd been born in a time when that choice would have been very hard. She might be angry with herself that she didn't make the choice anyway.

Emily was far from the only angry person in Faye's immediate vicinity. Kenny and Mickey had worked for forty years in jobs that paid criminally low wages for men of their intelligence. They'd both been divorced for nearly thirty years from wives that Faye presumed they had loved. They could be as lonely as Emily and just as angry.

Looking around Sylacauga for angry people took her directly to Carson. It seemed so unlikely that he could have murdered a woman when he was eleven, though looking at his size now, she guessed it was theoretically possible. Children who are that troubled rarely move on to a successful academic and professional career, but he clearly felt some anger now.

Carson hadn't mentioned a life partner and his home had felt like a place where a single man lived alone. His mother's single glance at Faye's left hand made her think that there was no partner and no immediate prospect of one. He could be just as lonely as his parents, Emily, and Kenny.

Faye couldn't see a straight line from Carson's anger and loneliness to shooting Kira Denton, but Carson was more than old enough to kill somebody now. He was not, however, a magician, so he couldn't possibly have fired those shots that had scared them so badly just a day before, not while he was crouched right next to Faye.

Kenny, too, was off the hook for that shooting. She'd seen him lying prone on the ground during the incident. Besides, Roy Cloud and Bleck would have surely found the gun, because Kenny wouldn't have had any way to get rid of it.

She pulled into the driveway of the shabby old house where her husband had finished growing up. She let herself in the back door and found Joe at the Formica-topped kitchen table in a green fake leather chair, smoking a cigarette. He didn't speak when she came in. He didn't even say hello. He just looked up at her.

Joe had taken his hair down from its customary ponytail and it hung loose around his slumping shoulders. He was wearing a stretched-out t-shirt that she didn't recognize. Maybe it had been in this house since he left it, all those years ago. His mouth was set and his eyes were shielded. He didn't even look like himself.

Joe was a quiet man, but he did talk to his wife. When he went mute with Faye, it meant he was in pain.

There were four cigarettes stubbed out in the gold-tone ashtray in front of him, and they weren't Sly's brand. The cigarettes underscored the message that something wasn't right with her husband.

Sometimes Joe smoked a cigarette, just one, while sitting outside enjoying the night air. He justified the habit to his worried wife as an ancient spiritual practice of his people, who gave the world tobacco. Faye thought it was cheating to use religion to settle an argument, and she didn't think tobacco was much of a gift.

They'd had this fight more than a few times. Faye's only consolation was that Joe never smoked indoors and he never smoked more than one cigarette at a time. The pile of cigarette butts in front of Joe told Faye that something was wrong. His silence told her that he couldn't even bring himself to tell her what it was.

"Joe. What is it?"

"I thought yesterday was bad when Dad wouldn't stop talking. Today? He ain't said a word to me since you left."

"Is he drinking again?"

"No."

"Thank goodness."

"But he ain't even drinking water. Or eating. He's been in that chair all day. The TV's on, but he ain't watching."

He stubbed out the cigarette and fumbled with the pack for another one. Faye wanted so badly to take it out of his hands.

"I come all this way to see him and now he won't talk to me? At all? I did something wrong, Faye. We've been doing real good, Dad and me, and I've done something to mess it up. I just don't know what it was."

He took a long drag on the cigarette, then let it go. There was enough smoke in the air to make Faye feel dizzy and sick.

Suddenly, Joe sat up a little straighter and set his burning cigarette into the groove on the ashtray's rim. His face turned toward the hallway.

The TV in the living room was still playing, but Faye could hear shuffling steps coming their way on the worn wood floor. She didn't like the sound of those steps. Her father-in-law was still vital and strong. He did not shuffle like an old man.

Sly trudged through the door and he looked worse than his steps sounded. His usual good posture was gone. His back slumped in a way that made him look shorter and heavier, and his worn t-shirt looked like Joe's, only twenty years older. His bronze skin was sallow. His black eyes were dull. Even his jaw-length black hair was dull. When he spoke, his voice was dull, too.

"Good to see you're back safe, Daughter. It's been a long day. I believe I'll head to bed."

He turned to leave before either of them could answer him, and he almost made it out of sight before he stopped walking. As Sly stood stock-still in the hallway, Faye was afraid.

Now she knew why Joe was distraught. This was like seeing someone fall into Alzheimer's disease in a single day. Could Sly be having a stroke while they watched?

They had both half-risen when he turned around, so they hovered awkwardly over their chairs when Sly turned around and began to speak.

"It ain't easy. Burying your mother, I mean. Been thinking about it all day. Where to put her. Where to spread her ashes. What to do with this damn urn that I've been living with for fifteen years."

Faye hadn't noticed that he was holding the urn in both hands.

"I just don't know how to do it. Never did. The Creek ways weren't her ways, no matter what the Dawes Rolls say. She stopped going to church right after she met me. You know we never went to church, Son. Didn't even get married in a church."

He seemed to be waiting for a response, so Joe nodded. "I remember, Dad."

"I'm thinking she felt like God sent her the wrong man, so she was gonna keep her distance from His house."

"Dad, I don't believe that."

"I never went to church at all in my whole life. I never learned the Creek ways, neither, nor the language, because they wouldn't let us be Creek at school. They cut our hair. Just cut it off like we didn't need it. They wouldn't let our parents be Creek before us, nor their parents. It's just…it's gone, that's what it is. The language, the religion, all of it's gone for me. I don't know nothing about how anybody buries their people. That's why I never buried her. And also, if I didn't bury her, I still had her."

"Dad," Joe said, "it's okay. I learned some Creek words that I'll teach you. It'll all be okay."

If Sly heard his son speaking, Faye couldn't tell it.

"It's not too late," Joe said.

Sly looked at him hard, but he didn't speak.

"Dad, it's not too late to grow your hair. Do you hear me? You can have your hair back."

Sly brushed his hand over the urn lightly. The gesture looked well-practiced.

"I got so confused and upset when the cancer took Patricia so quick that I told the people at the hospital to go ahead and cremate her. Then they come to me with her ashes. I'm supposed to know what to do with them?"

He turned and walked toward his bedroom. He passed the living room without a pause, so he must have intended to take the urn to his bedroom for the night. For all Faye knew, he took it to his bedroom every night.

He was speaking as he left, but Faye couldn't tell if he was talking to them or to himself.

"If I would've known what to do with Patricia, I would've made her happy while she was alive."

• • ● • •

Faye lingered at the kitchen table until Joe excused himself to go to the bathroom. As soon as she heard the door close, she went to the fireplace. Its mantel was cluttered with junk mail, coffee cups, and packs of cigarettes, but there was an open spot where Patricia's urn had been.

Faye checked that open spot first, then she broadened her search to the rest of the mantel, to the hearth, to the end table where Sly had left yet another coffee cup. She searched until she heard the bathroom door open. Then she dropped into Sly's easy chair before Joe came back, as if nothing whatsoever was on her mind.

She had no idea why she didn't want Joe to know what she was doing. She supposed it was because she thought her suspicions would cause him pain on a day when he'd had quite enough of it.

She knew one thing for sure, but she didn't know what it meant. Sly's potsherd was nowhere in the living room or the kitchen. It simply wasn't there. Joe had told her that it had laid around the house for most of his growing up years. Just twenty-four hours before, it had been on the mantel, as if Sly intended for it to be on display.

Now it was gone.

Chapter Sixteen

Faye had passed in and out of sleep for hours, fretting about Sly's missing potsherd when she was awake and visiting disturbed corners of her psyche when she wasn't. Her subconscious could put her anywhere it liked when she was asleep, and tonight it wanted her to dream about finding her loved ones buried deep in the ground. Tonight, being awake was far more pleasant than being asleep.

It was an odd coincidence that she'd found a sherd in Sophia Townsend's grave, one with a rainbow-and-feather pattern so similar to the design etched on Sly's sherd, but it wasn't out of the realm of possibility. If the Sylacauga site turned out to have housed a large city in Mississippian times, as Carson believed, then there could be many pots of similar design lingering underground in the area. Finding parts of two of them would be like a future archaeologists digging up Atlanta and finding two broken Coke bottles. It could happen.

But what were the odds that those future archaeologists would find two pieces of the self-same broken Coke bottle? Sure, it was possible to find all the pieces of a single broken Coke bottle by excavating the spot where the bottle had met its end, leaving all its pieces conveniently close together. Once those pieces were separated, though, it was like throwing a bunch of needles into a haystack as big as all outdoors.

Nevertheless, Faye thought she might actually have found two pieces of the same pot in two very different locations. The patterns were so similar. The sherds had felt the same in her hand, as if they were made from the same clay, tempered with the same shells, shaped into the same vessel by the same hands.

Both sherds had been a tiny bit convex, as if they came from two round vessels of the same size—or as if they came from the same vessel. Faye felt almost certain that the triangular projection at the top of the potsherd from the grave would fit neatly into the triangular notch that had made Sly's potsherd look like a heart. If she could just find the heart-shaped potsherd, she would know for sure.

In graduate school, Faye's assistantship had required her to reassemble broken pots for hours on end. Or to try to reassemble them. Real world puzzles are harder to solve than jigsaw puzzles sold in sealed boxes. Experience like Faye's leaves a person with a feel for pieces that fit and pieces that don't fit. She wanted to hold both sherds, one in each hand. She wanted to hold them against each other and see if they matched, but she couldn't. Somebody, probably Sly, had taken the sherd off his mantel today and put it someplace where it couldn't be seen.

She wanted to know why.

And yet when Joe had emerged from the bathroom to tell her good night, she didn't ask him who had moved the potsherd and she knew she wouldn't be asking Sly. Faye felt herself shying away from talking to the two most important adult men in her life about that little piece of ancient dried clay. She just didn't know why.

Maybe she didn't want to know.

● ● ● ● ●

Faye wasn't sure anybody in the house was sleeping.

Joe was lying still with his eyes closed when she crept out of their bedroom, but that didn't mean he was asleep. She could see light leaking from the crack at the bottom of Sly's door. Maybe he was still awake, or maybe he had forgotten to turn his lamp off.

In case someone in the house had succeeded in slipping into sleep, she moved quietly as she gathered Sophia Townsend's notebooks, her reading glasses, and a glass of milk. Since she was awake, she might as well work.

When she came on this trip, she'd planned to work for Carson the first day and then shift into vacation mode. She'd certainly never expected to be billable in the middle of the night. Roy Cloud might joke about paying her a low hourly rate, but money was money and she might as well spend her waking hours earning some. If Sly's physical and mental health continued with the nose dive they'd seen a few hours before, she and Joe might need to take care of him much sooner than they'd ever dreamed.

She settled herself at the kitchen table and opened the notebook on top. Sophia Townsend, despite having been dead for nearly thirty years, managed to shock Faye on the first page. Calling one's employees "Idiot" and "Stupidface" was ludicrously disrespectful, but openly carrying on affairs with married employees? Sleeping with multiple employees and using sex to manipulate them? Was this business as usual in 1987, or was Sophia Townsend a special case?

Faye was going to presume she was a special case.

The woman's brash words weren't pleasant to read. Reading them was part of Faye's job, but she was going to let it wait. At the moment, she only had enough brain power to look at pretty pictures. Fortunately, the notebooks were full of pretty pictures. Sophia Townsend had missed her calling as an archaeological illustrator.

Sophia's plot plans weren't just complete and factual. They were beautiful. She had included nonessentials like trees, grass, and gravel at a level of detail that was almost lifelike. These were not sketches dashed off in the field. They were evidence of love for her work, as an artist and as an archaeologist.

After flipping through all the notebooks and admiring Sophia's sketches, Faye found the drawing that she expected to find. It was near the end of the very last book. It was a potsherd, incised with a familiar feather-and-rainbow pattern. It was accompanied by notes saying that Emily Olsen had found it and immediately broken it into three pieces. Those notes were studded with Sophia-like epithets like "Ladybitch." The woman had not been pleased with Emily for breaking it.

Sophia had used colored pencils to draw the potsherd as it had been when it was found, inscribing two heavy black lines across the drawing to show where it had been broken. Faye was not surprised to see the shapes of two of the pieces. One of them was shaped like a heart, and the other was shaped like an envelope, with the triangular projection fitting neatly into the notch at the top of the heart. These two pieces seemed to come from near the rim of the vessel, which must have been ringed near the top with the incised decorations. The third piece came from a spot further down from the rim. It was smooth and plain and the color of dirt.

Like all of Sophia's illustrations, this image was expertly drawn, with the potsherds' contours represented by shading and fine-textured tippling. The illustrations were so detailed, so real, that Faye could feel the textures and contours of the original pieces in her hand.

Faye pictured Sophia sitting alone in the evenings, sketching and drawing until the illustrations suited her. She must have spent a great deal of her off-hours with her notebooks, when she wasn't sleeping with her employees. How else could she have generated the voluminous notes that included everything that professional archaeologists could be expected to record and so many things that no one would expect to read in a quasi-public document?

How public were field notes, really? Sophia might have included pages from her notes for the appendix of a final report, but she would be the one choosing the pages and doing the copying. Readers of the report would see her gorgeous drawings, not the dirty laundry she had aired on the previous page. Someone would have to be deeply interested in her work to delve into the original notes. This was something that might never happen in the original archaeologist's lifetime, but the possibility was always there.

It was possible that Sophia had enjoyed the danger of being revealed as unprofessional in her work life and unethical in her private life. Perhaps it gave her the same rush that lured people to jump out of airplanes again and again, risking their lives for the chemical surge that was an adrenaline junkie's drug.

In a peculiar way, these notebooks were her memoirs. They were a thorough blending of a woman's professional and personal lives. Faye remembered what she'd been taught about field notes. They were to be written with history in mind. They could feasibly survive the person writing them, the artifacts found, and even the archaeological remains that they described. They were history in the raw.

Field notes were the memoirs of an archaeological project. Sophia Townsend had merely enlarged the parameters, defining her whole life as an archaeological project.

Faye spent the rest of the night flipping through the notes again, reading selected entries but mostly marveling at the detailed contours and shading of every single illustrated chipped stone knife or spear point. Try as she might, though, Faye never found a drawing of a particular pottery figurine or a handful of old pearls.

• • ● • •

When the sun began to pink up the sky, Faye knew that she'd stayed up too long to go back to bed. She walked toward the mantel as she sleepily made her way from the bathroom to the coffee pot and the sugar bowl, despite the fact that Sly wasn't even up so the potsherd couldn't possibly be there.

Checking the mantel had become an instant new habit, and she knew that she'd be checking every time she passed by the fireplace. She checked. Still no potsherd.

The knock at the front door surprised her. It was nowhere near a civilized hour to arrive at someone's house, and it wouldn't be for quite some time. She slept in a t-shirt and gym shorts, so she was nominally dressed, but she hadn't put on her shoes. The uninvited guest would just have to look at her bare feet.

Coffee cup in hand, she made her way to the front door. Emily was standing on the doorstep. Her eyes were red and she looked like she'd slept in her actual clothes, a rumpled button-front shirt and a pair of jeans.

"I know it's early, but I just—I couldn't be by myself for a minute longer."

Faye could see who needed coffee the most, so she held out her full cup without asking Emily how she took it. Emily didn't even look at it. She just took a long sip of the dark and sugary brew.

After Faye got Emily settled in Sly's easy chair and sat down in the chair facing it, she realized that she'd forgotten to pour herself another cup. It would have to wait now, because Emily was in no shape to be left alone.

Faye stated the obvious. "I can see you're upset."

Emily nodded several times, still holding the steaming cup close to her mouth.

"Did you come here to tell me why?"

Emily gave her more nervous little nods. "Yes. Yes, I did. I need your help."

"I'm happy to help, but you have to tell me what you need."

"Coffee was a good start." Emily laughed at her own little joke, then dissolved into tears.

Joe and Sly had stuck their heads out of their bedroom doors to see who had come to visit. When Emily started to weep, Faye saw them pull their heads back in like two turtles confronted with a curious dog.

"Is it about Sophia Townsend's death?" she asked Emily. "You must have been close."

"Yes. No. Not close at all, really, but I admired her so. She was…indomitable. Yeah, that's how I'd describe her. Nothing and nobody could stop her from doing what she wanted to do. I've never known anybody like that. Certainly not me."

The sobs had stopped, but Emily's cheeks were still wet. "I wanted to be just like her. I wanted her to like me. I wanted to be her friend. I was jealous of her."

"Jealous of what?"

"Of her *freedom*. She didn't care what people thought of her. She said what she thought. She swore like a sailor, only with a much bigger vocabulary. Did you know she called me Ladybitch?"

Faye did know, because she had seen the notebooks, but she didn't say so. "Well, that's an unusual nickname."

"I liked it because she gave it to me."

"Did you ever spend time with her outside of work?"

Emily's eyes dropped to the coffee cup in her hands. "No. Well, I tried to. I was desperate to know where she went on Friday evenings. She'd get in her truck and tear out at a speed that would have gotten anybody else killed. Driving was just one more thing that she did well. All weekend, I would wonder what she was doing. One day when I couldn't stand it any more, I decided to follow her. I thought I was going to wreck my car and die in flames, but I kept up with her. I'm proud of that."

"You saw her cabin?"

"I did! I followed her almost all the way there and parked my car on a side road that was downhill from her driveway a little. After waiting a few minutes to give her time to change clothes and relax for a bit, I walked up the driveway and knocked on her door."

So Emily's habit of showing up unannounced went back a long way.

"How did it go? Did she invite you in? Ask you to dinner?" Faye asked, though she was pretty sure she knew how Sophia Townsend would have reacted to this kind of intrusion.

She gave a quick shake of the head. "That's what I'd hoped for, but no. When she opened the door, she was so angry. So, so angry. It was like she'd lost the ability to talk in sentences. She just screamed words at me, most of them swear words. She screamed and screamed while I ran to my car and drove back down the mountain."

"I'm sorry."

"I'm not. I got to see her away from work and I got to see her weekend place. It made her seem more real. More human. It knocked her off her pedestal and made me think that someday maybe we could be friends."

Given what Faye knew about Sophia Townsend, this seemed profoundly unlikely.

"What was her place like?"

"Beautiful. Just beautiful. She'd only had it about four years—I checked the courthouse records—but she'd made it her own."

"The courthouse? Do you remember which county she lived in? Could you find the cabin now?"

"Oh, heavens no. Do you know how long thirty years is? I couldn't drive there on a bet, but I remember what her property looked like as if I had just been there yesterday. She'd planted wildflowers and herbs in the yard, and she had a garden out back. I remember that she'd set a bunch of tomatoes on her kitchen windowsill to finish getting ripe. She had an outdoor shower, which only makes sense for an archaeologist. Maybe I'll get one, so I can wash the dirt off before I go in the house."

Faye reflected that it took a special kind of stalker to look up her beloved's property records. She didn't know that she blamed Sophia for screaming at Emily and calling her names.

Emily's statement that she had waited while Sophia changed out of her dirty work clothes grew more disturbing as Faye thought about it. Sophia would surely have showered before changing. Did Emily really wait in her car? Or did she lurk in the bushes and watch Sophia shower in the open air? Maybe that was the reason the woman had greeted Emily with incoherent screaming.

"I went back out there one more time after I heard she'd gone away. The cabin, the property, the long drive up the mountain—it was all just the same. So beautiful."

This revelation shifted Faye's attention from Emily's disturbing past behavior to the story she was telling in the moment. "You went back? When?"

She was going to ask "Why?" but then she remembered that stalkers don't need a reason for the things they do.

"It was a couple of days after she didn't come to work. I wanted to make sure she was okay."

"Did you see her?"

If Emily saw Sophia a few days after the disappearance, then the narrative Faye was using to picture the crime was completely wrong. She'd been going with the simplest explanation, which was that Sophia was killed at the end of the last day she came to work and buried immediately on the spot. If Emily saw her after that, this couldn't be true.

"No, I didn't see her. It was early, so I was embarrassed to knock."

If it was too early for Emily to knock, it was pretty freaking early.

Emily was still chattering. Faye noticed that her mood had brightened the instant her thoughts shifted to the past and Sophia Townsend. "I'm pretty sure she was up, though, because I could see a light in the bedroom window. I pictured her in there reading, and it was such a cozy image. The curtains were drawn, so I couldn't see in, except in the kitchen. There were more tomatoes on the kitchen windowsill, just getting ripe, so her garden must have come in. How can I describe it to you? It just looked like a place where someone was living her life, not like a place where the owner was never coming home."

"Did you see her car?"

"Her car? I don't remember anything about her car. I was only interested in whether she was okay. I saw as much as I could see without disturbing her, then I went home."

Emily sure knew a lot about Sophia's windows. How did she know which one was the bedroom if the blinds were drawn? Could she really have seen the vegetables on the kitchen windowsill without peeking in the window?

Emily might have used binoculars to study Sophia's cabin from a distance, but that was as creepy as standing outside a window and looking in.

"Did you tell anybody you'd gone out there?"

"I told Mickey, since he was the one who'd said she ran away to her cabin. He seemed relieved to hear that she seemed to be okay."

Emily wasn't finished rhapsodizing about her final uninvited trip to trespass on Sophia Townsend's private property. "It was such a beautiful sight—the house, the garden, the wildflowers, the vegetables in the window—that I decided Sophia was better off without a job and without us. She was certainly better off without me. There wasn't anything that I could add to her perfect life." Her fever-bright expression dimmed. "So I went home."

"This is all really interesting, Emily, but why exactly are you here? You said you needed my help."

Emily blushed and the tears started again. "You have a lot of influence with Roy Cloud."

Faye tried to brush it off, saying, "No, he just listens to me when it comes to archaeology. That's all. We only met day before yesterday."

"It's true. He respected you the very instant he saw you. You're like Sophia. You have the same competence, and you even have a little bit of her swagger. People respond to people like you and Sophia. You make them feel safe. I can see that Roy appreciates that about you."

Faye was more flattered to hear this than she would have expected. Was she becoming yet another Sophia fangirl?

"How exactly do you want me to use this influence I supposedly have over Roy Cloud?"

"I want you to ask him if I can have Sophia's necklace."

This request was so perfectly Emily that Faye was amazed she hadn't been expecting it.

"I'm sure he needs the necklace for evidence, and he'll have to answer to Agent Bigbee," Faye said. "When all's said and done, I guess they might try to find out if she had family who might want it."

Now the woman's hands were clasped as if she were begging. "There was no one. Not here and not in Alabama. No family. No friends. Nobody. I checked."

How had Emily checked? Court records? A private detective? Was there no limit to this woman's willingness to intrude?

"I cared about her and I was the only one who did. I would treasure her necklace forever. Please."

"I can mention it to Chief Cloud and Agent Bigbee, but I can't imagine—"

"Oh, thank you! This means so much to me. I don't even have a picture of her. Back then, we didn't take pictures all the time the way people do now. We probably would have taken a group shot at the end of the summer, but we didn't make it to the end. Not as a group. Not all of us."

"I'll ask him. No guarantees."

"You shouldn't let anyone fade away into nothingness." Emily's expression dared Faye to argue. "There shouldn't come a time when you have nothing left of them but memories."

Faye couldn't help thinking of Sly, who had never let Patricia's ashes go. She knew without looking at the fireplace behind her that the urn was still gone. The potsherd, too.

"Emily, can I ask you something unrelated?"

"Sure."

"Sophia's notes mentioned that you found a potsherd toward the end of the dig. About palm-size. Incised with curving patterns. Do you remember it?"

Emily's face fell. "I do remember. I found it and I broke it. I felt so terrible for letting Sophia down. I thought she was never going to finish yelling at me."

"Do you remember a clay figurine? Small and shaped like a woman? Or any pearls?"

"No, and I would have remembered something that exciting."

"Do you remember finding anything else out of the ordinary? Something that might fit in a box this size?"

Faye held out her arms as if she was carrying a load of firewood.

"No, nothing that big. But there was that one bone."

"A bone? Was it human? When did you find it?"

"It was late, sometime during the last week before Sophia left, sometime after we found the potsherd. Mickey said it was human, but she just told him he was wrong and set it aside.

Then she made fun of him for thinking a middle school biology teacher might know more than she did."

"Do you know where it was found?"

Emily shook her head. "No. I wasn't there. Maybe I'd gone to the bathroom. I did see it, though. It looked like a rib bone, broken into two or three pieces. Maybe it wasn't human, but Mickey should know, don't you think?"

Faye knew that finding a human bone on tribal land could have triggered antiquities protection laws, even in 1987. Sophia might have had a vested interest in saying that the bone wasn't human if she wanted to avoid government red tape slowing down a project that was already over budget. But there was another issue at play. Bone, human or otherwise, can be carbon-dated. According to the papers Carson had published, Sophia never found anything that she could use to date the site.

Maybe Sophia had been willing to miss the chance of dating the bone if it was human and could put the project that was her bread-and-butter on hold. Hiding the fact that she'd found it was unethical and illegal, but Sophia Townsend didn't seem to respect much. Why should Faye expect her to respect the law or even human decency? Arguing against that was the extreme professionalism of Sophia Townsend's documented work.

And what about the pearl? Faye was no expert on the subject, but she knew pearls were still hard to date. Radiocarbon results were affected by events as arcane as the upwelling of water from the ocean depths and DNA testing had only recently become available. The analysis would have been even harder in 1987, if it could have been done at all.

Still, if Faye understood Sophia's obsession with dating the Sylacauga site, she thought Sophia would have at least tried to find a lab willing to work with an ancient pearl. Based on Carson's papers and her limited time with the field notes, Faye knew of nothing that proved Sophia had ever seen the pearls.

Could it be that she never got a chance to document the bone, the figurine, and the pearls in her notes because they were found on her very last day? No, that couldn't be true, not if Emily was right that Sophia had been at her cabin days after her last day at the dig. If she did indeed find them, it seemed out-of-character for her to fail to document them in her notes. What happened on Sophia Townsend's last day at work to cause her to abandon the job where she'd lavished so much care?

Chapter Seventeen

"Damn straight I want to know more about that bone," Cloud said. "I also want to know whether Emily is getting professional help. That woman does not sound stable."

"What? You don't approve of following people for hours so you can find out where they live? Or hiding outside the house to watch them shower? Stalkers need love, too."

Faye liked Cloud's laugh. It even sounded good over the phone. His laugh was just right for his personality. It was solid. Warm. It made you feel safe about letting down your guard. She would not want to be a criminal who was trying to keep a secret from Roy Cloud.

"Did you say Emily said the bone turned up about the time Dr. Townsend died? On the very last day anybody saw her alive? I'm glad Bigbee wanted to call everybody in again today to talk about Sophia's cabin, because I want to ask them about that bone. I don't know why I didn't hammer harder on whether any of them had ever been to the cabin themselves. Everybody talked like it was her retreat from people, which did suit the antisocial woman everybody said she was. I was an idiot not to think that she maybe took her lovers out there."

"It's a weird case. You were flying by the seat of your pants on the first day."

"Yeah," he said. "I'm sure that's what it was. How's this? Emily got you up at an ungodly hour, so why don't we go ahead and start the day?"

Faye looked longingly at the untouched cup of coffee in her hand. Well, she owned a travel mug.

"Can you come on down to the station and help us with the interviews, Doctor Faye? Bigbee is very good at intimidating witnesses by staring at them and saying exactly nothing. And I'm plenty capable of asking a bunch of people the same questions over and over, just to see what they say. I even throw in a new one now and then to keep them on their toes, but I don't know a damn thing about ancient bones and potsherds. That's what you call those little bits of broken pots? Potsherds?"

"Yes. You're saying it right."

"Potsherds. Okay. Let's start with Kenny Summers, because you tell me that the notebooks say he was arguing with his boss during that last week."

"Hang on," Faye said, searching through the loaded dish rack for her travel mug. "What about Mickey? Emily says he's the one who told her their boss had run off to her mountain cabin. I'd like to know who told him."

"So you think we should chase this rumor until somebody tells us where it came from? Or until somebody says something that can't possibly be true? I like it, Doctor Faye. And yeah. We can start with Mickey."

"I can be there before you and Bigbee get Mickey in the hot seat."

Faye put the travel mug on the table and started sliding papers into her briefcase with the hand that wasn't holding the phone. She'd be able to leave as soon as she broke the connection and put on some clothes that she hadn't slept in.

"You do that. I believe I'll bring Alba Callahan in to talk to us, too. Besides the fact that she's still a suspect, I want to hear what she has to say about everybody else. Kenny, Mickey, and Emily—they're all book-smart but people-dumb. Alba's book-smart, too, but she's a small-town attorney. She's almost as people-smart as a small-town police chief like me."

"Almost but not quite?"

"Heh. You got that right. We'll talk to all of them, but we'll do Carson Callahan last. He's the only living person that we know of who has read all those field notes. I trust that you plan to remedy that?"

"I was up with them most of the night. I'll go back to them as soon as we finish with the interviews." She slid one binder full of Sophia's notes into her briefcase, hoping she got a break during the day when she could do some more reading.

"How often do I work a murder case where the victim wrote a few books about what she was doing in her last days? Tell me how you're getting along with reading them when you come."

Faye said good-bye and gathered her things. She gave Joe a good-bye kiss, then went looking for Sly. He was back in his easy chair, motionless and silent. When she told him she was leaving, he nodded but didn't answer.

As Faye headed out, she gave the mantel one last glance. The urn was back among the clutter, right where it had been the day before, but the sherd was nowhere to be seen. She couldn't have explained why she didn't just ask Sly where it was, but she didn't. Instead, she hurried out the door so that she didn't have to stay in the same room as her father-in-law's suffering eyes.

• • ● • •

"Did you ever visit Sophia Townsend's weekend cabin?"

Cloud had beaten around the bush for nearly half an hour before delivering the question Faye knew he wanted to ask the most. Bigbee had spent that time proving that he did indeed have an intimidating stare. When the witnesses weren't there, he was an affable enough guy. When they came around, she could have sworn he turned to stone.

When Cloud asked if he'd ever visited the cabin, Mickey Callahan said, "Do what?" as if he didn't understand the question, but he quickly recovered his cocky attitude. "Of course, I did. I took the cops out there after she went missing."

Cloud looked at Mickey like he didn't understand his response. "That's not possible. I checked our files for any paperwork on missing persons reports from the time after Dr. Townsend disappeared. I found none, and all of you people have been telling me that you didn't ever realize that she was missing. Explain."

"Something just smelled fishy to me. Kenny and Emily disagreed with me about that, so I decided to go check on her myself. I went to the sheriff's office in the county where she lived and told them they needed to do a welfare check. They sent somebody up the mountain to check on her and I tagged along."

Faye felt sorry for Cloud, trying to wrap his head around a scenario he hadn't expected. Bigbee was still wearing his rock face.

"If you called the law to help you look for her, there should be a record of it," he said. "We've had somebody call every county in this end of the state that has a hill big enough that somebody might call it a mountain. Maybe I should have done it myself."

"Did you check Arkansas? Because that's where her property was."

Bigbee let his face twitch.

Cloud swallowed visibly and tried to recover. "It's a good distance to Arkansas. I never would've thought she'd drive that far just for weekends."

"Sophia liked to drive."

Cloud quickly regrouped enough to respond to the unexpected information. "Apparently she did. Can you tell me why you took the police to check on a woman you knew very, very well? Why didn't you just go on your own?"

Mickey didn't flinch at the insinuation behind Cloud's "very, very" statement. "I got the police to go with me because I was afraid I might find her dead. Or maybe I was afraid she'd shoot me when she saw me coming. I thought she'd probably hold her fire if I came with the police, although you could never be sure about anything with Sophia."

"She had guns?"

"Sure she did. You haven't learned enough about her yet to know that she was quite serious about protecting herself?"

Faye could see that Cloud was still processing the fact that Sophia had lived in Arkansas.

"Surely the folks at the sheriff's office in Arkansas let the people here know that they'd checked on her."

"Why? Nobody here had reported her missing, not even me. For the deputies who went with me, it was a simple welfare check. Once they knew she wasn't lying dead on the floor, they were out of there. For all any of us knew, she'd decided she was tired of people. It would have been just like her. If we would've found something that didn't seem right, the Arkansas people would've called the police here or I'd have done it myself. Didn't happen."

Mickey delivered this explanation slowly. He enunciated every syllable, like he was talking to a misbehaving eighth grader. Faye disliked sarcastic people, and she thought Cloud was probably about ready to slap Mickey for his tone of voice. She also thought Cloud was ready to slap himself for not considering that Sophia Townsend might have considered Arkansas to be a reasonable weekend drive from Sylacauga.

"So what did you and the folks from the Arkansas sheriff's department see? Was Dr. Townsend at home?"

"No. She wasn't there."

"You went in without a warrant?"

"She didn't answer when we knocked. The door was unlocked. Like I said, she could have been dead in there, so yeah. We went in."

"She wasn't there?"

"Nope. Neither was her car. We found a receipt on the kitchen counter that said she'd bought gas a few days after her last day at work. That seemed like a pretty good indication that she'd at least made it home safe. The cabin looked like it was shut down for the winter, which was weird in August. The shutters were closed. There were sheets on the furniture. Things like that."

"You're sure she didn't always keep sheets on the furniture?" Bigbee asked.

"Sophia? She might have lived in a tiny house, but she wanted things just so. Sheets would have been too sloppy. Anyway, here's the most important thing. There wasn't a suitcase in the house. I knew she had one, because we all saw it taking up the whole back seat of her car every Friday. It was old. Blue. Hard-sided. No wheels. I'd have known it anywhere."

"Are you saying you think she was on a trip? That's why you didn't call the police here?"

"That's exactly what I'm saying. Emily had told me what she saw when she drove out there after Sophia disappeared. By the time I took the Arkansas cops to check on her, everything was different. The house was shut up. The lights were off. Her car was gone. Her suitcase wasn't under the bed. In my shoes, wouldn't you have thought she'd gone on a trip?"

Cloud couldn't argue with Mickey's very logical point, but Faye could see that he was peeved by the biology teacher's snarky tone. He looked as serene as ever, but the pen he was using to doodle in the margins of his notepad was cutting deep grooves into the paper.

Mickey was enjoying his moment of unassailable logic. "The Arkansas officer agreed with me. There was plenty of evidence that said she was fine. Judging by the gas receipt, she'd come home after her last day of work and kept living her life. Judging by the shutters and the sheets and the lack of a suitcase or car, she'd packed up and gone on a trip sometime after that. We figured that's why she bought gas. Neither of us saw any need to give you people a call because *she wasn't missing.* At least, she wasn't missing as far as we knew. We thought she was an adult who had decided she didn't want to be where she was. She had that right."

Cloud continued to doodle in the margins of his notepad. Faye could hear his pen scratching on the yellow pad. Sometimes he stopped writing and fiddled around with his phone.

For reasons she couldn't pinpoint, she was as nervous as a cat. The scratching of Cloud's pen made her want to reach over and smack it out of his hand. Without looking up, Cloud said, "Dr. Longchamp-Mantooth, would you like to ask Mickey a question about some things that he might have seen dug up at the Sylacauga site?"

She wasn't sure whether word had gotten out about the figurine and pearls, because she didn't know how close-mouthed the medical examiner was. She'd just asked Emily about them, but she hardly thought Emily had immediately called Mickey to tell him. They didn't seem like best buddies. She knew Cloud wouldn't have told anybody about the potsherd, and the federal forensics people had left shortly after it was found. She decided to ask questions that gave no information away.

"Do you remember finding anything unusual while excavating the Sylacauga site?"

"You mean other than tons and tons of dirt?"

"You know that I do."

Her voice was calm and cool. Mickey looked surprised that she hadn't laughed or been offended at his ham-handed attempt to evade the question. She hadn't reacted at all. At that point, he apparently decided to take her question seriously.

"I found a couple of arrowheads that were real pretty. I think all of us found those sometime during the summer. There were also a lot of chipped-up and ground-down pieces of stone that didn't look like much until Sophia explained them to you. She'd show you that this one was sharp on one edge, like a knife, and that one had a dent in it where somebody rested their finger while they used it for grinding. I won't lie. It was an interesting job. I'd gotten a second major in anthropology in college, but I didn't really understand a lot of what I learned until Sophia explained it to me."

"You don't recall finding any pottery? Jewelry? Bones? Anything like that?"

"No, but Sophia sure did want us to."

"Nothing else memorable?"

"Nope. Just chipped-up rocks. Some of them were pretty."

Finally, Cloud looked up from his yellow pad and held Mickey's gaze for a moment. If he'd been waiting for the man to get nervous or fidget, he was disappointed. "Am I right to suppose that you are the one who spread the rumor that Dr. Townsend had left Sylacauga, retreating to her weekend cabin?"

"I didn't start that rumor. That wasn't me. I'd already heard it before I headed out to Arkansas. If I didn't have an inkling that she'd gone to her cabin for good, I would have been a lot more worried before I went out there. When I did go out there, it looked to me like the rumor had been true at first, but then she'd packed up and gone someplace even further away from Sylacauga. Can't say I blame her. I should've left this town years ago."

"Do you remember who told you the rumor first?" Bigbee asked.

"Nope. If I had to guess, I'd say it was Emily."

"Not Kenny?" Roy's tone said that he was going to ask specifically by name about everybody who might have spread that key piece of gossip.

"Nope. Kenny doesn't talk much, so I remember it when he does talk. Now that I think about it, I'm sure it was Emily that told me." He leaned forward with a conspiratorial air. "Is it just me, or does Emily seem a little unbalanced?"

• • ● • •

It wasn't just Mickey and Faye who thought Emily was unbalanced. Cloud's body language told Faye that he felt the same. The man was obviously uncomfortable sitting across the table from Emily and asking her questions. Bigbee looked about as off-balance as Cloud did.

Every time Emily revealed an inappropriate behavior like "I was the first one to come to work *every* morning so that I could have a little alone time with Sophia" or "She pretended like she didn't like me, but I knew different by the way she looked at me," Cloud leaned a little further back in his chair. It was as if he were running away from her while still staying in the same room.

He asked her to repeat the story she'd told Faye about her trip to the cabin, and she gave him details that were completely consistent with what she'd said before. Mickey had backed up some of her story, so Emily was turning out to be Cloud's star witness. Too bad she creeped him out completely.

Faye pressed Emily to remember anything historically interesting that the team had dug up. Emily reminded Faye about the potsherd and bone that they'd already discussed, and she remembered that they had all uncovered stone tools. And that was all.

Emily's response to the question of the day—"Are you sure it was Mickey who told you that Sophia Townsend had left her job to stay at her weekend home full-time?"—wasn't at all helpful.

"Now that I've thought about it, I believe it was Kenny. I'm pretty sure about it, because I asked him a lot of questions about why she left and how she was doing and whether she was coming back. He just kept saying, 'I don't know.'"

Just before Kenny was ushered in, Faye whispered, "What do you bet he says that Mickey told him? That would send the rumor in a complete circle."

But Faye had forgotten to account for one suspect. After Kenny had stated for the record that he never visited Sophia's cabin and that he didn't remember any particularly interesting finds, Cloud asked him a confusing array of questions about what Sophia Townsend had been like as a boss. When the repetitive questions finally cracked the even-tempered Kenny's cool, Cloud asked Kenny that all-important question.

"How did you hear the rumor that Dr. Townsend had left the project to live in her weekend place?"

"Alba Callahan was the one that told me she'd gone to her cabin. She said that everybody knew that was where Sophia took her lovers. Alba said she figured that having a job had cut into the time Sophia needed for sleeping with other women's husbands, so she'd quit it so she could wreck homes full-time. And before you ask, yeah. That's what my wife thought of Sophia, too."

The rumor circle was eventually completed during the next interview, when Alba answered their questions with, "Yes, that is exactly what I said to Kenny about Sophia and her philandering, and it's exactly what I thought of her as a human being."

This time Cloud wasn't retreating in his seat. He had regained the confidence born of many years on the force, and he was leaning forward with his eyes locked on Alba. "But who told you that Sophia had gone to the cabin?"

"My husband, of course. Mickey was always very concerned with where Sophia Townsend was and what she was doing."

Chapter Eighteen

Faye wasn't sure how much longer she could watch Roy Cloud scribble. It seemed to be taking him longer to organize his notes than it had taken to interview the subjects in the first place. Bigbee was using the time to catch up on his e-mail, but Faye didn't like to handle business in front of a client.

While waiting, she had nearly memorized the contents of Cloud's office. There was a map of Creek lands on the wall, next to a historical map of Oklahoma when it had been the old Indian Territory. There was an array of neatly shelved books. Some of them were law books and forensics texts, but there were a few novels tucked among them. Faye could picture Roy spending the occasional lunch break flipping through the pages of a book that took him to faraway places, but not to stay. She couldn't imagine Roy Cloud living anywhere but east Oklahoma.

There was only one personal photo in the room, a small one in a frame covered with tiny, handset beads. It showed a younger Roy and a woman who must have been his late wife. Between them stood a teenaged girl dressed in a cobalt blue dress. It was high-necked with a square yoke and a ruffled floor-length skirt. The beaded crown on her head made her nearly as tall as Roy. Her oval face and full mouth were very like her mother's, but her relaxed bearing and warm eyes were all Roy.

"You got any grandkids, Roy?"

He didn't even look up. "I wish. Evelyn isn't even thirty yet, so there's still lots of time."

Faye got the message that she should quit interrupting him or he'd never finish, so she spent a few minutes admiring the lovely Evelyn and her sweet-faced mother.

Finally, Roy looked up from his notepad. He looked remarkably calm for a man who had to be kicking himself for forgetting that there was an Arkansas.

"You heard them all, Roy. Nobody can agree on who started the rumor about Sophia running off to her cabin," Bigbee said.

"Emily can't even agree with herself," Faye pointed out. "Nobody remembers finding the figurine and pearls. And nobody but Emily remembers finding the potsherd and the bone. Did we just waste the whole day interviewing four people who told us nothing we need to know?"

"You haven't spent much time questioning people, have you? You have to learn to read between the lines." Cloud pushed his notepad across the table to her. Bigbee, looking over the police chief's shoulder to read his notes, started to laugh.

Cloud had written pages about what the witnesses had said, then he had summarized the key points on a page all by themselves.

1. Mickey Callahan went to Sophia Townsend's cabin after she died. Now that I know it was in Arkansas, I can go there myself. I imagine Bigbee's going to want to go, too.

2. Mickey Callahan obviously went to the cabin before Sophia disappeared at least once, or he couldn't have found it. Oh, I guess he could have followed her the way Emily did or maybe Sophia had told him where it was, but let's go with the simple answer. Seems like a man who maybe took at least one weekend trip with his lover. Presumably he went to the cabin with her or she told him how to get there.

3. Emily Olsen went to the cabin both before and after Sophia disappeared. Sophia did not tell her

how to get there, and she was not pleased when Emily followed her there the first time. Emily has been carrying a torch for Sophia for nearly thirty years, and she was very happy to finally be able to unload on us. Most witnesses are not happy to talk to me, but Emily stayed for two hours, even when I was actively trying to get her to leave. This is not the behavior of your average guilty person, but Emily is certainly not average.

4. Alba Callahan was pretty confrontational this afternoon, considering that I've got nothing on her. Her husband was the one that did wrong, not her. Lots of people get cheated on, but not many of them commit murder. Why was she so touchy?

5. Kenny Summers is hiding something.

6. Emily Olsen couldn't hide anything if she tried.

7. I would not care to be alone in a room with Emily Olsen. I'm not sure I'd care to be alone in a room with any of them, but especially not her.

8. None of them will admit to seeing the figurine or the pearls. Only Emily will admit to seeing a bone that might have been human.

9. Emily remembers finding that potsherd. The others don't seem to remember it, but I don't want to read too much into that. It might not have seemed all that exciting to them and it's been nearly thirty years. A bone, though. Finding a bone that might be human seems pretty memorable.

10. Dr. Longchamp-Mantooth is pretty sure that we found a piece of Emily's potsherd in the hole with Sophia. It wasn't there when we first dug her up, but it showed up after the killer dug around in her grave. Not sure what that means.

11. They all want us to believe that they thought Sophia just took off, but none of them seems the least bit surprised to find out that she's dead. None of them even seem sorry about it, except for Emily.

12. Sometimes I just want to wipe that smug grin off Mickey Callahan's face. It pleases me to no end that he knows what it's like to have and lose a woman like Alba.

Faye slid the notepad back across the table toward Roy. "Your notes remind me of Sophia's."

"I didn't curse as much as her."

"You didn't curse at all."

"Sometimes I do."

Bigbee chuckled again.

A tentative knock sounded.

"Yes?" Roy said.

It was Emily. "I was thinking—"

She took a step into the room. "I thought maybe, um—"

She edged a little closer and Faye felt herself solidly in Roy's camp. Emily weirded her out and she felt herself physically drawing away from the woman, just as Roy had. Faye wouldn't relish being alone with Emily any more than he would. The time she'd spent with her that morning had been more than sufficient.

"We should have a funeral," Emily said. "For Sophia."

"Maybe we should leave that to her family."

Emily took a big step forward, moving directly across the table from them.

"She doesn't have any family. Didn't, I mean. No brothers or sisters. No aunts or uncles or cousins that she ever spoke to. Her work was her life. We worked with her, so we were her family. We were the last family she ever had."

Now that she'd begun speaking, the words poured out. "Kenny, Mickey, and me—we should hold a memorial service. It should be at the site, because that's where we were all together with her and that's where her grave has been. We'll have to find another place to bury her when the investigation is over but—oh, I'll think about that later. I'll organize the memorial service."

"Okay..." Roy dragged out the word as if to say, "I'm not sure why you're asking me this."

"I hope you'll both come. You, too, Agent Bigbee. You're trying to get justice for her, and I'm grateful. I want to do it tomorrow. I think it should be a sunrise service. She would have liked that. So many indigenous cultures timed their ceremonies with the motion of the sun, you know."

Sunrise. Of course, Emily would want to do this at sunrise. Rousting other people out of bed at dawn seemed to be what she did best.

• • ● • •

Faye, Roy, and Bigbee had firmed up some end-of-the-workday details, like looking up when the sun would rise the next morning. If they were going to go to Emily's sunrise service, getting there on time was the least they could do.

Faye was ready to leave Roy and Bigbee to their work. Bigbee seemed more than ready for her to leave.

She'd gotten the feeling that he considered her superfluous, and that was fine with Faye. Sophia Townsend's notebooks were calling her and she was starting to feel her lack of sleep, but she remembered one thing that she wanted to tell Roy before she went home.

"Emily wants to know if she can have Sophia's necklace when this is all over. You know, the silver necklace shaped like a sigma."

"Emily's not shy about asking people to do things or give her stuff, is she?" Roy said.

"Nope."

"I'll see what I can do." The hooded black eyes caught hers. "Most people would have blown Emily off. Not you. You invited her into your home. You listened to her story about her relationship with Sophia, which is more than a little disturbing. You spoke to her respectfully during questioning, and you did it again just now. You're even willing to be the go-between for Emily's weird little request for the necklace she just yanked off a dead woman's skeleton. You're a good woman, Doctor Faye. You have heart."

It felt almost like Roy was taking this opportunity to explain to Bigbee why she was on the job, and Faye was surprised by how much this touched her.

"You've been nothing but respectful to all these people, Roy. They're lucky to have you here to keep the peace."

Before Faye could excuse herself and go home, a man in a uniform opened the door.

"You texted that you wanted me to interrupt you when I got the information. Right, Chief?"

"I did. What have you got?"

"I talked to the sheriff's department in Crawford County, Arkansas. They dug up a report filed back in 1987 when they checked up on Dr. Sophia Townsend's wellbeing."

"No kidding? They found it this fast? It had to have been on paper, maybe handwritten. I figured they'd sent all their old stuff to some warehouse somewhere and we'd have to wait for them to dig it out of deep storage."

"Nope. They found it, scanned it, and e-mailed it to me. It was the very devil to read that officer's chicken-scratch handwriting on a computer screen, so I printed it for you. Here you go."

He handed a page to Roy who gestured to the man that he could leave.

After a moment, Roy handed it to Bigbee and said, "This report tracks with everything Mickey told us. Even better, there's enough information here to get us to that cabin. I think we should go tomorrow."

Bigbee nodded without looking up from the page.

"If there's any information left under those old sheets Mickey says she put on her furniture, we will find it," Roy continued. "For once, I'm glad you're here, Bigbee. No offense. It'll be a helluva easier for you to get us onto private property in Arkansas than it would be for me."

Taking the page back, he handed it to Faye. "Here. Take a look."

"Mind if I take a picture for my files?"

"It's public information. Be my guest."

Faye centered the document on her phone's screen and snapped a picture. Then she skimmed the document, which described a long series of backwoods roads that ended in a dead end in front of Sophia Townsend's former front yard.

He took the report back. "I suppose we might find something out on that mountainside that's in your bailiwick, Doctor Faye. I don't know—a potsherd or some more pearls or something. Can you come with us?"

She said, "Sure. After the memorial service, I guess?"

"Yeah. We'll be at the cabin before the morning's done. At least Emily's making sure we get an early start."

Bigbee snorted. "That woman needs a hobby. Or a boyfriend."

Roy studied the report some more. "According to the officer who wrote this, Mickey did call these people, just like he said. He did meet them and take them to the cabin. They did find the house shuttered and the car gone. There really were sheets on the furniture."

"So Mickey was telling the truth and he cared enough to check." Faye said. "Does that mean he's not a suspect?"

"Wouldn't it be smart of him to go out there, put her suitcase in her car and find a way to get rid of it, drape some sheets, close the shutters? Then call the sheriff? It makes him look a lot like a caring friend and not a bit like a suspect."

"You're a suspicious man, Roy Cloud."

"Just doing my job."

● ● ● ● ●

The afternoon and evening weren't much different from the day before. Faye came home to find Joe at the kitchen table, but at least he wasn't smoking. Sly was in the living room in front of the TV, looking at it but paying no attention to what was on the screen. He wasn't smoking, either. He was holding a cigarette that had gone out.

She and Joe made some sandwiches, but Sly said he wasn't hungry. Within the hour, he went to bed, carrying Patricia's urn.

Joe listened absently as Faye told him about her day. The ashtray in front of him was empty, but his forefinger tapped a nicotine-craving beat on the table next to it. Time and again, she saw him like this, proving to himself that he had willpower. Joe had spent all his adult years proving to himself that he was nothing like his old man. He had done this by, time after time, putting aside the cigarettes he'd like to smoke and the liquor he'd like to drink.

She found an excuse to go into the living room, hoping to see that the potsherd had been returned to its spot on the mantel. There was no need for the excuse, because Joe was paying no attention to what she said or did.

The potsherd was still gone.

After Joe went to bed, Faye found that she had passed from sleepiness into the kind of overstimulated hyperdrive that was terrible for her health but good for her ability to rack up billable hours. She spread Sophia Townsend's notes out on the kitchen table, poured herself a tall glass of milk, and got to work.

Chapter Nineteen

The sun was rising over the Sylacauga site when Faye and Joe arrived for the funeral. It was half-obscured by banks of slate-blue clouds, but it's hard to fully hide the sun. Its rays gilded the underside of each cloud, rimming it in red-gold. She had seen thousands of dawns from Joyeuse Island, and this one was no more colorful. The sky was no bigger than the blue dome that arched over her home and the surrounding Gulf of Mexico. Yet this sky, this cloud, this dawn were all different. Not better. Different. Faye couldn't have described how they were different. They just were.

Faye could see that Emily was beside herself with excitement. She'd succeeded in getting eight people to join her in honoring Sophia Townsend's memory. Even better, she'd managed to turn this kind gesture into an inappropriate intrusion by insisting that they get up at five o'clock in the morning to do so. For Emily, this was a red-letter day.

Faye and Joe left the parking area with Roy Cloud. Mickey, Alba, Carson, and Kenny arrived in separate cars and walked behind them. Agent Bigbee arrived last and hung back to watch everyone else. Emily hurried to greet them all as soon as they came into sight.

Roy shook her hand and thanked her for organizing the memorial service. "This was a nice thing for you to do, Emily. You're a good friend to Sophia. Can I ask you a favor?"

"Certainly. I'm so glad you're all here today."

"Do you mind if we take some time to remember Kira, too? It nearly killed me to hear that her folks are having her funeral in Albuquerque. I can't leave this investigation or I'd be on the plane tomorrow to be there for her. If you're willing, I can say a few words in her memory. It's the least I can do."

Emily looked like she didn't want Sophia to have to share the spotlight with Kira, but even she couldn't dismiss a police chief's request to honor his fallen comrade.

Cloud said, "I've got a lot of memories of Kira to share. Anybody else who wants to say something about her or about Dr. Townsend should have a chance. Right, Emily?"

Emily's nod was a little too late and a little too tentative, but she gave it. She led them to the rim of the excavation where she'd set up chairs. In front of the row of chairs was a card table covered with a white cloth and set with two candles.

Emily had to strike three matches to light the candles, because the constant wind kept snuffing the flames. Once lit, the candles guttered, always on the verge of going out. Emily kept her eyes on them as if willing them to stay lit.

"Welcome, everyone. I'm so grateful you all could come today. I think we should begin by remembering Kira Denton."

Faye knew she was being uncharitable, but it felt like Emily was clearly defining Kira as the opening act, making Sophia this funeral's headliner.

Cloud rose from his chair and said, "Kira Denton was utterly admirable for her honesty, her loyalty, her professionalism, and her selflessness. When the Andersons' house burned down, she organized the drive to get them back on their feet. She hounded people...oh, excuse me...she politely asked every last officer to donate clothes, food, toys, furniture, anything they thought a family might need. When people forgot the promises they made, she hounded...oh, excuse me...she politely reminded them that the people waiting had nothing but the clothes on their back."

The first "Oh, excuse me" brought chuckles. The second one was harder to hear, because Roy Cloud was in tears, but he kept going.

"Kira didn't forget people after she helped them. Not Kira. She calls the Andersons and all the others she helped all the time. I mean, she did call them. Before. She called to make sure their children had school clothes. She called to tell people that the price had dropped on a truck they wanted. If a family couldn't afford a ham at Christmas, Kira got one donated or bought it herself. The person who took her from us has deprived the world of someone who truly wanted to make a difference in people's lives. When we remember Kira, we have to remember the Andersons, too, and people who are in their shoes. If we do that, we'll keep her alive and with us, at least a little bit."

This time Roy wasn't able to keep going. He had to stop and wipe his eyes. "I will hunt the person who killed Kira Denton for the rest of my life, if that's what it takes to get justice for her. She should be here on this beautiful day. I will miss her."

After he spoke, there was silence. No one else present had known Kira, and Faye found that inexpressibly sad. She herself had no memories of either Sophia or Kira to offer. She was surprised to find herself blinking back tears for these women who were strangers to her. Unshed, they stung in her throat.

If this had been an ordinary funeral, she could have brought flowers for the graves. She could have baked a casserole for the families, because she found feeding people to be a satisfying way to show love and care. These outlets for grief weren't available today, so she just sat next to Joe and sniffled.

Emily sensed that no one else was going to speak for Kira, so she moved ahead to the reason she'd brought them all together. She said, "And now I'd like for us to remember Sophia Townsend, who has come back to us after twenty-nine years."

Her voice was high and quavery, as if she were struggling to be heard over the wind. Or perhaps it was because she was holding something back. It certainly wasn't tears that Emily was withholding, because they flowed steadily down her face and she never once reached up a hand to wipe them away.

"It is a hard thing," she said, "to memorialize someone who has been gone for so long, but Sophia deserves that. Anybody would deserve it after being murdered and buried in an un-marked grave for years and years."

She bit her lip.

"Anyone who ever met Sophia Townsend was struck by her sheer intelligence and her passion for life. I've heard people described as 'live wires' all my life, but I never understood the term until I met Sophia. She had a vital energy that is hard to describe. I only know that I couldn't look away."

She opened the pasteboard box in front of her. Inside of it was a stack of homemade booklets, folded and stapled. "Time has taken so much. There is almost nothing left of Sophia's life. Just her bones and a stack of archaeological papers that are still cited today and a dainty silver necklace."

Faye couldn't miss the meaningful look that Emily aimed at Roy. She might as well have said, "Give me the necklace and give it to me now."

Emily shifted her eyes from Roy Cloud's face to address the full group. "Sophia was at her best when she directed that vitality and energy toward her work. I started putting together a bibliography of her papers as a keepsake for her mourners, because I wanted us to remember the work that was the focus of her life. And also because I thought the papers were the closest things we would ever have to an enduring image of her. When I started this project, I thought that she didn't leave a photo of herself for us to remember her by."

Emily moved toward the seated guests, handing a booklet to each of them. "But then, as I looked through her work yesterday, I saw that she did leave a visual memory for us. I found these images in some of her published papers. Sharing them with you seemed like a fitting way to memorialize her."

Faye looked at the cover of the booklet in her hands. It was a regular, everyday photo, and the caption said that it was taken during an archaeological dig Sophia had done five years before she came to work in Sylacauga. The photo showed a collection of beads brought to North America by sixteenth-century Europeans.

Behind the beads was a hand included in the photo to provide scale. It took Faye a second to realize what she was seeing.

This was a photo of Sophia Townsend's hand, probably taken years before she even heard the word Sylacauga.

"I thought this picture of Sophia's hand was almost as personal and intimate as a close-up photo of her face would have been. That's why I put it on the cover, but be sure you look inside. I found other precious mementos to share with you."

Faye opened the booklet and was rewarded with a copy of one of Sophia's lovely illustrations.

Emily opened her own booklet and held out that page for people to see. "This is Sophia's rendering of what Poverty Point might have looked like thirty-five hundred years ago."

Sophia had drawn a bustling town stretching out along a creek bank where people were fishing. Behind them, sturdy houses stood on manmade soil berms. Silhouetted behind the houses was a tremendous earthen mound. The next time Faye was trying to explain to someone that it had been possible to live a comfortable and healthy life far in the past, she would be using this drawing as an illustration.

On the next page was a copy of another photograph. It was so unexpected that Faye drew a quick breath when her eyes landed on it.

"This photo was taken at a project Sophia did while she was still a graduate student. Behind her is a reconstruction of a Mississippian village that she helped design and build. She was twenty-three."

Fay could see that the photo had been taken to document the build phase of the project and that Sophia's presence in the shot was an accident. Yet she dominated the frame.

The camera had loved her glowing skin and her tousled black hair. She was looking at someone standing outside the frame of the photo and she was laughing.

Faye saw Kenny Summers reach out a hand to touch the image of her youthful face. Mickey and Alba Callahan, moving with the synchronicity of a married couple who hadn't spent the past twenty-nine years divorced, both gave the photo a quick glance and closed the booklet quickly.

The other pages were taken up by the bibliography that Emily had promised, and it was every bit as long and distinguished as she had led them to believe.

Faye leaned toward Roy Cloud and whispered, "You should give Emily that necklace." She gestured at the booklet in her hand that Emily had probably stayed up all night to make. "Have you ever seen love like this?"

Roy said, "She'll get it when we close the case, if I have to steal it out of the evidence file myself."

Emily stood before them, wringing her hands while everyone present studied her last gift to Sophia Townsend. She'd probably rehearsed a longer eulogy and she'd probably planned a more eloquent summing-up, but she had run out of steam.

After a long, awkward pause, she said quietly, "I just wanted you to know who she really was. Did anybody else have anything to share?"

Mickey, who was carefully avoiding eye contact with his ex-wife, said, "I'd like to say something." He rose and began, "Sophia was not someone you can describe in a sentence or a wonderful booklet like this one Emily made or even in a whole stack of books. She—"

The wind had stopped and the group had fallen so silent that the well-maintained engine of an approaching pickup truck seemed as loud as a military jet.

Someone was late to the funeral.

Chapter Twenty

Roy Cloud looked up as he heard the truck approach. His reflexes were fast, so the only person who turned his head quicker was young Joe Wolf Mantooth, sitting on the other side of his wife, the estimable Doctor Faye. An instant later, everyone else looked to see who was coming, except for Bigbee, who was keeping his eyes on the assembled crowd.

A battered white pickup, evenly coated with a patina of dust, pulled into the parking area and stopped. Roy had been with Muscogee Nation's Lighthorse Tribal Police long enough to know what all the local ex-cons drove. That truck belonged to Sly Mantooth.

Joe Wolf Mantooth looked at his wife and grunted in the way that married people do when there's no reason for words. Then he stood up and started walking fast in Sly's direction, like a man who was trying to intercept trouble before it arrived.

Roy remembered the Mantooth boy from some years back. He had grown into a fine-looking man. Mid-thirties, really tall, well-built without being bulky. Dark-brown skin and a black ponytail hanging halfway down his back. Quiet and confident, with a peaceful air about him. Doctor Faye had married well.

Roy remembered when Sly had looked like that, minus the ponytail and the peaceful air, and he remembered how far down Sly had spiraled when his wife died and his son tried to walk as far away as he could get from his no-account dad. Nobody within fifty miles had blamed Joe for going. Coming back now to deal with his dad and the past spoke highly of him, and so did his choice of a wife.

Sly Mantooth's son had come home as a successful business-man with a happy family. Who would have thought it?

Roy pitied young Joe, because he sensed that Sly's belated arrival did not bode well.

• • ● • •

Sly Mantooth had tried to stay away, but here he was. He knew he should have stayed at home with Patricia's ashes, since he would soon scatter them and lose his last physical connection with the love of his life, but Sophia Townsend had always been a complication.

She hadn't been the love of his life, not even close. He hadn't loved her at all, not much. He hadn't even liked her much, but there was no explaining the magnetism that sometimes fired between two people who had nothing more in common than lust. And sometimes it fired upon first meeting, which was even harder to explain.

Patricia had made him feel open and free. When their rela-tionship was good, and it had been good for a lot of years, she had made him feel like he was man enough to take on the world.

Sophia had made him feel like he was trapped in a hot room with an open flame. She was too dangerous to turn his back on, so he had no choice but to look at her. Nothing could make him forget she was there.

Where Sophia was concerned, Sly did things he shouldn't, like coming here today.

Patricia had surely known how he felt about Sophia. His pas-sion for her would have been obvious to anyone past puberty, and it would have been that much more obvious to the woman who shared his bed.

They had never talked about it, so he had never reassured her, never told her flat-out that she was the only woman for him. He'd been too much of a coward to own up to his feelings, so

Patricia had died without knowing where she stood. These were the things he thought about when he looked at the damnable urn that held all that remained of his wife.

All eyes were on him. They were all here, the combustible group who had surrounded Sophia in her last days, and he needed to be with them on the day of her memorial. Unfortunately, his son was here, too, so he would be a witness to whatever came next.

Joe had started walking his father's way before Sly even got the truck in park. Calm and steady Joe knew that trouble followed his father, so here he came, ready to help. How Sly loved that boy...that man. His son was a man now.

Since even hawk-eyed Joe didn't have eyes in the back of his head, his son couldn't see the tableau behind him. Nobody could but Sly, who was in a position to take in the full scene. Every single head had swiveled his way as soon as he stepped out of the truck.

Faye's sweet face said that she'd been afraid all along that Sly would eventually break her husband's heart.

Kenny, Mickey, and Emily looked surprised to see Sly. Shocked, even. This might have hurt his feelings under other circumstances. The turmoil of the weeks after he stopped being able to work under Sophia Townsend had bonded the three shovel bums who had stayed on the job, so much so that it had slipped their minds that he was ever among them. Twenty-nine years can do strange things to the mind, especially when there are things that the mind actively wants to forget.

Chief Roy Cloud was enough younger than Sly, Emily, Mickey, and Kenny that he'd never been part of their social circle. Cloud had no reason to know or suspect that Sly had worked among them. At least, he had no reason that Sly knew about. Still, he looked a lot less surprised to see him than Sly's former friends did.

Sly guessed that the chief knew when a man was trouble, and it was only natural to expect to see a troublesome man when life took a dark turn.

Sly watched his son approach with an unspoken question on his face. Sly didn't need to hear the question to know that it was "Why are you here, Dad?" More specifically, his question was "What business do you have at the funeral of this murdered woman?"

It was a hell of a thing for a man's son to ever wonder why he was there. To his credit, Sly understood that he deserved this. Also to his credit, he was trying to step up. It was just too bad that it had taken him all of Joe's life to do it.

Sly wasn't proud of much, but he was proud of getting on a plane and going to Florida to seek his son's forgiveness. Since that trip, he'd stayed the course. He'd invested in a cell phone plan with unlimited minutes and he'd used it until he was afraid the phone company was going to call him and say, "We didn't really mean *unlimited*." He'd even learned what a video chat was, so that he could visit with his grandchildren, face-to-face.

Did these things make up for the years he spent driving an eighteen-wheeler, instead of being home with his wife and son? Did they make up for letting Joe walk away and stay gone for all those years, when a real man would have turned the country upside down looking for his son? Did they make up for the shame of his penitentiary term?

They did not. But a man could only do the things that were possible. He couldn't fix the past, but he could use the hell out of his cell phone and its video chat capability, so that's what Sly did.

And speaking of the past, it was about to roar back into his life. When Sophia Townsend's bones surfaced, they had brought his past with them. There was every likelihood that this past was going to tear up the tender and fragile relationship he was building with his only child.

Sly might not be able to do anything to prevent that, but he was going to try.

• • ● • •

"Dad?"

This was the moment when Sly realized that he should have planned his words. He knew better than to walk into a situation half-cocked. The penitentiary had been full of men who did what they felt like doing and said what they felt like saying. That's why they were in the penitentiary.

Sly had vowed never to go back. To keep that vow, he had to change. And he had to stay changed.

"I wanted to—"

Sly felt around for the right words, and in that moment he lost.

"Sly! Damn, man. How've you been? Good to see you!"

Mickey embraced him in the kind of hug that manly men give, both fists pounding on his back. Sometimes it means "How've you been? Good to see you," but sometimes it means "Long time no see, asshole. This is the only socially acceptable way to punch you."

Kenny was neither a fist-pounder nor a hugger, so all Sly got from him was a nod and a brusque "It's been a while."

● ● ● ● ●

Roy watched Mickey, Kenny, Emily, and Alba file past Sly, dutifully shaking the ex-con's hand as he joined the group, or hugging him or scrupulously avoiding physical contact, as appropriate. Roy sensed that they weren't doing this because they were glad to see Sly Mantooth, but because that's how you behave at a funeral.

They all clearly knew Sly, but their faces were guarded. Alba's welcome seemed sincere, but no one else's did. Their smiles were wooden. From the looks of them, Roy couldn't tell whether his murder suspects were really glad to see the newly arrived ex-con, or whether they were just barely able to keep from killing him where he stood.

● ● ● ● ●

Joe asked, "Are you here for the funeral, Dad? Did you know Sophia Townsend?" and Sly wasn't quick enough to be the one to give his son an answer.

Mickey answered so quickly that Sly suspected him of cutting him off on purpose. "I forgot it until he drove up just now.

We all worked together. Right here, back when you and Carson were just kids. Just for a few days, I think. Right?"

There it was on his son's face. Doubt. Suspicion. Distrust. He'd seen them on Joe's face before, but not since they'd been reunited.

Sly hated Mickey Callahan for putting the ugliness back into his relationship with Joe, but the hatred wasn't really new. Sly had hated Mickey Callahan for a long time.

"Dad? You worked here? Back in eighty-seven?"

That was all Joe said, but Sly saw all the other questions in his eyes.

We've been talking about this job since Faye and I got off the plane, Dad. We talked about it all the next morning, wondering how Faye was doing and whether Carson was excited about being in charge. After Faye called and told us they'd found a body, we talked about that until I got so antsy that I had to come make sure she was okay. We've been talking about nothing else since then.

Why didn't you mention even once that you'd worked here, too? What are you hiding?

• • ● • •

Roy was an investigator to the core, so he hadn't taken his eyes off Sly Mantooth since the man stepped out of his truck. Sly had paused and squared his shoulders, and his body language had been so obvious that it was almost cartoonish. This was a man getting ready to do something hard.

Sly had watched Joe approach his father slowly, only to be overtaken by the back-slapping Mickey and his shadow Kenny. Then the four men had stood silent and stiff, like a pack of hunting dogs who weren't sure whether to tree a bobcat or to run from its claws. Roy decided to complicate their lives even more by joining them.

"Sly? Here to see your son?"

Roy saw Faye sidle up beside Joe, as if she too had read the group's body language and thought they might need her to keep the peace.

"No. I think I'm here to see you, Roy."

This was news in itself. Sly didn't ordinarily seek out the company of law officers.

"Ever since Faye called and told Joe that Sophia was dead, I've been thinking. Remembering. It's been a long time since I worked for Sophia, and I didn't work for her long, but I thought maybe I might remember something that would help you find out who killed her. Seems like I owe it to an old friend to help her get justice, you know? And it seemed like I owed it to an old friend to be at her funeral."

Roy wasn't sure Sly was telling the whole truth, but Sly wasn't looking at him for a response to his statement. He was looking at Joe.

Joe's face was a blank. Maybe Sly could read it, but Roy couldn't.

Faye looked like she wanted to take her husband by the hand but she wasn't sure it was a good idea. Roy thought he saw her right hand twitch, but she kept it by her side.

Agent Bigbee looked like he was thinking that this case had just gotten a whole lot more interesting.

Roy said, "You got something to tell me, Sly? We're going to spend a few more minutes remembering Sophia and Kira, but we can talk when the memorial service is over. I'd like to give over this whole day to remembering those two women, cut down in their prime, but I can't do it. The day's getting old and we have a killer to catch."

• ● ● ● •

Faye watched Joe as he watched his father. After the memorial service was over, Sly, Agent Bigbee, and Roy had sat down in three camp chairs that Carson had provided from his project's storage shed, the same chairs where Roy had sat when he interviewed all his witnesses and suspects.

Which was Sly? A witness? Or a suspect?

The men sat under a cedar tree that wasn't throwing much shade. They were just talking. In fact, they looked almost friendly, but Joe was looking at Sly like a man who thought his father was heading back to the pen, and soon.

● ● ● ● ●

"You got something you especially want to tell me?" Roy asked, looking at Sly Mantooth up close for the first time in a lot of years.

He could see that time was weighing light on Sly, who had to be ten or more years older than Roy. He had seen Sly with the sallow, clammy skin of an active alcoholic whose liver couldn't keep up. Not today. His face was almost unwrinkled, except for some faint lines at the corners of his eyes and mouth, and it was the warm brown of his youth. It seemed that Sly Mantooth had stopped drinking and that he'd done it in time to save his health. It was probably too much to hope that he'd given up cigarettes, too.

There were individual strands of gray in his straight hair, but it was still thick and most of it was still black. Roy saw that Sly's face was broader than his son's through the cheekbones and jaw. With that sturdy bone structure, Sly might never have the jowls of an old man. Roy, who was nearing fifty, resisted the urge to touch his jawline to check on the condition of his own jowls.

"I ain't got much to tell you, only that I was here, working, a couple of months before Sophia disappeared. I don't know what to tell you about it. It's not like I knew she was going to die, and I was only here for a couple of weeks, maybe three. I've had thirty years to forget things, and it looks like my friends have used those thirty years to forget me, but coming here seemed like the right thing to do. I'll answer any question you've got, best as I can."

Sly's words sounded right and honorable—although Roy did notice that he'd called his former boss by her first name—but it had taken him a long time to come here and say them. The logical thing for an innocent man to do would be to come right away, as soon as he heard that a body had been found. The logical thing for a guilty man to do would be to stay away.

This man had thought about it for days, and then decided to come. Did that make him a guilty man who'd decided he needed to cover his tracks? Or did it make him an innocent man who'd decided he'd better start acting like one?

Chapter Twenty-one

"Let's go."

Joe was watching his father talk to Roy Cloud and Agent Bigbee, so Faye repeated herself.

"Did you hear me? I said let's go!"

She hustled Joe to the passenger seat of the rental car and took the wheel.

"Where are you taking me?"

"To a mountain cabin in Arkansas."

"That sounds romantic."

"I wish."

Faye handed him her phone. On its screen, Joe could see the report from Mickey's 1987 visit to Sophia Townsend's cabin, including detailed directions to the spot where it hid on the side of a mountain.

"Help me navigate," she said.

"You plan to tell me why we're going there in such a big hurry?"

"I do, just as soon as I get out of Roy Cloud's sight and can stop driving like an old man."

Joe studied the screen for a minute. The Arkansas officer's sloppy scrawl made his dyslexia kick up something fierce. After he got the letters to settle down and stay in one place, he said, "Head for the interstate. That'll take us across the state border. After we get off the highway, we'll have to pay attention or we're going to miss some of these little roads. I'll pull up a map on my phone and see if I can plot out where those roads actually are. It'll be a lot easier than following these directions."

"Are they really bad?"

He watched Faye squeeze the accelerator toward the floor. She was a far more aggressive driver than he was. The road between them and the interstate was rough, but it was paved and straight, so he guessed they'd be okay.

"Naw, they're pretty good. Had to be. There wasn't any GPS back then. These directions tell you every little twist and turn. They even give you landmarks. But when they say 'Turn left at the third dirt road on the left,' how are we supposed to know they ain't built another dirt road in the last thirty years?"

"Or paved one of the ones that was already there."

"Yeah. Now do you want to tell me why we're doing this?"

"I suppose it's obvious that I just lost my consulting job with the Lighthorse Tribal Police."

"Because Dad's a suspect now?"

Faye nodded. He watched her nudge the accelerator a little closer to disaster.

"Faye, why do you think Dad hasn't said the first thing about working for Dr. Townsend? He should've told us."

"I don't know, but Roy Cloud is going to think that he waited so long to come forward because he's guilty. No, that's not right. Roy is fair. He's going to think that your dad might be guilty and he's going to try to get at the truth. But it doesn't help a bit that Sly's an ex-con. And heaven only knows what Bigbee is thinking right about now."

Joe looked out his window. He didn't like thinking about his father's past. He also didn't particularly like his wife saying nice things about the man who had been taking up so much of her time, the man who coincidentally might try to railroad his father. Faye continued talking as if she didn't notice his annoyed sigh.

"Someone with your father's past would naturally steer clear of the police. Cloud knows that, so it's good that Sly came forward on his own. But he just made himself a suspect until he and Bigbee sort everything out. We already know that Roy won't work with Carson because his father is a suspect. Now that my father's a suspect, there's no way he will continue to work with me."

At the word "father," Joe jerked his head around to look at his wife. Her lips were pursed together so hard that they were pale. "What did you say?"

"I never knew my father," Faye said. "Now that I've got one, do you think I want to lose him?"

"How will it help Dad for us to die in a burning car?" He leaned over to look at the speedometer as she merged on to the interstate. "Dang, Faye. Why've you got to go so fast?"

"I've read enough of Sophia's field notebooks to know that the last one is missing. We know she stayed at a motel during that last week, checking out on Friday like she always did. She went missing on a Friday when all her stuff would have still been in her car. If she made it home, there's a good chance that the notebook is there."

"And you think there might be something in that notebook that will tell us who did it?"

"Could be. Or maybe it will just tell us something about the figurine and the pearls and the bone. They all seem to be connected to her murder, though I can't imagine how. We need to know more about the last days of Sophia Townsend's life if we're going to clear your dad."

"You're not going to steal that notebook, are you? If we find it, I mean."

"And get charged with obstructing justice or tampering with evidence or being an accessory after the fact? No, thank you. But I can certainly take pictures of the pages and read them after we get out of there."

● ● ● ● ●

Faye's nerves were too frayed to sit with her husband in silence. She had driven twenty minutes since he last spoke, and that was long enough.

"Joe? You doing okay? About your dad, I mean. We're going to work this thing out. You don't have to worry about him so much."

Joe was thumbing something into his phone and he didn't look up. Faye moved into the left lane and gave the car some more gas, praying that there were no speed traps.

Finally, Joe spoke, but he didn't respond to her reassurance that he didn't need to worry about his dad.

"Faye? You think that Roy Cloud is going to come to the cabin today, too?"

Of course, Roy would be following them to Arkansas. This was the thing that was driving her to travel at such a suicidal speed. "I know he'll come. We were already planning to make a trip there. He'd already be on the road, except your father made himself first priority."

"That's what I thought, so I just texted Dad. Couldn't call him, because he probably wouldn't pick up. Besides, I couldn't risk Roy hearing what I had to say. Dad keeps his phone pretty loud. Don't know why. He can hear just fine."

"What did you tell him?"

"I told him to stall as long as he could, then to call us when Roy gets done with him."

When Faye heard that Joe had taken an action, any action, she felt better. Now that he had broken out of the strangely passive place he'd inhabited since they came to Oklahoma, she allowed herself to think that maybe their family was going to emerge from this crisis unscathed. As she thought about it, this was exactly what Sly had done that morning. He had walked away from passiveness and taken back control of his life.

"Excellent. Now let's just hope that your dad checks his texts. I might not if I were being questioned in a murder case."

"That's why I dialed his number after I texted. You know he never turns his ringer off. He'll pull out the phone and see that I texted. If we're lucky, he'll read it. He wouldn't have to be obvious about it. Just tapping the screen twice would pull up the text."

"He could send you back a text that says, 'K' with two more taps."

"He won't think of that. Just drive and hope he's busy talking Roy Cloud's ears off."

• ● ● ● •

The last gravel road leading to Sophia Townsend's cabin looked to Faye like it hadn't been graded since 1987. The underbrush reached out from both sides of the road, dragging against both sides of the car.

Joe rolled down the window to see what the scraping branches were doing to the car's paint job. "We're going to owe the rental company big bucks for those scratches."

"We're lucky to be able to get through at all," Faye said. "You would think we'd at least have had to stop and move some fallen limbs."

"Somebody else has come down this road lately. No way to do that without clearing anything blocking the road."

"You sure?" Faye said, although she knew better than to doubt Joe when he was tracking somebody or something.

"Yep. Some of these branches have been cut."

Seeing her nervous glance down the road, looking for someone lurking at the end of it, he said, "Don't worry. They aren't here today. The scars on these branches ain't that fresh. But somebody's been down this road, and it wasn't very long ago."

"Will Roy know that somebody was here today? Are we leaving tracks?"

Joe looked out the rear window. "Not bad. There's a lot of leaves and pine straw on top of the gravel. He'd be able to tell somebody'd been here if he got out and looked, but why would he do that? Is he expecting anybody to be out here?"

"Maybe, but I think he'd be surprised to find out I was the one trying to beat him to the evidence."

The road appeared to end abruptly at the edge of an overgrown clearing, but Faye could see that it had once turned sharply to the right, heading into the woods. She turned the wheel hard and eased the car down the completely overgrown side road.

"In case you hadn't figured it out," Joe said, "nobody's been cutting these branches. Nobody's been down this side road in a long, long time."

"Even I can see that. This must be where Emily waited in her car all those years ago. If I leave our car here, I'm guessing you can't see it from the road or from the house."

"You're probably right. Good thing it's green."

Faye picked her way through the row of trees separating the car from the clearing where Sophia Townsend's cabin must be. Or maybe it wasn't there at all now. Rot could have taken it to the ground. A lightning strike or a wildfire could have turned it to ash. Sophia had been dead so long that these woods could have burned and recovered more than once without a trace of scorched earth left behind.

"Try not to leave a trail," Joe said. "It's probably better to walk in the tall grass, as long as you don't knock too much of it down."

The overgrown grasses parted as Faye pushed her way through, but they hid bushes with stiff, woody branches that didn't yield so easily. The branches poked their sharp ends into her shins. If she hadn't been wearing long pants, they would have drawn blood as soon as she left the car.

Now that Faye was clear of the trees, she could see the cabin, but the rampant vegetation kept her from rushing to its front steps. Then she unexpectedly stepped into a strip of land where she felt less claustrophobic. She looked at Joe to see if he noticed.

He just pointed to hacked-off shrub branches and said, "Like I said, somebody's been here. They cleared a path through this mess, but it wasn't today and it wasn't this week. It's been weeks, maybe months."

"But not years?"

"No."

They were within a stone's throw of the cabin now, and Faye could see that it was largely intact. A fallen branch had caved in the roof at the back of the house, but the floor of the porch stretching across its front still looked sturdy enough.

As she walked across the overgrown land that used to be Sophia Townsend's front yard, she smelled mint as her feet crushed an untended herb garden. Morning glory vines crawled up the cabin's nearest wall and onto the roof. It was still early morning, so the purple and white blooms were like colorful trumpets. If someone had told Faye that those vines were holding up the cabin's walls, she would have believed them.

Milk-and-wine lilies sprawled in the weeds on either side of the porch stairs, quietly saying, "A gardener once lived here."

The stairs took Faye and Joe to the cabin's porch, where the front door stood open. Marks on the wood floor showed where someone had pushed hard on the damp-swollen door to get it to open. Was it the person who had cleared the road and slashed the branches that had blocked their path?

Even though every part of Faye was telling her that she mustn't intrude on the desolate privacy of this neglected cabin, she stepped onto the porch of Sophia Townsend's last home and peered in.

The cabin consisted of a large room that held a kitchen and a living area, with a partially enclosed bedroom at the back. The branch that had pierced the roof still protruded from the ceiling in the rear of the house. Today, it brought a bit of light into a space that had been unlit for a long time. Years of rainy days had turned the bed under the hole into a sagging, mildewed heap. The floor underneath would soon collapse.

Faye felt a sudden chill. It may have been real, or it may have been the realization that this had been a place where someone had been happy. Now there was no life here at all, other than the encroaching vines.

The front of the house, by contrast, was largely undamaged, other than the rot and mold around closed windows that had leaked steadily over the years. The furniture was still draped in mildewed sheets, just as Mickey had said. A thick layer of dust covered the kitchen counters, the desk, the floor, everything. To the right of the doorway stood Sophia's desk and three overfull bookcases. To the left was an old upright piano. It was intact, but its keys rested at uneven heights all across the keyboard, like bad teeth.

"It's gonna be hard to walk across that floor and not leave tracks in the dust," Joe said.

"No problem."

Faye's eyes were attuned to the precise shade of blue of Sophia's field notebooks, so her attention had gone straight to the desktop. The notebook lying there was unmistakable. No dust could completely dim that color of ultramarine.

"There it is. Right on top. It's either the last notebook she used or an empty one that she was going to use next. What do you bet me that it's the one we're looking for? Fifty-fifty shot."

"I'm not taking that bet," Joe said. "She used that one. Look at the dirt on the cover. You can see it even through the dust."

"You know what that means? It means that she made it home on that last Friday."

Faye didn't need to go into the cabin and leave her tracks on the dust-covered floor. She pulled a tissue out of her purse to keep from leaving fingerprints, then she leaned hard to the right and snagged the book, carefully lifting it from the dusty desk. She was surprised that it didn't feel dustier, damper, older. It seemed that the advertisements for weather-proof field note-books weren't lying.

Gesturing for Joe to follow her, Faye backed across the porch and dropped cross-legged in the tall grass to photograph the pages. It was awkward, using a tissue in the hand holding the book. Using a pencil to turn the pages took even more concentration, but she thought she could do it. She figured that there was a better likelihood that clues to Sophia Townsend's death would be found in the final entries, so she started with the last page with handwriting and worked forward.

When Joe saw what she was doing, he took the phone from her hand and started snapping pictures for her as she flipped the pages. Together, they made quick progress.

Four pages in, Joe almost dropped the phone. "Would you look at that?"

Sophia's drawing of the figurine was so realistic that Faye felt like the little pottery woman could step off the page. Faye had only seen parts of her right side, because the thief had taken away her chance to dig it up and study it. Sophia had seen the whole thing and she had illustrated its every detail.

On the facing page was a drawing of thirteen spheres arranged as if they'd been scattered across a tabletop. Sophia had shaded and stippled their surface texture, but she'd been working with a charcoal pencil, so it hadn't been possible to depict the pearls' red tinge.

A few more pages in, another of Sophia's lovely illustrations jumped out at her. It depicted the Mississippian potsherd that Emily had found, after it was broken into three pieces. The drawing that Faye had already seen had shown the complete potsherd, with lines drawn at the two fractures.

Faye stared at the picture of a plain potsherd, a heart-shaped sherd ornamented with incised curves, and a third sherd, also ornamented, with a point that would fit neatly into the notch of the heart.

She didn't want Joe to see this until she'd had time to tell him about the connection between his father and Sophia's final days. More than a month had passed between the day Sly quit the job and the day this picture had been drawn. She wished she could explain how the sherd had come into his hands, but she couldn't, and she was afraid that this was a bad thing for his dad.

She quickly took the phone from Joe's hand and snapped a picture, turning the page before he saw the drawing of the three potsherds. She feebly covered for taking over the job he'd volunteered to do for her by saying, "We've got to wrap this up before Roy and his people get here."

On cue, Joe's phone beeped. He glanced at the text and said, "It's Dad. Cloud just left. He said, 'I told Roy and Bigbee every story about Sophia and her shovel bums that I knew. Was about to start making up some lies but remembered I was talking to the cops. Thought I better let them leave.'"

"It took us a while to get here from Sylacauga," Faye said. "We have some time before they show up."

The words were hardly out of her mouth when they heard gravel crunch. In a heartbeat, Faye was up and on the porch, crossing it in a single step that she hoped didn't leave much of a footprint. She leaned in the door and replaced the notebook, leapt off the porch and ran for the woods, doing her best to keep to the strip cleared of brush by the mysterious person who had been there before them.

Joe caught up with her quickly and he could easily have passed her. Instead, he matched her step by step in their run for cover. Faye thought he might be planning to pick her up and throw her into the shadows, so she put on another burst of speed. Together, they dropped flat on the ground and let the underbrush hide them.

Sophia Townsend's mountain retreat was so quiet that the grinding sound of gravel under tires seemed nearer than it was. Faye would have sworn the vehicle should have arrived already, but all she could see was a cloud of dust. This must have been how she and Joe had looked as they approached. If a car kicked up this much of a mess just by rolling slowly down the road, they couldn't hope to leave unseen until Cloud and Bigbee had gone. She and Joe were going to be lying here in the dirt for quite some time.

"Your dad only texted that Cloud was leaving a minute ago," she said. "How is this happening?"

"Maybe the cell service is bad out here and the text didn't go right through? I'm surprised there's service out here at all."

Faye didn't like to think about what it would be like if Cloud found them. Sneaking out here and hiding in the woods made them look guilty, but of what? Neither she nor Joe were plausible suspects for the murder.

Would he suspect them of tampering with evidence to hide Joe's father's guilt? They'd kept their fingerprints off the notebook and they'd left the cabin undisturbed, but they had tampered with the evidence in a small way by simply moving and handling the notebook. If Roy Cloud found out they'd done that and if he wanted to make their lives hell, he probably could.

Faye didn't actually care, not at the moment, though she certainly might care later. For an archaeologist, finding the original notes from the first time the figurine and pearls were uncovered was worth a certain degree of hell. No one had seen those notes in twenty-nine years. Faye couldn't wait to read them.

The vehicle had parked on the far side of the line of trees bordering the road. Now it wasn't tires that were making gravel crunch. It was the work shoes of a federal agent and the chief of the Lighthorse Tribal Police.

Faye thought that Roy must have brought a machete, because she could hear the sound of a blade hacking a path to the cabin and Bigbee didn't seem like the machete type. Unlike Faye and Joe, they didn't mind making noise, because they didn't care if anybody knew they were there. And who could they reasonably expect to be here? Their work shoes trod on the patch of mint that had escaped from Sophia's garden so long ago.

The mint's sharp scent reached Faye's nose, but she paid it no attention. She was too startled by what she saw. There was no team of investigators passing in front of her and there were no work shoes. There was just a single set of boots, and there was just one machete hacking through the overgrown weeds. Neither the boots nor the machete belonged to Roy Cloud or to Agent Bigbee or to anyone from the Lighthorse Tribal Police.

They belonged to Carson Callahan.

• • ● • •

Carson had just slashed his way across Sophia Townsend's front yard and walked into the cabin. Faye didn't dare speak to Joe, but she turned her head enough to meet his eyes. He looked stunned to see his old friend.

Within seconds, Carson came out of the cabin, retracing his steps down the newly cleared path. She and Joe were well-hidden, but Carson was in such a hurry that he might not have noticed them if they'd been right out in the open. Faye's heart sank as he passed near where she hid. He had an ultramarine blue field notebook under his arm.

It was as if Carson, too, was trying to get in and out before Roy and Bigbee arrived. The only difference was that they hadn't come there to keep evidence out of the hands of the law, and Carson had apparently come for that express purpose.

They heard gravel under his feet again as he stepped onto the road. The sound of his truck door slamming echoed in the stillness. Then the truck roared to life and made its way back down the mountain, kicking up a pall of dust as it went.

"It would serve him right to run into Cloud on the way down," Joe said.

"Yeah, but it's not going to happen. Your dad said that Roy just left Sylacauga. Carson will be long gone by the time he gets here."

"Guess we should get going, too."

Faye shook her head. "We can't go."

"Are we going to lay here until Cloud and Bigbee come, watch what they do, then wait till they're gone before go home?"

"I have to talk to him. He'll be angry, but there's no help for it."

Joe's face had about a dozen questions on it. "What do we owe Roy Cloud? Let's get out of here."

She held out her phone, with the last picture they'd taken of the notebook on its screen. "If we leave, he won't know the notebook was here. He won't even know for sure that it exists. He won't know what was in it. And he won't know that Carson took it. We know all those things. I might be willing to push the law a little bit by reading the notebook and putting it back. I'm not willing to withhold evidence that could get justice for Sophia Townsend."

"Then can we get up off the ground and go sit in the car while we look at those pictures? We might as well find out what's in the notebook so we can tell Cloud as soon as he shows up. While we're telling him that we tried to do an end run around him by sneaking out here, I mean."

"Yeah. He won't be happy to hear that."

They got up, pulled twigs out of their hair, and walked back to the car. There was no more reason to hide, so they drove it out of its leafy hiding place and waited in the open spot at the end of the road where Carson had parked.

Faye held the phone in her hands, delaying the moment when they looked at the pages together. "Why do you think Carson came out here to get the notebook?" she asked. "And how do you think he knew it was here?"

"We know somebody drove out here lately. I saw where they'd cut those limbs. It could've been Carson. But how did he find it in the first place? To do that, he had to know the notebook existed, he had to know that it was here, and he had to know how to find this cabin."

"I've been thinking that through," Faye said. "Once Cloud knew the cabin was in Arkansas, he had the location in minutes. If Carson knew that much, then he could check property records and find this place just as easily. And I'm pretty sure he did know that much."

"Why?"

"Carson described the cabin to me, and he got it absolutely right, so he must have been here. Carson told me that Sophia had a garden and a piano and a lot of books, and all those things are true. When he told me about her cabin, I didn't realize that its location was such a state secret. I didn't realize what it really meant when he described its every detail."

Faye wondered how the land around her would look now if Sophia had lived to tend it. There would be no mildew in the cabin, no roadside underbrush obscuring her view of it, no weeds in the herb garden, no dust on the well-swept front porch. Sophia's absence was palpable here.

"Can you imagine getting that piano up here?" she asked. "You'd have to tie it down in the back of a pickup and hope for the best."

Faye looked down the road, waiting for the dust that would herald Roy Cloud's arrival.

"Why do you think Carson would have been out here when he was eleven years old?" Joe asked.

"Carson said that he remembered her, but he never really talked to her. We have no reason to think that Sophia liked children, so I don't think she was the one who brought him out here. We do know, however, that his father was having an affair with Sophia. It would be horrifyingly inappropriate to bring your child with you when you visited your lover, but people do inappropriate things when they're in love."

"Well, yeah. Or in lust."

"You're a dad, and you were a kid once. Think about it. An eleven-year-old would absolutely notice the sign that marked the state border. Kids are fascinated by that kind of thing. They keep a count of how many states they've visited. Carson would remember, and he'd have known to look for the cabin in Arkansas, even though Roy Cloud didn't. But I have no idea why Carson has come back here as an adult, probably twice, and I don't know why he took the field notebook, since he didn't take it the last time he was here. I'm guessing he got wind about the law coming out here, maybe because his dad told him Roy was interested in Sophia's cabin. There must be some reason he hightailed it to Arkansas almost as fast as we did. I just don't know why he wanted to keep that field notebook out of Roy Cloud's hands."

Joe reached for her phone. The last photo taken was still on the screen. He thumbed through the next few pages, stopping abruptly when he saw Sophia's drawing.

"That's Dad's potsherd. The little heart that he's kept for years. Faye. What's going on?"

The crunching gravel and billowing dust spared her from having to answer. She got out of the car and waited for the betrayed look on Roy Cloud's face when she told him what she'd done.

Chapter Twenty-two

"I can't believe you did this, Faye."

Roy looked just as betrayed as she'd expected, and it was no surprise that he'd dropped the endearing "Doctor Faye." They'd worked together for days, seeking justice. Then, as soon as she felt the need to defend a loved one, she had driven like a madwoman so she could be sure she had enough time to subvert justice.

Technically.

She was technically interfering with the investigation, but she wasn't trying to subvert justice. She just wanted to help Sly, a man she believed in her heart to be innocent. This did not make what she'd done right. And she'd dragged Joe into it, which didn't make her proud of herself, either.

Did good results mitigate an action that was wrong? Faye wasn't willing to wade into that ethical territory, but the result of her action was that Bigbee and Cloud now knew that the notebook existed. He also knew that Carson had some reason to want it. Part of that reason seemed to be that he didn't want the law to have it.

Most of all, Cloud and Bigbee now had copies of some of the pages from that missing notebook, because Faye had taken pictures of them. This was probably the reason they were still listening to what she had to say, instead of yelling at her or arresting her or something.

She had held her phone out to Cloud, saying, "It's only the

last few pages and I haven't had time to read them yet, but I think you'll recognize a couple of the drawings."

He'd whistled when he saw the drawings of the figurine and the pearls. When he got to the other drawing he said, "I'll be damned. There's the potsherd you found in the grave. The design on it is unmistakable."

When Joe heard Cloud say that Faye had found one of the other potsherds, she felt his eyes on her. She and Joe were lovers and partners. They shared everything. They had no secrets from each other. Rather, they'd had no secrets until she chose not to tell him that she'd found a sherd in an unmarked grave that matched the one his father had inexplicably hidden.

Knowing that this conversation could go nowhere good, Faye told Cloud and Bigbee what she knew anyway. She was done with being dishonest and secretive. She didn't do it well.

"I think I know where the other two pieces are," she said, looking into the eyes of three men who all had good reasons not to trust her any more.

"Do you plan to tell me?" Cloud asked.

"Do you remember how Sophia wrote that she'd argued with Kenny about lab tests? That's because they often require a sample of the object being tested. There are ethical issues with damaging or destroying something irreplaceable, just to find out how old it is. Kenny apparently objected to her doing that, possibly because he felt that it disrespected the ancestors who made these things. See this piece of the sherd, the plain one with no decoration?"

Cloud gave her a curt nod.

"Imagine you're Sophia. You want to test the sherd very badly. You're working with an experimental lab that may need even larger than usual samples. Emily considerately breaks it for you. Don't you think you might send the plain, boring piece of pottery to the lab? They could test it, destroy it, whatever, but the interesting part of the sherd is preserved. Even better, it wasn't you that damaged the object to collect a sample."

"So where's the third sherd? And why didn't you tell me you knew where it was, or that it even existed at all?"

This was going to be the hardest revelation of all. It would reveal to Roy that she'd been keeping an important piece of evidence from him to protect her father-in-law. It would reveal the same thing to her trusting husband. And it would vault Joe's father to the top of the suspect list.

It killed her to lose Joe's trust and Roy's respect, but it had to be done.

"Sly has the third potsherd. Well, he had it when we got here, but it's been days since I saw it. He's had it for a very long time."

"You're fired."

Roy's head whipped in the direction of Bigbee's voice.

The agent repeated himself. "You're fired, Dr. Longchamp-Mantooth. Insubordination is intolerable."

"She's not yours to fire." Roy's voice was clipped and cool. "She's my consultant. I'm the one paying her."

"Are you forgetting that this isn't your case, Cloud?"

"I am not. But that doesn't mean that she's yours to fire. I'll say if she works for me or not." Focusing his black eyes on Faye's, he said, "You're fired, Faye."

• • ● •• •

The ride home was long and silent. Joe didn't ask Faye why she hadn't told him that his father's potsherd linked him to Sophia Townsend's murder, and he didn't ask her why she'd kept the information from Roy Cloud, too.

About halfway back to Sylacauga, he looked at her and said, "Sometimes I think I don't even know you." Then he shifted his eyes back to the road and said nothing more.

When they got home, they found Sly sitting at the kitchen table, filling the ashtray full of ashes and cigarette butts. The wreath of smoke around his head made Faye queasy, and so did the smear of grease on the plate by his elbow. At least he had eaten something.

"If Cloud asked me once whether I'd ever had an argument with Sophia, he must've asked me a dozen times. I told him no. I got along with Sophia better than the rest of 'em did."

He brought the cigarette to his mouth, then held it suspended there without taking a drag. "I did. She said I was smarter than those two college boys put together. And almost as big as the two of 'em put together. Gracious, she worked us hard. There was a time when I thought I might die right there in the pit. Sunstroke. Heart attack. Something like that."

Sly finally put the cigarette between his lips and drew in a breath. "Is that why you quit, Dad?"

The smoke left Sly's lungs and Faye's eyes watered. He didn't look at his son, but he answered him.

"Nah. Whatever else I ever did wrong, I ain't never been scared of hard work. But I was a little scared of Sophia. When Cloud asked me why I quit that job I needed bad, I told him that married people who spent too much time with Sophia Townsend didn't generally stay married too much longer. I needed my wife more than I needed that job."

Joe, who had been looking at his hands folded in his lap, lifted his head. He met Sly's eyes, and Faye could see the anger at his father for keeping secrets fade. Whenever Sly needed to patch things up with Joe, now or in the future, all he would ever have to do would be to remind Joe that he had loved Patricia.

Faye didn't have that advantage. She had never seen Joe as angry with her as he was right now, and she had no idea what it would take to make things right between them.

"After Cloud left to go to Sophia's cabin, we all stood together—me, Mickey, Kenny, Emily. We talked like thirty years ain't passed. And nothing had changed. The three of them stood away from me in a little knot and said things that sounded nice but wasn't. Well, not Emily. She ain't never said a mean thing in her life. It was Mickey that said, 'You did the right thing to go. I think Sophia yelled at you every day that rolled.' I said it looked to me like she was yelling at all of us and he just grunted."

"Mickey was always full of himself," Joe said. "Even a kid can tell that. I used to feel sorry for Carson."

Now it was Sly's turn to look up from the hands that were tearing apart the cigarette he'd intended to light next. He looked like he wanted to say, "You're telling me that you thought some other kid had a worse dad than you did?"

Instead, he said, "Emily is an odd one, but sometimes she ain't far wrong. She said, 'You missed her after you left, didn't you?' I knew Mickey and Kenny would go running to Cloud and tell him I looked like the kind of man who would kill a woman he thought was sexy, but I didn't lie. I said, 'Yeah, Emily. I missed her. I missed all of y'all, and you can believe that or not. It don't make no matter to me.'"

Joe took the torn-up cigarette out of his father's hand and put it in the ashtray. "What did Kenny say?"

"He said, 'Things weren't the same after you left.' Maybe he meant he wished I'd stayed, but maybe he meant that his world looked a lot more cheery without me in it."

As bad as things were, Sly's clear-eyed understanding of his so-called friends made Faye want to smile.

Like most smokers, Sly never knew what to do with his hands when they were empty. He reached for his cigarette pack again. "Kenny said something else double-edged. He said, 'I never understood why you left,' when what he really meant was 'I never understood how you could leave her.' Then he just looked at me like he thought I killed the woman, when everybody standing there knew that he wrecked his own marriage for her. Mickey, too. And now they have the gall to let people think I might be the one that done wrong. God knows what they said about me to Cloud."

"You don't think they told him you killed her, do you? Dad?"

Sly fetched the frayed cigarette out of the ashtray and finished destroying it. Then he shook another one out of the pack and lit it. "I don't know what they said. I don't want to think about it and I don't want to talk about it."

Faye and Joe sat with Sly awhile and watched him smoke, but he had nothing more to say to them. It appeared that Faye's husband had nothing more to say to her, either. After a while, she decided she couldn't stand the silence any more, so she packed her briefcase and left. Neither man said good-bye.

• ● ◉ ● •

Faye had left Sly's house without a plan. She'd wanted to read the pages that she'd been able to copy out of Sophia's final notebook, but it wasn't like she had an office where she could work. She pulled into a parking space on Sylacauga's brick-paved Main Street, planning to burn a bunch of gasoline to keep the car cool so she could sit there and read.

The sky was tumultuous with blowing clouds and Faye was glad that Sophia Townsend's bones were no longer exposed to the elements. She would have said that it would rain any moment, but she'd thought that ever since they got back from Arkansas. Oklahoma clouds had a way of threatening rainstorms without delivering. That is, they made you think they weren't going to deliver, then they unleashed a deluge when you least expected it.

Just as she was getting settled, she noticed that the dress store shared space with a coffee shop. It even had Wi-Fi. Faye figured she'd rather give her money to a local business than to an oil company, so she turned off the gas-slurping car and went inside seeking air conditioning and a latte.

After uploading the notebook pages from her phone to her computer, she could finally get a detailed look at what they said, even to the details of Sophia's tight, controlled handwriting. Faye read about her frustration with the Canadian lab that couldn't retrieve DNA from a stone knife. She studied the meticulously detailed drawing of the three pieces of the broken potsherd. And then she reached the last entry, Sophia Townsend's last known written communication.

Excerpt from the field notes of Dr. Sophia Townsend
August 7, 1987

Why do the most interesting and troublesome finds always come on a Friday afternoon?

This afternoon, Ladybitch pulled a piece of a rib from the ground and miraculously failed to break it into smithereens. It was pretty big, and therefore it looked pretty startling lying there in the dirt. She asked me, in that tremulous voice that I find endlessly annoying, whether it was human.

It can be hard to tell with a single bone that you're not even finished digging up, so I said maybe. Or maybe it was from a deer or something, but yeah. I think it's human, and isn't that going to make my life hell? There are laws against burial desecration and that's just fine. I'm a law-abiding citizen, when I'm not behind the wheel of a car that has enough horse-power to really move, but I do not have the budget to wait for some bureaucrat to dick around. More to the point, I doubt the Creeks will go ahead with the project if they learn that this is a burial site. Why would they disturb the dead so they can build an archaeological park to honor the dead?

I need to know whether I have really uncovered a human burial before I involve the bureaucrats. Ladybitch will have a weeping fit if it turns out to be human. She might have a weeping fit, anyway, even if that rib does belong to a deer or—I don't know, maybe a bear. She cannot stay here while I do more digging to check out the situation.

Stupidface and his misplaced tribal pride would be equally troublesome. If we found a broken piece of a fish bone the length of my thumbnail, he would want to call in the authorities to make sure the little fishy's spirit wasn't disturbed. No. Just no. He has got to go, too.

I may let Idiot stay and help me, or I may send him home. He certainly does not have Stupidface's moral qualms and he's big enough to be of some actual use, but he likes to help with the detail work and he's simply not good at it. I may need to do this by myself.

● ● ● ● ●

Damn. The bone was human and it's got friends. I've moved more soil than I should have, enough to see that there's probably an entire skeleton here. And that's not all. It's almost certainly very old, because there were the most amazing things buried with it.

There were pearls scattered around the throat area, serious pearls, big ones that show that these people had a trade network extending to the Gulf of Mexico. Even better, there was a museum-quality clay figurine an arm's-length away from the skeleton. For the record, I will say that I found it before I knew there was a burial here. I will also say, for the record, that the pearls also turned up before I had confirmed that this was a burial. Otherwise, I would have left the grave goods where they lay.

These things are now locked safely in the shed, but they are too valuable to stay there for long. I need to get them to the Creeks and help them decide where to curate them and everything else I found all this summer. They are the most spectacular finds of my career. They're going to sink this project, but those are the breaks. If these were my people, and I guess they are, I would want them to protect their past.

I might as well call it a night. I'm already pushing my luck with the law, so I'm just going to throw a tarp over the bones and call my client.

But first, I want to enjoy this last quiet evening in a most beautiful spot. I want to watch the fireflies come out and I want to listen to the night sounds begin. I want to put the finishing touches on this sketch of the figurine and the pearls, so that I'll have something to remember this place by. And I want to work some more on the sketch of three broken pieces of an old, old potsherd that will never be reunited in this life. I sent one piece to a lab, where they destroyed it for nothing. Fool that I am, I gave another piece away. I, Sophia Townsend, who never gave her heart to anybody, has given it away to a man with a wife and child.

I suppose I'll never get it back.

When this long day is finally done, I'll go home and start hustling up another job. My heart's not in it this time. Maybe this is what happens when you get older, or maybe it's because there's someone here that I'd rather not leave. I have so gloried in my solitude and independence that it has taken me a long time to get lonely, but I'm lonely now.

So before I face the long ride home and the long days in a house built for one, I will let my paper and pencils keep me company. We have traveled a long road together and there are more miles to come.

I'm feeling low tonight, but I will rise to the occasion come morning. I always do.

Chapter Twenty-three

Faye's latte was cold. She'd neglected it while reading Sophia Townsend's last field notes, but she was too cheap not to drink it. She was down to the dregs when her phone rang.

Instead of hello, Carson said, "I'm sorry I've been an asshole. Sorry. Really sorry. I mean it. Sorry."

Her first thought was *I really shouldn't have to put up with drunk calls from a man who is not an ex.*

She looked at her watch. It was past four. Carson sounded like he'd been in his cups since he got home from Sophia's cabin, maybe since he left the funeral.

She flailed around for something to say. "You haven't been that bad. You—"

"Yeah, I have. Maybe I wasn't out-and-out mean, but I sure wasn't nice. I could have helped you out. Should've helped you out. I could have been nicer—yeah, that's the word, nice—and I wasn't. Nice, I mean. It's not your fault my project got shut down. We found the body of a murdered woman, for God's sake. What did I think was going to happen?"

She heard the telltale gurgle of a man who was making a drunk call even worse by continuing to drink.

"Well, I accept your apology, whether or not it was necessary." Faye said this in a firm, we-don't-really-have-to-talk-about-this-now voice that she hoped would end the call while Carson was still making some sense and before he started crying.

Carson was long past being able to take a hint, so he kept talking. "Oh, it was necessary. Necessary. Did I really think Roy Cloud would trust me when my own dad was one of his murder suspects? I did not. No, not good ol' Roy, not when he's got the clout to get me barred from my own job. I could've helped him with the murder investigation, but he's shut me out. Totally."

There was another gurgling swallow.

"I'm sure Roy didn't—"

"Hey, speaking of shutting me out, I'm guessing he did the same to you. After Sly showed up at the funeral this morning, I mean. My dad and your—um—dad-in-law have put us both in a bad spot. Did I ever tell you that Old Sly used to drive me around in his truck, just like Kenny did? There were probably whole years when I spent more time with Sly and Kenny than I did with my own dad."

Faye could picture her father-in-law taking an interest in a boy whose dad was too busy sleeping around to pay him much attention. "Did Joe go with you?"

"Yeah. Me and my little buddy and his dad, riding around Sylacauga and eating cheeseburgers. Never knew why Sly stopped coming around, not till today. My mom explained it all. *Everything.* Well, almost everything. Told me she and Dad would still be married today if Sophia Townsend hadn't come along. Not sure what Sly had to do with all that, because I know for damn sure he wasn't sleeping with Mom, but there you go. My parents tore up my life, but they can't manage to explain why in a way that makes sense. Not even after all this time."

Faye was beginning to think that Carson shouldn't be alone, but calling his mother to go check on him seemed like a terrible thing to do to a forty-year-old man. "So how can I help you? Did you really just call me to apologize?"

"Nope. I called you because I have a plan. And it's a good one. It's a great plan."

"Do tell. What kind of plan are we talking about?"

"You've got a lot more experience working with law enforcement than I do. A lot more. Because I have none. I want you to meet me at my dad's house. Maybe he'll tell me things he won't tell Roy Cloud. Maybe we can get to the bottom of this, just us. Not Roy. Yep. To the bottom of it. That's where we need to get."

"This probably isn't the best time—"

"If you won't come with me, I'm going myself. Right now. I've got my truck keys in my hand."

Faye could hear the keys jingle. That sealed it. Carson couldn't safely drive his car down his own fifteen-foot driveway in this condition.

"No, I'll go. Let me come get you."

Carson was in bad shape, even worse than he sounded. He answered the door wearing one boot, then spent ten minutes looking for the other one. He found it in the kitchen.

The sock was in the bathroom. After five tries to get it turned right-side-out, he gave up and wore it the way it was. He talked throughout the long process of getting himself shod. Faye let him take his time, figuring when he finished putting on his boot, he'd be fifteen minutes closer to sober. Unless he started drinking again.

While Carson struggled with his boot, Faye spent the time scanning the room for a telltale bit of aquamarine. Carson probably would have hidden the notebook he'd filched from Sophia's cabin that morning, but he wasn't expecting guests and maybe alcohol had made him careless.

No luck. She kept hoping he'd go to the bathroom and give her a chance to look around, but Carson continued lacing and re-lacing his boot, and he kept talking.

"Can't make anything make sense. Couldn't have been Kenny shooting at us that first morning. Dad can be an asshole, but he loves me, so I don't think it was him. If Emily Olsen knows how to shoot a gun, I'll—"

It took him a while to come up with something that would fully communicate his doubt of Emily's gun skills.

"—I'll drink to that."

He jumped up from the couch, boot still untied, and lurched toward the refrigerator. Faye grabbed his arm and steered him toward the door. "We need to go talk to your dad. Remember?"

"But I want a beer."

She reached up and put her hands on his shoulders, pushing him toward the door. "No open containers in the car and no time to wait. Let's get to your dad's house and see what he has to say for himself."

"Yeah. What's he got to say for himself? It better be good."

Faye devoutly hoped so.

● ● **●** ● ○

Faye thought she'd been pretty smooth in her efforts to find out about the notebook that Carson had stolen. As soon as they got settled in her car, she'd started steering the conversation in that direction.

She'd opened with a casual mention of the field notebooks she officially knew about. "I finally got a chance to read my copies of Sophia's field notes. Thanks for giving me those."

"Don't thank me too much. You know Roy Cloud would've made me give 'em to you if I hadn't done it on my own. And I didn't like doing it. Get your own project. You're capable. No need to take mine."

She let that bit of bitterness slide. "It was interesting to read them after having read your papers on her work. I could see how you'd managed to make some well-argued conclusions based on those notes, without muddying the conversation by mentioning how…unorthodox…they were."

"I don't like to insert myself into my work. Distance. Objectivity. Gotta have those. Sophia didn't feel that way. Obviously."

"Did you ever notice that the notes stop days before she left? She was so careful to record everything. Surely she made notes during those last few days."

Carson was not drunk enough to admit that he knew about the last notebook, much less that he had it. But he was too drunk to cover his feelings. The cagey expression on his face was laughable.

"Sure she did, but it's been a long, long time. Nearly thirty years. That's a long time. Things get lost. If that notebook got separated from the others somehow, it could be gone forever. Gone. Thrown away, probably. When I wrote my papers on her work, I knew I had to go with what I had."

Faye personally thought that Carson should have mentioned the discrepancy in dates when he wrote those papers. It would not have harmed their scientific reliability to mention that more data might have existed. She wondered why Carson had wanted to keep the possible existence of another notebook a secret. If she understood why he'd done that, she might have a fighting chance to understand why he'd stolen it. As for the question of how he knew where it was or why he hadn't stolen it already, that was anybody's guess.

"I texted my mom to tell her we're coming," he said, holding out his phone to see. The screen said simply 'K.'

His laugh hurt Faye's ears. "That's my mom. She texts like a teenager."

Carson poked a quick message into his phone and waited. There was no return text.

"Typical. She texts like a teenager, but she manages her phone like an old person. She probably left it in the bathroom. She does that all the time."

"I don't always do so well with my phone, either."

He leaned close to her ear and fake-whispered, "I bet she always answers when Dad texts. Right away. I mean it. Right away. All these years, she's stayed single, a pretty woman like that. You know you're pretty when your son can see it. Right?"

Faye nodded and kept her eyes on the road.

Carson wasn't finished making uncomfortable revelations about his mom. "She goes out. Sly even took her out a time or two after Joe's mom died. But she comes home early so Dad won't worry. Is that messed up or what?"

Faye wasn't sure it was much more messed up than the thought of sleek Alba and rough-around-the-edges Sly. But she wasn't surprised to hear that they'd gone out. He was Sly, after all. He liked the ladies and the ladies liked him.

"Sophia got a lot of things right, Faye. You know that? As many times as I read those notebooks, I could never poke a hole in her logic. Any of it."

"I bet you tried. Proving somebody wrong is a good way to get your work noticed."

Carson's drunken giggle made Faye cringe. "You got that right, just like Sophia got a lot of things right. Want to know the rightest thing she wrote in those notebooks?"

"Sure," Faye said, hoping that Carson was about to make the revelation that would crack this case wide open.

He leaned over close to her and the smell of beer was so strong that she could almost identify the brand he drank.

"Sophia was a hundred percent right when she called my father an idiot."

● ● ● ● ●

There were display cases on all four walls of Mickey's living room. They held an eye-popping array of arrowheads, ceramic vessels, silver and gold coins, and old bottles. Faye wondered if he'd found all these things himself, or if he spent a lot of time in pawn shops and on eBay.

Above the cases hung his gun collection and souvenirs from the animals he'd shot. Deer heads didn't bother Faye overmuch. Joe had shot many deer over the years to feed their family, and the only reason he didn't mount the heads was that he didn't like all those eyes looking at him. A person who was willing to eat meat had to be realistic about the animal who died for it.

Mickey's other trophies—a carefully posed bobcat, a swan stuffed to look like it was in flight, a fox with a pheasant carcass in its mouth, a squirrel mounted on a branch—seemed to have been shot for show rather than for food. Faye had serious ethical issues about killing for sport. Maybe Mickey had eaten the squirrel and the pheasant, but she doubted that a swan was good for eating. Certainly not a bobcat.

Try as she might, she could not picture Alba living with this profusion of stuff. Mickey must have used twenty-nine years of singlehood to hone his idiosyncratic sense of style.

Mickey had greeted his son with a "Howdy," and an overlong hug. Unless Faye missed her guess, Carson wasn't the only one who had been drinking heavily. He was not, however, too drunk to notice Carson's condition.

His "Glad you're here," segued quickly into "Carson. Son, are you all right?"

"Fine. I'm just fine, Dad," Carson said, dropping into a chair to hide the fact that he was staggering. Mickey did the same, and probably for the same reason.

"We're here because...um...Faye and I are here because we've both been dismissed by Roy Cloud, so we had nothing better to do than come see you. And all...this..." He gestured vaguely at the antiquities collection, the taxidermy, and the guns. "We're thinking maybe we should turn ourselves into citizen cops."

Faye and Mickey simultaneously said, "What?"

"Neither of us like Cloud sniffing around our dads. Dads-in-law. Whatever. And I include Kenny and Sly on my list of dads. Faye and me, we're gonna find out who really killed Sophia Townsend and Kira Denton. I'd also like to know who it was that shot at me and Faye and Kenny. Faye and me, we're smart. We can get to the bottom of this mystery, just like Scooby-Doo. Like the Hardy Boys. Right, Faye?"

Carson leaned forward, resting his elbows on his thighs, and fastened his gaze on Mickey's face. Deepening his voice to sound like a television detective, he said, "Dad, tell us what you remember about August 7, 1987."

"It was just a day, just another day," said Mickey, who didn't seem to mind being the subject of his son's mock interrogation. "I didn't know it would be the last day I saw Sophia. How could I? If I'd known, I'd have paid more attention."

"Seems like you paid her plenty of attention. That's what Mom says."

Mickey blinked once before he answered. "It was a long time ago, and I paid for it. I lost your mother, and I could have lost you. Maybe I did. Did I?"

Carson said nothing but, "Do you have a beer to spare? I bet you do."

Mickey said, "Not tonight," then he gave Faye a look that said, *Help me.* She obliged by diverting the subject from beer.

"I understand that Sophia sent her crew home early on that last day," she said. "I've been wondering—"

Mickey recoiled. "How do you know that? You couldn't know that."

Faye began to explain, but Mickey wasn't listening. At first, she thought she'd screwed up in revealing that she knew something about Sophia's last day on the job. Then she decided that any question that got this much of a reaction out of a murder suspect couldn't be all bad.

"It's not possible for you to know that. I didn't even remember it until you mentioned it."

Mickey rose in a huff and walked through a door toward the rear of the house, slamming it shut behind him. Faye looked at Carson and mouthed, "What now?"

An instant later, the sound of a gunshot reached her, followed by a grunt and the sound of a body hitting the floor, Faye had a moment—only an instant, really—when reality seemed to blink out. It was a moment when she thought, "Somebody's shot Mickey. Or maybe he's shot himself," and she thought it in such a calm, everyday fashion that she wondered if it were possible to get accustomed to such a thing.

Another shot sounded, and then there was silence.

This time, Carson was the one pushing her in the direction he wanted her to go. He slung a heavy arm across her shoulders and forced her to hit the floor as hard as he did. The impact of her body on the cold tile floor shook her back to reality. Carson was already crawling on his elbows, like a soldier inching toward enemy lines while under heavy fire.

"Dad? Dad, are you okay?"

Mickey said something that was unintelligible through the closed door. Carson reached up for the doorknob. "Dad?"

Another shot sounded. Carson shoved the door open, then dropped back on his stomach. He slithered through the door, trying to get to his father.

"I'm okay," Mickey was saying, over and over. "I'm okay, son. I'm okay."

Faye couldn't see any blood on Mickey, so maybe he really was okay. Carson didn't seem to question his father's claim to be okay, because he'd turned away and started crawling across the floor toward the window.

Faye wasn't sure why she felt so responsible for Carson. It might have been because he was drunk or it might have been because he seemed like a broken-hearted little boy trapped in a forty-year-old body. For whatever reason, Faye crawled after him, slapping him on the back to get his attention.

"Stop! Are you crazy? There's somebody out there with a gun! Somebody's *shooting* a gun."

He reached the wall and grabbed onto the windowsill to heave himself up. When his head rose above that windowsill, Faye had a horrifying vision of a bullet hitting him in the face. The first shot had come just as Mickey entered the room and turned on the light, silhouetting himself in the window. Now Carson was trying to make himself into the same kind of target.

Faye reached up, but instead of using the windowsill to haul herself off the ground, she used Carson's shoulders, hoping to use her weight to throw him off-balance. She wasn't nearly heavy enough to pull off that maneuver, so when Carson stood up, he dragged her with him.

Still sprawled on the floor, Mickey spoke sharply and with the authority of a teacher or a father. "Carson. Get down."

Carson sank back to the floor, taking Faye with him, but not before she got a glimpse of the scene outside the window. She saw no shooter, no neighbor's house, no road, no sign of any civilization at all. Mickey's back yard sloped down to a thickly wooded area, just like the woods that had harbored the shooter on the day she met Carson. Every house on the short dead-end road where he lived backed up to the same woods. It was going to be very difficult to track the shooter through all that undergrowth.

As soon as Faye hit the floor, she pulled her phone out of her pocket. Perhaps she should have called 911, but that would have required three keystroke to dial the number, plus a fourth to place the call. Instead, with a single keystroke, she let speed dial connect her directly to Chief Roy Cloud.

Another shot sounded. She hoped Roy would come to help them soon.

Chapter Twenty-four

"Alba. I have to get to Alba."

Mickey was still on all fours, but now he was crawling toward the front door of his house. Faye listened to Roy Cloud's phone ring, wondering if Mickey was planning to crawl all the way to his ex-wife's house.

"Dad, are you insane? You can't go out there."

"She's by herself. All alone. I have to get to Alba."

Carson was hanging onto his father's shirttail with both hands. "Call her, Dad. Call her and see if she's okay. You've got a cell phone in your pocket."

"Oh, yeah." Mickey pulled a clamshell phone out of his rear pocket and used his index finger to punch in a phone number.

Faye was barely two feet away from Mickey, so she could hear Alba's phone ringing almost as clearly as she heard Roy's.

When Roy picked up, Faye said only, "I'm at Mickey's. Somebody's shooting again. They're in the woods out back. I heard one of the bullets hit the house."

"We're on our way."

"Bring Bleck."

"Damn, woman. You really like that dog."

• • • • •

"You're okay? You're really okay?"

Mickey stopped talking and Faye could hear Alba's voice wafting out of Mickey's phone. The volume on Mickey's cell phone suggested that maybe his hearing was starting to go. Alba was saying something about Kenny.

"Yeah. Yeah, I need to check on him, too."

Faye looked at Carson. "Is he going to call everybody he knows? There's a nut shooting at him, but it's not like there's an earthquake or a hurricane that's trying to take out the whole county. Why would he think anybody else would be in danger?"

"He's just checking to see if any stray bullets came their way. They live next door."

"Together?" Faye asked. Then she realized what Carson was saying. "They live on both sides of Mickey's house?"

Carson nodded. He pointed to his right. "Kenny." Then he pointed to his left. "Mom."

Faye remembered that Carson had said that Kenny and Mickey lived next door to each other and always had, but it would never have occurred to her that they lived side-by-side next to Alba in the only three houses at the end of a long country road. Could these people possibly be more emotionally enmeshed? How could Mickey stand to live next door to both his ex-wife and the man who was his rival in a long-ago love affair?

"Your divorced parents live next door to each other?"

"Welcome to my life."

Mickey poked in another number and Faye thought that Carson should probably show him how to use speed dial. She had no doubt that Mickey, Kenny, and Alba talked to each other several times a day.

Faye could still hear everything coming through Mickey's phone, and Kenny's voice was clearer than Alba's had been because he was yelling. Kenny skipped right over hello and went straight to "Holy shit, there's a hole in my wall. A bullet came right through my wall and hit my kitchen cabinet."

"Hang tight, buddy," Mickey said. "The police are on their way."

• • ● • •

After they were cleared to leave the house, Faye, Mickey, and Carson stood with Roy Cloud in Mickey's back yard. Cloud was officially telling them nothing about the investigation, but they could plainly see what was going on. Bigbee had elbowed Cloud aside, pointedly taking charge of the effort to find the shooter. Bleck had helped the officers clear out the woods, and they had all moved on to searching the back yards of the only other houses on the road, Alba's and Kenny's.

Kenny stood in the yard to Faye's right, talking intently with Bigbee. When they finished, he came straight over to talk to Mickey.

"You okay, man? What in the hell? There's a bullet hole in the wall of my living room. It was from the second shot. I know that because I was counting shots and I watched it make a crater in my sheetrock. That bullet's still in my kitchen cabinet. If I'd been sitting in a different chair, it would've got me."

"Do you think it was a wild shot or was that bullet meant for you?" Mickey said. "I just thought—I mean, it was so obvious that the first shot happened right when I turned on the light that I was sure all those bullets were aimed at me. Cloud's people found a bullet in my basement wall. I've never been so glad somebody was a terrible shot in my entire life."

"It was for Alba," Mickey said. "I bet the third shot was for Alba. What was I thinking? I bet it hit her house, too. She says she's okay, but she's gotta be terrified."

Mickey went running toward his other next-door neighbor's house. Cloud, Kenny, and Faye followed close behind.

Faye would have known which house was Alba's without being told. The yard was overrun with flowers. Pink roses climbed up a white trellis over the back door, flanked by billowy blue hydrangeas, and there were daisies everywhere.

"Alba! Are you okay? Open the door right now."

Faye looked at Carson, who was doing his best not to watch his father make a spectacle of himself.

Mickey stood under the flower-laden trellis and fumbled with his keys.

Cloud muttered, "No, you don't," as he sprinted toward the door where Mickey stood. "Get out of there, Mickey! Right now!

We're still searching that yard. Alba is staying put inside her house because that's what I told her to do. You need to do the same."

Alba picked that moment to answer her door and say, "I just told you that I was okay. On the phone, remember? You need to get a grip, Mickey."

"There's a hole in Kenny's house. A hole clear through the wall. Cloud tells me there's a bullet lodged in my basement wall. The third shot must have been meant for you. Did it hit your house? Are you sure you're okay?"

Alba held out her arms and looked each of them up and down, then she bent over and surveyed the rest of her body. "I don't see any blood." She turned around and said, "Do you see any bullet holes in my back. No? I guess I'm fine, Mickey."

"I just thought—"

"Why would any of those bullets be aimed at me? I didn't know Sophia, but I loathed her. I didn't have to know her to see her for what she was. Even if I knew anything that would convict her killer, I wouldn't say anything, so why would I be a target?"

Roy leaned over and whispered in Faye's ear. "He's carrying a torch for his ex-wife after all these years. Not surprised." He might have been angry enough to fire Faye, but at least he was still speaking to her.

Mickey turned around and walked away from his ex-wife without another word. He ambled back to his own back yard as casually as if he hadn't been firmly put in his place by the woman who had left him thirty years before.

• • ● • •

Faye had fully expected the search to find nothing. This shooting was so similar to the first one she and Carson and Kenny had experienced. The shooter was invisible, hidden in a densely wooded area. There were no injuries. The motive was unclear. It was unclear who the target was. It was even unclear whether anyone was being targeted. Why would she expect that there would be more clues this time, beyond a couple of bullets lodged in walls?

She hadn't taken into account Bleck's legendary nose. This time, he turned up a weapon.

Roy was coming to the end of his questions and Faye was thinking maybe she'd be able to get Carson home soon so he could sleep off all those beers, when a young officer walked out of the woods and handed Roy his phone. He said nothing but "Hunting rifle."

Roy snatched it out of his hand, and said, "You couldn't text me this? Does Bigbee know?"

"It's not far. Didn't take me a minute to walk it. And, yeah, he knows."

Roy leaned his head meaningfully in the direction of Carson, Mickey, and Faye. The look on his face said, "Shut up in front of the witnesses," so the young man did.

Cloud used his fingers to enlarge the photo and examine details. Carson leaned over for a glance. Cloud pulled the phone away, saying only, "Evidence," but Faye could tell that Carson had seen something that surprised him.

Bigbee hustled across the yard toward them. "Dr. Callahan, Dr. Longchamp-Mantooth. You two shouldn't be here. I've already asked you all my questions for now. You should go." He flapped his hand toward Faye's rental car and walked away.

Mickey's back yard was on a sharp incline, and its surface was uneven. Carson was hours away from being able to walk straight. Within five steps, he had fallen to his knees. It took both Mickey and Roy to get the big man to his feet.

"I'll get him home tomorrow," Mickey said. "He can sleep it off here."

Carson began to argue that he wanted to go home right then.

"The both of you need to sleep this off in your own beds," Roy said. "Maybe you might think about cutting down on your drinking."

Alba announced that she'd take Carson home. Kenny, talking over her, said the same thing.

This made Faye think to give Alba and Kenny a thorough

look. If she had to guess, they were both stone cold sober. They certainly weren't visibly drunk.

Roy gave them a cool look, and Faye could almost read his mind. He wasn't sure if they could be trusted. Faye was beginning to wonder whether anybody in Sylacauga could be trusted. Everything about Roy Cloud said that he, at least, could be trusted, but how well did she know Roy? Not well at all.

Roy didn't even acknowledge that Kenny and Alba had offered their help. "If you can wait a little while longer, Doctor Faye, I'll help you get him home."

• • ● • •

By the time they reached Carson's house, he had passed from being a loud drunk to being a sleepy drunk.

"Can you walk or do you need help getting to bed?" Roy asked.

"You think I need help walking, old man?" Carson weaved his way up his own sidewalk and nearly fell three times. "Oh, okay, maybe you'd better help me get in the house."

Faye and Roy steadied him as he shuffled along. She wasn't sure whether they should put him on the couch or help him to bed. Roy saw her indecision and said, "This man's too big to spend the night on that little couch," so they walked him into his bedroom and helped him off with his shoes.

Closing the bedroom door behind them, Faye said, "He invited you in. Here's your chance to see if the notebook's here. You can do what you like with it."

"We get search warrants for a reason, Faye."

"I didn't say 'Why don't we go through Carson's desk and kitchen cabinets?' but I don't see anything wrong with looking around without touching anything."

"I'm too tired to argue ethics with you, but I'll admit to letting my own ethics slide a bit just now. I looked around that bedroom pretty good while we were pulling off Carson's boots. If the notebook is in that room, it's not in plain sight."

"I agree." Faye gave one last look around Carson's living room, because she knew that Roy Cloud was about to hustle her out the door. "I don't see it in here, either."

"Me neither."

"Alba and Kenny don't have alibis for this afternoon's shooting."

"You think they shot up their own houses?"

"Maybe. Something's not right about what happened today. I'd suspect Mickey himself if I hadn't seen him with my own eyes, lying on the floor listening to somebody else shoot a gun at him. It's not possible that those shots came from inside his house. You could at least test Kenny and Alba for gunshot residue."

"I did." The disapproving air that had hung around Cloud since he caught her at Sophia's cabin lifted a little. In fact, there was a smile playing around his wide mouth.

She punched him on the arm. "You were making fun of me for thinking they shot up their own houses, and the whole time you had the exact same suspicions. You're a sneaky one, Roy Cloud."

"It's my job, Doctor Faye. I want you to understand that the gunshot residue data will be worthless in court. The residue hangs around forever. It stays on the clothes you wear to the shooting range. It accumulates in your house over time if you shoot a lot. You saw Mickey's gun collection. Kenny's may be bigger. A defense attorney will shred any evidence we present, but we still have to take the samples. If we didn't, the defense attorney would say we must not really have believed the accused had shot a gun."

"You really think Alba's house is a hotbed of gun residue?"

"A woman living alone for twenty-nine years? Who prides herself on her independence? Who was married to a gun lover? In Oklahoma? Alba has a gun in her house and she keeps in practice. I guarantee it."

"Did somebody check on Emily?" She was ashamed that this hadn't already occurred to her.

"She cut her hand making a sandwich at lunchtime. Pretty bad. Her knife slipped off a big block of cheese and nearly took the end of her thumb off. She's been in the ER until just a few minutes ago. So nobody shot at her and she didn't shoot at anybody. She lives in the back of beyond, just like Alba, Kenny, and Mickey, so I sent somebody out to her house to check things out. Didn't find anything."

She hated to ask the next question, but it hung in the air like a thunderhead. "Sly?"

"Your husband vouches for him. I wish we had a witness that wasn't family, but this is better than nothing."

"My husband is not a liar."

"Yeah," Roy said. He put his hands in his pockets and stood there as if considering his words but, in the end, he said nothing but, "We should go."

Faye looked around Carson's living room longingly.

"Don't you worry, Doctor Faye. I'll get a warrant and come back here for a proper search. I've looked over your photos of the last pages of that notebook, and I know that I need to read the whole thing eventually."

"Yes, you do. We both do. We have to find out what Carson did with it."

He continued speaking as if he hadn't heard her. "I also need to understand why Carson wanted that notebook badly enough to interfere with a murder investigation. Which you, by the way are no longer working on. Remember?"

Chapter Twenty-five

Faye got to Sly's house in time for supper, but she wished she hadn't. Joe didn't have anything to say to her, and she was beginning to wonder if he ever would again. They even washed the dishes together in silence, and she ached for all those evenings when they had used that time to laugh and talk. When her phone rang, she was relieved to have the chance to go outside and take it.

"I am so sorry. I feel like a fool. You must think I'm a total drunk."

Carson's liver hadn't finished processing all that alcohol yet, but he'd sobered up enough to enter the remorse phase of a bender.

"It's okay, Carson. Sometimes people drink a little too much. You'll be fine tomorrow." Thinking of the coming hangover, she said, "Or maybe the next day."

"When I heard that gunshot, I thought I'd lost my dad. He's not perfect, but I love him. I really do love him. I can't help it."

"You're not supposed to help it. Mickey is your father."

He was sobbing now. "I don't know what to think about my mother. Maybe the asshole was aiming at her, too. Maybe she did the shooting herself, but she favors a revolver, not a rifle. Maybe she took that rifle out of Kenny's house and opened fire at him and my dad both. It wouldn't be hard to walk down that ravine behind the house and take an easy shot. There's trails all through there. I spent whole days out back when I was a kid and I know exactly where I'd stand if I wanted to aim at all three houses."

"Could Kenny have done the same thing? Gone down one of those trails, shot the rifle, hid it, then come out of the woods? It would have been pretty safe to shoot a hole through his own wall, since he wasn't in there. I notice the shots at Mickey's and Alba's houses went wild, so they would have been pretty safe, too."

Carson snorted. "It's easier to imagine Mom with murder in her eye than Kenny, but yeah. There's paths out in those woods that would take you where you needed to go."

He started to laugh and seemed to be having trouble stopping.

"Carson. Carson, are you okay?"

"Yeah, but I just thought of something. Mom would never put a hole in the side of that house that she likes so much. Besides, what if she accidentally shot a rose bush? It would be just like her to mess up her alibi by shooting wild so none of her flowers came to harm."

"Roy is an excellent investigator. I haven't known him long, but I can tell. He's going to get to the bottom of this. It's important to him." She wasn't sure she could say the same things of Bigbee, who was, after all, in charge.

"But what if he's too late?" His voice was thick with tears. "I can't lose any of them, Faye. Not my parents and not Kenny. They're all I have. I can't let them die and I can't stand it if any of them goes to jail. Do you think maybe Emily did the shooting?"

"She has an excellent alibi and a lot of witnesses that say she couldn't have done it."

The sobs stopped and his voice grew quiet, as if he was just too tired to talk any more. "There's somebody else who could have done it, but you won't like it."

"Sly has an alibi." She neglected to mention that Sly's alibi was given to him by his loving son.

"I don't really want it to be Sly, either. It's been years since I was a little kid riding in his truck, but I still care about him. Bottom line, I am completely certain it wasn't Mom or Kenny. Neither one of them would have ever shot into a house with me in it."

"Carson. We were in my car. How would they have known that you were there?"

This thought brought the sobs back.

"Listen. We both have loved ones to protect, and we both want to get to the truth. I have an important question and I need for you to get yourself calm so that you can answer it. Can you do that?"

A deep breath. "I can."

"Just now, you said something about your mother going to Kenny's house to get the rifle. Why did you say that?"

"I told you. Her gun is a revolver."

"But why Kenny's house? Couldn't she have bought it or taken it from your dad's house? It would take him a while to notice that one gun out of his huge collection was missing."

"You'd think that but no. He'd notice. Anyway, it wasn't one of Dad's guns, I know that for sure. It was Kenny's. Faye, I can't be the one to testify against him. I can't."

"Maybe you won't have to. The police can look up the registration—"

Carson's laugh was explosive. "Kenny inherited that gun from his dad who got it from his dad who probably bought it from a friend during the Great Depression. Do you think one of them got up one day and said, 'I think I'll go register all my guns?'"

"Maybe it's not his. Are you sure?"

"Just because I'm drunk, it doesn't mean I'm not right. Kenny taught me to hunt and that's the first rifle I ever shot. I'm sure."

• • • • •

When Faye went back into the house, it was with the express intent of getting Sly and Joe to talk to her. There were too many shootings and too much fear, injury, and death. Everyone in Sylacauga must want to see an arrest immediately. Any arrest. Fear made it too easy to look for a scapegoat. Her family needed to pull together.

She was surprised to realize how much she trusted Roy Cloud to be fair to Sly but, sooner or later, Bigbee was going to decide it was time to pay more attention to the suspect who had already done time in a penitentiary.

She came in the door and walked straight to Sly's easy chair, where he was spending yet another night pretending to watch TV.

"Do you keep your old trucking logs?"

Sly looked at her. His eyes were so bleary that she almost suspected him of drinking again.

"Yeah," he said, but he didn't budge from the chair.

"This is important, Sly. How else do you plan to establish an alibi for a murder that happened nearly thirty years ago?"

His expression was flat, emotionless, unreadable. She wondered if he really didn't care if he got sent back to the penitentiary. Then the moment passed and he looked like a man who was scared to death of being railroaded because he looked conveniently guilty.

Sly heaved himself to his feet, opening a narrow closet door that opened into the hall. It was filled with logbooks stacked in disorderly heaps. When he reached in for one, several of those heaps teetered, spilling logbooks onto the hall floor.

"Are they labeled?"

"Nope."

"How many years did you drive?"

He looked at her like he didn't understand the question. "Always."

She crouched down and picked up a couple of logbooks at random. Opening them, she saw that they were as different from Sophia Townsend's notebooks as was possible for them to be. There were no musings and no drawings lovingly rendered. Sly's records showed only the dates of each job, the mileage, the fuel burned, the time spent on the road, and the money earned. Stapled to the back cover were receipts for the fuel that had taken him all those miles.

They were the work of a man who was in a hurry, a man who would dearly love to never see another logbook, a man who deep down just wanted to drive home. They were the work of a man who hated his job as much as Sophia Townsend had loved hers.

She ran a finger over the page, feeling the depressions left by ballpoint pens in whatever color Sly had handy. Blue, red, black. Once, even purple, which led her to wonder where a man without a teenaged daughter got a purple pen. Some pages were dotted and rippled as if their words had been written in the rain.

"These look real," she said.

"You thought I was lying?"

"No, I was trying to think like a judge and jury, and a judge and jury is going to love these dated receipts. They're not going to wonder whether these logbooks are something that you fabricated to cover your tracks."

Sly opened the back of one notebook and riffled through the receipts as if he could remember every mile that he drove and every gallon of diesel that he burned.

"Sly, can you look through these for proof of where you were during the period of time after Sophia Townsend went missing? Preferably from the beginning of August through the end of the month, when they closed that excavation with her at the bottom of it. Please tell me you were out-of-state."

"I did a lot of runs out to California back then. I hope that's where I was at."

"Me, too."

Joe's face was unreadable, but she thought maybe he was grateful to her for helping his father get himself out of a tough spot. He didn't seem ready to speak to her yet. He had never stayed angry with her for this long.

A person could be pushed too far, and no one could ever be completely sure where another person might draw the line. She shouldn't have been surprised to learn that Joe's line lay on the boundary between openness and secrecy or between truth and deceit. She had pushed that boundary harder than she'd intended.

As his father took stacks of his old logbooks into his room to review, Joe picked up the book he'd been reading. He took it with him to their room, and he closed the door.

• • ● • •

Faye had forced Sly into action, urging him to find any record that remained from 1987 that might prove where he was and what he was doing at the time. Maybe it was time to ask herself to do the same thing. She needed to find out what Sly was doing in 1987. No, not just Sly. She needed to see what she could find out about the activities of all the people who surrounded Sophia Townsend in her last days.

Faye still had library access at the university and she could access it from her laptop. That access included old newspapers. Which newspapers were available was catch-as-catch-can and the time spans covered were spotty, depending on whether someone had decided it was worthwhile to scan them. Still, it was a start.

Of all the suspects, only one of them had been actively courting publicity at the time of Sophia Townsend's death, and that person was Alba Callahan. Beyond the question of whether she might have killed Sophia Townsend or Kira Denton, Faye was a little bit fascinated with this woman who had been rabble-rousing way back when Faye was just hitting puberty. If anybody was savvy enough to get newspaper coverage for her protests, it would be Alba Callahan.

Faye put her computer on the kitchen table and went to the university website. Accessing its library database was painfully slow, given Sly's turtle-speed Internet service, but she would never ever complain to him about it. She suspected that he'd signed up for it solely because she and Joe were coming to visit.

Eventually, the index for the Sylacauga newspaper finished downloading, telling her that the paper had not yet digitized its morgue, so she turned to Tulsa. Once she made that choice, it was a simple matter of navigating to 1987.

Or not. The people in Tulsa must be busily scanning their old papers, with no end in sight, because full text copies of editions from 1911 to 1922 were available and then there was a huge gap before coverage resumed from 1988 to the present. If she had to guess, she'd say that they had begun by scanning the years framing the 1921 race riots, giving historians the opportunity to study the years leading up to the tragedy. They had probably scanned papers as they were printed after 1988, but it was going to take a long time to digitize the long decades between the Tulsa riots and the fall of the Berlin Wall.

Faye stared at the number 1988, taunting her by going almost far enough back in history but not quite.

No matter. Faye was completely sure that Alba did not fade into obscurity after Sophia Townsend had her arrested for protesting her dig in 1987. And Faye was right.

A search for the single word "Alba" brought up a dozen or more hits. Faye was never so glad she wasn't searching for a woman named "Susan." There weren't many Albas in the world.

And there weren't many activists as photogenic as Alba Callahan.

Almost every one of the articles that mentioned Alba Callahan by name included a photograph. Alba had resisted the 1980s trend of "big hair," keeping her blond locks straight and very long. It must have been so hot, wearing that cape of hair in the Oklahoma sun while protesting at the state capitol, and it must have stayed in her eyes when the spring winds were whipping.

But what an asset Alba's hair and face and form had been. What news photographer could resist a photo of lean, strong Alba forcing her way through a crowd of people grabbing at her hair and her tight black jeans? They might try and hold her back, but Alba's energy was unstoppable.

One photographer had won a regional news award for a photo of Alba in action, but that wasn't the one that held Faye's attention. The photo of Alba that Faye would always remember showed her as an angry woman who was shaking her fist at authority and paying no attention at all to the twelve-year-old in the background. Carson lingered under a tree, bent over an open book.

This photo clarified a couple of things for Faye.

First, it answered the question of how big Carson had been when his dad was working with Sophia Townsend. The answer was "big." In this photo of his mother taken less than a year later,

Faye could see that Carson was already taller than many grown men, with the beginnings of the broad torso and tree-like legs of the man she knew. She couldn't imagine Carson caving in a woman's head now, much less at age eleven but, for a boy with this much body mass, all it would have taken was a lucky blow. But did a child that age have what it took to bury a dead body in a place it might never be found?

This was a horrible thought that she pushed away, but another horrible one crept into its place. What would a father do to protect a son who had killed someone, accidentally or not? Would he help his son bury the body? Would the boy's mother help him bury it? What would a secret like that do to a marriage?

The second thing that the photo of Carson and his mother did was to give her a glimpse into the man's formative years. Faye hoped her children never saw her as angry as Alba was in this picture, and she hoped they never felt as lonely as Carson looked.

She remembered that Carson had said that the rifle found behind his father's house had belonged to Kenny, and she remembered that he'd said that Alba's gun was a revolver. The conclusion that she drew from the discovery of Kenny's rifle was not necessarily that Kenny was the killer. Faye's takeaway was that Alba seemed like as reasonable a suspect for the killings as Kenny or Mickey. Most damning was her ready access to the arsenals in Kenny's and Mickey's houses.

Faye knew that Alba owned a revolver and knew how to shoot it. She also knew that Mickey moved in and out of Alba's house at will. Was it too much to speculate that all three of them were the closest of neighbors, casually popping into each other's houses to borrow a cup of sugar or a couple of eggs? Or a rifle capable of dropping an animal the size of deer? Or of dropping a human being?

When Faye signed off the library site, more than an hour had passed. Joe was still in bed reading and Sly's door was closed. She should go to bed. More than that, she should go try to make peace with her husband, but she was dreading it. She put it off a few more minutes by deciding that she had one last thing to do.

She typed up a summary of what she'd learned about Alba Callahan from the Tulsa paper. She added a few paragraphs summing up her conversation with Carson, which made her sadder every time she thought about it. Then she constructed a timeline based on Sophia's field notes:

Late May: The dig began, but interesting finds were scant and remained so, because Sophia was still griping about the lack of datable materials in July.

Mid-June: Sly can be presumed to have been absent from the dig for any later event, because of his testimony that he only worked for Sophia for three weeks.

Prior to July 30: Sophia argued with Kenny about laboratory dating, and he expressed particular reservations about destructive dating techniques. She sent samples to a lab in Canada during this period, with no luck getting reliable dates.

July 31: Emily found and broke a potsherd. It is unclear whether she made her first trip to the cabin before or after this event, but it cannot have been long after, as Sophia was last seen on August 7.

Early August: Sophia grumbled about the lab in Canada's failure to get any data from the potsherd or the lithics she had sent.

August 7: The pearls, the figurine, and a skeleton were found and the entries end. Sophia seemed convinced that this burial was so significant to the Creeks that the project would be stopped, perhaps forever. She sent her workers home early, with the possible exception of Mickey, who would have helped her excavate the artifacts found with the skeleton. No witness has admitted to seeing Sophia Townsend alive after this date. Emily and Mickey state that they visited her cabin after she disappeared and came away with the impression that she was still alive, but they did not see her.

August 31: The excavation is closed with Sophia Townsend at the bottom. This is the last possible date of her death.

Faye attached both of her summaries and the timeline to an e-mail and addressed it to Roy Cloud.

Dear Roy,

I spoke with Carson today, and I thought you would want to know what he said. I know that I'm not working on the case now, but I feel obligated as a citizen to let you know anything I learn that could help you find the killer. And the shooter, if they are not the same person. If Carson is right that the gun is Kenny's, that is a literal smoking gun pointing at him. But Carson, who knows all of these people better than you or I do, did not think that finding Kenny's gun cleared Alba of suspicion.

Based on that conversation, I did some digging around to see what Alba was doing around the time of Sophia Townsend's disappearance. I found no smoking gun, but I've attached some newspaper articles that tell us something about what Alba was like in the eighties. I keep coming around to the question of what any of these people might have been like when they were younger. We can only know them now, and that's a hindrance to getting to the truth.

Speaking of the truth, you were correct that I was wrong to betray your trust by going to Sophia's cabin and taking the risk that I might destroy evidence. It occurs to me that I have not said that I am sorry. I was wrong and I apologize.

I'm sure there are clues in Sophia's notes that I have failed to catch, and I'm sure you will want to go through them yourself. I'll drop my copies off at the station tomorrow.

For what it's worth, I hope you find the bastard who did this to Sophia. After reading her notebooks, I have grown quite attached to her. When you read them, I suspect you will feel the same.

All my best,
Faye

By writing that e-mail, Faye found that she could make peace with losing her job as Roy Cloud's consultant. The more important thing was to regain his respect. Why should that be? She'd only known the man a few days. Why did she care so much what he thought?

Deep down, Faye knew the answer. Until she'd been immersed in the maelstrom of adultery that had surrounded Sophia Townsend, she might have denied that people could develop such strong feelings so quickly, and she might have denied that she could ever be tempted by any man who wasn't Joe. This was no longer true.

Roy Cloud was not Mickey Callahan, nor was he Kenny Meadows, but a woman knows when a man admires her. And Faye was not Sophia Townsend. Joe was the love of her life, but she no longer felt smug in her fidelity. Only now did she realize that it had never before been tested.

It was time for Faye to admit that she was human. It was time to admit to herself that if there hadn't been a Joe in her life, there might have been a Roy. She would never act on that and neither would Roy, but that didn't mean she didn't feel a tinge of sadness at what might have been.

Sophia had possessed an uncanny understanding of human emotions and she'd used that knowledge for her own entertainment. Faye, on the other hand, had a lifelong history of being oblivious to matters of the heart. Being oblivious had brought her to some terrible decisions, but maybe she had learned something over the years.

After reading the final, wistful entry in Sophia's notebook, Faye understood her better. She'd been judging Sophia's behavior for days, but her capacity for judgment was all burnt out. All she had left was pity.

Sophia had led Mickey and Kenny to hurt their wives and each other. Sadder still, they had all hurt Carson, who had been a defenseless child. Faye didn't intend to go down that road. It was time to go patch things up with her husband.

She pressed "Send" and her message to Roy Cloud went out into the mysterious tangle of communication that was the Internet. Then she got up and walked away.

Chapter Twenty-six

Faye had her hand on the bedroom doorknob when Sly came out of his room.

"I found my logs for 1987, Faye. All of 'em, even August."

He wanted to sit right down at the kitchen table and show her what he'd found. Faye didn't want to wait any longer to talk to Joe, but she couldn't bring herself to push Sly aside when he had information that might clear him of murder. He looked more alive than he had in days.

"Show me."

"I wasn't in town when Sophia died. Look. I left town at noon on August 7, and she was working at the dig all afternoon. Mickey, Kenny, and Emily were all with her. Nobody saw her after those three went home that day, but my receipts show that I was down past Houston by that time. Early the next day, I headed west toward New Mexico and kept going for two weeks. See?" He held out a sketch showing his route, marked with dates and times. "I never looped back close enough to Oklahoma to run home and kill her, not and get back to my route, and these logs say I stayed on it the whole time. Receipts, too. Do you think the weigh stations keep their records for this long?"

"I don't know. But even if they don't, these logbooks look solid. They give you an alibi from noon on August 7 until…" She checked the sketch. "Until six o'clock on the evening of August 21. You never saw her after that trip?"

"No. By the time I got home, she'd left her job, and I never saw her after that."

"That's good. Really good."

"Do these logs this fix things, Faye? Even if the weigh stations or the trucking company can't back me up?"

"They sure help. Especially these receipts. You did well for yourself tonight, Sly."

He ducked his head at the praise. "I've got grandchildren. I don't have time to go back to the pen."

Faye looked at the meticulous map Sly had made of his August 1987 travels, drawn to scale with an architect's care. The distance of each leg on the route was labeled in numbers that looked more drawn than written. His handwriting had the elegant neatness of people old enough to have been taught penmanship. Like Joe, Sly had a mental acuity and an attention to detail that put the lie to those who underestimated their intelligence.

This map almost cleared her father-in-law, but not quite. Sophia had been seen alive late on the afternoon of August 7, 1987. Sly was firmly in the clear for that day and for most of the rest of the month. But the excavation was not closed until August 31, and nobody could be absolutely sure she was dead before that day when she was buried beneath five feet of red clay.

The conflicting descriptions from the people who visited her cabin after August 7 suggested that she had lived for at least a few more days, closing up the house and leaving with a packed suitcase. If she'd survived to the evening of August 21, then Sly would in theory have had ten days to kill her, but Faye couldn't bring herself to tell him that. Maybe later, but not while he was sitting here victorious over finding his trucking logs and sorting out what they meant.

"This will really help, Sly," she said as he stepped back into his room and closed the door.

She immediately regretted not telling him that he wasn't in the clear yet. Keeping that painful knowledge to herself was the kind of omission that Joe would condemn as deceptive. She knew Joe would think she was wrong, but she just couldn't bear to wipe that proud, hopeful look off her father-in-law's tired face. Clutching Sly's sketch, she opened the door to the bedroom she shared with Joe and stepped in.

• • ● • •

"I thought you weren't coming."

Joe sat up in bed with a book in his hand. Was he waiting up for her? Had he been doing that all week while she obsessed over the fate of Sophia Townsend?

"I was talking to your dad. Well, I was futzing around on the Internet and then I was talking to your dad. I'm sorry it's so late."

She wanted to say, "What have you done to make me think you wanted me to come to bed?" but she swallowed that testy comment.

As much as Joe might want to believe that nothing less than undiluted truth was acceptable, Faye knew that there were times when silence was better than saying the wrong thing. At the moment, there was only one thing she could say that was better than silence. She'd already said it to Roy Cloud when she should have said it to Joe first.

"I'm sorry."

"Sorry for what? Some of it? All of it?"

"All of it. I'm sorry I didn't tell you that your dad's potsherd linked him to Sophia and maybe to her murder. I just…I just didn't want you to know. I didn't want it to be true."

"You didn't tell Cloud, either. What if my dad *is* guilty? You didn't know him back then and he's done some bad things. Maybe he did kill Sophia Townsend. Would you be happy if Dad got away with murder because you didn't tell Cloud and Bigbee what you knew?"

"I didn't want that to be true, either."

Joe sat up straighter and pulled the covers up to his waist, but he didn't invite her join him.

"Dad didn't tell me he worked for her. You didn't tell me that he's been keeping a potsherd she found for all these years. You didn't tell Cloud about it, either. Carson didn't tell anybody about that notebook he stole. As best I can tell Roy Cloud hasn't done any lying, but he's the only one."

"You're both very honest people." *And maybe I just found out what attracts me to a man.*

"I didn't want to hurt you," she continued. "Or your dad. Not even Roy Cloud. The funny thing is that I did those deceitful things while I was trying so hard to get to the truth."

"Is that why you're so obsessed with this woman's death? I couldn't figure it out, myself."

"Be fair. Until this morning, helping find Sophia's killer was my job. Maybe I got carried away because I was afraid for Sly. And, knowing me, you know there was probably some unhealthy obsession with solving an unsolvable puzzle. Is that so wrong?"

"No, not too much." Joe pulled back the covers and fluffed up the pillow next to him. "Come over here?"

She didn't have to be asked twice.

"Faye, look at all these people. Kenny. Mickey. Sophia. Carson. Secrets are their sickness. Don't be one of them."

She stretched her full length along Joe's body and pressed her lips to his neck. "Are we going to be okay?"

He didn't speak at first, and her heart stopped. Then he said, "Yes. Forever," and reached for her with both hands.

● ● ● ● ●

Faye knew all was well with the world when Joe greeted the morning with a griddle and his incomparable French toast, moist and eggy and heaped with powdered sugar.

The smell of cinnamon and vanilla had also roused Sly, who was talking a blue streak and chugging down coffee. He seemed to have had enough of being Old Man Sly, because there was no shuffle in his feet and no stammer in his mouth. He was busy telling Joe about every single highway he'd traveled in 1987, and he was doing it in excruciating detail, but Joe didn't seem to mind. He was, in fact, encouraging him.

"Want some cream and sugar? So tell me more about driving across Death Valley in a truck with an iffy radiator."

Joe was a good listener, so he had both eyes fastened on his dad, but he held out a plate heaped high with carbs without looking and Faye grabbed it.

"You two go ahead with your talk about Death Valley and eighteen-wheelers and don't mind me. I haven't done anything important this morning. I just figured out how to get in touch with somebody who probably talked to Sophia Townsend about her work in 1987 and, even better, probably remembers it. It may even be somebody who can help us prove that she was dead before you got home from your trip, Sly."

There. She'd admitted to Sly that his logbooks weren't enough to clear him on their own. He didn't even flinch. He was plenty smart enough to figure out the truth without her help. She'd been babying a grown man for no reason. She was going to have to stop protecting people.

"Daughter, how do you plan to find somebody that remembers talking to her after all this time?" Sly said, tapping his empty plate with his fork so that Joe knew to reload it.

"In her notes, she said that she was getting labwork that would have been very specialized at that time. Maybe even experimental. For whatever reason—either because American labs weren't doing the test or because they charged too much—she had to use a Canadian lab to get the job done. How many analytical labs in Canada do you think were trying to test blood residue on ancient stone tools in 1987?"

"I don't know," Sly said. "Do you?"

"I've got the Internet and a telephone. Somebody knows and I will find them."

● ● ● ● ●

By the time Faye had finished her French toast in the Central Time Zone, Canadians in the Newfoundland, Atlantic, and Eastern Time Zones were at work. After she ran through all the analytical laboratories in those time zones, she could head west to the Mountain Time Zone and beyond. It was time to start rolling back the years to 1987.

All morning, she talked to twenty-two-year-old lab techs who didn't have much to say beyond "Eh?" but, by noon, she'd hit paydirt in the form of an illustrious professor who had been a grad student in 1987. He had worked in his dissertation advisor's lab, doing work that was cutting edge, even experimental. When he told Faye that, she knew that all those phone calls had paid off.

"I remember Sophia," the professor said. "She had the most wonderful voice. I've forgotten most of our other clients, but I remember her."

Faye was getting a little tired of hearing about Sophia Townsend's phenomenal sex appeal. At least it was proving helpful now.

"I remember calling her to say that we'd failed to get enough blood residue to carbon date the spear point she sent." He sounded like he was still sorry he'd disappointed her.

"She would have sent it in late July of 1987. Is that the sample you're talking about?"

"Sounds right. I remember that it was a hot summer. And I remember that she sent a tiny little potsherd—plain, nothing fancy—for thermoluminescence testing sometime after that. Maybe the end of July? Early August? Anyway, I actually came up with a date for her on that. About a thousand years back, I think. I tried to call her several times to tell her the good news, but I never got through. Just left messages on her machine. Eventually, I mailed the report, but I never heard from her again."

Faye wondered if the report had languished in a post office box until it was thrown away. Maybe it was there still. Or maybe it was hiding in a deep-storage file kept by the Muscogee (Creek) Nation.

"She never sent you a pearl or a sample taken from a clay figurine?"

"Nope. I'd remember something like a pearl. And I'd remember if I had ever heard her voice again."

• • ● • •

So Sophia had disappeared from phone contact with the Canadian lab after she sent the plain potsherd for testing. Her notes were very clear that she had sent that potsherd a week before she disappeared. Faye thought that pointed to a death date shortly after she stopped writing in the journal, perhaps on the very day of the last entry, although that didn't explain why two different people had reported evidence that she'd been home after that. She wasn't too keen on talking to Roy Cloud, possibly ever again, but she really did need to tell him about the Canadian lab.

Maybe she could get away with an e-mail.

When she opened her e-mail, she saw that Roy had already written to her.

> Dear Doctor Faye,
>
> Sometimes I am hasty when I'm under stress. In your shoes, I might have been just as quick to hightail it to Arkansas to look for clues if I thought it would save my father-in-law. Why don't we hit the reset button? I need your skills.
>
> I'm probably smart enough to notice if you're trying to cover for Sly, and I think you're honorable enough not to do that. (Again.) If you promise to be straight with me from here on out, I'd like you to stay on as my consultant, even though it will naturally more get Bigbee's goat if you do. Perhaps we shouldn't tell him.
>
> Since I believe you'll be willing to come back and help me out, I'm not going to waste time waiting for you to decide. Come to the station when you can. I'll be there, buried under paperwork that is not doing a damn thing to solve this case for me. Bigbee says he's spending the morning at his hotel trying to dig out from some of his other cases, so we will not have his judgmental eyes on us. That should be a relief.
>
> All the best,
> Roy

PS—Keep your copies of the notes. It will be days before I have time to read them, and I probably wouldn't understand the archaeological stuff anyway. You, on the other hand, are fully capable of teasing enough evidence to convict a murderer out of a stray mark Sophia Townsend left in the margin in 1987. Please do that soon, okay?

• ● ● ● •

Joe leaned against the kitchen door and watched Faye pack her briefcase. "Did you have any luck talking to Canada? Cloud will want to know."

"I did. And I think the answers I got should help your dad. Cross your fingers on that. Otherwise, Sly's in a bad spot."

He saw her scratching around in the bottom of her purse, so he reached in the kitchen drawer and handed her a pen.

"Remember the broken potsherd? Well, the Canadian professor said that Sophia sent him a small, plain potsherd just before she went silent. Don't you think she would have sent him the least interesting part of the broken sherd? And don't you think that the one I found was one of the engraved pieces, which she would have kept?"

"And you think Dad's got the third sherd? How'd he get it?"

"He's going to have to tell us that."

Joe was still leaning on the door like it needed him to hold it up. "That's all real interesting, but what are you getting at?"

"Why did I find a potsherd in Sophia's grave? Why wasn't it in one of those boxes of artifacts that had been stored all those years? We've been thinking that she might have surprised a thief with a canvas bag full of valuable artifacts—the pearls, the figurine, maybe more. By that logic, this person was probably the person who killed her, maybe by accident and maybe on purpose. Then the killer buried the artifacts with her, because selling them would make it possible to trace them back to the killer."

Joe thought for a moment. "The potsherd would have been packed up and in the shed by that time. The killer would have had to go through the storage boxes, find the potsherd, and put it in the bag with the other stolen stuff. Which wouldn't have been that hard to do, but why? It's not valuable, is it?"

"Nope. We really need to find out whether one of her workers worked late with her that day. Nobody else but Sophia and her helper, if she had one, could have known they'd uncovered valuable grave goods. She says in her notes that she was planning to ask Mickey and maybe she did. Or maybe she changed her mind and asked Kenny or someone else. Or maybe she sent them all home and did the work by herself. If she wasn't alone, then the person who stayed late might have killed her or told someone what they'd found. Word would have gotten around fast enough for somebody else to kill her. All indications, though, are that it was Mickey."

Joe announced, "I've thought he did it all along," with a certainty that surprised Faye. Joe wouldn't accuse a man of murder lightly. "Emily wasn't the helper that day. That's for sure. I don't think she's a good enough liar to convince Roy Cloud that she didn't know about the pearls and the figurine."

"What about Kenny? I think he could tell Roy lies with a straight face. So could Mickey. Adulterers are usually very good liars."

"Could be. I'd rather think it was Mickey, because I don't like him, but I've got a better reason for thinking it wasn't Kenny. Stealing those things would go against his beliefs about disturbing burials goods."

"What if he really needed money?"

"Nope. Don't think so. What I do think is that he would have told Sophia straight-out that she was wrong to send that potsherd to a lab that was going to make dust out of it. I also don't think he knew about the bone."

"I think they all knew about the bone."

"Yeah, but Sophia told them she thought it came from a deer. If Kenny thought for sure it was human, he would have reported it right away."

Faye couldn't say that she disagreed. If she were Sophia and she had something to hide, it was the ethically flexible Mickey that she'd invite to help her. She shouldered her briefcase and gathered an armful of her copies of Sophia's field notebooks.

"Where do you think Alba fits into all this?" she asked. "The dead woman was having an affair with Alba's husband. Roy's got to be more suspicious of Alba than he lets on."

"No joke."

"If I were Alba, and if Sophia was fooling around with you, I might have killed her myself."

• • ● • •

On her way out of the house to meet Roy, Faye did her habitual morning check of the mantel and found that the potsherd was still not there. She needed to find out how Sly got it, even if the conversation was painful for him. She knew of no other candidate for the man Sophia called the Hulk. It had not escaped Faye's attention that the Hulk was the only employee that she had never insulted.

In her last entry, Sophia had said that she gave a piece of her heart to a man with a wife and child. She had also said that she gave him a piece of the potsherd.

The sequence of events between Sophia and Sly seemed pretty clear. Faye knew now how he got the potsherd, and she knew that Sly was a state away when she was last seen. He said he never saw her again after leaving on that trip, so she must have given him the sherd sometime after Emily broke it and before he left for California. Did Faye really need to know the details of his relationship with Sophia? Maybe. Those details could point to the killer.

Asking Sly pointed questions about his relationship with Sophia could cause him pain, but Faye couldn't afford to respect his secrets. Secrecy had upended her own life over the past few days, and it had protected Sophia's killer for a lot of years. When Faye got home that evening, she and Sly needed to have a heart-to-heart talk.

• ● ● ● •

Roy Cloud was an obstinate man.

Faye, for the fourth time, tried to explain to him that her conversation with the lab-tech-turned-professor proved that Sophia Townsend died on or shortly after August 7. More personally important to her was proving to Roy that she died while Sly was far away, and he knew it. Roy was having none of it.

"She stopped responding to calls from the lab long before Sly got home," she said. "You know she would have called the lab tech back, especially since he left messages telling her the good news."

"Maybe she had her reasons. Maybe she'd already left on that mysterious trip. Maybe she knew he'd eventually mail the report. Maybe she didn't go quiet on him because she was dead. Maybe she had better things to do."

Faye slapped her hand on a printout of the last few pages of the last notebook. "Listen to this, Roy, because it's even more important. Pearls are a whole different thing from potsherds and spear points. They were once alive. In a perfect world, they could be carbon-dated. There are complicating factors, especially with 1980s technology, but still. She was working with a lab willing to try experimental analyses at the very edge of what was possible. If she had multiple pearls, and we know she did, I'm sure she would have sent one and asked them to go for the gusto. But she didn't. She had to have been killed right after those pearls surfaced. I just know it."

Roy shook his head.

Faye tried another tack. "Having read her notebooks, I see that writing in them was part of the fabric of her life. The best explanation for the lack of entries after August 7 is that she was dead after that."

"I hear what you're saying and it's good logic, but it's not proof. Maybe she started another notebook that we don't know about."

"Oh, fine. Be that way." As a parting shot, Faye said, "If you're wondering why the project budget was overspent with very little to show for it in the field, here's your answer. She paid for multiple lab tests, and we know that they were experimental. Doesn't that say to you that she was obsessed, possibly to an unhealthy degree, with putting an objectively measured date on the site? She wouldn't have gone silent on the man who was helping her do that."

"Still not proof. If you want to change my mind, you're going to have to do better than that, Doctor Faye."

"But Roy, you can't—"

The door behind her burst open. Alba strode in, followed by a stammering clerk telling her to stop doing what she had already done. "Ma'am, Chief Cloud is in a meeting and can't be disturbed. I told you to wait outside. You can't go in there. Ma'am!"

Alba, as put-together as always, was rocking a pencil skirt, leather jacket, and ankle boots, all of them pale yellow. The boots' tall, chunky heels did not slow her down.

"Roy Cloud, I demand to know what you're doing to protect my ex-husband and my son from the nut who's running around Sylacauga with a gun. If you don't keep them both safe, I'll make you miserable for the rest of your life."

"I'm on it," Roy says. "And what about you? Don't you need protecting?"

She waves a hand. "There weren't any bullet holes in my house. Just Kenny's and Mickey's. Why would anybody come for me?"

"I can't say anything to you about an ongoing murder investigation."

This statement startled Alba into a rare moment of silence, but she recovered. "Are you presuming that this has something to do with Sophia Townsend's death?"

Cloud gave her the flick of the eyelid that said, *Are you nuts? Of course I'm presuming that.*

"I'm not going to share sensitive information with you," he said, "but why wouldn't you think those bullets had anything to do with her death? When have you ever known this many bullets to fly in this county? Other than bullets aimed at deer, I mean.

It can't be a coincidence that all this shooting is happening the very week we uncovered Sophia Townsend."

"The first shooting happened before she came back to haunt us all, so I don't think it's related. I've been terrified for my son's safety ever since he told me about it."

"What about Kenny?" Cloud said. "He was there, too. And now somebody's shot up his house. You're not worried about the man who's been your neighbor for your entire adult life?"

"Nobody's going to hurt Kenny. He's never home any more. I'm actually surprised he was there yesterday. He's got a new girlfriend and he spends his time with her. I'm glad for Kenny. It's taken him all these years to get over his wife—what was her name? Maria? He's pined for Maria ever since she joined the Peace Corps because it would take her half a world away from him."

"When did she do that?"

"The very day she found out that Kenny was sleeping with Sophia Townsend. And before you drag her into this, know that she was gone at least a month before the woman disappeared. I doubt Maria came back from Ecuador long enough to do the killing."

"And you know this because...?"

"This is a small town. Everybody knows everything."

"Then sleeping at his girlfriend's house doesn't make Kenny all that safe, does it?" She shrugged in acknowledgement.

"To answer the question that brought you here," Cloud said, "I've got an officer watching Mickey's house. Kenny's, too. If you'll tell me where he's sleeping, I can send the officer to the house where he actually is."

"Her name's Chloe Darwin. She lives on Market Street, near the courthouse."

"I'll send somebody right away. It wouldn't hurt anything for your ex-husband to go stay someplace else, too. You got any ideas?"

"He's not in that house your people are guarding. I told him to go stay with our son. Maybe the shooter won't find him there. If so, at least they can protect each other."

Faye wasn't sure how they were going to protect each other from bullets tearing through walls, but if imagining that made Alba feel better, so be it. She also wasn't sure she'd want to be Alba, staying alone on a street that both her neighbors had fled.

"If all these shootings are truly about Sophia's death," Alba said, "then maybe the killer is trying to shut up the people who might pose a threat. That's who's being targeted. Kenny on the first day, if you can blame that shooting on a body that hadn't surfaced yet. That evening, Kira was shot while she was guarding the grave. And today, Mickey and Kenny."

"And maybe you."

Alba didn't even acknowledge Cloud's interruption. "Poor Kira. Maybe she was just too close to the truth." After a pause that hung on too long, Alba announced, "I have to go."

"Go where?" Faye asked.

"To find Emily." Alba did not say, *To find Emily, dummy*, but her tone said it for her. "Emily knows as much as anybody about Sophia Townsend's last days. Kenny, Carson, Mickey—they've all got people who care for them. Have you checked on Emily?"

She turned an appraising stare on Cloud.

"I sent some people around to her place yesterday evening, right after the shooting on your street."

Alba was moving toward the door as quickly as she had come through it. "Not yesterday. Today. Have you checked on her today? That poor woman lives alone in the big fine house her husband built for her. It's smack in the middle of fifteen acres. You know that, Roy. It's not like our street where Mickey drops a hammer on his toe and Kenny comes running when he howls. Nobody would hear shots at Emily's house."

She was out the door. Roy called out, "Alba, wait. We'll go with you," but his office door was already slamming behind her.

As Faye and Roy scrambled to catch her, Faye said, "Who's carrying a torch for whom?"

"Maybe. Or maybe she came to tell us where Kenny and Mickey are hiding. Could be that she wants the word out. Maybe she hopes the killer finds them."

Chapter Twenty-seven

Alba had parked out in front of the station in the visitor's lot, but Roy's vehicle was in out back behind a security gate. By the time they reached the street, Alba was out of sight.

"Don't worry," he said. "I know where Emily lives."

Faye was unaccountably afraid. Nothing had changed. Emily's situation was exactly the same as it had been before Alba burst into his office, but now she knew that Alba thought Emily was in danger.

Maybe Alba was right. But if she was right that Emily could be in danger, then she was driving toward that danger as fast as she could go. Roy Cloud clearly did not intend to let Alba do that alone.

• ● ● ● •

Roy Cloud and Alba Callahan were both excellent drivers who knew the back roads around Sylacauga, but Alba had a head start. Roy did his best to catch up, careening around blind curves that only a Sylacauga native could navigate. Faye had lost count of the steep hills they climbed at top speed toward a waiting curve that was invisible until the moment they crested the summit.

Were they gaining on Alba? Faye had no way to know.

At last, she got a glimpse of Alba's cherry-red sedan ahead as Roy drove toward it much faster than Emily's long gravel driveway wanted him to go.

She saw Alba park the car and run for Emily's porch. She slammed the front door open like a woman who was certain that nobody in Sylacauga locked their doors. Maybe they didn't.

Faye and Roy were close behind her, running hard, but they had only reached the front step when they heard Alba wail.

"Oh, no no no. Oh, sweetie, no."

They found Alba in the kitchen, sitting in a puddle of clotted blood with Emily's head in her pale yellow lap. Roy rushed to check Emily's pulse, but Faye could see how things were.

He stepped back and dialed his phone. Faye heard him murmuring words like "gunshot to torso" and "dead within minutes," and she knew he was telling Bigbee what had happened.

Alba rocked Emily's body and sobbed. "She never hurt anybody in her whole life. You know that, Roy."

Dropping the phone to his side, Roy said, "I do."

Alba looked at him with eyes that were as angry as they would have been if he'd shot Emily himself. "We all knew her well enough, but we avoided her. We thought she was clingy. Needy. Nobody wanted to be the next person that Emily loved too much. Nobody had time to let her be the best friend they ever had."

Roy dropped to a squat and put a hand on Alba's shoulder. She shook it off.

"I take responsibility," he said. "I should have sent somebody to keep an eye on her."

"Well, I'm not letting you have the responsibility. I want it. The police can only do so much. The rest of us have to do our part. I could have come out here to take care of Emily. I am a damn fine shot."

Faye didn't doubt her.

A wound in the center of Emily's chest was responsible for all that blood. Alba ignored the gore and wrapped her arms tighter around the dead woman.

"We're so very proud of being a small town where everybody knows everybody. But that doesn't mean we treat everybody like a human being. I should have thought about Emily yesterday when somebody shot at Kenny and Mickey. She was the only other person who knew Sophia at the end. Of course, she was a target. Maybe she was *the* target all along. I should have seen it."

"What are you saying?" Faye asked.

"Did anybody get hurt when Carson and Kenny were being shot at? And you, Faye."

"No."

"Did anybody get hurt yesterday? The shot at Mickey went wild. Kenny got lucky. Again," Alba said. "All of the people who knew Sophia—Mickey, Kenny, Emily, Carson, me—have been near at least one of the shootings. Well, except Sly, and I don't know what to think about him. The rest of us have all been shot at but, until today, none of us has even been hurt."

"I haven't thought of it that way. We're dealing with a pretty incompetent shooter," Faye said.

"No joke. I could have stood in the woods and taken Mickey out through his bedroom window. No problem. Don't think I haven't considered it." Alba brushed Emily's hair off her bloody forehead and kissed it. "But why Emily? Who would want to kill her? There was nothing scary about her."

Faye was silent, reviewing Sophia's field notes in her head and trying to figure out what made Emily different. "Roy, Emily told us about something that happened on the last day and Sophia's notes confirmed it. Sophia said she sent everybody home early. Why hasn't anybody else mentioned that? When I mentioned it to Mickey, he got upset and asked how I could know about it. I read it in Sophia's journal, but I didn't say so. He must have thought I heard it from Emily. Maybe that's when he decided that she remembered too much and he couldn't leave her alive."

Cloud was moving toward the door with his keys in one hand and his phone in the other. "Where's Mickey? Alba, where's Mickey? Are you sure he's at Carson's house?"

Faye tried to follow him, but he said, "Oh, no. Take a look at that woman on the floor and tell me you think I'd let you come near that man. I shouldn't have let you come with me just now. Alba will give you a ride back to town. I'll send backup and the medical examiner to look after Emily. And can you make Alba get out of my crime scene? I'd do it, but I have to go catch the man who shot this poor woman."

Alba wrapped her arms tighter around Emily's neck. "I'll give her up when the medical examiner comes and not before."

Roy threw up his hands and left. Neither Faye nor Alba spoke as they listened to him start his car. Faye drew back to give Alba time alone with her friend. She pulled out her phone and silenced it so that the sound wouldn't disturb Alba. She typed

Emily's dead. Shot.

and pushed Send.

"What are you doing? Did you text somebody? Stop that."

Alba struggled under the weight of Emily's body, finally shifting it off her lap and standing up. "Was that your husband you texted?"

Faye nodded her head, not sure why Alba was bothered by a simple text.

"He'll tell Sly and—oh, it doesn't matter. Sly knows. He's the one who did this. He has to be."

"Why would you say that?"

"I heard you just now. You think Mickey did this because you told him about something that happened that last day. Did you tell your husband the same thing? Because Joe is a pipeline straight to Sly. If Emily was killed by someone who was afraid she remembered too much, it had to be Sly, not Mickey. I won't have him railroaded for crimes he didn't commit."

Faye could imagine Alba standing in a courtroom before a jury, competent and in charge, defending the ex-husband she still loved.

Gravel scratched under Cloud's spinning wheels as he backed down the long driveway. As soon as the sound of his engine faded, Alba crouched beside Emily and gently placed the woman's hands across her wounded chest. She stepped back to get a good look. After a second, she reached down and closed the dead woman's eyes.

"There. She looks comfortable, don't you think? Now I have to go talk to my son and my ex-husband."

"Roy's on his way to Mickey and he—"

"Did you think I told him the truth about where Mickey is? And my son? There's a killer running around Sylacauga. I'm not telling anybody where to find Mickey and Carson. Not even Roy Cloud."

Alba was walking to her car so quickly that Faye had to work to keep up.

"But Roy thinks Mickey *is* the killer. At least, he thinks he killed Emily."

"Then who shot a hole in his house yesterday? Kenny? If Kenny did it, then who was shooting at him and you and Carson on that first morning that Sophia's body was discovered? Who else is left that could have killed Sophia? Sly? My money's on Sly. He's the only one involved who hasn't been shot at yet. Other than Roy Cloud."

"What evidence do you have that points to Sly, other than that he once worked for Sophia Townsend? What was his motive? He has alibis for the shooting at your house and the one at the Sylacauga site. Nobody can put him anywhere near the scenes of the crimes. Something doesn't add up."

"His motive is to cover up the fact that he murdered Sophia. He was obviously trying to scare Carson into shutting down his project on that first day. That's probably what he was doing on the night Kira Denton was killed. He needed to obscure some evidence and Kira got in the way."

As far as Faye knew, word of the pearls and figurine had not gotten out, nor did anyone know that something in a box seemed to have been taken. Alba was dead-on when she ascribed Kira's killing to someone who wanted to hide evidence. Faye just couldn't believe that it was Sly.

"Did you know that Sophia sent her crew home early on that last day?" Faye asked. "Do you remember if Mickey ever came home early? I have to think you were keeping close tabs on his comings and goings at that particular time in your marriage."

Alba said nothing. She just shook her head and kept shaking it. Oddly, Faye didn't think she was shaking it at her question about Mickey's whereabouts. She seemed to be shaking it at a voice inside her head that was saying things she didn't like.

"I have to believe that Mickey knows something," Faye said. "You should have seen him when he found out that I knew Sophia sent them home early on that last day."

"Mickey will tell me the truth. He always does."

"Except for when he was sleeping with Sophia."

"Well, yeah. And he learned his lesson, didn't he?"

They reached Alba's car and Faye could see that she was having no success in getting Alba to stay put. "Where are you going? I thought you were going to hang on to Emily's body until somebody peeled her out of your hands?"

"That's what I told Roy. You really do believe people when they talk, don't you? Faye, that's a bad life strategy. Why would I tell Roy that I was planning to wait here while he rushed off to find Mickey, who is absolutely not where I told Roy he was? Why would I volunteer that information?"

"Because honesty is a virtue?"

Alba snorted.

Faye decided to stop arguing facts with an admitted liar and said, "You do what you need to do. I'll wait here and talk to the medical examiner when he comes. Joe will come get me later."

Alba put an impatient hand on her hip with a gesture that made her look like a supermodel, only covered in blood and sixty years old. "You don't think I'm going to leave you here to call Roy Cloud, do you? You'll tell him I'm on my way to let Mickey know he's a murder suspect, and that just won't work. It won't work at all. Give me your phone and get in the car."

"Why would I do that?"

"Are you carrying a gun?" Alba tapped her blood-stained yellow boot while she waited for an answer.

"Of course not."

"Well, I am. And it's loaded." She gestured to the oversized leather tote hanging from her shoulder. "I think I need some company on this trip. Get in the car."

• ● ● ● •

Faye tried to piece together what Cloud would do when he got to Carson's house and found nobody home. He would call Alba. When he got no answer, he would call Faye.

Alba had Faye's phone and the ringer wasn't on, so she wouldn't know if Roy called and she wouldn't know if Joe texted her back. After a little time had passed, they would wonder why she hadn't answered, but there would be no urgency to finding her.

Was there any urgency? Alba had said she was just taking Faye along for a ride to demand the truth from her ex-husband. Faye presumed she intended to let her go afterward but she didn't know that for sure. If Faye turned out to be a threat to any of the people Alba cared about—Mickey, Carson, Kenny, or herself—Faye could believe that Alba would shoot her.

Was there any sequence of events that would bring help?

She'd texted Joe that Emily was dead. He had probably already texted her back. At first, he would assume that she was busy at the crime scene, either as Roy's employee or as a witness. As time went on, he would worry, but she could think of no reason for him to look for her at Alba's house.

What about Roy Cloud? If he called her after he failed to find Mickey and then went back out to Emily's house to check on them when she didn't answer, he would find that Faye and Alba were gone. This was to be expected since he'd told her that Alba would take her home. If he kept trying to reach her without getting through, would he eventually call Joe to make sure she'd arrived safely?

The most comforting answer Faye could muster was "Maybe."

How dangerous was Alba? Was she the killer? Had she committed any of the shootings?

At Emily's house, Alba had convinced Faye that she was an innocent bystander, concerned only with the safety of her husband and son. But Alba's entire life was performance art. Was anything she did or said real? How would anybody know?

Supposing Alba was truly innocent, what were the odds that she was taking Faye into a face-off with the real killer?

As the evidence stood, Faye could only make sense of the crimes if she took them individually. Taken individually, she would suspect Mickey of the first shooting, since Kenny was one of the victims and couldn't have done it. But she would suspect Kenny of the most recent shooting, since Mickey had been in the house with her. Carson was right beside Faye during both incidents. She had seen these things with her own eyes. She herself was a witness to these people's innocence.

The only witness to Sly's innocence was Joe, but she believed in Joe's integrity to her very core. He wouldn't lie, not even to save his father. Try as she might, Faye could come up with no theory that pointed to any one of Sophia's former employees. Who else was there?

The blood-covered woman sitting beside Faye was pushing her expensive European sedan to its limit. She also had a gun in her purse, and she'd just threatened Faye with it. Faye knew of no alibi for Alba for any of the crimes. The only argument against Alba's guilt was her convincing grief at Emily's death. But that grief could be real, even if she did kill Emily. Maybe a murderer really would feel that much pain when confronted by the victim's dead body.

Should Faye be afraid of Alba?

The woman had suffered visible shock when she saw Emily's body. Perhaps she killed her. If not, and maybe even if so, Alba must be driven by the need to protect her son and prove that the man she still loved wasn't guilty of murder.

The proper question was not whether she should be afraid of Alba. The proper question was whether she should be afraid of a single-minded and adrenaline-charged woman who was frightened for her loved ones and armed. Faye decided that she should indeed, and the fact that she'd had to think about it suggested that Faye's own adrenaline was messing with her mind.

To make matters worse, a powerful wind was blowing thunderclouds in from the west.

"Weather's looking bad," she said.

"It's that time of year," Alba said, never taking her eyes off the road. "You get used to it when you live in Oklahoma."

Alba's driving had gone past aggressive and was firmly in the reckless zone. Faye could feel the rising wind shoving the car sideways and she could see how hard Alba was gripping the steering wheel to maintain control. If the green-gray clouds looming over them started dropping rain or, from the looks of it, hail, even iron-willed Alba wouldn't be able to make the car behave on the slick road.

Faye had lived through hurricanes, but she'd never seen a tornado's violent funnel. She had seen how a hurricane could flatten a long swath of coastline, demolishing everything manmade and washing it out to sea, but tornadoes went beyond even that. They dealt in impossibilities. Tornadoes left washing machines in trees. They piled cars into neat stacks. They deposited the naked corpses of their victims on the roofs of their neighbors' houses.

"You can tell me where we're going," Faye said. "There's nothing I can do about it in this car and without a phone. It seems like we're going to your house?"

"Yes. Nobody would think Mickey was dumb enough to hide on the same street where the bullets flew yesterday, so it's the perfect place for him to wait out the danger. Am I right?"

Faye gave her a weak "Yeah?" and Alba took that as confirmation.

"I thought that was a brilliant idea, if I do say so myself. Carson didn't want to leave his own home, but he's staying at mine anyway. He doesn't spend a lot of time arguing with his mother."

Faye believed that.

"I put them in my basement. It's completely underground, so they'll be safe if somebody starts taking potshots again. I picked them up, so their trucks are in front of their own houses, like decoys."

Faye guessed that was as good a plan as any. Looking at the way the roadside trees were bending sideways, she asked, "Do you have a storm shelter?"

"I'm a native Oklahoman. I store my Christmas decorations in my storm shelter. If the tornadoes wanted me, they would have gotten me by now."

The wind was piling the anvil-shaped thunderheads higher. Faye tried to focus on the need to get away from Alba, but which should she fear more? The armed woman beside her or the gathering storm outside?

Chapter Twenty-eight

Joe stood at the front window of his father's house. It was so dark outside that the streetlights had come on. "I don't like Faye being out in this."

"Me, neither." Sly walked up behind him to get a look. "You know where she is?"

The phone in Joe's pocket beeped. He glanced at it and said, "Nope, I don't know where she is, but this is awful." He held it out for his father to see.

"Well, text her back and find out where she is and what happened to Emily." Sly held the phone in both hands and stared at the screen like a man who thought the message it displayed would change. Maybe reality would change with it. "I'd like to kill the bastard that did this. As a matter of fact, I think I will."

"How are you planning to do that? You got a gun?"

"I'm a convicted felon who doesn't want to go back to prison. No, I don't have a gun. Besides, I won't need one. I can take Mickey Callahan apart with my bare hands."

"You're sure it's him?"

"I've known Mickey all my life. I've been sure all along."

"Then why do you need to kill him today?"

"Because I've known Emily Olsen all my life, too. Kira Denton had the police department to make sure she got justice and they haven't managed it yet. Emily's son can't even be bothered to drive over here from Tulsa and spend an afternoon with her. Emily ain't got a soul to make sure the lowlife that shot her pays."

"Where are you planning to look for Mickey?"

"His house. Carson's house. His wife's house. Ex-wife. He doesn't go all that many places. If somebody figures out that I'm looking for him so I can kill him, I might get a little help to find him. Nobody likes that know-it-all creep."

Joe followed him out the door. He said, "I thought you didn't want to go back to prison."

"I didn't want to swap my freedom for a gun. Emily? Yeah, I'll swap my freedom for the life of the asshole who took hers."

"Dad, please don't do this."

"You can't stop me. Don't try."

"Then I'm coming with you."

"Are you armed?"

Joe's hand went to the leather bag at his waist where he kept a handy stone weapon that he'd chipped himself. "Always."

"Then come on. Let's go."

• • ● • •

Faye's brain couldn't stop chewing on the events of the afternoon of August 7, 1987. As Alba drove and refused to talk, Faye tried and failed to make all the pieces fit. The pieces of the potsherd. The pieces of all the shattered lives that surrounded Sophia Townsend. The bony pieces of Sophia's body that she'd seen with her own eyes.

And what about the bone that was found on that last day? Was it just one piece of another skeleton that still haunted the Sylacauga site? How did it fit into the puzzle?

Where had that old skeleton been over all the years since Sophia found it? In her journal, she'd said that the existence of the skeleton would sink her project, because the Creeks would shut it down before they'd disturb an ancient burial. She'd seemed resigned to leaving Sylacauga and starting again. What if she had changed her mind?

Would she really have destroyed the old skeleton to save this project that had become an obsession for her? Would she have hidden it someplace where it still hadn't turned up? Where could that possibly be? Not at the curation facility where the rest of the project's finds had been stored. At her cabin, maybe? Had Carson found it there?

The Arkansas police report from Mickey's last visit to her cabin suggested that Sophia had spent time there after the project shut down but before she died. It was possible that she'd hidden the bones there, but it just didn't sound like something Sophia would do.

Faye laughed at herself for thinking she could know a woman from this distance in time, even after reading pages and pages of the woman's private thoughts. This made no more sense than thinking she knew her because she'd seen her bones lying in her grave.

This thought called to mind an image of Sophia's grave, just as they'd found it, and it told Faye what she needed to know. It told her exactly where the other bones had been all this time.

They had been in the box buried beneath Sophia's body.

Faye could picture the size and shape of the rectangular hole dug by the person who had shot Kira. It was absolutely big enough to hold the disarticulated bones of a human skeleton, especially since this skeleton had been so old that many of its bones were likely broken or missing.

Faye believed this to be true, because it gave the chain of events a narrative that was at least slightly more coherent. Sophia had been killed sometime after she disappeared and before the excavation was backfilled.

The killer had dug her grave in the bottom of the excavation. The killer had then dug a deeper hole in the middle of the grave, reinterring the old skeleton at the bottom of it in a large box. A canvas bag holding the pearls, the figurine, and the engraved potsherd had been laid on top of the box before soil was shoveled around it all. Sophia's body had been laid on top of all those buried things, and then more dirt was shoveled in to cover her under two feet of dirt. Soon afterward, the excavation was backfilled with another meter of soil, virtually guaranteeing that nobody would ever find Sophia and the treasures buried with her.

It had been a perfect plan—until it failed. The killer must have been terrified to learn that the excavation was to be reopened.

With this scenario in mind, it made sense that the killer had, in 1987, gone into the shed being used by the project, retrieving a stray potsherd. It made perfect sense if that someone had purposely reinterred the skeleton with all of the original grave goods that were available.

The killer's care in making sure the burial was returned to the ground with all of its associated goods didn't speak of Mickey Callahan. It spoke of Kenny Meadows, the man who had pestered Sophia Townsend for her entire last summer because he respected the artifacts too much to condone damaging them for lab tests.

Then why did she still suspect Mickey Callahan? Perhaps because she didn't like him, but perhaps it was because he was said to have been crazy about Sophia. The woman was carrying on with his best friend right in front of him. Domestic violence was a story as old as time.

If he'd been jealous enough to hit her, anything could have happened. He could have beaten her to death outright, or she could simply have fallen and hit her head on a rock. In either case, Faye absolutely thought he would have buried her and all the evidence, then gone around doing things like calling the Arkansas sheriff so he could hide his tracks. He could even have gone out to the cabin to fake a trip for Sophia by closing up the house and putting a dated gas receipt on her kitchen counter. Nobody ever said Mickey wasn't smart.

The trouble with both these theories is that they flew in the face of facts that Faye had witnessed for herself. She herself was Kenny's alibi for the first shooting and Mickey's alibi for the second one. This left her wondering again whether the woman driving the car where she sat was the one guilty of murderous domestic violence, or whether her son could have managed murder while still very young.

It did not escape her attention that any objective observer would say, based on all the evidence, that Sly was still the most likely suspect.

• • ● • •

As Alba steered the car onto the bumpy road where she lived, Faye kept trying to picture the killer. First, she imagined Kenny walking through Emily's unlocked door and murdering her. Then she tried imagining Mickey doing the same thing. She even tried to picture Sly driving to Emily's house with a gun. Faye couldn't come up with a scenario that allowed any of those people to do all the crimes that haunted Sylacauga, yet she did believe all the crimes were related.

It was only when she broadened her thinking a single notch that the answer came to her and she said it out loud.

"It was both of them."

Alba jerked her head at Faye. Her attention was completely removed from the road, where it was much needed. "Both of who?"

"What if Mickey was doing the shooting on the first day? Afterward, he could have gone on foot as far as the church where Roy says somebody parked. It would have been easy to double back from there and drive to work. He wouldn't have had to come all that close to us to do the shooting. If the two of them were working together, he would only have needed to be close enough to see Kenny. Kenny could have judged the most effective times for shots to be fired and given Mickey hand signals. If Mickey was shooting from further away than was possible for a man without an accomplice, then the police would have had trouble finding his trail."

She was ridiculously glad to clear Bleck from missing something so obvious as the trail of a smelly human being.

Alba snorted again, but she didn't argue with Faye.

"And what if Kenny was doing the shooting yesterday?" Faye went on. "He could have dropped the rifle before he ran back to his house. He might even have thought it wouldn't be traced to him. It was unregistered. If Carson hadn't recognized it—"

"I don't like Carson being mixed up in any of this."

"Me either, but he is. Anyway, if Kenny dropped the unregistered rifle, then walked in the creek to get back to his house, Bleck wouldn't have found a trail."

"I don't believe it," Alba said. "Why would either Mickey or Kenny do these terrible things, much less do them together?"

"Something happened in 1987 on that last afternoon of the project, and it was important enough to rattle Mickey when he found out we had information about it. I asked him a question that showed that I knew things I shouldn't know. He might have thought that Kenny was the one who talked, but Emily's the one who's dead. As far as we know, Kenny's not, so Mickey seems okay with letting Kenny stay alive with damning information. If they're working together, he doesn't have to worry about what Kenny knows."

Faye wouldn't have thought it possible that Alba could grip the wheel more tightly or push the car to go even faster. She said, "You're making this more complicated than it needs to be."

"Think about it. Name a reason why somebody would shoot Emily. With all the shooting that's been going on around here, I'm going to presume that her death is related to whatever is driving the shooters."

"Shooter."

"Have it your way, but I'm still going to presume that her death isn't something random, like a robbery gone wrong or…I don't know…an attack by a violent prison escapee. Will you grant me that much?"

"Maybe."

This was a reasonable enough response, and Faye was always happy to see evidence of reasonable thought in a person who was packing heat. "Can you imagine Emily doing something that would drive somebody to murder? Do you think this could be a revenge killing?"

"Revenge against Emily? Don't be stupid."

"Can you imagine her blackmailing someone? If Emily had known who killed Sophia Townsend, would she have kept it to herself so that she could extort money from the murderer?"

"Heavens, no."

"Why else do people get killed? Domestic violence? Could Emily have been having an affair with someone dangerous?"

"Please."

"So tell me how a sweet, loving, nonconfrontational person who doesn't hang around with dangerous people gets murdered? I say it's because she knew something dangerous."

Finally, Alba allowed herself to think like an experienced attorney instead of a passionate person defending her loved ones. "You're right. Either she had something valuable or she knew something dangerous. Those are the only motives that make sense."

For the rest of their breakneck trip, nothing Faye could do would prompt Alba to say a single word.

• ● ● ● •

Alba skidded to a stop and slammed the car into park. "Get out."

Faye thought of running, but where would that get her? Maybe Alba was hoping for a reason to shoot. If Faye made a break for it now, Alma could put several holes in her before she could find a safe place to hide.

Would she do that? Probably. Alba didn't seem like someone who would carry a gun she wasn't willing to shoot.

As they walked down Alba's front path, the woman's lovingly tended flowers blew in the rising wind. In the dim sunlight, filtered through heavy clouds, they seemed to glow. A rose bush reached out a branch that snagged the blood-stained sleeve of Alma's jacket. Downy leaves of pineapple sage brushed their ankles and smelled wonderful.

On the front doorstep sat a massive display of flowering plants. Alba paused there to pluck a dead begonia leaf and Faye thought, *There it is. Proof that this situation has driven her around the bend. She's taken a hostage as she carries a gun on a mission to confront her ex-husband who may be a murderer, yet she needs to stop and make sure that her flowers are perfect.*

There were many ways the crimes could have been accomplished by multiple killers. Perhaps Alba was the one conspiring with Mickey. Or with Kenny. Carson could have been involved. But only Alba could have been working alone. Or Sly.

Alba's front door opened into a single massive living space, stylish and recently renovated. The far wall was all windows, with a row of French doors opening onto the back yard. No one was in the room, but Faye could see two people enjoying the patio.

Carson was relaxing in a wrought-iron chair with his back to them. Mickey had taken a fatherly stance behind him, leaning against his son's shoulder. They were looking at something, but their bodies blocked Faye's view.

As Faye and Alba crossed the room and as they each put a hand on the doorknob of a French door, Faye's subconscious was saying, *Something's wrong. Look around you. Something is very wrong.*

The wind snatched the door out of her hands, banging it against the house so hard that Faye half-expected some of its panes to shatter. The sharp crack of the doorknob hitting wood got the attention of the men in front of her, and it reminded her of the thing that was very wrong about this tender father-and-son gathering in front of her.

It was no day to be sitting outside.

This is what had bothered her as she and Alba had made their way to the patio and Mickey and Carson. The whipping wind stirred their hair and their clothes, and it did little to cool the stifling heat. Deep in the woods, she heard a crash as a massive limb broke off a tree and fell to the ground. It was long past being an uncomfortable time to be outside. It had become dangerous.

She had no time to ask herself why Mickey and Carson were outside in such violent weather before she and Alba passed through the open doors and stepped outside. She only had time to see that they were not alone. Kenny, still and unsmiling, was facing them.

• ● ● ● ●

Mickey and Kenny hadn't moved since Faye and Alba stepped out onto the patio. Their hair whipped in the wind, but their bodies were motionless. The two men stood just as they had, face-to-face, each of them staring down the barrel of a handgun aimed directly at the heart of his best friend.

Both guns might as well be aimed at Carson. If Kenny shot first, the slightest quiver in his aim could put a bullet into Carson as easily as Mickey. If Mickey shot first, Kenny would shoot back, unless he was killed instantly. The aim of a wounded man was iffy so, again, he was as likely to hit Carson as he was to hit Mickey.

"What's happening?" Alba clutched the purse that held her own weapon.

Kenny twitched his gun in Alba's direction. "Put the purse down, Alba. We all know what's in there."

She eased her satchel to the patio's concrete surface.

Both Mickey and Kenny were comfortable handling a gun. They each stood straight holding their weapons with both hands at arms' length, aimed squarely at each other's chest.

Carson, sitting in a chair between them, was trembling. Faye was trembling, too. Thunder rumbled so far away that she couldn't hear it, but she felt it in her chest.

Faye didn't know where she found enough breath to speak, but her voice was surprisingly strong. "Neither of you wants to pull the trigger with Carson in the crossfire. Put the guns down."

Yes, that was right thing to say. Both men loved Carson. He could be the key to getting them to stand down.

And if he wasn't the key? He still deserved to be taken out of the line of fire. Carson had lived his whole life in the crosshairs of these people. She had no doubt they all loved him—Mickey, Alba, Kenny—but that hadn't stopped them from using him as a pawn.

"I need you to stand down until Carson can get to a safe place." She slid her left foot slowly forward. "Come here, Carson. Kenny and your dad don't want to shoot you."

"If either of them thought shooting me would make it easier to shoot the other one, he'd do it in a minute."

"Carson," Alba said, following Faye's lead and taking a small step forward, "that isn't true. Your father and Kenny love you. Mickey? Kenny? Don't you? You have to stop this."

As Alba spoke, Faye took another minute step to the left. Alba responded with an equally small step to the right. Faye wasn't sure what her plan was, but Alba was acting as her backup. In time, they would be standing on either side of Mickey, close enough to touch him, but what good would it do? Even if they could subdue him, Kenny's gun would still be aimed in their direction.

"If either of you shoot my boy," Alba said, "you're going to have to shoot me, too. You know it's true. You think you hate each other? You've never had an enemy like me."

"Tell us what happened, Carson," Faye said in the calmest voice she could muster.

"I'm not sure. I was sitting out here watching the storm come up and waiting for Dad to come home. When he showed up, Kenny came running up yelling something like 'I saw you leave and come back. Where did you go?' He wouldn't stop yelling 'Where did you go?' Before I knew what was happening, they had their guns out. They've been standing like this ever since."

"Yeah, Mickey," Kenny said, "where did you go? You sure weren't gone long. Can you tell me why your ex-wife is covered in blood?"

Mickey said nothing.

"Alba," Kenny said, "would you get Emily Olsen on the phone? I want to make sure she's okay."

Alba's hand moved toward the satchel at her feet, but Mickey said, "Hold still. We already said we know what's in there."

"Why wouldn't Emily be okay?" Faye asked, sliding a foot forward. This time Kenny saw her and shook his head while glancing meaningfully at the gun in his hand.

"Mickey said she was dangerous," Kenny said. "He—"

"Emily?" Carson's disbelieving voice made it clear how dangerous he thought Emily was.

"Mickey said word was getting around about things that happened on that last day with Sophia. He said that we couldn't afford to let Emily tell anyone what she might remember. It could sink us."

Kenny didn't look good. His face had gone gray and it was damp, too damp to be explained away by the wet wind.

"What do you mean when you say 'it could sink us'?" Carson demanded. "Sink who? What does Emily know?"

Faye moved her hand in a gesture intended to communicate to Carson that he should stay put, but she did it ever so slightly. The last thing she wanted was to startle two jumpy men into shooting her.

Carson saw the twitch of her hand. He stayed in his seat and nobody shot anybody.

"Kenny thinks we should check on Emily. Dad? Should somebody call her?"

"Yeah, Mickey," Kenny said, "should somebody call Emily? Or maybe go over there and check on her?"

Mickey said nothing.

"Can we stop this, Mickey?" Kenny was shouting now. "It's not like we're hardened criminals. We're teachers, for God's sake. How are we supposed to know how to cover up a killing?"

Faye heard the patter of light hail on the roof behind her and remembered that hail often preceded a tornado. Bits of ice that were hardly bigger than salt crystals stung her face.

"What are you and Mickey trying to cover up?" Faye asked.

"Kenny," Mickey said, giving his gun a long glance, "you don't know what in the hell you're talking about. So you should stop talking."

"I know very well what happened on that last day with Sophia, and so do you. You and I saw that bone come out of the ground. If Emily told Roy Cloud, well…you couldn't let her do that, could you? People might've started wondering where that bone was. They might have started asking Emily more questions. That's what you said last night. I told you I'd kill you if something happened to that woman."

Kenny glanced at Faye and Alba to see whether they believed him. "I did. I said I'd kill him and then I'd go tell Roy Cloud everything before I'd hurt Emily. Mickey, we've done enough. Sophia, Kira…we didn't plan what happened to them. They were in the wrong place at the wrong time, but we're still to blame. The time comes when you have to admit you've done wrong."

"Done wrong? What did you do? Dad?" For the first time, Carson moved. He turned around in his chair. His face almost brushed his father's belly.

Mickey said nothing.

"Mickey stayed late that last day," Kenny said. "He'd like everybody to forget it, but I remember. I guess he's killed Emily now, so nobody living but me knows the rest of it, but I'm telling you now. Mickey helped Sophia dig up a treasure. That's what it was to him. A treasure. To me, it was something holy. A beautiful little statue made by my ancestors and a double-handful of pearls. He was going to steal them, thinking I'd keep quiet."

Mickey broke his silence. "You were my best friend. If I hadn't offered to cut you in, we wouldn't be standing here. Sophia would be alive. Emily would be alive. And I could've used the money from selling that junk—that's what it is, Kenny, somebody else's trash—I could have used it to give my son a better life."

"Those things weren't yours to sell. Nor mine."

Carson leaned back to get a clearer look at his father's face. "Emily?"

Mickey gave a single nod.

More hail fell. The beads of ice had grown, but they were still hardly bigger than apple seeds. If they were to reach the size of the old pearls, each hailstone would bring a jolt of pain.

Faye hoped for heavier hail. Mickey and Kenny weren't going to be able to hold those heavy weapons at arm's length much longer, so this standoff had a ticking clock. Maybe a hailstorm would end it before the time bomb blew.

Through the clatter of ice, Faye heard something familiar. It sounded like Joe's voice calling her, but that was impossible. He didn't even know where she was.

The voice called out a little louder. It really was Joe's voice, but he wasn't looking for her. He was in the yard next door, calling out for Mickey. Behind Joe's voice, she heard a lower rumble that she recognized as Sly yelling something unintelligible. Beneath those voices was a deeper rumble. She hoped like hell that it was a train.

There was only one thing to do and it might well get her shot. Faye did it anyway.

"Joe! Sly! We're back here."

She'd crept so close to Mickey that he flinched at her voice, but he couldn't afford to shoot her. If he took his gun off Kenny to put a bullet in Faye, then Kenny would be clear to shoot him. Faye's calculated risk had evidently panned out because she didn't get shot. She was, however, close enough for Mickey to hook a vengeful foot around her leg and throw her onto her face.

When she saw that her head was going to strike the ground, her fear cranked up a notch. Once she was unconscious, anything could happen. She turned her head just as it banged into the concrete patio, avoiding a broken nose but suffering a hard blow. Still, she hung on to consciousness.

Sly's voice boomed as he and Joe rounded the back corner of the house. Joe had his bolo in his hand, and Sly was carrying a tire iron. Faye wanted to tell them to drop their weapons, but she couldn't get her mouth to work.

"Callahan," Sly bellowed at Mickey, "did you kill that woman?"

Faye was so stunned by her fall that she thought he was talking about her. She tried to say, "No, he didn't. I'm fine," but Mickey interrupted her.

"Which woman? I only killed two. That man in front of me killed the other one."

Chapter Twenty-nine

Joe was literally restraining his father, one hand on each shoulder. The cords of his bolo draped across Sly's chest.

"What other woman? Sophia?" Sly called out. "One of you killed Sophia and the other one killed Kira and Emily? Is that what you're saying? Then I need to kill you both, but I want you to tell me who did what. If I'm going to kill a man—two men—I need to know why."

"Dad, don't," Joe said, throwing both arms around Sly and pinning his father's arms to his sides.

Carson was still twisted around in his chair, staring at Mickey. "Dad?"

Kenny was taking in long drags of air. He shifted his feet into a wider stance to brace his weakening legs. Still, he gripped his gun. "I'd gone back out to the site after Mickey told me about the bones and the pearls and the little statue. I was down in the pit, trying to explain to Sophia how finding a human bone changed everything. It meant we were digging in a grave and we needed to stop."

"Good luck convincing Sophia of something that stupid." Mickey said.

"She said okay. She agreed with me. All these years, I've been telling you that she agreed with me."

Mickey was as resolute as he'd been when Faye first saw them, but Kenny's grip was failing. He pulled the gun in, resting the hilt against his chest while still holding it with both hands. This was a terrible position for accuracy, but how good did his aim have to be at this distance?

"I thought everybody had gone home." Mickey said in a rational voice designed to convince them all that Sophia's death was accidental or justified or preordained. "I'd gone to the store and bought a bag to carry the treasure in. I'd swiped her key to the shed, thinking I could grab what I wanted and be gone in maybe a minute. I saw your cars, but the shed was way yonder away from the two of you. I thought I could grab the loot and drive away before either of you knew it."

"A looter. That's what you are. A scummy good-for-nothing looter," Kenny said. "All this time, I had to pretend to be your friend and you had to pretend to be mine, because we couldn't afford to let anybody think something was wrong."

The wind was drizzly and wet, but it didn't seem to be reviving Kenny. The man was fading in front of them. "The shed door creaked. Always did. Sophia heard it and we came looking for a thief. We caught you red-handed, Mickey. It pleases me to know that she saw you for the grave robber you were, even for just that minute before she died."

Faye held out her hand. Carson grasped it and she felt the comfort of human contact. The instant she thought it was safe, she planned to yank him right out of that chair and onto the ground beside her.

"Maybe I was a thief that night, Kenny, but it was you who tried to kill me. It wasn't so smart to sling that heavy toolbox at my head, was it? All I did was defend myself. I put up my hands to block the blow and Sophia was standing in the wrong place. It wasn't me that killed her."

"It was an accident. It—"

"You weren't so sure it was an accident that you wanted to chance ending up on Death Row. You know we do more executions here in Oklahoma than just about anybody. Hell, we invented lethal injection. Could've happened."

"You could've wound up on Death Row instead of me," Kenny said, "depending on what we said and what the jury believed. All these years, I thought we got away with it," Kenny said. "I'd almost put it out of my mind until your own son got the excavation reopened."

"Leave my son out of this."

Kenny looked at Carson sitting vulnerable between them. "He's been in it since the beginning. You had him out at that site so much, filling his head with how glorious it was to dig up the past. He's never wanted to be anything but an archaeologist. He was bound to dig up what we did someday."

"That was a cute idea you had on the first day, Kenny, telling me to scare my son off from his own excavation with gunshots while you pretended you were a victim. You know that? You're a great victim. You thought a few loud noises would get Carson to give up his project, but you should have known better. He's no victim. Those warning shots worked great in the daytime, but not so great at night when I couldn't see that Kira was running toward me instead of away from me."

"I just wanted you to scare her away long enough for me to get the evidence out of the hole."

"I did. And I did it for you. That toolbox was full of bones and it had your name on it. Might've even still had Sophia's blood on it."

"And it might've had your fingerprints, so don't tell me you did it just for me."

And now Faye understood what box had held the bones.

"If my son wasn't so bullheaded and so damn book-smart, we wouldn't be standing here. If he was smart in the other ways besides books, the bullets would have scared him off. Kira and Emily would still be alive."

Carson's face was unreadable. He was listening to his father brag about how smart he was, while simultaneously saying that Kira and Emily would still be alive if he were a quitter.

"The first two deaths were accidents," Kenny said, "but Emily Olsen was a sweet, harmless human being, and you killed her in cold blood. Nothing will ever be right again."

And then Kenny crumbled. His body spasmed, both hands went to his chest, and the gun dropped from his hands. He fell to his knees and was still falling when the bullet struck him.

The most obscene instant for Faye was the tiny hesitation between Kenny's collapse and the sound of a gunshot. It was a gap in time that told the difference between a reflexive jerk on the trigger and a measured, studied squeeze. Mickey had watched a man he'd known all his life begin to fall, he had thought about what to do next, and then he had pulled the trigger.

That silent instant before the gunshot was the sound of premeditation. It left no doubt that Faye had just witnessed murder in the first degree.

Faye yanked on Carson's arm and he leapt in her direction. For an instant, they were side by side on the ground, staring at Kenny's crumpled body. Then Mickey grabbed Faye by the leg and yanked her toward him, dragging her over the hard wet concrete patio.

Faye could hear Joe and Sly running toward her, and she could hear the word, "No." The humming in her ears was drowning out all other sound.

Or maybe it was the roaring of the wind that filled her ears. The rain had stopped, and the hail, or maybe it had all blurred into the black spots in front of her eyes. The clouds were blotting out the sun just as fast as shock was blotting out her mind.

Mickey jerked Faye to her feet. She felt a cold hard circle pressing against her temple. The strength in her legs left her, and she would have slumped to the ground if Mickey hadn't held her up with one arm wrapped around her chest. Keeping her body between him and the cluster of onlookers, he started backing away from Alba, Carson, Joe, Sly, and the body of Kenny Summers.

"She's going with me. If you people try to stop me, she dies. Tell Roy Cloud that if his people try to stop me, she dies. Highway Patrol, border guards, anybody that tries to get in my way, she'll die and I'll take a few of them out, too. Cloud will make sure they stay away from me. He'd be as sorry to see this one go as I was when Sophia went. I do believe he's crazy about her."

Faye's hearing faded and took her vision with it. Her head lolled onto Mickey's shoulder. She barely had the strength to speak, but she did speak, and she was surprised to hear what she said.

"She loves you." Her voice was so low that it would have been inaudible if her lips hadn't been brushing his ear.

The arm around her chest squeezed her harder. Faye couldn't breathe. The light dimmed again and the noise in her ears roared still louder.

"Who? Who loves me?"

All she could do was turn her fading eyes toward Alba, who was kneeling on the ground in her bloody yellow suit with both arms around her son. Mickey turned his head toward his ex-wife and Faye was never able to describe the look she saw there.

Maybe it was love and maybe it was hate. Faye wanted to say that it was self-hatred, but that was too easy. Just because she was horrified by the things Mickey had done didn't mean that he was. It was possible that Mickey had never given up on justifying his actions to himself, to Alba, to everybody.

But he didn't try to justify himself in that moment. He didn't say any of the expected things, like "It's not what you think," or "I couldn't stand the thought of going to jail," or "I didn't want to let my son know what I'd done." He said only, "I wish—" without ever saying what it was that he wished.

The next moment was one that Faye would try for the rest of her life to forget. And she would fail.

The cool circle on Faye's skin where the gun's muzzle was resting suddenly warmed as he pulled it away from her cheek. Still looking at Alba, he put it to his own head, and pulled the trigger.

• • ● • •

It was a long while before Faye fully came to herself. Later, she would recall falling to the ground with Mickey's dying body, scrabbling on her hands and knees to get away from it. She would remember Carson holding his mother back from his father's corpse with all the strength in his massive arms, and still Alba had nearly broken free.

Faye would always be able to call up the image of her husband running to her, dropping to his knees and taking her in his arms. She would never forget the sight of Sly standing among the carnage with a tire iron in his hand and nobody to smite with it. In those memories, Roy Cloud would always be barreling into view behind Sly at the very moment Mickey Callahan put his gun to her temple, because her unanswered phone and Alba's had told him there was trouble, and his fine mind had told him where to go looking for it.

She would remember Roy's face, as dark and troubled as the sky above them, and she would remember the sound of the tornado siren screaming for them to take cover. She would always be able to call up the roaring noise coming from all around her. It had made the ground shake. It had caught in her bones and stayed there.

After that she recalled nothing but darkness for a time, but clarity had returned in Alba's dark basement. There had been no time to empty the storm shelter of its Christmas ornaments, and not enough room for them all, anyway. Alba's basement had been forced to fill the need.

Faye supposed Joe had carried her there, though she'd never asked him. She would never speak of that day to anyone ever again. She was sure that Carson had carried Alba, who never stopped screaming for Mickey, not even when the twister tore her roof away and they looked up into the underside of death.

If the tornado had dropped the roof on them, none of them would have left the basement alive, but most of Alba's roof was found the next day in the front yard of her late ex-husband's house. A few scattered shingles were found at the Sylacauga site, miles away, and Faye would always suspect that they were Alba's.

Agent Bigbee spent the life of the tornado lying facedown in a ditch miles away from them, praying for it to pass over him, and it did. He had driven out into the rising storm, trying to respond to Cloud's call reporting Emily's death, only abandoning that goal when the twister nearly rolled his car off the road.

Pieces of Mickey's house were scattered all the way to town, and so were his guns. Faye would always imagine that his collected artifacts had been given back to the land that they never should have left.

Kenny's house had suffered a gas leak and burned to the ground before the rain even stopped falling. She would never learn the fate of the little figurine and the handful of pearls and the old skeleton that Kenny had stolen on the night that Kira Denton died. No trace of them was found in the house's burned-out shell, nor was there any sign of Kenny's old toolbox.

Faye had never believed the figurine and pearls and bone were still aboveground when the tornado struck. As soon as Kenny recovered them from Sophia Townsend's grave, she knew he would have reburied them in a place where they could rest in peace. Somewhere near Sylacauga, they lay underground, together, as they had always been and as they should be.

Perhaps they were somewhere near the Sylacauga site, where the storm had flooded Carson's excavation nearly to the rim. A fallen tree bridged it. There were more fallen trees than standing ones in the woods around the open hole, and the standing trees had lost half their branches. A sandy bluff had slumped into the creek where people had fished for generations.

Some time later, representatives of the Muscogee (Creek) Nation would survey the site and judge that it would no longer make a very good park. Instead, they would place a historical marker on the highway nearby, documenting the presence of Mississippian-era cultural remains there and crediting the discovery to Drs. Sophia Townsend and Carson Callahan. The historical marker would also document the date and location of the most destructive tornado in Sylacauga's history. The town itself, it would note, was unscathed.

Faye would always disagree.

Chapter Thirty

Only four days after the tornado, Faye awoke to a loud, happy morning. Michael and Amande had flown in the night before, and Michael was lying on the kitchen floor doing what toddlers do when they've had too much excitement and too little sleep. He was screaming something about how much he missed the pony he'd ridden for his lessons. Faye was terrified that Joe was going to decide that this was an excellent time to buy him one. Rewarding this kind of behavior would ensure daily tantrums for the rest of their lives.

Amande, who was pretty confident that she had destroyed the SAT before getting on the airplane, was swapping questionable jokes with Sly. Faye was trying not to listen or to laugh, but she was keeping her mouth shut. Her adopted daughter was practically grown. It was far too late for Faye to police her sense of humor.

The unexpected knock on the front door reminded Faye of Emily, and she felt a pang. The knock came at a more humane hour than Emily might have chosen, but Faye and her family were still sitting around the breakfast table, so it was early enough. Faye opened the door and found Carson waiting outside.

He skipped "Hello," and began with, "I've let my employer know about the old burial and the pearls and the figurine. I've told the Muscogee Nation everything. It seems that they are probably going to let me keep my job as their tribal archaeologist, though for the life of me I couldn't tell you why."

"The Creeks are gracious people. You know that." Faye gestured for him to come in, but he was still talking and he seemed to want to do it while standing on the doorstep.

"The Creeks are in touch with the preservation office and the wheels of NAGPRA are starting to roll, but it's all a legal formality. They'll never let anybody put a shovel in the ground at the Sylacauga site, not ever again. Fortunately, they've got a lot of ordinary everyday archaeology on other tribal lands that will keep me busy for as long as I want to work here, but I can't tell you how long that will be."

Faye was glad to know what the Creeks were going to do, but she was looking at a man who had just watched his father and his almost-father die horribly. It didn't seem right to be talking business. "How are you, Carson? Really, how are you? Come in."

Carson stepped through the door, but he was more in a mood to talk than listen. "I know you've figured out what happened with the notebook, which is the reason I deserve to lose my job."

"The last notebook?"

He nodded.

"Correct me if I'm wrong," she said, "but I think the last notebook was never lost. It waited for years at the curation facility with all the other notebooks and with the artifacts found in 1987. When you grew up, it only made sense that you'd gravitate toward the project that fascinated you as a kid. As soon as you started your graduate work, you would have found those notebooks and devoured the information in them. When was that? About 1999? 2000?"

"Something like that. I looked everywhere for the pearls and the figurine that she drew in that last notebook. And those bones. They weren't at the curation facility. I ransacked the warehouse where the Creeks store things they don't use but don't want to throw away. I did the same thing at the university, which has a lot more places to store things and forget about them than the Creeks do. I really thought I'd find them. I mean, a skeleton? Come on. Who would have thrown that away without a word?"

"But you never told anybody. I figure it's because you knew that those bones could complicate the work you wanted so much to do. As you just said, the Creeks know about them now and they've stopped all work at the site."

Carson dropped his gaze. Studying his feet was preferable to meeting Faye's appraising eyes. "I told myself that I'd pull the plug if I found those bones. Until I had them, though, they weren't real. All I had were a few words on a page."

"So you hid the page."

He raised his eyes and there was challenge there. "I could have destroyed the page and we wouldn't be having this conversation. I couldn't do that, so Sophia's cabin seemed to be the perfect answer. Nobody was going to find it there. Even if they did, they wouldn't know its significance. And even if someone did understand its significance, they wouldn't know I put it there. Why would they suspect it? It was Sophia's notebook and it was in Sophia's house."

"But if the situation ever changed, you could fetch the notebook and have the information you needed. And you wouldn't be carrying the guilt of destroying something irreplaceable."

No answer. Just the same challenging gaze.

"Was there anything else in that notebook that you didn't want the world to know?"

"No. Not at all. Actually, there was something wonderful in it. I know you've only seen the last few pages of the notebook, so you can't know what else Sophia found that day."

Faye couldn't stay angry with Carson when he let his enthusiasm show. "What?"

"A hearth. She found the charcoal she needed to date the site. That's why I've been burning to dig here. Don't look at me that way. As far as I knew, the pearls and figurine were long gone, boxed up and stored somewhere. The bones might still have been somewhere in one of those thirty-meter trenches, but what were the odds that one five-meter-square pit was going to uncover them?"

"How did you choose that particular five-meter square?"

"Like I told you, I did some magnetometry, and there it was. It was as clear an anomaly as you can hope to see with remote testing, too big and obvious to be a few old bones. At least that's what I told myself. I thought it was the hearth. I thought I could do a quick dig, small and cheap, and bring up inarguable proof of the site's age without much chance of disturbing the old burial."

In Carson's shoes, she would have been just as excited, and she might have been just as reckless. She hoped not.

"Hiding that notebook wasn't a completely ethical solution," he said, "but I thought it was ethical enough. You're free to spread the word to all our colleagues and let them pass judgment."

"I'm inclined to think that you've been through enough hell lately."

The challenge on his face melted and Faye was glad for a moment, until he broke into tears. Fear and anger had been propping him up, and she'd taken it away.

Joe heard the sobs and came to help. Together, they led him into the kitchen and poured him a cup of strong coffee that was not going to heal his troubles at all, but the routine of sweetening it and adding cream did stop his tears. Joe handed him a tall pile of pancakes doused in sorghum syrup, which wasn't going to fix anything either, but the concern of the people around the table just might.

"How's Alba?" Sly asked. Faye cringed, thinking that a reminder of his bereaved mother might start Carson's tears again, but the man held it together.

"Not too bad, considering. She's been staying with me since—" He drew a deep breath. "Since, well, you know. I'm sure she'll sell the land where her house used to be, and I'll probably sell Dad's."

"Will you stay here?" Faye asked.

Sly looked at her with a why-would-they-not? expression, but Joe didn't. Faye's husband knew that there were times when you just had to go.

"I think Mom and I both know that staying here means we'll probably be single for the rest of our lives. I've known for a long time that I want this." He gestured at the cluttered kitchen, the screaming toddler, and maybe even the crappy rental house. "I want a family. If I haven't already met the right woman here, I never will. Mom will probably move to Oklahoma City, where she can harass our public servants on a more regular basis. She doesn't deserve to be alone forever, so I hope there's somebody for her there. I don't know where I'll go. When I think about what it will be like to leave, I remember you, Joe. You left and you made it work. Just look around." He raised his coffee cup in Joe's direction and then Faye's, Amande's, Michael's, and Sly's. "Maybe I can get lucky enough to have a family like this."

"If you can find a woman dumb enough to have you," Joe said, sitting down to his own breakfast. "And blind. She'd need to be blind."

"Like Faye, little buddy. Like Faye. Look what she married."

"Stay for lunch," Sly said.

Carson looked at his plate, which was loaded with about a million calories. "I probably won't be able to eat again until next week sometime."

"Stay till you're hungry. I reckon it's been about thirty years since I bought you a cheeseburger."

• ● ● ● •

The call came while Faye was putting Michael down for a nap, so she waited until he was quiet before she returned it.

"You did good, Doctor Faye."

"It doesn't feel like I did good. How many people are dead?"

"Did you pull any triggers? I didn't see you pull any triggers. I carry some blame for Emily, for sure. I didn't see what kind of danger she was in. What did you do wrong?"

Faye leaned against the wall outside Michael's room and slid slowly down to sit on the floor. She needed to keep her voice down so that she didn't wake her son. "There had to be some way to get the truth out of Mickey and Kenny that didn't end with them being dead."

"I've been running scenarios in my head since the day it happened. I could've done this thing. I could've done that thing. If I'd done this other thing, maybe I'd have figured everything out right away and Kira would still be with us. It's my job to carry guilt like that. It's not yours. Let it go."

She stared at the wall where Sly had hung the pictures of the kids that she'd sent him. "Maybe someday."

"You're the one who knew what to say to Mickey. In your shoes, with that gun to my head, I would've said the wrong thing and you might be dead. Carson. Alba. Sly. Me, too, I guess."

She wanted to answer, but all she could give him was a long sigh.

"I've been thinking about Sophia's necklace." Roy's voice was cool, almost casual, as if he'd like her to believe that thinking about the necklace didn't break his heart.

Faye could do cool and casual, so she pretended that she didn't know what necklace he could possibly mean. "The silver one with the little sigma?"

"Yeah, that one. I think it's going to go missing from the evidence file. Not tomorrow and not next week, but someday."

"Say something like that went missing. Where might it go?"

"It belongs in Alabama on the Creek reservation where Sophia lived for all of her growing-up years, the place where good people who never knew her are making sure she gets a proper burial. I can't tell you why I don't want to give them the necklace, too, but I don't."

"It's as much a memorial to Emily as it is to Sophia. I think it should be in the keeping of somebody who understands that."

"Yes," he said.

Somehow, she knew that he wasn't finished speaking so she waited for what came next.

After a good long pause, Roy proved her right, "There's bound to be a good place to bury Sophia's necklace somewhere on that reservation."

Faye nodded her agreement, as if Roy were there to see. Then she made herself speak up so that he could hear her. "I live in the Florida Panhandle, not so far from Alabama. If somebody wanted help burying that necklace, I own a shovel."

"Good to know."

Again, Roy waited a moment to speak, and the quiet interval felt to Faye like Roy's own elegy for the people who had been lost.

"Tell you what," he said, breaking the silence. "I get oddball cases like this sometimes. This probably won't be the last time I need an archaeology doctor to help me. When I do, I'll hire your company and you'll get a free trip to come see Sly. You can bring his grandkids to see him. Joe, too. Everybody wins, right?"

"Everybody wins. I like that."

"Good. Me, too. You take care of yourself, Doctor Faye, you and your family. Be safe and happy."

Faye knew something was wrong, because Sly had asked Amande to take Michael to town for ice cream. Ice cream and his grandchildren were Sly's favorite things, so what would possess him to send them to eat banana splits without him?

As Amande pulled out of the driveway in Sly's truck, he beckoned for Faye and Joe to join him at the kitchen table. Patricia's urn sat in front of him. Sly had postponed her memorial service for a few days so that Amande and Michael could be there, but he couldn't postpone it forever. Today was the day.

When Faye dropped into the chair next to Sly, she found that there was nowhere but the urn to put her eyes. After they scattered the ashes that day at sundown, would Patricia be anywhere any more? When was a person really gone?

Sly held out his hand and there was a heart-shaped potsherd on its palm. "I need to decide what to do with this."

"Do you want to tell us where you got it?" Faye asked.

"You know where I got it. I'm damn sure you do. Sophia gave it to me the day before I left for Houston. It was the day before she died."

Joe's face was so still that Faye would have sworn he wouldn't say a word, no matter what. She was wrong.

"Why, Dad? Why did she give it to you?"

Sly flipped the potsherd over in his hand and studied the other side. "A woman has a lot of ways to let a man know she wants him. From the day I met her, Sophia tried every one of those ways to get my attention. Truth is, she had my attention. She was trying to get me to do something about it. When I didn't take the bait, she tried harder."

"But Mickey and Kenny—" Joe started.

"Maybe I'm an egotistical son-of-a-bitch, but I always thought she was carrying on with them because she thought it would get to me."

Faye had seen how women looked at her husband. There had been a time when Sly had looked like Joe.

"I've done a lot of bad things. Truth told, I've been a terrible person, sometimes. One thing I never did was cheat on my wife. I thought Sophia didn't understand why I took myself away from her. But on that last day, she told me that she did. She gave me this heart and told me she loved me."

He flipped the potsherd again and studied its design. "Before that, I would've said that you can't love somebody in just a few weeks. Maybe you can't. But you can feel something. You can feel a lot, to tell the truth. What I didn't understand until I met Sophia was that you can feel a lot for somebody, even when you're in love with somebody else. I can't tell you how it broke my heart to hear what happened to that woman."

He held out the little pottery heart on his open palm. "I thought about burying this on the creek bank where we're going to scatter your mother's ashes, but that don't feel right. I thought about burying it at that dig she loved so much, but she was murdered and buried there and now it's just awful to me. Can either of you tell me what to do with this?"

Faye didn't even have to think. "Donate it, so people can enjoy seeing it."

"You mean to a museum?"

"Not just any museum. Give it to the museum at Spiro Mounds. They've lost so many treasures there. If you tell Roy you're doing it, I bet he'll dig the other potsherd out of his evidence files and donate it, too. You know, the one that fits right into the notch on top of that heart. I love the idea of reuniting them someplace where they can stay together forever. Don't you?"

• • ● • •

This was the creek, the shallow rippling endless stream of water where Joe's mother had taught him to fish. Faye couldn't say how many times Joe had told her about it. He was a man who loved nature and the sweetness of its quiet spaces, but none of those spaces had ever lived up to this grassy bank and these trees and that brown water.

There wasn't a blade of grass around them or a drop of water in the creek that had been here when Joe and Patricia sat on this bank. Everything was new but the trees, some of them, but this was still the place. It had a quiet holiness and it was an altogether worthy place to remember one's dead.

Joe had picked some herbs out of the woods. Only he knew their significance, but he threw them on the water and watched them float away, never saying a word.

Sly tried to say the words he'd been practicing, but all he could manage was, "Kids, I wish your grandmother was still here. She would have loved you so much. And your mother. She would have adored this woman standing here beside your father."

Sly turned to the creek and upended the urn over its flowing water. His family gathered tight around him and, together, they let Patricia go.

Guide for the Incurably Curious

This is the place where I give a bit of background for readers who are interested in the facts behind Faye's fictional adventures. Teachers and book group leaders say that this kind of information spurs discussion. Also, I find that book-lovers are incurably curious. After we finish reading a book, we almost always want to know more. Here are some things I turned up in my research that I think my readers might find interesting.

- If you check the website for the Muscogee (Creek) Nation's Lighthorse Tribal Police, you will find that they really do have a K-9 named Bleck: http://www.mcn-nsn.gov/services/lighthorse-police/

- The Oklahoma Historical Society's website has an excellent overview of the historical use of schools, particularly boarding schools, to forcibly assimilate Native American children by depriving them of their cultures' languages and customs. This is the basis for Sly's painful memories of having his hair cut while he was away at boarding school. As I wrote those memories, I thought that I might be pushing the boundaries of truth a bit, as I thought that Sly, who would have been in high school in the 1970s, might be too young to have had those experiences. As I finished writing *Burials*, I found Mary Harjo's memoir of her boarding school experiences during those years and I learned that children continued to suffer separation from their families and their cultural traditions well into the time period when Sly would have been in school. She speaks of returning home unable to understand her family when they spoke, saying that she felt sad because "Creek/Seminole should be my first language." Her memories can be read on Southeastern Oklahoma State University's website at http://www.se.edu/nas/files/2013/03/NAS-2011-Proceedings-Harjo.pdf.

• The story of the destruction of Spiro Mounds is true. There is a brief history of the site and a description of the archaeological park there on the Oklahoma Historical Society's website at http://www.okhistory.org/sites/spiromounds. You'll also find a fascinating description of the University of Oklahoma's efforts to conserve 600-year-old lace found at Spiro here: http://samnoblemuseum.tumblr.com/post/50367318964/historical-heroes-saving-the-spiro-lace.

Longtime readers of the series will remember that I established in *Artifacts* that Joe had a father in Oklahoma whom he needed to call. In *Isolation* (2015), he finally reestablishes that connection and now, in 2017, Joe finally comes home. *Artifacts* was published in 2003, so these two Oklahoma-related books were a long time in coming. This makes sense, because family dynamics often build walls between loved ones that are hard to break down. I'm glad Joe and Sly finally managed it.

On a personal note, I had no idea when I planted the notion in *Artifacts* that Joe would eventually need to go to Oklahoma that I would eventually live in Oklahoma myself. I didn't even know that I'd be living here when I wrote *Isolation*. *Burials* would have been a different book if I weren't now an Oklahoman, and I'm very grateful for the twists of fate that brought Joe, Faye, and me to this beautiful place at the same time. The three of us are looking forward to our next adventure.

To see more Poisoned Pen Press titles:

CPSIA information can be obtained
at www.ICGtesting.com
Printed in the USA
BVOW03s1818050217
475347BV00002B/120/P

9 781464 207525